Orville A. Roorbach

Volume 4 of the Bibliotheca Americana

a catalogue of American publications, reprints and original works - from March,

1858, to January, 1861.

Orville A. Roorbach

Volume 4 of the Bibliotheca Americana
a catalogue of American publications, reprints and original works - from March, 1858, to January, 1861.

ISBN/EAN: 9783337251123

Printed in Europe, USA, Canada, Australia, Japan

Cover: Foto ©Andreas Hilbeck / pixelio.de

More available books at **www.hansebooks.com**

VOLUME IV.

OF

The Bibliotheca Americana,

A

CATALOGUE

OF

AMERICAN PUBLICATIONS,

(REPRINTS AND ORIGINAL WORKS,)

FROM

MARCH, 1858, TO JANUARY, 1861.

COMPILED AND ARRANGED

BY ORVILLE A. ROORBACH.

NEW YORK:
ORVILLE A. ROORBACH.
LONDON: TRUBNER & CO.

1861.

ABBREVIATIONS.

ara..Arabesque—Embossed.
bds...Boards.
cf..Calf.
cl..Cloth.
cl. ex..Cloth full gilt and gilt edge
emb...Embossed—Arabesque.
flex. cl..Flexible cloth.
hf. ara...Arabesque backs.
hf. r...Half roan.
hf. rus...Half Russia.
hf. cl..Cloth backs.
hf. bd..Sheep backs.
ill'd pap...Illuminated paper.
im. mor...Imitation morocco.
Lib...Sheep, Philadelphia style.
mor...Morocco.
pap...Pap.
r...Roan.
r. cl. sides......................................Roan back, cloth sides.
shp...Plain sheep.
shp gt..Sheep, gilt backs.
Saxy..Saxony.

RESIDENCE OF PUBLISHERS.

Abbey & Abbott . . . . . New York.
Amer. Bap. Pub. Society . New York.
" Bible Union . . . . "
" Sunday School Union . Philadelphia.
" Tract Society . . . . New York.
" Unitarian Association . Boston.
Anners, H. F. . . . . . . Philadelphia.
Anderson, D. . . . . . . "
" Gates & Wright . Cincinnati.
Applegate & Co. . . . . "
Appleton, D. & Co. . . . . New York.

Bailey & Noyes . . . . . Portland, Me.
Baird, H. C. . . . . Philadelphia.
Baker & Godwin (printers) . New York.
Bailliere Brothers . . . . "
Ballou & Loveland . . . . Montpelier, Vt.
Barnes, A. S. & Burr . . . New York.
Bartlett, John . . . . . . Boston.
Bazin & Ellsworth . . . . "
Boardsley, J. E. . . . . . Buffalo, N. Y.
Biddle, E. C. & J. . . . . Philadelphia.
Blackie & Son . . . . . . New York.
Blanchard, C. . . . . . . "
" & Lea . . . . Philadelphia.
Board of Pub. of Ref. Dutch Ch. New York.
Bond, J. W. & Co. . . . . Baltimore.
Bradley, J. W. . . . . . . Philadelphia.
Brady, F. . . . . New York.
Bridgman & Childs . . . . Northampton.
Briggs, Geo. W. & Co. . . . Boston.
Brooks, D. B. & Bro. . . . Salem, Mass.
Brotherhead, Wm. . . . . Philadelphia.
Brown & Gross . . . . . . Hartford, Conn.
" Loomis & Co. . . . New York.
" & Taggard . . . . Boston.
Buffum, J. . . . .
Burdick, A. B. . . . . . . New York.
Burke, A. . . . . Buffalo, N. Y.
Burnham, T. O., H. P. . . . Boston.
Burt, Hutchinson & Abbey . New York.
Bushnell, Lynde . . . . . St. Louis.
Butler, E. H. & Co. . . . . Philadelphia.
Butts, J. R. . . . . Boston.

Calkins, D. & M. . . . . . Worcester, Mass.
" & Stiles . . . . . New York.
Carlton & Porter . . . . . "
Carter, Robert & Bros . . . "
Case, Lockwood & Co. . . . Hartford, Conn.
Challen, Jas. & Son . . . . Philadelphia.
Chase, Nichols & Hill . . . Boston.
Childs & Peterson . . . . . "
Clapp, David . . . . Boston.
" E., Jr. . . . . . . "
" Otis . . . . "
Clark, Austin, Maynard & Co. New York.
" Elisha & Co. . . . . Bath, Me.
" & Meeker . . . . . New York.
" Robt. & Co. . . . . Cincinnati.
Cleveland, C. H. . . . . . "

Cobb, J. B. & Co. . . . . . Cleveland, O.
Colby, A. & Co. . . . . . Boston.
Collins, Robt. B. & Bro. . . New York.
" T. K., Jr. . . . . . Philadelphia.
Colton, J. H. & Co. . . . . New York.
Cong. B. of Pub. . . . . . Boston.
Cooke, D. B. & Co. . . . . Chicago.
Cooper, J. M. & Co. . . . . Savannah.
Copeland, A. E. . . . . . Middlebury, Vt.
Comby, W. F. . . . . . . Dayton, O.
Cotton, M. . . . . Boston.
Courtenay, S. G. & Co. . . . Charleston, S. C
Cowperthwait, H. & Co. . . Philadelphia
Cozans, P. J. . . . . New York.
Crocker & Brewster . . . . Boston.
Crosby, Nichols, Lee & Co. . "
Crowen, T. J. . . . . . . New York.
Crown, L. P. & Co. . . . . Boston.
Cunningham, P. F. . . . . Philadelphia.
Cushing & Bailey . . . . . Baltimore.

Damrell & Moore . . . . . Boston.
Dana, D., Jr. . . . . New York.
Darrow & Bro. . . . . . . Rochester.
Davidson, J. S. . . . . . . Pittsburg, Pa.
Davids, Thaddeus & Co. . . New York.
Davis, A. J. & Co. . . . . . Boston.
" C. H. . . . . . . Philadelphia.
" R. S. & Co. . . . . Boston.
Dayton, H. . . . . New York.
Deagen, H. V. & Son . . . . Boston.
Delisser & Proctor . . . . New York.
Derby & Jackson . . . . . "
Desilver, Charles . . . . . Philadelphia.
Dewey, D. M. . . . . Rochester.
De Witt, R. M. . . . . . . New York.
Dexter, H. & Co. . . . . . "
Dick & Fitzgerald . . . . . "
Dinsmore & Co. . . . . . . "
Ditson, O. . . . . Boston.
Dodd, M. W. . . . . New York.
Doolady, M. . . . . "
Donahoe, P. . . . . Boston.
Doughty, Straw & Co. . . . Detroit, Mich.
Draper, W. F. . . . . Andover, Mass.
Dunigan & Bro. . . . . . . New York.
Duren, E. F. . . . . Bangor, Me.
Durrie & Peck . . . . . . New Haven.
Dutton, E. P. & Co. . . . . Boston.

Eastman, E. C. . . . . . . Concord, N. H.
Eggert, D. & Son . . . . . New York.
Ellenger, M. & Co. . . . . . "
Ensign, Bridgeman & Fanning . "
Epis. Sunday-school Union . "
Ernst, Jacob . . . . Cincinnati.
Evans, Chas. T. . . . . . . New York.
" G. G. . . . . Philadelphia.

Feuchtwanger, L. . . . . . New York.
Fleming & Hamill . . . . . Xenia, O.

Follett, Foster & Co.	Columbus, O.
Fowler & Wells	New York.
Francis, C. S. & Co.	"
French, James & Co.	Boston.
" S.	New York.
Gaut & Volkmar	Philadelphia.
Goetzel, S. H. & Co.	Montgomery, Ala.
Gould & Lincoln	Boston.
Gowans, William	New York.
Graves, A. F.	Boston.
Gray, John A.	"
Green, B. H.	Boston.
Griffin, Joseph	Brunswick, Me.
Griggs, S. C. & Co.	Chicago.
Hale, E. J. & Son	Fayetteville, N. C.
Hamersley, W. J.	Hartford.
Harper & Bros.	New York.
Harriman, F. D.	"
Haverty, P. M.	"
Hayes, S. C.	Philadelphia.
Hays & Zell	"
Hazard, W. P.	"
Heath & Graves	Boston.
Higgins & Perkenpine	Philadelphia.
" Bradley & Dayton	Boston.
Holbrook, George	New York.
Homans, J. S.	"
Hooker, H.	Philadelphia.
Howe & Ferry	New York.
Hoyt, Henry	Boston.
Hunt & Son	Philadelphia.
Huntington, F. J.	New York.
Hutchinson, O.	"
Ide, G. H. & N. L.	Claremont, N. H.
Ingham & Bragg	Cleveland, O.
Ives & Smith	Salem, Mass.
Ivison, Phinney & Co.	New York.
James, U. P.	Cincinnati.
Jewett, J. P. & Co.	Boston.
Jones, W. L.	New York.
Johnson, T. & J. W. & Co.	Philadelphia.
Kay & Bro.	Philadelphia.
Keith & Woods	St. Louis, Mo.
Kelly, Hedien & Piet	Baltimore.
Kurtz, T. N.	Philadelphia.
Leary, Getz & Co.	Philadelphia.
Leavitt & Allen	New York.
Leonard, J. W. & Co.	"
Lewis & Blood	New York.
Libby, E. O. & Co.	"
Lindsay & Blakiston	Philadelphia.
Lippincott, J. B. & Co.	"
Littell, Son & Co.	Boston.
Little, W. C. & Co.	Albany.
" Brown & Co.	Boston.
Lloyd, H. H. & Co.	New York.
Lloyd, J. T.	Philadelphia.
Lockwood, R. & Son	"
Long, E. D. & Co.	"
Longstreth, H.	Philadelphia.
Loring, A. K.	Boston.
Lucas Bros.	Baltimore
Lutheran Bd. of Publication	Philadelphia.
Lyon, Henry	New York.
Macoy & Sickles	New York.
Magee, J. P.	Boston.
Marsh, Bela	"
Martien, W. S. & A.	Philadelphia.
Martin & Johnson	New York.
Marvin, T. R.	Boston.
Mason Bros.	New York.
Massachusetts Sab. School Soc.	Boston.
Mayhew & Baker	"

McCarter & Dawson	Charleston, S. C.
McClure, W. O.	Utica, N. Y.
McCormick, S. J.	Portland, Oregon.
McGrath, H.	Philadelphia.
McPherson, J. & Co.	Atlanta, Ga.
Mondum, J. P.	Boston.
Mentz, W. G.	Philadelphia.
Merrill & Metcalf	Lowell, Mass.
Methodist Book Concern	Cincinnati
"	New York.
Miller, James	"
Miller, J. & H.	Columbus, O.
Minifie, William	Baltimore.
Moffet, John	New York.
Moore, C.	Cincinnati.
" J. W.	Philadelphia.
" Wilstach, Keyes & Co.	Cincinnati.
" & Nims	Troy, N. Y.
Morris, A.	Richmond, Va.
Morton & Griswold	Louisville, Ky.
Moss, Bro. & Co.	Philadelphia.
Munroe & Co.	Boston.
Munsel, Joel	Albany.
Munsell & Rowland	Albany.
Munson, S. T.	New York.
Murphy, J. & Co.	Baltimore.
Murray, Young & Co.	Lancaster, Pa.
Nelson & Sons	New York.
New Church Publishing Assn.	"
Newton, Geo. M.	"
Nicholson, V.	Cincinnati.
Norton, Anson P.	New York.
" C. B.	"
" Jno. W.	"
Oaksmith & Co.	New York.
Osborne & Delamater	"
O'Shea, P.	"
Parry & McMillan	"
Partridge, Chas.	New York.
Pattison, Geo. P. & Co.	Memphis, Tenn.
Pauson & Nicholson	Philadelphia.
Peck & Bliss	Philadelphia.
Pennington, John & Son	"
Perkinpine & Higgins	"
Perry, J. B.	"
" C. P.	"
Peterson, T. B. & Bros.	"
Philips & Solomon	Washington, D. C.
Phillips, Sampson & Co.	Boston.
Phinney, Blakeman & Mason	New York.
Pollock, M.	Philadelphia.
Pooley, W. I. & Co.	New York.
Pomeroy, W. L.	Raleigh, N. C.
Poor, A.	Haverhill, Mass.
Potter, John E.	Philadelphia.
Pratt, Oakley & Co.	New York.
Presbyn. Bd. of Publication	Philadelphia.
Price, Henry B.	New York.
Pritchard, Abbott & Laurence	Augusta, Ga.
Prot. Ep. Sun. School Union	New York.
Pudney & Russell	"
Pugh, T. B.	Philadelphia.
Purse, E. J.	Savannah, Ga.
Putnam, Geo. P.	New York.
Quinby, G. W.	Cincinnati.
Radde, William	New York.
Randolph, A. D. F.	"
" J. W.	Richmond, Va.
Read, J. L.	Pittsburg, Pa.
Redding & Co.	Boston.
Redfield, J. S.	New York.
Reardon, Jno. E.	Little Rock, Ark.
Reynolds, W. J. & Co.	Boston.
Richardson, C. B.	New York.
" N. F.	Boston.

Rickey, Mallory & Webb . . Cincinnati.
Riley, J. H. & Co. . . . . Columbus, O.
Roe, Chas. . . . . New York.
Rollo, S. A. . . . . . . "
Roorbach, O. A., Jr. . . . . "
Ross & Tousey . . . . . . "
Rudd & Carleton . . . . . "
Rulison, D. . . . . Philadelphia.

Sab. Sc'l Ref. Prot. Dutch Ch. New York.
Sadlier, D. & J. & Co. . . . "
Sanborn, Bazin & Ellsworth . Boston.
Sexton & Barker . . . . New York.
Scribner, Charles . . . . "
Sheldon & Co. . . . . . "
Shepard, Clark & Brown . . Boston.
Shepard, C. & Co. . . . . New York.
Skelly, Wm. . . . . . . New York.
Smith, English & Co. . . . Philadelphia.
" James B. & Co. . . . "
Smithson, W. T. . . . . Washington, D. C.
Southern Bab. Pub. Society. Charleston, S. C.
Sower, Barnes & Co. . . . Philadelphia.
Spencer, W. V. . . . . . Boston.
Sprague & Co. . . . . . Albany, N. Y.
Stanford & Delisser . . . New York.
Stevenson & Owen . . . . Nashville, Tenn.
Stockton, T. H. . . . . Philadelphia.
Strickland & Co. . . . . Milwaukee.
Stroug. T. W. . . . . . New York.
Swan, Brewer & Tileston . Boston.
Swormstedt & Poe . . . . Cincinnati.

Tappan & Whittemore . . . Boston.
Thatcher & Hutchinson. . . New York.
Thayer & Eldridge . . . . Boston.
Thomson Bros. . . . . . "
Tibbals, N. & Co. . . . . "

Ticknor & Fields . . . . . Boston.
Tilton, J. E. & Co. . . . . "
Tompkins A. . . . . . . "
Townsend, W. A. & Co. . . New York.
Truman & Scofford . . . Cincinnati.
Tuttle, Geo. A. & Co. . . . Rutland, Vt.

Usher, J. M. . . . . Boston.

Van Nostrand, D. . . . . . New York.
Virtue, Emmins & Co. . . . "
Voorhies, John S. . . . . New York

Walker, E. . . . . New York.
" Wise & Co. . . . . Boston.
Walsh, J. P. . . . . . . Cincinnati, O.
Waters, Horace . . . . . New York.
Webb, Gill & Levering . . . Louisville, Ky.
Weed, Parsons & Co. (printers) Albany.
Welk, J. . . . . Philadelphia.
Wentworth & Co. . . . . Boston.
West & Johnston . . . . Richmond, Va.
Westermann, B. & Co. . . New York.
Wheeler & Williams . . . "
Whipple, S. K. & Co. . . . Boston.
Whitney, George H. . . . Providence, R. I.
Widdleton, W. J. . . . . New York.
Wiley, John . . . . . . "
" & Halsted . . . . . "
Williams, A. & Co. . . . Boston.
Wilson & Crockford . . . Geneva, Ill.
" J. M. . . . . . . Philadelphia.
Wood, S. S. & W. . . . . New York.
Woodhouse, James & Co. . . Richmond, Va.

Young, R. T. . . . . . . New York.

Zell, T. Elwood . . . . . . Philadelphia.

BIBLIOTHECA AMERICANA;
Volume IV.

———◦•◦———

A

A Will and a Way. Translated from the German. 16mo. cl.		0 75	*Crosby, N., L. & Co.*
Abbott, Jacob, American History. Vol. I. Aboriginal America. Vol. II. Discovery of America. Vol. III. The Southern Colonies. 16mo. cl. each. . . .		0 75	*Sheldon & Co.*
——— "	Excursion to the Orkney Islands. 16mo. cl.	0 60	"
——— "	Florence and John. 18mo. cl. . .	0 60	"
——— "	History of Genghis Khan. 16mo. cl.	0 60	"
——— "	History of King Richard the Second of England. 16mo. cl.	0 75	*Harper. & Bros.*
——— "	History of Peter the Great, Emperor of Russia. With Engravings. 16mo. cl.	0 60	"
——— "	Rollo in Rome. 16mo. cl. . .	0 50	*Brown & Taggard.*
——— "	Stories of Rainbow and Lucky. Rainbow's Journey. 16mo. cl. . .	0 50	*Harper & Bros.*
——— "	Selling Lucky. 16mo. cl. . . .	0 50	"
——— "	The Three Pines.	0 50	"
——— "	Up the River.	0 50	"
——— "	Handie. 16mo. cl.	0 50	"
Abbott, J. S. C., South and North, or, Impressions received during a Trip to Cuba and the South. 12mo. cl. . . .		0 75	*Abbey & Abbott.*
——— "	The French Revolution of 1789, as viewed in the light of Republican Institutions. 8vo. cl.	2 50	*Harper & Bros.*
——— "	The Monarchies of Continental Europe. The Empire of Austria; its Rise and Present Power. 12mo. cl. . . .	1 50	*Mason Brothers.*

1

Abridgment of the Debates of Congress, from 1789 to
     1856. From Gale's and Seaton's Annals
     of Congress; from their Register of De-
     bates, and from the Official Reported
     Debates, by John O. Rives. By the Au-
     thor of "The Thirty Years' View." 8vo.
     15 volumes published, each. . . . 8 00   *D. Appleton & Co.*
About, E., Germaine. 12mo. . . . . . 1 00   *J. E. Tilton & Co.*
—— " The King of the Mountains. 12mo. cl. . . 1 00   "
—— " The Roman Question. 12mo. pap. . . 0 45   "
—— " The Roman Question. 12mo. cl. . . . 0 60   *D. Appleton & Co.*
Acadia; or, a Month with the Blue Noses. By Frederic
     S. Cozzens. 12mo. cl. . . . . . 1 00   *Derby & Jackson.*
Actress (The) in High Life; an Episode in Winter Quar-
     ters. 12mo. cl. . . . . . . 1 00   "
Adam Bede. By George Eliot. 12mo. cl. . . 1 00   *Harper & Bros*
—— Graeme of Mossgray. By Mrs. Olyphant. 12mo.
     cl. . . . . 1 00   *Dick & Fitzgerald.*
Adams, C., The Poet Preacher; A Brief Memorial of Chas.
     Wesley, the Preacher and Poet. 16mo. cl. . 0 65   *Carlton & Porter.*
—— " Words that Shock the World; or, Martin
     Luther his own Biographer. 16mo. cl. . 0 75   "
—— J. C., The Adventures of James Capen Adams,
     Mountaineer and Grizzly Bear Hunter, of Cali-
     fornia. By Theodore H. Hittell. Illustrated.
     12mo. cl. . . . . 1 25   *Crosby, N., L. & Co.*
—— J. T., The Lost Hunter. A Tale of Early Times.
     12mo. cl. . . . . 1 25   *M. Doolady.*
—— N. (D.D.), The Great Concern; or, Man's Relation
     to God and a Future State. 12mo. cl. . . 0 85   *Gould & Lincoln.*
Addie Anshey; or, How to make Others Happy. 18mo. 0 35   *Henry Hoyt.*
Addresses to the Candidates for Ordination, on the Ques-
     tions in the Ordination Service. By the Bishop
     of Oxford. 12mo. cloth . . . . 1 00   *R. Carter & Bros.*
Adele. By Julia Kavanagh. 12mo. cloth . . 1 25   *D. Appleton & Co.*
Adelia, the Octoroon. By Hez. L. Hosmer. 12mo. cl. 1 00   *Follett, Foster & Co.*
Adelmar, the Templar: a Tale of the Crusades. By Abbe
     H***. Translated from the French. 18mo. 0 25   *Kelly, H. & Piet.*
Adler, G. J., History of Provencal Poetry. By C. C. Fauriel.
     Translated from the French, with notes and
     introduction. By G. J. Adler. 8vo. cloth. 2 00   *Derby & Jackson.*
—— " A Practical Grammar of the Latin Language,
     with perpetual Exercises in Speaking and
     Writing, for the use of Schools, Colleges, and
     Private Learners. Second edition. 12mo. . 1 25   *Sanborn, B. & E.*

Adopted Heir (The). By Miss Pardoe. 12mo. cloth. . 1 25   *TB Peterson & Bros*

Adventures (The) of Mr. Verdant Green. By Cuthbert
    Bede. 8 vols. in one. 12mo. cloth. .   . 1 00   *Rudd & Carleton.*

—————— and Observations on the West Coast of Africa,
    and its islands, in 1855, 1856, and 1857. By
    Rev. Charles W. Thomas, M. A. 12mo. cloth. 1 25   *Derby & Jackson.*

Advice to Young Ladies. By T. S. Arthur. 12mo. cloth, 1 00   *G. G. Evans.*

—————— " Young Men. By T. S. Arthur. 12mo. cloth. 1 00   "

Æschylus Ex-novissima recensione Frederici A. Paley.
    Accessit Verborum quæ precipue notanda sunt
    et nominum Index. 18mo. cloth. .   . 0 40   *Harper & Brothers.*

—————— The Agememnon of, with notes. A new edi-
    tion, revised by C. C. Felton. 12mo. .   . 1 00   *Munroe & Co.*

Africa, Travels and Discoveries in North and Central. *See*
    Barth H.

African Bible Pictures; or, Scripture Scenes and Customs
    in Africa. By Rev. M. Officer. 18mo. .   *Luth. Bd. of Pub.*

After Dark: A Novel. By Wilkie Collins. 8vo. pap. . 0 50   *Dick & Fitzgerald.*

Afternoon (The) of Unmarried Life. 12mo. cloth. 1 00   *Rudd & Carleton.*

Against Wind and Tide. By Holme Lee. 12mo. cloth. 1 00   *WA Townsend & Co*

Age (The): a Colloquial Satire. By Philip James Bailey.
    18mo. cloth. .   .   .   . 0 75   *Ticknor & Fields.*

—————— " of Chivalry. By Thomas Bulfinch. 12mo. 1 25   *Crosby, N., L. & Co.*

Agnes, A Novel. By the author of " Ida May." 12mo. 1 25   *Phillips, S. & Co.*

—————— Hopetoun's Schools and Holidays. By Mrs. Oli-
    phant. 16mo. cl. .   .   .   .   . 0 63   *Gould & Lincoln.*

—————— Lee, and other Tales. By Charles Dickens. pap. 0 50   *F. A. Brady.*

Aguecheek, Essays and Letters. 12mo. cl. .   . 1 00   *Shepard, C. & B.*

Ahn, F., A New, Practical, and Easy Method of Learning
    the Spanish Language. 12mo. .   . 0 75   *D. Appleton & Co.*

Aimwell, W., Jessie; or, Trying to be Somebody. 16mo. 0 63   *Gould & Lincoln.*

Ainsworth, W. H., The Miser's Daughter. 2 vols. pap. 1 00   *Peterson & Bros.*

Alcohol; its Place and Power. 16mo. cl. .   . 0 50   *Lindsay & B.*

Alden, J., The Light-Hearted Girl; a Tale for Children.
    18mo. cl. .   .   .   .   .   . 0 34   *J. E. Tilton & Co.*

Aldrich, T. B., The Ballad of Babie Bell, and other Poems.
    12mo. cl. .   .   .   .   .   . 0 75   *Rudd & Carleton.*

Alexander, J. A. (D. D.), Memorial of. 18mo. cl. . 0 25   *W. S. & A. Martien.*

——————   "   "   Sermons. 2 vols. 12mo. cl. 2 50   *C. Scribner.*

—————— J. W.   "   Bring Me up Samuel. 18mo. . 0 15   *A. D. F. Randolph*

——————   "   "   Forty Years' Familiar Letters
    of, constituting, with the Notes, a
    Memoir of his Life. Edited by the surviv-
    ing correspondent, Rev. John Hall, D. D.
    2 vols. 12mo. cl. .   .   .   .   . 8 00   *C. Scribner.*

Alexander, J. W. (D. D.), Sacramental Discourses. 12mo.
cl. . . . . 1 00   *A. D. F. Randolph.*

———— S. D. (Rev.), History of the Presbyterian Church
in Ireland. Condensed from the Standard
Work of Reid and Killen. 12mo. . . 1 00   *R. Carter & Bros.*

———— W. D. S., The Hermit of the Pyrenees, and
other miscellaneous Poems. 18mo. pp. 126.   *Washington, D. O.*

Alford, H., The Greek Testament: with a critically revised Text; a Digest of Various Readings; Marginal References to verbal and idiomatic usage;
Prologomena; and a Critical and Exegetical Com-
mentary. Vol. 1, containing the Four Gospels. 8vo. 5 00   *Harper & Bros.*

Alice Learmont; or, A Mother's Love. By Miss Muloch.
16mo. cl. . . . . . . 0 50   *Mayhew & Baker.*

—— Sherwin; a Tale of the Days of Sir Thomas More.
By O. J. M. 12mo. cl. . . . 0 75   *D. & J. Sadlier & Co.*

—— and Adolphus; or, Worlds not Realized. By Mrs.
Alfred Gatty. 18mo. cl. . . 0 80   *Carter & Bros.*

Alison, A., The History of Europe, from the Fall of Napoleon in 1815, to the Accession of Louis Napoleon in 1852. Vol 4. 8vo. . . . 1 50   *Harper & Bros.*

Alice's Dream. By Mary Ann Whitaker. 18mo. . 0 50   *Walker, Wise & Co.*

All about It; or, the History and Mystery of Common
Things. 12mo. cl. . . . . 1 00   *Townsend & Co.*

Allen, R. L. (M.D.), An Analysis of the principal Mineral
Fountains at Saratoga Springs. 24mo. . 0 25   *Ross & Tousey.*

—— W. (D.D.), A Book of Christian Sonnets. 12mo. .   *Bridgman & Childs*

Almost a Heroine. 12mo. cl. . . . . 1 00   *Ticknor & Fields.*

Alphabet of Birds. 12mo. cl. . . . . 0 50   *D. Appleton & Co.*

Althaus, J., A Treatise on Medical Electricity, Theoretical and Practical; and its Use in the Treatment of Paralysis, Neuralgia, and other
Diseases. 12mo. . . . . 1 50   *Lindsay & Blak'n.*

Alurid Lind. By Mrs. C. M. Fort. 18mo. . . 0 25   *J. Challen & Sons.*

Am I a Christian? and how can I Know it? 32mo. . 0 25   *Pres. B. of Pub.*

American Christian Record, (The) containing a Classified
Statistical Record of Religious and Moral
Associations in the United States and
Europe; the History, Confession of Faith,
and Present Statistics of each of the Relig-
ious Denominations of the United States. . 1 25   *Sheldon & Co.*

———— Form Book, and Legal Guide, for every State
in the Union. By a Member of the Cincin-
nati Bar. 12mo. law sheep. . . . 1 00   *U. P. James.*

American Historical and Literary Curiosities.   Second
  Series.   Edited and arranged, with the assist-
  ance of several autograph collectors, by
  John J. Smith.   Imperial 4to. . . . 8 00 *C. B. Richardson.*
———— Home Garden.   By Alexander Watson. 12mo. 1 50 *Harper & Bros.*
———— Horse Tamer.   By J. Bentwright.   12mo. . 0 50 *George Holbrook.*
———— Normal Schools.   Their Theory, their Work-
  ings, and their Results.   8vo. . . . 0 75 *A. S. Barnes & B.*
———— Numismatical Manual of the Currency and
  Money of the Aborigines, and Colonial,
  State, and United States Coins, with His-
  torical and Descriptive Notices of each Coin
  or Series.   By Montroville Wilson Dickeson,
  M. D.   4to. . . . . . . 6 00 *Lippincott & Co.*
———— Practical Cookery Book.   By a Practical
  Housekeeper.   12mo. cl. . . . *Geo. G. Evans.*
———— Racing Calendar, and Trotting Record, from
  Sept. 1, 1856, to Jan. 1, 1858.   Compiled
  from Porter's Spirit of the Times.   8vo. . 1 00 *Porter's Sp. T., NY*
———— Wit and Humor.   Illustrated by John M'Lenan.
  8vo. pap. . . . . 0 50 *Harper & Bros.*
Amoor, Travels in the Regions of the Upper and Lower.
  See Atkinson, T. W.
———— a Voyage down the; with a Land Journey
  through Siberia, and Incidental Notices of
  Manchooria, Kamschatka, and Japan.   By
  Perry McDonough Collins.   12o. cl. . . 1 25 *D. Appleton & Co.*
Amy and her Brothers; or, Love and Labor.   By Aunt
  Friendly.   18mo. cl. . . . . . 0 80 *A. D. F. Randolph*
An Inquiry into the formation of Washington's Farewell
  Address.   8vo. cl. . . . . 1 25 *Parry & McMillan*
Ancient Spanish Ballads.   Historical and Romantic.
  Translated by J. G. Lockhart, Esq.   A new
  revised edition.   12mo. cl. . . . 0 75 *Ticknor & Fields.*
———— Mineralogy; or, An Inquiry Respecting Mineral
  Substances, mentioned by the Ancients, with
  Occasional Remarks on the Uses to which they
  were applied.   By N. F. Moore, LL. D.   A
  new and revised edition.   16mo. cl. . . 0 75 *Harper & Bros.*
Andersen, H. C., The Sand-Hills of Jutland.   12mo. cl. . 0 75 *Ticknor & Fields.*
Anderson, F., Zenaida.   12mo. cl. . . . 1 25 *Lippincott & Co.*
———— J., The Constitutions of the Freemasons, con-
  taining the History, Charges, Regulations,
  etc., etc.   For the Use of the Lodges. . . 1 00 *J. McPherson & Co.*

Anderson, J. R., Sermons for the Sick Room and Fireside. 12mo. . . . .   *Higgins & P.*

———— R. (Major, U. S. A.), Evolutions of Field Batteries of Artillery. Translated from the French, and arranged for the Army and Militia of the United States. Published by order of the Department. 64mo. . .   1 00   *D. Van Nostrand.*

Anecdotes of Love. By Lola Montez. 12mo. cl. . . 1 00   *Dick & Fitzgerald.*

Angel (The) of the Iceberg; and other Stories. By John Todd. 16mo. cl. . . . .   0 75   *Bridgman & Childs*

———— " and the Demon. By T. S. Arthur. 12mo. cl.   *J. W. Bradley.*

Anjou, L. A., The History of the Reformation in Sweden. Translated from the Sweedish by Henry M. Mason, D.D. 12mo. cl. . . . . . 1 25   *Sheldon & Co.*

Ann Ash; or, the Foundling. 18mo. cl. . . . . 0 88   *Daniel Dana, jr.*

Anna Clayton; or, the Inquirer after Truth. By Rev. Francis Marion Dimmick, 12mo. cl. . 1 25   *Lindsay & B.*

———— the Leech-Vender. A Narrative of Filial Love. By O. Glaubrecht. 18mo. . . . . .   *Presb. Bd. of Pub.*

Annals of Luzerne County: a Record of Interesting Events, Traditions, and Anecdotes. From the First Settlement at Wyoming to 1860. By Stewart Pearce. Illustrated by a Map and Engravings. 8vo. cl. . . . .   2 50   *Lippincott & Co.*

———— of Newberry District, S. C. By John Belton O'Neall, LL. D. . . . . . . 1 25   *Courtenay & Co.*

Annan, W., The Difficulties of Armenian Methodism. A Series of Letters addressed to Bishop Simpson, of Pittsburg. Rewritten and enlarged. 12mo.   0 75   *W.S. & A.Martien*

Annesley, M. (Miss), Light in the Valley; or, the Life and Letters of Mrs. Hannah Bocking. 18mo. cl.   0 80   *Carlton & Porter.*

Annondale. A Story of the Times of the Covenanters. 18mo. . . . .   *Presb. Bd. of Pub.*

Annotated Paragraph Bible, containing the Old and New Testaments, according to the authorized Version. Arranged in Paragraphs and Parallelisms, with explanatory Notes, Prefaces to the several Books, and an entirely new selection of References to Parallel and Illustrative Passages. (The New Testament). 8vo.   1 50   *Sheldon & Co.*

Annual for Boys, for 1860. By William H. G. Kingston. Small 4to. . . . .   1 75   *Ticknor & F.*

———— Obituary Notices of Eminent Persons who have Died in the United States. For 1857. By Hon. Nathan Crosby. 8vo. cl. . . . . . 1 75   *Phillips, S. & Co.*

Annual of Scientific Discovery; or, Year Book of
  Facts in Science and Art for the years 1858, '59,
  '60. By D. A. Wells, A. M. 12mo. cl.   each 1 25 *Gould & Lincoln.*
—— Report of the Chamber of Commerce of the State
  of New York, for the year 1858. With Maps.
  I. Of the Bay and Harbor of New York, showing
  the Sounding from Harlem River to Sandy Hook.
  II. Of the Canals and Railroads in the State of
  New York. 8vo. . . . . . . 3 00 *Wheeler & Wil'ms.*
Anthem Book (The), A Collection of Anthems, Choruses,
  Opening and Closing Pieces. By William B.
  Bradbury. Music 8vo. . . . . . 1 25 *Mason Brothers.*
Anticipations of the Future, to serve as Lessons for the
  Present Time. 12mo. cl. . . . 1 00 *J. W. Randolph.*
Antisell, T. (M. D.), The Manufacture of Photogenic or
  Hydro-Carbon Oils, from Coal and other Bitu-
  minous Substances, capable of supplying
  Burning Fluids. 8vo. cl. . . . 1 75 *D. Appleton & Co.*
Antoinette, the original of "The Child Angel." By Mrs.
  Mary A. Dennison. 16mo. cl. . . . 0 65 *Henry Hoyt.*
Apelles and his Cotemporaries. By the Author of "Er-
  nest Carroll." 16mo. cl. . . . . 0 88 *T. O. H. P. Buru'm.*
Appleton's Companion Hand Book of Travel. 12mo. Pa-
  per, 50; cl. . . . . . 0 75 *D. Appleton & Co.*
—— Cyclopædia of Drawing. Edited by W. E.
  Worthen. 8vo. . . . . . 6 00 "
Aquarelles; or, Summer Sketches. By S. Sombre. 16mo. 0 62 *Stanford & D.*
Arago, F., Biographies of Distinguished Scientific Men.
  Second Series. 16mo. cl. . . . 1 00 *Tickner & Fields.*
Arctic Adventure by Sea and Land, from the Earliest
  Date to the Last Expedition in Search of Sir
  John Franklin. Edited by Epes Sargent. 12mo. cl. 1 25 *Brown & Taggard.*
—— Boat Journey in the Autumn of 1854. By Dr. I.
  I. Hayes. 12mo. . . . . . 1 25 "
Armstrong, G. D. (Rev.), The Theology of Christian Ex-
  perience. 12mo. . . . 1 00 *C. Scribner.*
Army Life on the Pacific. By Lawrence Kip. 12mo. 0 50 *J. S. Redfield.*
Arnold, A. (Rev.), Prerequisites to Communion. 16mo. 0 88 *Gould & Lincoln.*
—— S. G., History of the State of Rhode Island and
  Providence Plantations. 2 vols. 8vo. cl. 5 00 *D. Appleton & Co.*
—— T. (D. D.), The Life and Correspondence of. By
  Arthur P. Shanley, M. A. Third American
  from the last London Edition. 2 vols. 12mo. cl. 2 00 *Tickner & Fields.*
Arnold Leslie; or, the Young Skeptic. 18mo. cl. . 0 35 *Carlton & Porter.*
Art (The) of Elocution. By Prof. H. A. Day. 12mo. 1 00 *Moore. W., K. & Co*

Art (The) of Extempore Speaking. By Prof. M. Bautain.
    12mo. cl. .   .   .   . 1 00 *Charles Scribner.*
Arts (The) of Beauty; or, Secrets of a Lady's Toilet, with
    Hints to Gentlemen on the Art of Fascinating.
    By Madame Lola Montez. 16mo. cl. .   . 0 50 *Dick & Fitzgerald.*
Arthur, T. S., Advice to Young Men. New and enlarged
    edition. 12mo. cl. .   .   .   .   . 1 00 *G. G. Evans.*
——— " Advice to Young Ladies. New and enlarg-
    ed edition. 12mo. cl. .   .   .   . 1 00   "
——— " Lizzie Glen; or, the Trials of a Seamstress.
    12mo. cl. .   .   .   . 1 25 *Peterson & Bros.*
——— " Steps towards Heaven; or, Religion in
    Common Life. 12mo. cl. .   .   . 1 00 *Derby & Jackson.*
——— " The Angel and the Demon: a Tale of Mo-
    dern Spiritualism. 12mo. cl. .   .   .   *J. W. Bradley.*
——— " The Hand but not the Heart; or, the Life-
    Trials of Jessie Loring. 12mo. cl. .   . 1 00 *Derby & Jackson.*
——— " Twenty Years Ago, and Now. 12mo. cl. 1 00 *G. G. Evans.*
——— W., Italy in Transition; Public Scenes and Pri-
    vate Opinions in the Spring of 1860. Il-
    lustrated by Official Documents from the
    Papal Archives of the Revolted Legations.
    12mo. cl. .   .   .   . 1 00 *Harper & Bros.*
Arthur and Constance. A Poem. By J. F. D. Cornell.
    12mo. cl. .   .   .   . 0 50 *Wiley & Halsted.*
——— and his Mother; or, the Story of a Child that be-
    longed to the Church. 18mo.   .   .   . 0 25 *Carlton & Porter.*
Artillerist's Manual (The), compiled from Various Sources,
    and adapted to the Service of the United States.
    Illustrated by Engravings. By John Gibbon,
    Capt. 4th Artillery, U. S. N. 8vo.   . 5 00 *D. Van Nostrand.*
Ashton, S. G. (Mrs.), The Mothers of the Bible. With an
    Introductory Essay, by Rev. A. L. Stone. 12mo.   *J. E. Tilton & Co.*
——— T. J. (M. D.), The Diseases, Injuries, and Mal-
    formations of the Rectum and Anus, with
    remarks on Habitual Constipation. From
    the Third and Enlarged London Edition.
    With Illustrations. 8vo. shp. .   .   . 2 00 *Blanchard & Lea.*
As It Is. 12mo. cl. .   .   .   . 1 00 *Munsell&Rowland*
Aspirations of Nature. By I. T. Hecker. Third edition,
    revised and corrected by the author. 12mo. cl. 0 75 *Dunigan & Bro.*
Astronomical Geography, with the use of the Globes.
    By Emma Willard. 12mo. .   .   .   . 0 75 *Moore & Nims.*
Atkinson, J. (Rev.), Memorials of Methodism in New
    Jersey. 12mo. cl. .   .   .   .   . 1 00 *Carlton & Porter.*

Atkinson, J. H. (Rev.), The True Path; or, The Young
         Man Invited to the Saviour. 12mo.   0 60   *Presb. Bd. of Pub.*
———— T. W., Oriental and Western Siberia; a Narra-
        tive of Seven Years' Exploration and
        Adventures in Siberia, Mongolia, the
        Kirghis Steppes, Chinese Tartary, and
        Part of Central Asia 12mo. cl,   . 1 25   *J. W. Bradley.*
—- - " Travels in the Regions of the Upper and
        Lower Amoor, and the Russian Acqui-
        sitions on the Confines of India and
        China, with Adventures among the
        Mountain Kirghis; and the Manjours,
        Manyaras, Toungours, Touzemts, Gol-
        di, and Gelyaks, the Hunting and Pas-
        toral Tribes. With a Map and numer-
        ous Illustrations. 8vo. cl.   . 2 50   *Harper & Bros.*
Atonement (The). Discourses and Treatises by Edwards,
        Smalley, Maxcy, Emmons, Griffin,
        Burge, and Weeks. With an Intro-
        ductory Essay, by Edwards A. Park,
        Abbot Professor of Christian The-
        ology, Andover, Mass. 8vo.   . 2 00   *Cong. Bd. of Pub.*
———— " in its Relations to Law and Government.
        By the Rev. Albert Barnes. 12mo. 1 00   *Parry & McMillan*
Atson, Wm., Heart Whispers. 12mo. . . . .   *H. Cowperth. & Co.*
Aunt Charity. By Mrs. E. L. Northrop. 16mo. cl.   . 0 75   *F. D. Harriman.*
Aunt Friendly. Amy and her Brothers; or, Love and
        Labor. 18mo. . . . . .   0 30   *A. D. F. Randolph.*
—— Gracie's Library for Little Folks who want to be
        Good. By Grace Murray. 10 vols. 32mo. . 1 00   *Carlton & Porter.*
—— Judy's Tales. By Mrs. Alfred Gatty. 18mo. cl.   . 0 50   *R. Carter & Bros.*
Austin, J. G., Fairy Dreams; or, Wanderings in Elf-Land.
        Sq. 16mo. cl. . . . . . .   0 75   *J. E. Tilton & Co.*
Autobiography of Dan Young, a New England Preacher
        of the Olden Time. Edited by W. P. Strick-
        land. 12mo. cl. . . . . .   1 00   *Carlton & Porter.*
Autocrat (The) of the Breakfast Table. Every Man his
        own Boswell. 12mo. cl. . . .   1 00   *Phillips, S. & Co.*
Autograph Etchings. By American Artists. Illustrated
        by Selections from American Poets. Crown
        folio. Assorted bindings, $8, $10 and . 12 00   *Townsend & Co.*
Avenger (The) a Narrative; and other Papers. By
        Thomas DeQuincey. 16mo. cl. . .   0 75   *Ticknor & Fields.*
Avolio; A Legend of the Island of Cos. With Poems,
        Lyrical, Miscellaneous, and Dramatic. By Paul
        H. Hayne. 16mo. cl. . . .   0 75   "

Aztecs (Land of the); or, Two Years in Mexico. By A.
K. Shepard. 12mo. . . . .   *Weed, P. & Co.*

B

Babcock, S. A., Hidden Treasure; or, The Secret of Success in Life. 16mo.	0 60	*Carlton & Porter.*
Babes (The) in the Basket; or, Daph and her Charge.	0 50	*A. D. F. Randolph.*
Baby Night-Caps. By the author of "Aunt Fanny Stories." Sq. cl.	0 50	*Appleton & Co.*
Bachelor's Story. A Book of Love, Philosophy, and Humor. 12mo. cl. . .	1 00	*Rudd & Carleton.*
Backus, I. (Rev.), A Memoir of the Life and Times of. By Alvah Hovey, D. D. 12mo. .	1 25	*Gould & Lincoln.*
Bacon, F., Essays, with Annotations by Richard Whately, D. D., Archbishop of Dublin. 8vo. cl. .	2 50	*Crosby, N., L. & Co.*
—— " The Works of Francis Bacon, Baron of Verulam, Viscount St. Albans, and Lord High Chancellor of England. Collected and edited by James Spedding, M. A., of Trinity College, Cambridge; Robert Leslie, M. A., late fellow of Trinity College, Cambridge; and Douglas Denon Heath, barrister-at-law, late fellow of Trinity College, Cambridge. (*Now publishing.*) 12 vols. 12mo. cl. Per vol.	1 50	*Brown & Taggard.*
—— T. S. (Rev.), Both sides of the Controversy between the Roman and Reformed Churches. 12mo.	1 00	*Delisser & Procter.*
Badeau, A., The Vagabond. A volume of piquant Sketches. 12mo.	1 00	*Rudd & Carleton.*
Bailey, J., The Age; a Colloquial Satire. 16mo. .	0 75	*Ticknor & Fields.*
Baillie, J. (Rev.), St. Augustine; a Biographical Memoir.	0 75	*R. Carter & Bros.*
Baird, S. J. (Rev.), The Elohim Revealed in the Creation and Redemption of Man. 8vo. cl. .	2 50	*Lindsay & B.*
—— W. (Rev.), Duty and Reward; or, the Blessedness of Doing Good. 18mo.	0 20	*A. D. F. Randolph.*
Baker, D. (Rev.), The Life and Labors of. Prepared by his son, Rev. William M. Baker. 12mo. .	1 25	*W. S. & A. Martien.*
—— W. G., The Christian Lawyer; being a Portraiture of the Life and Character of William George Baker. 12mo.	1 00	*Carlton & Porter.*

Bakewell, F. C., Great Facts. A popular History and
    description of the most remarkable
    Inventions during the present century.
    12mo. cl. . . . . . . 1 00   *D. Appleton & Co.*

Baldwin, G. C. (Rev.), Representative Men of the New
    Testament. 12mo. . . . . 1 00   *Phinney, B. & M.*

Balfern, W. P. (Rev.), Glimpses of Jesus; or, Christ Ex-
    alted in the Affections of his Peo-
    ple. 18mo. cl. . . . . 0 60   *Sheldon & Co.*

———— " "   Lessons from Jesus; or, the Teach-
    ings of Divine Love. 16mo. . 0 75   "   "

Ballad (The) of Babie Bell, and other Poems. By Thomas
    Bailey Aldrich. 12mo. . . . 0 75   *Rudd & Carleton.*

Ballads (The) of Ireland. Edited by E. Hayes. 8vo. . 1 00   *P. Donahoe.*

Ballantyne, R. M., Hudson's Bay; or, Every-Day Life in
    the Wilds of North America. 16mo. 0 75   *Phinney, B. & M.*

———— "   Snow-Flakes and Sun-Beams; or, the
    Young Fur Traders, a tale of the Far
    North. 16mo. . . . . 0 75   "   "

———— "   The Coral Islands; a Tale of the Pacific
    Ocean. 16mo. . . . . 0 75   "   "

———— "   Ungava; a tale of Esquimaux-Land.
    16mo. . . . . . 0 75   "   "

Ballyshan Castle; a Tale founded on Fact. By Sheelah.
    12mo. . . . . . . 1 00   *Delisser & Procter.*

Balmanno, Mrs., Pen and Pencil. Illustrated with 120
    engravings. Small 4to., extra cl. gilt. . 5 00   *D. Appleton & Co.*

Balmes, Jno. (Rev.), European Civilization; Protestant-

Balzac, H. De, The Greatness and Decline of Cæsar Birot-
    teau. From the French of Honore De
    Balzac. Translated by O. W. Wight
    and F. B. Goodrich. 12mo. . 1 00   *Rudd & Carleton.*

———— "   The Petty Annoyances of Married Life.
    From the French of Honore De Balzac.
    Translated by O. W. Wight and F. B.
    Goodrich. 12mo. . . . 1 00   "   "

    ism and Catholicity compared. 8vo. . 2 00   *Murphy & Co.*

Bancroft, G., History of the United States, from the Dis-
    covery of the American Continent. Vols.
    7 & 8. 8vo. cl. each. . . . 2 25   *Little, Brown & Co.*

Baptist (The) Church Directory. A Guide to the Doc-
    trines and Discipline, Officers and Ordinances,
    Principles and Practices of Baptist Churches,
    embracing a concise view of the Questions of
    Baptism and Communion. By Edward T.
    Hiscox, D. D. 18mo . . . . 0 80   *Sheldon & Co.*

Baptology. My Bootmaker and I, on Modes of Baptism.
     By an Old Student. 12mo. cl.   . ; 0 40   *Daniel Dana, jr.*
Bar (The) of Iron, and the Conclusion of the Matter. By
     the Rev. Charles B. Taylor, A. M. 18mo. . . 0 25   *Presb. Bd. of Pub.*
Barbee, W. J. (M. D.), Physical and Moral Aspects of Geo-
     logy. 12mo. . . . . . 1 00   *J. Challen & Son.*
Barclay, S., Personal Recollections of the American Revo-
     lution. A Domestic Diary. 12mo. . . 1 00   *Rudd & Carleton.*
Barclays (The); or, Trying to Serve Two Masters. 0 45   *Am. S. S. Union.*
Barefooted Maiden (The): a Tale. By Berthold Auerbach.
     12mo. . . . . . . 0 75   *J. Munroe & Co.*
Barker, F. M., The Mountain Violet; or, the Charms of
     Early Piety, as displayed in the Memoir of
     Margaret Rust Bayne. 18mo. . . 0 20   *So. Bap. Pub. So.*
Barley Wood, A Tale. By Mrs. J. M. Parker. 16mo. . 0 75   *Daniel Dana, jr.*
Barnes, A. (Rev.,) Inquiries and Suggestions in regard to
     the Foundation of Faith in the Word of God.
     12mo. . . . . . . 0 80   *Parry & McMillan.*
                                           Presb. Pub. Com.
—— " How Shall Man be just with God. 12mo. .
—— " Life at Three Score. A Sermon Delivered in
     the First Presbyterian Church, Philadelphia,
     Nov. 28th, 1858. By the Rev. Albert
     Barnes, cloth. . . . . . 0 88   *Parry & McMillan.*
—— " Prayers for the use of Families; chiefly select-
     from various authors. 12mo. . . 1 00   *Chas. Desilver.*
—— " The Atonement in its Relations to Law and
     Government. 12mo. cloth. . . 1 00   *Parry & McMillan.*
Barrett, B. F., Letters on the Divine Trinity, addressed to
     Henry Ward Beecher. By B. F. Barrett.
     12mo. . . . . . . 0 50   *Mason Brothers.*
—— P., The Deaf Shoemaker. 18mo. cl. . . 0 50   *M. W. Dodd.*
Barth, H., Travels and Discoveries in North and Central
     Africa. Being a Journal of an Expedition
     undertaken under the auspices of H. B. M.'s
     Government in the years 1849–1855, 3 vols.
     8vo. cl. . . . . . 6 00   *Harper & Brothers.*
Bartlett, D. W., Paris with Pen and Pencil; its People
     and Literature, its Life and Business.
     12mo. . . . . 1 00   *Saxton & B.*
—— " Presidental Candidates : containing
     Sketches, Biographical, Personal, and
     Political, of Prominent Candidates
     for the Presidency in 1860. . 1 00   *A. B. Burdick.*
—— " The Heroes of the Indian Rebellion.
     8vo. . . . . .   *Follett, Foster & Co.*

Bartlett, J. R . Dictionary of Americanisms. A Glossary
of Words and Phrases usually regarded
as peculiar to the United States. Second edition, enlarged. 8vo. . . 2 25 *Little, Brown & Co.*

Barton, W. S., Easy Lessons in English Grammar, for
Young Beginners. 16mo. . . . 0 50 *Gould & Lincoln.*

Barton's History of a Suit in Equity, revised. By Jas. R.
Holcombe. 8vo. . . . . 2 25 *Robt. Clarke & Co.*

Bartol, O. A. (Rev.), Church and Congregation: a Plea
for their Unity. 16mo. . . 1 00 *Ticknor & Fields.*

——— " " The Word of the Spirit to the Church.
16mo. . . . . . 0 50 *Walker, Wise & Co.*

Barwell (Mrs.), Gilbert Harland, or, Good in Everything;
Being the Early History of a City Boy.
18mo. . . . . . 0 50 *Carlton & Porter.*

Bascom, J., Political Economy: designed as a Text-Book
for Colleges. 12mo. . . . . *W. F. Draper.*

Base Ball (The) Player's Pocket Companion; containing
Rules and Regulations for forming Clubs,
Directions for playing, &c. 18mo. . 0 25 *Mayhew & Baker.*

Bastile, Chronicles of the. Illustrated. 8vo. .. . 2 25 *Stanford & Delisser*

Batchelder, S., The Young Men of America. A Prize
Essay. 16mo. . . . . 0 40 *Sheldon & Co.*

Bate, W. T. (Capt. R. N.), A Memoir of. By the Rev. John
Baillie. 16mo. . . . . 1 25 *Carter & Brothers.*

Bateman, W. O., The General Commercial Law as Recognized in the Jurisprudence of the United
States. 8vo. . . . . . 5 50 *Johnson & Co.*

Bates, S. P., Lectures on Moral and Mental Culture. 12mo. 1 00 *Barnes & Burr.*

Battle Roll (The). An Encyclopædia containing descriptions of the most famous and memorable land
battles and sieges in all ages of the world,
arranged alphabetically and chronologically
illustrated. 8vo. . . . . . 3 50 *Mason Brothers.*

Bautain, M., The Art of Extempore Speaking. Hints for
the Pulpit, the Senate, and the Bar. 12mo. 1 00 *Charles Scribner.*

Baxter, R. (Rev.), Gildas Silvianus. The Reformed
Pastor. 8vo. . . . . . 2 00 *Carter & Brothers·*

Bayne, P., Essays in Biography and Criticism. 2 vols.
First Series and Second Series. 12mo. Each, 1 25 *Gould & Lincoln.*

Beach, W. (M. D.), The American Practice Condensed;
or, The Family Physician. Nineteenth ed.
Revised with the latest improvements. 8vo. 4 00 *Moore, W., K. & Co.*

Beale, O. A. S., George Lee; or, The Boy who became a
Great Artist. 18mo. . . . . 0 25 *Carlton & Porter.*

Beauties of the Sanctuary. From the French of Hubert
    Lebon. 18mo. . . . . 0 50 *Kelly, H., & P.*

Beautiful (The) Home, and Other Letters to a Child. By
    the author of "Ministering Children," &c.
    18mo. . . . . 0 30 *Carter & Brothers.*

Beck, T. R. & J. B., Elements of Medical Jurisprudence.
    Eleventh edition. With notes by an Associa-
    tion of the Friends of Dr. Beck. The whole
    revised by Prof. C. R. Gilman, M. D., of the
    College of Physicians and Surgeons of New
    York. 2 vols. 8vo. Law and Medical Styles. 10 00 *Lippincott & Co.*

Becket, Thomas-a- Life of. By Henry Hart Milman.
    18mo. cloth. . . . . . 0 50 *Sheldon & Co.*

Beckets, S. B., Hester. A Poem. 12mo. . . . 0 75 *Bailey & Noyes.*

Bede, A., Letters to an Episcopalian, on the Origin, His-
    tory, and Doctrine of the Book of Common
    Prayer. 12mo. . . . . . 0 75 *Kelly, H., & P.*

——C., The Adventures of Mr. Verdant Green. 12mo. 1 00 *Rudd & Carleton.*

Bedford, H., The Life and Times of St. Vincent de Paul.
    12mo. . . . . *D. & J. Sadlier.*

Bedortha, N., Practical Medication; or, The Invalid's
    Guide; with directions for the treatment of
    Disease. 12mo. cloth. . . . . 1 00 *Munsell & Row'd.*

Beecher, Catherine E., An Appeal to the People, in behalf
    of their Rights as authorized Interpreters of
    the Bible. 12mo. . . . . . 1 00 *Harper & Bros.*

——Edward (Rev.), The Concord of Ages; or, the
    Individuals and Organic Harmony of God and
    Man. 12mo. . . . . . . 1 25 *Derby & Jackson.*

—— Henry Ward (Rev.), New Star Papers; or, Views
        and Experiences of Religious
        Subjects. 12mo. . . 1 25 "

——   "   " Plain and Pleasant Talk
        about Fruits, Flowers, and
        Farming, 12mo. . . 1 25 "

Bees and Bee-keeping; a plain, practical Work, from years
    of experience. By W. C. Harrison. 12mo. cl. 1 00 *Saxton & Barker.*

Beggar's Closet (The), and other stories. 18mo. cloth. 0 35 *Henry Hoyt.*

Belcher, J. (Rev.), Historical Sketches of Hymns, their
    writers and their influence. 12mo. cl. . 1 25 *Lindsay & Blak'n.*

Believer's Daily Treasure of Texts of Scripture for Every
    Day in the Year. 32mo. . . . . 0 25 *Presby. B. of Pub.*

Belisle, D. W., History of Independence Hall, Philadel-
    phia. Also, Biographical Sketches of the
    Signers, &c. . . . . 1 25 *J. Challen & Son.*

Bell, A. N. (M. D.), A Knowledge of Living Things, with
the Laws of their Existence. 12mo. . . 1 50 *Baillière Brothers*
—— " Records of Daily Practice, A Scientific Visit-
ing List for Physicians and Surgeons. 12mo.
Tuck binding. . . . . . . 0 75   "
—— O. D., The Children's Mirror; or, Which is my
Likeness? 16mo. cl. . . . . . 1 25 *T. Nelson & Sons.*
—— J. (M.D.), A Treatise on Baths; including cold, sea,
warm, hot, vapor, gas and mud Baths; also
on Hydropathy, and Pulmonary Inhalations.
Second edition. 12mo. cl. . . . . 1 25 *Lindsay & Blak'n.*
Belle; or, The Promised Blessing. By the Author of
" Timid Lucy." 16mo. . . . . . 0 50 *Daniel Dana, jr.*
Belle (The) of Washington; a True Story of the Affec-
tions. By Mrs. N. P. Lasselle. 12mo. cl. . 1 25 *Peterson & Bros.*
—— Britain on a Tour at Newport, and Here and There.
12mo. . . . . 1 00 *Derby & Jackson.*
Bellows, H. W., Rev., Re-statements of Christian Doc-
trine, in Twenty-five Sermons. 12mo. . 1 25 *D. Appleton & Co.*
Ben Ratcliffe, the Wrecker. By M. J. Errym. 8vo. pap. 0 25 *F. A. Brady.*
—— Sylvester's Word. By the author of " The Heir of
Redclyffe. 18mo. . . . . . . 0 37 *D. Appleton & Co.*
Bengel, John Albert, Gnomon of the New Testament,
pointing out from the Natural Force of the
Words the Simplicity, Depth, Harmony and
Saving Power of the Divine Thought. A New
Translation. By Charlton T. Lewis, M. A., and
Marvin R. Vincent, M. A. Vol. 1. 8vo. . 2 50 *Perkinpine & H.*
Benedict, D., Rev., Fifty Years among the Baptists.
12mo. . . . . 1 00 *Sheldon & Co.*
———— E. C., A Run through Europe. 12mo. . 1 25 *D. Appleton & Co.*
Beneficium Christi, The Benefits of Christ's Death; or,
The Glorious Riches of God's Free Grace,
which every true believer receives by Jesus
Christ, and Him Crucified. 18mo. . . 0 38 *Pres. Pub. Com.*
Benjamin, M. G., Mrs., The Missionary Sisters; a Memo-
rial of Mrs. Seraphina Haynes Everett, and
Mrs. Harriet Martha Hamlin, late Missionaries
at Constantinople. 12mo. cl. . . . 0 75 *Am. Tract So.*
Bennett, E., Wild Scenes on the Frontiers; or, Heroes of
the West. 12mo. cl. . . . . . 1 25 *H. Dexter & Co.*
—— O. H., Old Nurse's Book of Rhymes, Jingles, and
Ditties. 4to. . . . .   *Munroe & Co.*
—— J. H., Clinical Lectures on the Principles and
Practice of Medicine. 8vo. . . . 6 00 *J. B. & W. Wood.*

Bennett, J. H. A Practical Treatise on the Inflammation
    of the Uterus, its Cervix and Appendages, and
    on its connection with Uterine Disease. Fifth
    American edition. To which is added a Review
    of the PresentState of Uterine Pathology. 8vo.   4 25   *Blanchard & Lea.*
Bentwright, J., The American Horse Tamer. 12mo.   0 50   *George Holbrook.*
Berriman, M. W., The Militiaman's Manual, and Sword-
    Play without a Master. 12mo.   0 75   *James Miller.*
Bertha Percy; or, L'Esperance. By Margaret Field.
    12mo.   1 25   *D. Appleton & Co.*
Bertrand Noel; a Story for Youth. By E. J. May.
    12mo.   0 75   "
Bessie Duncan; or, the First Year out of School.
    18mo.   0 30   *Am. S. S. Union.*
Bessie Grant's Treasure. By Aunt Dora.   0 50   *Walker, Wise & Co.*
—— Melville; or, Prayer Book Instructions carried
    out into Life. By M. A. C. 16mo.   0 75   *F. D. Harriman.*
Bethlehem and Bethlehem School. By C. B. Mortimer.
    16mo.   0 63   *Stanford & Delisser*
———— " her Children. By the author of "That
    Sweet Story of Old." Square 32mo.   0 25   *Am. Tract So.*
Better Land (The), A Book for the Aged. By Rev.
    James Smith. 18mo.   0 20   *Presb. Bd. of Pub.*
Beulah. By Augusta J. Evans. 12mo. cl.   1 25   *Derby & Jackson.*
Bible History; a Text-Book for Seminaries, Schools, and
    Families. By Sarah B. Hanna. 12mo.   1 00   *Barnes & Burr.*
—— Stories in Verse for the Little Ones at Home. By
    Anna M. Hyde. 4to.   0 50   *J. Challen & Son.*
—— Pictures for Children. 18mo.   0 22   *Carlton & Porter.*
—— Stories, in Bible language. Small 4to.   1 00   *D. Appleton & Co.*
—— (The) and Social Reform; or, the Scriptures as a
    Means of Civilization. By R. H. Tyler.   1 00   *J. Challen & Son.*
—— " in the Levant; or, the Life and Letters of
    the Rev. Chester N. Righter. By the Rev.
    S. Irenæus Prime, D. D. 18mo.   0 75   *Sheldon & Co.*
Biblical (The) Reason Why; a Family Guide to Scripture
    Readings, and a Hand-Book for Biblical Students.
    12mo. cl.   1 00   *Dick & Fitzgerald.*
Bickersteth, E. H., The Book of Ages; or, Scripture
    Testimony to the One Eternal Godhead.
    12mo. cl.   0 63   *E. P. Dutton & Co.*
Big (The) Nightcap Letters. By the author of "The
    Six Nightcap Books." Square cl.   0 50   *D. Appleton & Co.*
Bigelow, J., A History of the Cemetery at Mount
    Auburn. 18mo.   0 75   *J. Munroe & Co.*

Bigelow, J., M.D., Brief Expositions of rational Medicine.
18mo. . . . . 0 50 *Phil., Samp. & Co.*

Binney, W. G., The Terrestrial Air-Breathing Mollusks
of the United States and the Adjacent Territories of North America. Vol. IV. Supple-
ment. Six Plates. Small 4to. pap. . . 8 00 *Westermann & Co.*

Biographies of Distinguished Scientific Men. By Fran-
cois Arago. Second Series. 16mo. . . 1 00 *Ticknor & Fields.*

Biography of Self-Taught Men, with an Introductory
Essay. By B. B. Edwards. 16mo. . . 0 88 *J. E. Tilton & Co.*

Bird, G., Urinary Deposits, their Diagnosis, Pathology,
and Therapeutical Indications. A New American
from the fifth London edition. With 80 illustrations on Wood. 8vo. . . . . . 2 00 *Blanchard & Lea.*

Bishop, Every Woman her own Lawyer and Legal Ad-
visor. 12mo. . . . . 1 00 *Dick & Fitzgerald.*

—— J. P., Commentaries on the Criminal Law. Vol.
2, second edition, revised and enlarged. 5 50 *Little, Brown & Co.*

—— P., Commentaries on the Law of Marriage and
Divorce, and Evidenced in Matrimonial Suits.
Third edition, revised and enlarged. 8vo. . 5 50 "   "

Bissell, O., The Panic as seen from Parnassus, and other
Poems. By Champion Bissell. 12mo. . 0 75 *T. J. Crowen.*

Black Diamonds! Gathered in the Darkey Homes of the
South. By Edward A. Pollard, of Vir-
ginia. 12mo. . . . . . . 0 50 *Pudney & Russell.*

—— Gauntlet, The: A Tale of Plantation Life in South
Carolina. By Mrs. H. R. School-
craft. 12mo. . . . . . 1 25 *Lippincott & Co.*

Blackburn, W. M., The Holy Child; or, the Early Years
of our Lord Jesus Christ. 18mo. . 0 40 *Presb. B. of Pub.*

Blackie, W. G. (Rev.), Bible History in Connection with
the History of the World. 12mo. cl. 0 75 *T. Nelson & Sons.*

Blackstone, W., Commentaries on the Laws of England.
With Notes selected from the editions of Arch-
bold, Christian, Coleridge, Chitty, Stewart,
Kerr, and others, Baron Field's Analysis, and
Additional Notes, and a life of the Author.
By George Sharswood. 2 vols. 8vo. . . 6 00 *Childs & Peterson.*

Blair, Robert, The Grave. Illustrated with Blake's Designs. 4to. cl. . . . . . 2 50 *Stanford & D.*

Blake, W. P., Report of Geological Reconnoissance in
California, made in connection with the Expedition to survey routes in California, to connect with
the surveys of Routes for a railroad from the Mis-

sissippi River to the Pacific Ocean, under the command of Lieut. R. S. Williamson; with an Appendix, containing descriptions of portions of the collection by Professor Agassiz, Gould, Bailey, Conrad, Torrey, Schaeffer and Easter. Profusely illustrated. 4to. . . . . . . 8 00 *H. Baillière.*

Blake, W. O., The History of Slavery and the Slave Trade. 8vo. . . . . . *J. & H. Miller.*

Blakeley, A. (Rev.), The Sabbath; a Sermon in Poetry. 12mo. pap. . . . . . *E. Darrow & Bro.*

Blatchford's United States Circuit Court Reports for the Second Circuit. Vol. 2. 8vo. . . . 5 50 *John S. Voorhies.*

Blessington, Countess, A Journal of Conversations with Lord Byron. With a Sketch of the Life of the Author. 12mo. . . . , . . 1 00 *Crosby, N., L.&Co.*

Blind Bartimeus; or, the Story of a Sightless Sinner, and his Great Physician. By Rev. Wm. J. Hoge. 18mo. 0 75 *Sheldon, B. & Co.*
Ethan. A Story for Boys. 18mo. . . . 0 20 *Henry Hoyt.*
—— Lilias; or Fellowship with God. A Tale for the Young. By a Lady. 16mo. . . . . 0 75 *Carter & Brothers.*
——Man's Holiday; or, Short Tales for the Nursery. By the author of "Mia and Charlie." 18mo. . 0 50   "   "

Bliss, M. H., Little Tiger Lily, and her Cousin Alice; or, how a Bad Temper was cured. 18mo. . 0 28 *Carlton & Porter.*
—————— Margaret Maxham. A Book for Young Ladies. 18mo. . . . . 0 25   "   ".

Blonde and Brunette; or, the Gothamite Arcady. 12mo. 0 75 *D. Appleton & Co.*
Blood, B., Optimism; the Lesson of Ages. 16mo. cl. . 0 60 *B. Marsh.*
Blue Laws of Connecticut. A new edition, edited, with an Introduction. By Samuel M. Smucker, LL. D. 12mo. cl. . . . . . . 1 00 *D. Rulison.*

Boardman, H. A. (Rev.), Quarter Century Discourse, delivered in Philadelphia, Nov. 7th, 1858. Cl. 0 38 *Parry&McMillan*
—————— W. E. (Rev.), The Higher Christian Life. 12mo. . . . . . 1 00 *Henry Hoyt.*

Bob and Walter; with the Story of Breakneck Ledge. 16mo. . . . . 0 50 *Phinney, B. & M.*

Bodenhamer, W. (M. D.), A Practical Treatise on the Ætiology, Pathology, and Treatment of the Congenital Malformations of the Rectum and Anus. 8vo. . . . . 2 00 *S. S. & W. Wood.*

Bogatzky, C. H., A Golden Treasury for the Children of God. 18mo. cl. . . . . . *Lutheran Bd.Pub.*

Boismont, A. B., On Hallucinations; a History and Explanation of Apparitions, Visions, Dreams, Ecstasy, Magnetism, and Somnambulism. 12mo. *J. H. Riley & Co.*

Bolles, J. A. (Rev.), The Family Altar; or Prayers for
Family Worship: compiled from the Book
of Common Prayer, and arranged to suit
the four Principal Seasons of the Ecclesiastical Year. 24mo. pp. 97. . . . 0 50 *Daniel Dana, jr.*

Bomberger, J. H. A. (Rev.), Infant Salvation in its Relation to Infant Depravity, Infant
Regeneration, and Infant Baptism.
12mo. . . . . *Lindsay & B.*

——— " The Protestant Theological and
Ecclesiastical Encyclopedia: being a condensed Translation of Herzog's Real Encyclopedia. With additions from other
sources. 3 vols. 8vo. Vol. 1. . . " "

Bonar, A. A. (Rev.), Christ and His Church in the Book
of Psalms. 8vo. . . 1 75 *Carter & Brothers.*

Bond, G. P., An Account of Donati's Comet of 1858. 4to. 0 50 *John Bartlett.*

Bonnet, L., The Family of Bethany; or, Meditations on
the 11th Chapter of the Gospel of John. 18mo. 0 40 *Carter & Brothers.*

Bonnie Scotland. Tales of her History, Heroes and Poets.
By Grace Greenwood. 16mo. cl. . . 0 75 *Ticknor & Fields.*

Book of Ages; or, Scripture Testimony to the One
Eternal Godhead. By E. H. Bickersteth,
M. A. 12mo. cl. . . . . 0 63 *E. P. Dutton & Co.*

—— " Christian Sonnets. By William Allen, D. D.
12mo. . . . . . *Bridgman & Childs*

—— " Humorous Poetry. Comprising Selections from
the Most Popular Humorists of England and
America. 12mo. . . . 1 00 *G. G. Evans.*

—— " 1,000 Comical Stories (The). By the author of
"Mrs. Partington's Carpet Bag of Fun." 12mo. 1 00 *Dick & Fitzgerald.*

—— " Plays for Home Amusement; adapted for Private
Representation. By Silas S. Steele. 12mo. 1 00 *G. G. Evans.*

—— " Popular Songs. Selection of Songs, Ballads, &c.
12mo. . . . . . 1 00 "

—— " the First American Chess Congress; containing
the Proceedings held in New York, in the year
1857. By Daniel Willard Fiske, M. A. 12mo. 1 50 *Rudd & Carleton.*

—— (The) and its Story; a Narrative for the Young.
By L. N. R. 16mo. . . . 1 00 *Carter & Bros.*

Books and Reading; a lecture by W. P. Atkinson. 18mo. 0 20 *Crosby, N., L. & Co.*

Boone, Daniel. Life and Times of. Including an Account
of the Early Settlement of Kentucky. 12mo. 1 00 *G. G. Evans.*

Boot and Shoe Manufacturers' Assistant and Guide.
Compiled and edited by W. H. Richardson, Jr.
12mo. . . . . . 1 25 *Higgins, B. & D.*

Booth, M. L., History of the City of New York, from its
    earliest Settlement to the Present Time. 8vo. 3 50 *Clark & Meeker.*
——— " The King of the Mountains. From the
    French of Edmond About. 12mo. cl. . 1 00 *J. E. Tilton & Co.*
——— M., New and Complete Clock and Watchmaker's
    Manual. 12mo. .   .   .   . 1 50 *John Wiley.*
Border War; a Tale of Disunion. By J. B. Jones. 12mo. 1 25 *Rudd & Carleton.*
Botany for Young People. By Asa Gray, M.D. Small 4to. 0 75 *Ivison & Phinney.*
Botta, Anne C., Hand Book of Literature. .   . 1 50 *Derby & Jackson.*
Bound Out; or, Abby at the Farm. By Aunt Friendly. 0 25 *A. D.F.Randolph.*
Boutwell, G. S., Thoughts on Educational Topics. 12mo. 1 00 *Phillips, S. & Co.*
Bowen, The Life of Bishop Bowen, of South Carolina.
    By John N. Norton. 18mo. .   .   . 0 30 *F. D. Harriman.*
Bower, J., The New Public School Singing Book. 32mo.   *Leary, Getz & Co.*
Bowman, Anne, The Kangaroo Hunters; or, Adventures
    in the Bush. 16mo. .   .   . 0 75 *Crosby, N., L.& Co.*
Boy Missionary. By Jenny Marsh Parker. 18mo. cl. . 0 30 *F. D. Harriman,*
——— Tar (The); or, a Voyage in the Dark. By Capt.
    Mayne Reid. 16mo. .   .   .   . 0 75 *Ticknor & Fields.*
——— (The) of Principle: The Man of Honor: or, The
    Story of Jack Halyard. By William S. Cardell.
    18mo. cl. .   .   .   .   .   . 0 63 *U. Hunt & Son.*
Boy's (The) Book of Modern Travel and Adventure. By
    Meredith Johnes. 12mo. .   .   . 0 75 *D. Appleton & Co.*
——— Own Toy-Maker. By E. Landells. Square 16mo. 0 50   "   "
——— Pump Book: showing how to make several kinds
    of Minature Pumps and a Fire Engine. 12mo. 0 25 *A. D.F. Randolph.*
——— and Girls' American Annual. Edited by T. Martin.
    12mo. .   .   .   .   .   . 1 50 *D. Appleton & Co.*
——— (The) and Girls' Own, an Annual for Youth, con-
    taining Fact, Fiction, History, Biography, Arts,
    Science, etc., for 1860–61. 2 vols. 12mo., each. 0 75 *William L. Jones.*
——— Book of Industrial Information. By Elisha Noyce.
    12mo. .   .   .   .   .   . 1 25 *D. Appleton & Co.*
Boyd, J. R. Elements of English Composition. 12mo. . 1 00 *Barnes & Burr.*
Brackenridge, H. M. History of the Western Insurrection
    in Western Pennsylvania, commonly called
    the Whisky Insurrection,1794. 8vo. . 1 25 *W. S. Haven.*
Bradbury, W. B. Anthem Book. A Collection of An-
    thems, Choruses, Opening and Closing
    Pieces. Music 8vo., ... 1 25 *Mason Brothers.*
——— " Cottage Melodies; or, Hymn and Tune Book
    for Prayer and Social Meetings, and the
    Home Circle. 16mo. .   .   .   . 0 50 *F. J. Huntington.*
——— " Oriola, a New and Complete Hymn and Tune
    Book, for Sabbath Schools. 16mo. .   . 0 37 *Moore, W., K.& Co.*

Bradbury, W. B., The Eclectic Tune Book. 8vo. . . 1 00 *Mason & Bros.*
Bradford, Sarah H. The Linton Family; or, The Fash-
    ion of this World. 12mo. . . . . 1 00 *Pudney & Russell.*
Brady, Jas. T. A Christmas Dream. Illustrated by Ed-
    ward S. Hall. 16mo. . . . . 0 75 *D. Appleton & Co.*
Brandon; or, A Hundred Years' Ago. A Tale of the
    American Colonies. By O. Tiffany. 12mo. 1 00 *Stanford & Delis'r.*
Braun, C. R. (M. D.), Urænic Convulsions of Pregnancy,
    Parturition, and Childbed. Translated from
    the German, with Notes, by J. Matthews Dun-
    can, F. R. C. P. E. 12mo. . . . . 0 75 *S. S. & W. Wood.*
Breakfast, Dinner, and Tea; viewed Classically, Poetical-
    ly, and Practically. Square 12mo. . . 1 50 *D. Appleton & Co.*
Breckinridge, R. J. (Rev.), The Knowledge of God, sub-
    jectively considered. 8vo. . . . 2 50 *R. Carter & Bros.*
Bremer, F. Father and Daughter; a Portraiture from
    Life. 12mo. cl. . . . . . 1 25 *T.B.Peter'n&Bros.*
Bresciana, A. (Rev.) Lionello. A Sequel to the Jew of
    Verona. 12mo. . . . . . 1 00 *Kelly, Hidean &P.*
Brewer, D. R. (Rev). The Rector's Offering. Selections
    from the Sermons of the Rev. D. R. Brewer. 18mo. 0 50 *A.D. F. Randolph.*
Brewster, Anne M. H. Compensation; or, Always a
    Future. 12mo. . . . . . 1 00 *Lippincott & Co.*
Bride (The) of Love, or, The True Greatness of Female
    Heroism. By Ruth Vernon. 12mo. cl. . . 1 00 *Duane Rulison.*
Bridge, J. The Practical Miner's Own Book and Guide,
    with Additions. By J. Atkins. 12mo. . 2 00 *J. W. Randolph.*
Bridges, C. (Rev.) An Exposition of the Book of Eccle-
    siastes. 12mo. . . . . . 1 00 *R. Carter & Bros.*
Brief Biographies. By Samuel Smiles, author of "Self-
    Help," &c. 12mo. . . . . . 1 25 *Ticknor & Fields.*
Briggs, C. F., & Maverick, A., The Story of the Tele-
    graph and a History of the Great Atlantic Cable. 1 00 *Rudd & Carleton.*
Brigham, Amariah, A Biographical Sketch of. . .   *W. O. McClure.*
———— J., Twelve Messages from the Spirit of John
    Quincy Adams, through Joseph C. Stiles,
    medium, to Josiah Brigham. . . . 1 50 *Bela Marsh.*
Bright, W., Single Stem, Dwarf and Renewal of Grape
    Culture, adapted to the Vineyard, the Grapery,
    and the Fruiting of Vines in Pots, on Trellises,
    Arbors, etc. By William Bright, 16mo. . 0 50 *Saxton & Barker.*
Brightly, N., Biennial Digest for 1857 and 1859, on the
    plan and in continuation of Brightly's Analytical
    Digest of the Laws of the United States, and
    completing it to the present date. . . .   *Kay & Brother.*

Brightwell, C. L., Palissy, the Huguenot Potter. A True
     Tale. 16mo. . . . . 0 55   *Presb. B. of Pub.*
     The Same. 16mo. cl. . . . . 0 75   *Carlton & Porter.*
Brinton, D. G., Notes on the Floridian Peninsula, its
    Literary History, Indian Tribes, and Antiqui-
    ties. 12mo. . . . .   *Joseph Sabin.*
British Novelists and their Styles. By D. Masson, M. A. 1 00   *Gould & Lincoln.*
Brittain, Harriet G., Scenes and Incidents of Every-Day
    Life in Africa. 12mo. . . . . . 1 00   *Pudney & Russell.*
Brock, C., Mrs., Home Memories; or, Echoes of a
     Mother's Voice. 12mo. cl. . . . 0 75   *D. Appleton & Co.*
————   "   Working and Waiting; or, Patience
     in Well-Doing. 16mo. . . . 0 50   *W.S.& A.Martien.*
———— H. F., Mrs., Old Robin and his Proverb. 18mo. 0 40   *Am. Tract So.*
Broken Cisterns; or, the Story of Jessie Worthington, 0 75   *Am. S. S. Union.*
———— Ramrod (The); or, the Bible, History, and Com-
    mon Sense, in Favor of the Moderate use of Good
    Spirituous Liquors. Showing the advantage of a
    License System in preference to Prohibition and
    "Moral" in preference to "Legal Suasion." . 1 00   *Albert Colby & Co.*
Brook Farm; the Amusing and Memorable of American
    Country Life. 18mo. . . . . . 0 60   *Carter & Brothers.*
Brooks, A., A Cluster of Fruits from the Tree of Heavenly
    Wisdom. 18mo. . . . . . . 0 35   *Presb. B. of Pub.*
———— C. T., Rev., Simplicity of Christ's Teachings, set
    forth in Sermons. 12mo. . . . . 1 00   *Crosby,N.,L.& Co.*
———— N. C., Epitome Historiæ Sacræ, Auctore L'Ho-
    mond. Second edition. 16mo. . . 0 50   *Barnes & Burr.*
———— " Julius Cæsar's Commentaries on the
     Gallic War; elucidated by English
     Notes, Critical and Explanatory, with a
     Lexicon of all the words contained in
     the Text. 12mo. . . . . . 1 25   "
———— " The School Harmonist; comprising Psalm
     and Hymn Tunes in general use. 16mo. 0 50   , "
Brotherhead, W. (Editor), The Book of the Signers;
    containing Fac-simile Letters of the Signers of
    the Declaration of Independence. Illustrated,
    also, with sixty-one Engravings, from Original
    Photographs and Drawings of their Residences,
    Portraits, etc. From the Collection of an Asso-
    ciation of American Antiquaries. Folio. . . 8 00   *W. Brotherhead.*
Brother's (The) Watchword. 16mo. . . . . 0 75   *Carter & Brothers*
Brown, D., Rev., The Four Gospels, according to the
    Authorized Version, with Original and Selected

Parallel References and Marginal Readings, and
an Original and Copious Critical and Explana-
tory Commentary. 16mo.   .   .   .   .   0 50   *W.S.& A.Martien.*

Brown H. S., Rev., Lectures for the People.   First
Series, with a Biographical Introduction, by Dr.
R. Shelton Mackenzie. 12mo. .   .   .   .   1 00   *G. G. Evans.*

—————— John, The Public Life of Captain John Brown.
By James Redpath. With an Autobiogra-
phy of his Childhood and Youth.   12mo.   1 00   *Thayer& Eldridge.*

—————— "   The Life, Trial, and Conviction of Capt.
John Brown, with a full account of the
attempted Insurrection at Harper's Ferry.
8vo. pap.   .   .   .   .   .   .   0 25   *Robert M. De Witt.*

—————— "   Sixty Years' Gleanings from Life's Harvest.
A Genuine Autobiography.   By John
Brown, proprietor of the University
Billiard Rooms, Cambridge. 12mo.   .   1 00   *D. Appleton & Co.*

—————— "   M. D., Rabb and his Friends. 16mo.   .   0 15   *Ticknor & Fields.*
—————— J. S., The Bouquet, and other Poems. 24mo. .   *Murray, Y. & Co.*

Browning, E. B., Napoleon III. in Italy. And other
Poems. 16mo.   .   .   .   .   .   .   0 50   *C. S. Francis & Co.*

Brownlow, W. G., and Pryne, A., Ought American Slavery
to be perpetuated? A Debate between W. G.
Brownlow and Rev. A. Pryne, held at Phila-
delphia, September, 1858. 12mo. cloth.   .   1 00   *Lippincott & Co.*

Brünnow, F., Tables of Victoria, computed with regard to
the Perturbations of Jupiter and Saturn. 4to.   1 00   *B. Westerm'n & Co.*

Bryant, H. B., & Stratton's National Book-keeper.   Prepared as a book of reference for the counting-
house: and, also, as a text-book in High
Schools and Academies. 8vo.   .   .   .   1 75   *Ivison, Phin'y & Co.*

—————— J. D., Redemption: a Poem. 12mo. .   .   .   1 00   *Pennington & Son.*
—————— W. C., A Discourse on the Life, Character, and
Genius of Washington Irving, delivered before
the New York Historical Society, at the
Academy of Music, in New York, on the 3d
April, 1860. 12mo.   .   .   .   .   .   0 40   *G. P. Putnam.*

—————— "   A Forest Hymn. By William Cullen Bryant.
With Illustrations by John A. Hows. Small
4to. cloth, extra gilt.   .   .   .   .   3 50   *W A Townsend & Co*

—————— "   Letters of a Traveler. Second Series. By
William Cullen Bryant. 12mo.   .   .   0 25   *D. Appleton & Co.*

Buchanan, James (Rev.), The Office and Work of the
Holy Spirit.   .   .   .   .   .   .   *Carter & Brothers.*

Buchanan, R. (D. D.), Notes of a Clerical Furlough, spent chiefly in the Holy Land, with a Sketch of the Voyage in the Yacht "St. Ursula." 12mo.   1 50   *Blackie & Son.*

Buckland's Curiosities of Natural History. 12mo.   .   1 25   *Rudd & Carleton.*

Buckle, H. T., History of Civilization in England. Vol. 1. From the Second London Edition. To which is added an Alphabetical Index. 8vo.   .   2 50   *D. Appleton & Co.*

Budget (The) Closed. By Jane A. Eames. 12mo.   .   1 00   *Ticknor & Fields.*

Buds from Christmas Boughs. By Virginia F. Townsend. 12mo.   .   0 63   *R. L. Delisser.*

Bulfinch, T., The Age of Chivalry. Part I. King Arthur and his Knights. Part II. The Mabinogeon; or, Welsh Popular Tales. 12mo.   .   1 00   *Crosby, N., L.&Co.*

Bulwer, E. L., Novels *now publishing*, with illustration. 12mo. cloth. Per volume.   .   .   .   1 00   *Lippincott & Co.*

Bumstead, F. J., A Treatise on the Venereal Disease. By John Hunter, F.R.S. With copious additions. By Dr. Philip Ricord, Surgeon of the Hospital du Midi, Paris, &c. Translated and edited, with Notes. By Freeman J. Bumstead, M.D. Second Edition. Revised. 8vo.   .   .   .   .   3 25   *Blanchard & Lea.*

Bunbury, S., Fanny, the Flower Girl; or, Honesty Rewarded. 18mo.   .   .   .   .   0 30   *Carter & Brothers.*

Bunting, Jabez (Rev.), The Life of, with Notices of Contemporary Persons and Events. By his Son, Thomas Percival Bunting. Vol. 1. 12mo.   1 00   *Harper &Brothers.*

Buntline, Ned, The White Wizard; or, The Great Prophet of the Seminoles. 8vo. paper.   .   .   0 25   *F. A. Brady.*

Burdett, C., Dora Barton, the Banker's Ward . a Tale of Real Life in New York. 12mo.   .   .   1 00   *S. A. Rollo.*

——— "Margaret Moncrieffe: the First Love of Aaron Burr. A Romance of the Revolution. 12mo.   1 25   *Derby & Jackson.*

Burlamaqui, J. J., The Principles of Natural and Politic Law. 8vo.   .   .   .   .   .   .   *J. H. Riley & Co.*

Burnet, P. H., The Path which led a Protestant Lawyer to the Catholic Church. 8vo.   .   .   2 50   *D. Appleton &Co.*

Burns, Robert, Life of. By Carlyle and others. 18mo.   0 50   *Sheldon & Co.*

——— The Centennial Birthday of, as celebrated by the Burns Club, of New York, Jan. 25, 1859. Edited by John Cunningham. 8vo.   .   .   .   .   1 00   *Lang & Laing.*

Burrell, A. M., A Law Dictionary and Glossary. 2d edition. 2 vols. 8vo.   .   .   .   10 00   *John S. Voorhies.*

Burrowes, Geo. (Rev.), Commentary on the Songs of Solomon. Second edition, revised. 12mo.   .   .   .   1 25   *W. S. & A. Martien.*

Burton, The Anatomy of Melancholy. By Democritus
    Junior. With a Satirical Preface, conducing to
    the following. A new edition, corrected and
    enriched by Translations of the numerous Clas-
    sical Extracts. By Democritus Minor. 8 vols.
    12mo. . . . . 4 00   *Crosby, N., L. & Co.*
—— R. F. (Capt.), The Lake Regions of Central Afri-
    ca; a Picture of Explorations.
    With Illustrations. 8vo. cl. . 2 50   *Harper & Bros.*
—— W. E., The Cyclopœdia of Wit and Humor; con-
    taining choice and characteristic Selec-
    tions from the Writings of the most
    eminent Humorists of America, Ireland,
    Scotland, and England. 2 vols. 8vo. . 7 00   *D. Appleton & Co.*
Bush, Geo., Notes Critical and Practical on the Book of
    Numbers. 12mo. . . . . . 1 00   *Ivison & Phinney.*
Bushnell, Horace (Rev.), Sermons for the New Life. 12mo. 1 25   *Charles Scribner.*
Butler, Bishop Butler's Ethical Discourses and Essay on
    Virtue, arranged as a Treatise on Moral Philoso-
    phy. Edited with an Analysis, by J. T. Champ-
    lin. 12mo. . . . . 0 75   *John P. Jewett & Co.*
—— H. D., The Family Aquarium; or, Aqua Vivarium.
    16mo. . . . . , . . . 0 50   *Dick & Fitzgerald.*
—— O. M. (Rev.), Lectures on the Book of Revelation.
    12mo. . . . . 1 25   *Carter & Bros.*
—— R., Jessie Cameron; a Highland Story. 8vo. pap. 0 25   *Robt. M. De Witt.*
—— W. A., Two Millions. 16mo. . . . . 0 50   *D. Appleton & Co.*
Butt, Martha H., Leisure Moments. 12mo. . . 1 25   *F. D. Long & Co.*
By-and-By. By Virginia F. Townsend. 12mo. . . 0 63   *R. L. Delisser.*
Byers, Wm. N., A Hand-Book to the Gold Fields of Ne-
    braska and Kansas. 16mo. . . . 0 50   *D. B. Cooke & Co.*

C

Cabell, J. L., The Testimony of Modern Science to the
    Unity of Mankind. With an Introductory
    Notice. By James W. Alexander, D. D. 12mo. 1 00   *Carter & Brothers.*
Cæcilia (The), A collection of Vocal Music for Seminaries,
    Institutes, &c. By Sigismond Lasar. 4to. .   *Mason Brothers.*
Caird Jas., Prairie Farming in America, with Notes by
    the way on Canada and the United States.
    12mo. . . . . 0 50   *D. Appleton & Co*
—— J. O. (Rev.), Sermons. 12mo. . . . 1 00   *Carter & Brothers*

Caldwell, D. (Rev.), Parochial Lectures on the Psalms.
8vo. . . . . 1 50   *W.S. &A. Martien.*
Calkins, N. A., The Universal Speaker, Containing a
Collection of Speeches, Dialogues and Recita-
tions. 12mo. . . . . . . 1 00   *Brown & Taggart.*
Calvin, John., Letters of. Compiled from the Original
Manuscripts, and Edited with Historical Notes.
By Dr. Jules Bonnet. Volume III. Trans-
lated from the Latin and French languages.
By Marcus Robert Gilchrist. 8vo. . . 1 50   *Presby. B. of Pub.*
Camille ; or, The Camelia-Lady. 12mo. cl. . . . 1 25   *T. B. Pe'son&Bro.*
Camp's Geography. . . . . 1 00   *Moore & N.*
Campbell, A. J. (Rev.), The Power Jesus Christ to Save
unto the Uttermost. 16mo. . . . 0 75   *Carter & Bros.*
———— C., History of the Colony and Ancient Do-
minion of Virginia. 8vo. . . . 2 50   *Lippincott & Co.*
———— C., The Orderly Book of that portion of the
American Army stationed at or near Wil-
liamsburgh, Va., under the command of
General Andrew Lewis, from March 18th,
1776, to August 28th, 1776. Printed from
the Original Manuscript, with Notes and
Introduction. By Charles Campbell, Esq.,
author of " Introduction to History of
the Old Dominion," "History of Virginia,"
&c. Small 4to. . . . . . 2 00   *Richmond, Va.*
———— H. F. (M. D.), Essays on the Secretory and
.the Excito - Secretory System of
Nerves in their Relations to Physiol-
ogy and Pathology. 8vo. . .   *Lippincott & Co.*
———— John (Lord), Shakespeare's Legal Acquire-
ments Considered. 12mo. cl. . . 0 75   *D. Appleton & Co.*
———— J. L., A Manual of Scientific and Practical
Agriculture for the Farm and the
School. 12mo. . . . . 1 00   *Lindsay & B.*
———— S. (Mrs.), The Practical Cook Book. 12mo. 0 38   *Munsell & Rowl'd.*
Candlish, R. S. (D. D.), Life in a Risen Saviour. 12mo.
cl. . . . . 1 25   *Lindsay & B.*
Cape Cod, The History of the Annals of Barnstable Coun-
ty, and of several Towns, including the Dis-
trict of Marshpee. By Freeman. 2 vols. 8vo.
Vol. I. . . . . 0 00   *Rand & Avery.*
Capt. Russel's Watchword ; or, "I'll Try." 16mo. . 0 75   *Henry Hoyt.*
Captive (The) Orphan ; Esther the Queen of Persia. By
Stephen H. Tyng, D. D. 12mo. . . 1 00   *Carter & Bros.*

Cardell, W. S., The Boy of Principle: The Man of Honor; or, The Story of Jack Halyard. 18mo. cl. . . . . . . U. *Hunt & Son.*

Carden, R. A. (Rev.), The Heavenly Pathway: or, Going Home. 12mo. . . . . . 1 00 *Lippincott & Co.*

Carey, Alice. Pictures of Country Life. 12mo. . . 1 00 *Derby & Jackson.*

—— H. C. Letters to the President, on the Foreign and Domestic Policy of the Union, and its Effects, as exhibited in the Condition of the People and the State. 8vo. Paper. . . . 0 38 *M. Polock.*

———— Principles of Social Science. 3 vols. 8vo. . 0 00 *Lippincott & Co.*

Carleton, W. The Evil Eye; or, the Black Spectre. 12mo. . . . . 1 25 *Patrick Donohue.*

Carll, M. M., Child's Book of Natural History. 16mo. . 0 40 *A. S. Barnes & B.*

Carlyle, T., Critical and Miscellaneous Essays. 4 vols. 8vo. 5 00 *Brown & Taggard.*

—— History of Frederick the Second, called Frederick the Great. 2 vols. 12mo. . . . . 2 50 *Harper & Bros.*

—— The Life of Frederick Schiller, comprehending an examination of his works. 12mo. cl. . 1 00 *Sheldon & Co.*

Carnochan, J. M. (M. D.), Contributions to Operative Surgery, and Surgical Pathology. 4to. pp. 32. 0 75 *Lindsay & Blakist.*

Carolina Sports by Land and Water; including Incidents of Devil-Fishing, Wild Cat, Deer, and Bear Hunting, &c. By the Hon. Wm. Elliott. 12mo. 1 00 . *Derby & Jackson.*

Caroline Perthes, the Christian Wife. Condensed from the Life of Frederick Christopher Perthes. By Mrs. L. C. Tuthill. 12mo. . . . 1 25 *Carter & Brothers.*

Carpenter, H. S., Here and Beyond; or, The New Man— The True Man. 12mo. . . . . 1 00 *Mason Brothers.*

Carroll, B. R., Catechism of United States History of the Nation, from its earliest Period to the Present Time. 12mo. . . . . *McCarter & Co.*

Carson, Christopher, The Life and Adventures of Kit Carson, the Nestor of the Rocky Mountains, from Facts narrated by himself. By DeWitt C. Peters, M. D. 8vo. . . . . . 2 50 *Clark & Meeker.*

—— Life of the same. By Charles Burdett. 12mo. 1 00 *G. G. Evans.*

Cartee, C. S., Elements of Map Drawing. 4to. . . *Crosby, N., L.& Co*

Carter, Thos. (Rev.), History of the Great Reformation in England, Ireland, Scotland, Germany, France, and Italy. 12mo. . . . . . 1 00 *Carlton & Porter.*

—— W. S., The Code of Procedure of the State of Wisconsin, as passed by the Legislature in 1856, and amended in 1857, '58 '59, with an Appendix, containing the Rules of the Supreme and

Circuit Courts, the Time of holding the Terms
of Court in the various Circuits, and of the U.
S. District Court; also, a new and complete
Index. Compiled by Walter S. Carter, Coun-
selor-at-Law. 8vo. . . . .   *Strickland & Co.*

Cassin, J., Mammalogy and Ornithology of the United
States Exploring Expedition, under Commodore
Wilkes. 1 vol. 4to. With a Folio Atlas of
over Fifty Colored Steel Engravings. Prepared
under the superintendence of John Cassin,
Member of the Academy of Natural Sciences. . 50 00 *Lippincott & Co.*

Cassique (The) of Kiawah: a Romance of Carolina. By
William G. Simms. 12mo. . . . .   1 25 *J. S. Redfield.*

Castle Richmond; a Novel. By Anthony Trollope. 12mo. 1 00 *Harper & Bros.*

Cat and Dog; or, Memoirs of Puss and the Captain. A
Story founded on Fact. Sq. 18mo. . .   0 40 *A. D. F. Ran'lph.*

Cathara Clyde, A Novel. 12mo. . . . . .   1 00 *Charles Scibner.*

Catharine. By the author of   12mo. . . . .   0 75 *J. E. Tilton & Co.*

Cavendish, Clara (Eady), Lisa; or, The Mesmerist's Victim. 8vo. . . . .   0 50 *E. D. Long & Co.*

———— The Woman of the World. 8vo. . . .   0 50   "

Caverly Family (The); or, Mrs. Linden's Teachings. By
H. H. H. 16mo. . . . .   0 63 *D. Dana, Jr.*

Centennial Memorial. A Record of the Proceedings on
the Occasion of the Celebration of the One
Hundredth Anniversary of the A. R. Presbyterian Church of Little Britain, N. Y. Edited by
Archibald C. Niven. . . . .   1 00 *R. Carter & Bros.*

Chadbourne, P. A., Lectures on Natural History; its Relations to Intellect, Taste, Wealth, and Religion. 0 75 *Barnes & Burr.*

Challen, J. (Rev.), Baptism in Spirit and in Fire. 18mo. 0 40 *J. Challen & Son.*

———— Christian Morals. 18mo. . . . . .   0 50   "   "

———— Igdrasyl; or, the Tree of Existence. 12mo. cl. . 1 00 *Lindsay & Blak'n.*

———— Frank Elliott; or, Wells in the Desert. A Religious Novel. 12mo. . . . .   1 00 *J. Challen & Son.*

Chambers, T. W. (Rev.), The Noon Prayer Meeting of the
North Dutch Church, Fulton st., New York.
Its Origin, Character, and Progress, with Some
of its Results. 12mo. . . . . . .   *B. of P. of R. P. D. C.*

Champlin, J. T. (Rev.), Text-Book in Intellectual Philosophy, for Schools and Colleges. 12mo. . .   0 75 *Crosby, N., L. & Co.*

Chanter, Charlotte, Over the Cliffs. 12mo. . . .   1 00 *Ticknor & Fields.*

Chapin, E. H. (Rev.), The Crown of Thorns. A Token
for the Sorrowing. 12mo. . . . . .   *A. Tompkins.*

Chapin, E. H., (Rev.), Extemporaneous Discourses, delivered in the Broadway Church, New York, Re-
ported as Delivered, and Revised and Corrected
by the Author. First Series. 12mo. .   1 00   *O. Hutchinson.*

—— " Select Sermons preached in the Broadway
Church. 12mo. . . . . 1 00   *Henry Lyon.*

Chaplin, J. (Rev.), The Evening of Life; or, Light and
Comfort Amidst the Shadows of Declining
Years. 12mo. . . . . . . 1 00   *Gould & Lincoln.*

Chapman, G. W., A Tribute to Kane; and other Poems. 0 75   *Rudd & Carleton.*

—— Helen, Paul Winslow; or, Blessings in Disguise. 0 25   *Pres. B. of Pub.*

Chapters on Wives. By Mrs. Ellis, author of "Mothers
of Great Men." 12mo. . . . . . 1 00   *Harper & Bros.*

Charity Barnes, the Cobbler's Daughter. 18mo. . . 0 30   *Am. S. S. Union.*

—— Green; or, Varieties of Love. By Theodore
Hartmann. 12mo. . . . . . . 1 25   *John W. Norton.*

—— and Truth, or Catholics not uncharitable in Saying
that None are Saved out of the Catholic Church.
By Rev. Dr. Edward Hawarden. 12mo. . 0 68   *P. F. Cunningham.*

Charles Barton; or, the Mission Garden. 32mo. . . 0 15   *Presb. B. of Pub.*

—— Norwood; or, Erring and Repenting. By C. M.
Trowbridge. 16mo. cl. . . . . . 0 75   *W. S. & A. Martien.*

—— XII., History of. By M. De Voltaire; with a
Life of Voltaire by Lord Brougham, and Critical
Notes by Lord Macaulay and Thomas Carlyle.
Edited by O. W. Wight. 12mo. cl. . . 1 25   *Derby & Jackson.*

Charlesworth, Maria L., The Ministry of Life. 12mo. . 1 00   *D. Appleton & Co.*

Chase, O. T., The Prairie Fruit Culturist; or, What to
Plant and How to Cultivate in the West. 16mo. 0 25   *S. C. Griggs & Co.*

—— E. B., Teachings of Patriots and Statesmen; or,
The Founders of the Republic on Slavery.
12mo. . . . .   *J. W. Bradley.*

Chassay, F. E., The Touchstone of Character. 12mo. . 0 63   *P. O'Shea.*

Chateaubriand, M. De, The Martyrs. A revised translation. Edited by O. W. Wight, A. M. 12mo. . 1 25   *Derby & Jackson.*

Cheever, G. B. (Rev.), Right of the Bible in our Public
Schools. 16mo. . . . . . . 0 75   *Carter & Brothers.*

Cherry Blossom; or, Love Thy Neighbor as Thyself. By
Edward Schiller. 12mo. . . . . 1 00   *R. M. De Witt.*

Chess Handbook (The). Teaching the Rudiments of the
Game, and giving an Analysis of all the Recog-
nized Openings, played by Morphy, Harrwitz,
Anderssen, Staunton, Paulsen, Montgomery,
Meek, and many others. By an Amateur. 16mo. 0 75   *E. H. Butler & Co.*

Chevalier, M., On the Probable Fall in the Value of Gold:
the Commercial and Social Consequences which
may ensue, and the Measures which it Invites.
By Michael Chevalier, Member of the Institute
of France, &c., &c. Translated from the French,
with Preface, by Richard Cobden, Esq. 8vo. . 1 25 *D. Appleton & Co.*

Chief's Daughter (The); or, the Settlement of Virginia. 12mo. cl. .   .   . . 0 30 *F. D. Harriman.*

Child, A. B., Whatever is, is Right. 12mo. cl.   .   . 1 00 *B. Marsh.*

Child's (The) Book of Natural History. Illustrating the
Animal, Vegetable, and Mineral Kingdoms;
with Application to the Arts. By M. M. Carll. 0 40 *Barnes & Burr.*

———— (The) History of the Apostle Paul. 16mo.   0 50 *Am. Tract So.*

———— (The) Illustrated Scripture Question Book. 18mo. 0 15 *H. Hoyt.*

———— (The) Own Picture and Verse Book. With 100
engravings. Square 12mo, cloth.   0 88 *James Miller.*

———— (The) Pleasure Book. With colored plates. 12mo. 0 75 *Sheldon & Co.*

Childhood and the Church. By T. F. R. Mercein. 18mo. 0 30 *A. D. F. Randolph.*

Children (The) of the Church, and Sealing Ordinances.   *Presb. Bd. of Pub.*

———— (The) on the Plains. By Aunt Friendly. 18mo. 0 40 *Carter & Brothers.*

Children's (The) Mirror; or, Which is my Likeness? By
Catherine D. Bell. 16mo, cloth.   1 25 *T. Nelson & Sons.*

———— (The) Picture Book of Birds. Square 16mo.   0 75 *Harper & Bros.*

———— (The) Picture Fable Book, containing One Hundred and Sixty Fables. Square 16mo.   0 75 "

China Mission (The), embracing a History of the Various
Missions of all Denominations among the Chi-
nese, with Biographical Sketches of Deceased
Missionaries. By William Dean, D. D. 12mo. 1 00 *Sheldon & Co.*

Chloe Lankton; or, Light beyond the Clouds. 12mo. . 0 70 *Am. S. S. Union.*

Choate, Rufus, Reminiscences of. By Edward G. Parker. 1 50 *Mason Brothers.*

Chrisna; the Queen of the Danube. By the author of
"Pieciola." 8vo. pap. .   .   .   .   . 0 25 *Delisser & Procter.*

Christ in History. By Robert Turnbull, D. D. New
and revised edition. 12mo.   .   .   . 1 25 *Gould & Lincoln.*

———— the Spirit; being an Attempt to state the Primi-
tive View of Christianity. By the author of
"Alchemy and the Alchemists." 12mo. .   .   *L. Bushnell.*

———— our Life. The Scriptural Argument for Immor-
tality through Christ alone. By C. J. Hudson. 0 75 *J. P. Jewett & Co.*

———— and his Church in the Book of Psalms. By Rev.
A. A. Bonar. 8vo. .   .   .   .   . 1 75 *Carter & Brothers.*

Christian, L. H. (Rev.), The Accepted Time for securing
the Gospel Salvation, and from the Analogy between Temporal and Spiritual Affairs, answer-
ing certain Doctrinal Excuses sometimes urged
for neglecting it. 12mo. .   .   .   .   . 0 60 *Joseph M. Wilson.*

Christian Home (The); or, Religion in the Family. By
the Rev. Joseph A. Collier, Kingston, New
York, author of the "Right Way." 12mo. . 0 60 *Presb. Bd. of Pub.*

—— Hope (The). By John Angell James. 16mo. . 0 75 *Carter & Brothers.*

—— Law of Amusement. By Rev. J. L. Corning. . 0 38 *Phillips, S. & Co.*

—— Maiden (The). Memorials of Eliza Hessel. By
Joshua Priestley. 16mo. . . . . . 0 75 *Carlton & Porter.*

—— Morals. By Rev. James Challen. 18mo. . . 0 50 *J. Challen & Son.*

—— Songs, Translations, and other Poems. By the
Rev. J. G. Lyons, LL. D. 12mo. . . . 0 80 *Smith, Eng. & Co.*

—— Union and the Protestant Episcopal Church in its
relation to Church Unity. By William H. Lewis,
D. D. 16mo, cloth. . . . . . 0 38 *F. D. Harriman.*

Christian's Mirror (The); or, Words in Season. By A.
L. O. E. 18mo. . . . . . . 0 50 *Carter & Brothers.*

Christianity and Modern Infidelity, their relative Intellectual Claims compared. By the Rev. R. W.
Morgan. 12mo. . . . . . . 1 25 *Daniel Dana, jr.*

Christmas Dream (A). By James T. Brady. 16mo. . 0 75 *D. Appleton & Co.*

—— Holidays at Cedar Grove. By Mrs. William
Wood Seymour. 18mo. . . . . . 0 03 " "

—— Hours, by the author of the "Homeward
Path." 12mo. cl. . . . . . 0 50 *Ticknor & Fields.*

—— Vigils: or, Kitty Clark's Dream. 18mo. cl. . 0 25 *F. D. Harriman.*

Chronicles of the Bastile. Illustrated. 8vo. . . 2 25 *Stanford&Delisser*

Church Choral Book. 4to. . . . . . 1 00 *Crosby, N.,L.&Co.*

—— Melodies; a Collection of Psalms and Hymns,
with Music. By T. & T. S. Hastings. 12mo. cl. 0 75 *A. D. F.Randolph.*

—— (The) Identified, by a Reference to the History of
its Origin, Perpetuation, and Extension into the
United States. By the Rev. W. D. Wilson,
D. D. 12mo. . . . . . . 1 00 *Daniel Dana, jr.*

—— of the First Three Centuries; or, Notices of the
Lives and Opinions of some of the Early Fathers,
with Special Reference to the Doctrine of the
Trinity. By Alvan Lamson, D.D. 8vo. . . 1 75 *Walker, Wise&Co.*

—— and Congregation: a Plea for their Unity. By
Rev. C. A. Bartol. 16mo. . . . . 1 00 *Ticknor & F.*

Cicero de Oratore. Translated or edited by J. S. Watson. 12mo. . . . . . . 0 75 *Harper & Bros.*

Ciceronis de Officiis Libri Tres. With Marginal Analysis
and an English Commentary. Edited by the
Rev. Hubert Ashton Holden, M. A. First
American Edition, Corrected and Enlarged by
Charles Anthon, LL. D. 12mo. . . . 0 75 " "

Citizen's Manual of Government and Law. By Andrew
    W. Young. 12mo. . . . . . . 1 25   *H. Dayton.*
Claiborne; being Vol. III. of the Oakland Stories. By
    Geo. B. Taylor. 16mo. cl. . . . . 0 50   *Sheldon & Co.*
Clark, Alex., The Old Log School-House. . . .   *Leary, Getz & Co.*
——— G. F., A History of the Town of Norton, Bristol
    . county, Massachusetts, from 1668 to 1859. .   *Crosby, N., L. & Co.*
——— H. (M. D.), Sight and Hearing, how Preserved
    and how Lost. New edition. 12mo. . . , 1 25   *C. Scribner.*
——— M. B. S., The Scripture History of our Blessed Lord
    and Saviour, Jesus Christ; arranged to illus-
    trate his Divinity, Doctrine, and Mission. 18mo. 0 30   *Daniel Dana, jr.*
——— R. W. (Rev.), Romanism in America. 16mo. . 0 64   *J. E. Tilton & Co.*
——— "   "   The True Prince of the Tribe of
    Judah; or, Life Scenes in the Messiah. 12mo. cl. 1 25   *Alberl Colby & Co.*
——— T., Practical and Progressive Latin Grammar.
    Elementary Course. 12mo. . . . . . 1 00   *C. Desilver.*
——— " Sallustri Crispi Opera, adapted to the Hamil-
    tonian System by a Literal and Analytical Trans-
    lation, by Jas. Hamilton, revised and corrected
    by Thomas Clark. 12mo. . . . . 1 50   "
Clarke, Adam (Rev.), The Life of. By J. W. Etheridge,
    . M. A. 12mo. . . . . 1 00   *Carlton & Porter.*
Claude to the Rescue; or, the Escape of Duval and the
    Maniac Heiress. Pap. 8vo. . . . . 0 25   *R. M. De Witt.*
Cleaveland, C. H. (M. D.), The Physician's Pocket Memo-
    randum for 1861. . . . . . . 1 00   *Author.*
——— Parker (LL. D.), Life of. By Leonard Woods,
    D. D. 8vo. . . . . 0 40   *Joseph Griffin.*
Clelland, Thomas (Rev.), The Life of. 12mo. cl. . .   *Moore, W., K. & Co.*
Clemens, J., The Rivals; a Tale of the Times of Aaron
    Burr and Alexander Hamilton. 12mo. . . 1 00   *Lippincott & Co.*
Cler (Gen.), Reminiscences of a General Officer of Zouaves.
    Translated from the French. 12mo. . . 1 00   *D. Appleton & Co.*
Cleveland, C. D., A Compendium of American Literature;
    chronologically arranged, with Biographical
    Sketches of the Authors. On the plan of the
    Author's "Compendium of English Literature,"
    and "English Literature of the Nineteenth Cen-
    tury." 12mo. . . . . 1 50   *E. C. & J. Biddle.*
Clevelands (The), Showing the Influence of a Christian
    Family in a New Settlement. By Mrs. E. M.
    Sheldon. . . . . 0 20   *Am. Tract So.*
Cloud (The) Dispelled; or, The Doctrine of Predestina-
    tion Examined. By John Kirk. 12mo. . . 0 75   *N. Tibbals & Co.*

Clover Glen; or, Nellie' First Summer in the Country.   0 25   *A. D. F. Randolph.*
Cluster (A) of Fruits from the Tree of Heavenly Wisdom.
    Compiled by Annie Brooks. 18mo. .   .   .   0 35   *Presb. Bd. Pub.*
Cobb, S., The Maniac's Secret; or, the Privateer of Mas-
    sachusetts Bay. 8vo. pap.   .   .   .   .   0 25   *F. A. Brady.*
——— " The Patriot Cruiser; a Story of the American
    Revolution. Paper. .   .   .   .   .   0 25   "
——— T. R. R. (of Georgia), An Historical Sketch of
    Slavery from the Earliest Periods. 8vo. .   .   *Johnson & Co.*
——— T. R. R., An Inquiry into the Law of Negro
    Slavery in the United States. 8vo. .   .   .   "
Cochran, John, The Revelation of St. John its own Inter-
    preter, in Virtue of the Double Version in which
    it is delivered. 12mo. .   .   .   .   .   1 00   *D. Appleton & Co.*
Cocke, W. A., The Constitutional History of the United
    States, from the Adoption of the Articles of Con-
    federation to the Close of Jackson's Administra-
    tion. 8vo. .   .   .   .   .   .   2 50   *Lippincott & Co.*
Codex Alexandrinus, Novum Testamentum Græce, ex an-
    tiquissimo codice Alexandrino. A. C. G. Woide.
    Olim desoriptum: ad fidem ipsius codicis denuo
    accuratius editit. B. H. Cowper. 8vo. cl.   .   3 00   *Westerman & Co.*
Coggeshall, G., Historical Sketch of Commerce and Navi-
    gation from the Birth of our Saviour down to
    the Present Date (1860.) 8vo. .   .   .   .   2 00   *G. P. Putnam.*
——— W. T., Home Hits and Hints; a Book for the
    Fireside. 12mo. .   .   .   .   .   .   1 00   *J. S. Redfield.*
Coit, T. W. (Rev.), Lectures on the Early History of Chris-
    tianity in England. 12mo. .   .   .   .   1 00   *Daniel Dona, jr.*
Collections of the Maine Historical Society. 8vo. .   1 75   *Pub. by the So.*
——— of the Massachusetts Historical Society. Vol.
    IV. of the Fourth Series. Published at the
    Charge of the Appleton Fund. 8vo.   .   .   2 50   *Little, Brown & Co.*
Collier, J. A. (Rev.), The Christian Home; or, Religion
    in the Family. 12mo. .   .   .   .   .   0 60   *Presb. B. of Pub.*
Collins, P. M., A Voyage down the Amoor, with a Land
    Journey through Siberia, and Incidental Notices
    of Manchooria, Kamschatka, and Japan. 12mo.   0 25   *D. Appleton & Co.*
——— T. W., Humanics. 8vo. .   .   .   .   1 75   "
——— " After Dark: A Novel. 8vo. pap.   .   0 50   *Dick & Fitzgerald.*
——— W., The Queen of Hearts. A Novel. 12mo. cl.   1 00   *Harper & Bros.*
——— " The Woman in White. A Novel. 8vo.
                 Cloth, $1 00; paper   0 75   *Harper & Brothers*
Colona, Vittoria (Life of). By T. Adolphus Trol-
    lope. 18mo. .   .   .   .   0 50   *Sheldon & Co.*

3

Colton, H. E., A Book containing Descriptions of the most noted Points in the Scenery of Western North Carolina, and North-western South Carolina.   0 60   *W. L. Pomeroy.*

—— G. W., School Atlas. 4to.   .   .   .   1 25   *Ivison, Phin. & Co.*

Columbkille, St. (Life of). 18mo.   .   .   0 25   *P. Donahoe.*

Columbus, Christopher (Life of). By Alphonse Lamartine. 18mo.   .   .   .   .   .   0 50   *Sheldon & Co.*

Colwell, Stephen, The Ways and Means of Payment: a Full Analysis of the Credit System, with its Various Modes of Adjustment. 8vo.   .   2 50   *Lippincott & Co.*

Coming Home. By the author of "A Trap to Catch a Sunbeam." 18mo. limped cl.   .   .   *Jas. Munroe & Co.*

Commentary on the Songs of Solomon. By George Burrowes, D. D. Second edition, revised. 12mo.   1 25   *W.S.& A.Martien.*

Communicant's (The) Spiritual Companion; or, An Evangelical Preparation for the Lord's Supper. By the Rev. Thomas Howeis, D. D.   .   .   0 38   *Prot. Ep. Book So.*

Comprehensive Farm Record (The); with Directions for its Use. Arranged by Franklin B. Hough. 8vo.   3 00   *Saxton & Barker.*

Conant, W. C., Narratives of Remarkable Conversions and Revival Incidents. 12mo.   .   .   1 00   *Derby & Jackson.*

Concord (The) of Ages; or, the Individuals and Organic Harmony of God and Man. By Edward Beecher, D. D. 12mo.   .   .   .   .   .   1 25   "

Conduct of Life. By Ralph Waldo Emerson. 12mo.   1 00   *Ticknor & Fields.*

Confederate Chieftains (The): a Tale of the Irish Rebellion of 1641. By Mrs. J. Sadleir. 12mo.   .   1 25   *D.&J.Sadlier&Co.*

Confessions (The) of Augustine. Edited, with an Introduction, by Rev. Wm. G. T. Shedd, D. D. 12mo.   1 00   *Warren F.Draper.*

Constance and Edith; or, Incidents of Home Life. By a Clergyman's Wife. 12mo.   .   .   .   0 75   *Thomson Bros.*

Constitutional History of the U. States, from the Adoption of the Articles of Confederation to the Close of Jackson's Administration. By William A. Cooke. 2 vols. 8vo. Vol. I.   .   .   2 50   *Lippincott & Co.*

Constitutions (The) of the Freemasons; containing the History, Charges and Regulations of that Fraternity, for the use of the Lodges. 16mo. cloth.   0 50   *Robert Macoy.*

Convalescent (The). By N. P. Willis. 12mo. cl.   .   1 25   *Charles Scribner.*

Cook, T. J., and Perkins, T. E., The Olive Branch. A Collection of Sacred Music. 8vo.   .   .   0 75   *F. J. Huntington.*

Cooke, J. E., Henry St. John, Gentleman, of Flower of Hundreds, in the County of Prince George, Virginia. A Tale of 1774–'75. 12mo.   .   .   1 00   *Harper & Bros.*

—— J. P., Elements of Chemical Physics. 8vo.   .   8 00   *Little, Brown & Co.*

Cooke, H. B., Memories of My Life Work. The Autobiography of Mrs. Harriet B. Cooke. 12mo. 1 00 *Carter & Brothers.*

Cooley, T. M., Reports of Cases heard and decided in the
Supreme Court of Michigan, from January 1st to
November 12, 1858. By Thomas M. Cooley,
Reporter. Vol. I., being Vol. V. of the Series. *Doughty, S. & Co.*

Cooper, J. F., The Works of. Illustrated from Drawings
by F. O. C. Darley. 12mo. cl. . . Per vol. 1 50 *Townsend & Co.*

—— S. F., Pages and Pictures from the Writings of J.
Fennimore Cooper. Edited by Miss Susan Fenni-
more Cooper. Illustrated with Forty Steel En-
gravings, from Original Designs, by Darley,
Hamilton, &c., and one hundred and thirty
Sketches on Wood. 4to. . . . . 12 50 "

Cooper Gent, and Other Sketches, from "The Country
Pastor's Visit to his Poor." 18mo. . . . 0 40 *Am. S. S. Union.*

Copcutt, F., Leaves from a Bachelor's Book of Life. . 1 00 *S. A. Rollo.*

Copeland, R. M., A Hand Book of Horticulture, Agriculture, and Landscape Gardening. 8vo. . . 2 50 *J. P. Jewitt & Co.*

Copland, James (M.D.), A Dictionary of Practical Medicine. Edited by Chas. A. Lee, A. M., M. D.,
Vol. 3. 8vo. . . . . 5 00 *Harper & Bros.*

Copley, J., Thoughts of Favored Hours, upon Bible Incidents and Characters, and other subjects. . 0 50 *Lippincott & Co*

Coppee, H., Elements of Rhetoric. 12mo. . . 1 00 *E. H. Butler & Co.*

—— New School Academic Speaker. Small 8vo. . 1 50 "

Coral Island (The), a Tale of the Pacific Ocean. By R.
M. Ballantyne. 16mo. cl. . . . 0 75 *Phinney B. & M.*

Cordova, J. D., Texas; her Resources and her Public
Men. 12mo. . . . . . . 1 25 *Lippincott & Co.*

Corinne; or, Italy. By Madame De Stael. Translated
by Isabel Hill; with Metrical Versions of the
Odes, by L. E. Landon. 12mo. . . . 1 25 *Derby & Jackson.*

Corn in the Blade. Poems, and Thoughts in Prose. By
Orammond Kennedy. With an Introduction by
C. B. Conant. 12mo. . . . . . 1 00 "

Cornelius, M. H. (Mrs.), The Young Housekeeper's
Friend. New and revised edition. 12mo. cl. 0 75 *Brown & Taggard.*

Cornell, J. F. D., Arthur & Constance. A Poem. 12mo. 0 50 *Wiley & Halsted.*

—— S. S., First Steps in Geograph. Square 16mo. 0 25 *D. Appleton & Co.*

—— " Grammar School Geography. 4to. . 0 80 "

—— W. M. (M. D.), How to Enjoy Life; or, Physical
and Mental Hygiene. 12mo. . . . . 1 00 *Challen & Son.*

—— W. M. (A. M.), Life of Robert Raikes, the Founder of Sabbath Schools. 18mo. . . . . 0 20 *Henry Hoyt.*

Corner (The) Cupboard; or, Facts for Everybody. By
    the author of "Inquire Within." 12mo. . .   1 00   *Dick & Fitzgerald.*

Corning, J. L. (Rev.), The Christian Law of Amuse-
    ment. 18mo. . . . . . . 0 38   *Phillips, S. & Co.*

Cornwallis, K., Sackville St. Lawrence, an Autobiogra-
    phy. 12mo. . . . . . . 1 50   *M. Doolady.*

Corwin, Thomas, Speeches of Thomas Corwin, with a
    Sketch of his] Life. Edited by Isaac Strohm.
    8vo. cl. . . . . 2 00   *W. F. Comby & Co.*

Cosmo's Visit to his Grandfather. By M. A. H., author
    of "Goodly Cedars," &c. 18mo. . . . 0 40   *Carter & Bros.*

Cottage Melodies; or, Hymn and Tune Book for Prayer
    and Social Meetings, and the Home Circle. By
    William B. Bradbury. Assisted by Sylvester
    Mann. 16mo. . . . . . . 0 50   *F. J. Huntington.*

———— (The) and its Visitor. By the author of "Minis-
    tering Children," &c. 16mo. . . . 0 60   *Carter & Brothers,*

Cottages (The) of the Alps; or, Life and Manners in Switz-
    erland. By Miss Anna C. Johnson. 12mo. cl. 1 25   *Chas. Scribner.*

Cotton is King, and Pro-Slavery Arguments; comprising
    the writings of Hammond, Harper, Christy,
    Stringfellow, Hodge, Bledsoe, and Cartwright,
    on this important subject. By E. N. Elliott.
    LL. D. 8vo. Law sheep. . . . . 5 00   *Pritchard, A. & L.*

Coultas, Harriet, What may be Learned from a Tree. 8vo. 1 00   *D. Appleton & Co.*

Counterparts; or, the Cross of Love. By the author of
    "Charles Auchester." 8vo. paper. . . 0 50   *Mayhew & Baker.*

Courtney, W. S., The Gold Fields of St. Domingo; with
    a Description of the Agricultural, Commercial,
    and other Advantages of Dominica. 12mo. . 0 75   *Anson P Norton.*

Courtship (The) and Adventures of Jonathan Homebred.
    By Sam Slick, Jr. 12mo. . . . . 1 00   *Dick & Fitzgerald.*

———— and Matrimony; with other Sketches from
    Scenes and Experiences in Social Life. By
    Robert Morris. 12mo. . . . . 1 25   *Peterson & Bros.*

Cousin, V., Secret History of the French Court under
    Richelieu and Mazarin; or, Life and Times of
    Madame de Cheureuse. Translated by Mary L.
    Booth. 12mo. cl. . . . . . 0 63   *Delisser & Procter.*

———— Bertha's Stories. By Mary Noel Meigs. 16mo. 0 50   *A.D.F. Randolph.*

———— Guy. By George B. Taylor, of Virginia. 16mo. 0 50   *Sheldon & Co.*

———— Harry. By Mrs. Grey. 12mo. . . . 1 25   *Peterson & Bros.*

———— Maude and Rosamond. By Mrs. Mary J. Holmes. 1 00   *Saxton & Barker.*

Cowdin, V. G. Mrs., Ellen; or, the Fanatic's Daughter.   *S. H. Goetzel & Co.*

Cowes, S. E., Study of the Earth. 4to. pp. 98. . .   *Philip & Solomons*

Cozzens, F. S., Acadia; or, a Month with the Blue
   Noses. 12mo. cloth. . . . . . 1 00 *Derby & Jackson*
Craig, N. B., Exposure of a few of the Misstatements in
   H. M. Brackenridge's History of the Whisky
   Insurrection. 18mo. . . . . . 0 88 *John S. Davison.*
Craik, Jas. (Rev.), Old and New. 12mo. cloth. . . 0 80 *Daniel Dana, jr.*
Cranston House. A Novel. By Hannah Anderson
   Ropes. 12mo. . . . . 1 00 *Otis Clapp.*
Crary, C., The Law and Practice in Special Proceedings
   and in Special Cases within the Courts, &c., of
   the State of New York; with an Appendix of
   Forms. 8vo. . . . . . . 5 00 *John S. Voorhies.*
Crawford, M. S., Life in Tuscany. 12mo. . . . 1 00 *Sheldon & Co.*
Crescent (The) and French Crusaders. By G. L. Dit-
   son. 12mo. . . . . . .   *Derby & Jackson.*
Cricket Field (The); or, the History and Science of
   Cricket. 12mo. . . . . . . 1 00 *Mayhew & Baker.*
—— (The) Player's Pocket Companion. Containing
   Plans for laying out the Grounds, forming
   Clubs, &c., &c. 18mo. . . . . 0 25 *Mayhew & Baker.*
Crockett, David (Col.), Life of, written by Himself. To
   which is added an account of Col. Crockett's
   glorious Death at the Alamo, while fighting in
   Defense of Texan Independence. By the
   Editor. 12mo. . . . . . . 1 25 *G. G. Evans.*
Cromwell, Oliver, The Life of. By Alphonse de Lamar-
   tine. 18mo. cl. . . . . . . 0 50 *Sheldon & Co.*
Crooks, G. R. and Schem, A. J., A New Latin-English
   School-Lexicon, on the Basis of the Latin-Ger-
   man Lexicon of Dr. G. F. Ingersley. 8vo. .   *Lippincott & Co.*
Crosby, F., Everybody's Lawyer and Counselor in Busi-
   ness. 12mo. . . . . 1 00 *John E. Potter.*
—— N., Annual Obituary Notices of Eminent Persons
   who have Died in the United States. For
   1857. 8vo. . . . . 1 75 *Phillips, S. & Co.*
Cross, J. (Rev.), A Year in Europe. Edited by Thomas
   O. Summers, M. D. 12mo. . . .   *So. Meth. Pub. H.*
Croswell, W. (Rev.), Poems: Sacred and Secular. Ed-
   ited, with a Memoir and Notes, by Rev. A.
   Cleveland Coxe, D. D. 18mo. . . . 1 00 *Ticknor & Fields.*
Crown of Thorns. A Token for the Sorrowing. By
   Rev. E. H. Chapin. 12mo. . . .   *A. Tompkins.*
Cruise of the Betsey; or, a Summer Ramble among the
   Fossiliferous Deposits of the Hebrides. By
   Hugh Miller, LL. D. 12mo. . . . 1 25 *Gould & Lincoln.*

Crusades (The) and the Crusaders. By John G.
Edgar. 16mo. . . . . 0 75   *Ticknor & Fields.*

Cruttenden, D. H., The Philosophy of Sentential Language; or, Language an Exact Science. 12mo. 0 75   *C. Shephard & Co.*

Cuba (To) and Back : A Vacation Voyage. By Richard
Henry Dana, jr. 12mo. . . . . . . 0 75   *Ticknor & Fields.*

—— for Invalids. By R. W. Gibbes, M. D. 12mo. . 0 75   *Townsend & Co.*

Culprit (The) Fay. By Joseph Rodman Drake. 12mo. 0 50   *Rudd & Carleton.*

Cumming, John (Rev.), The Great Tribulation; or, Things
Coming on the Earth. First Series, and Second
Series. 2 vols. 12mo. Each . . . . 1 00   *Rudd & Carleton.*

—— W. H. (M. D.), Food for Babes ; or, Artificial Human Milk, and the Manner of Preparing
it and Administering it to Young Children. 18mo 0 35   *A. D. F. Randolph.*

Cummings, J. W. (Rev.), Italian Legends and Sketches. . 0 75   *Dunigan & Bro.*

Curiosities of Natural History, First and Second Series.
By Francis T. Buckland, M. A. 12mo. each . 1 25   *Rudd & Carleton.*

Curtis, George T., Equity Precedents, Supplementary to
Mr. Joseph Story's Treatise on Equity Pleading.
Third edition. 8vo. . . . . . . 5 00   *Little, Brown & Co.*

—— Geo. T., History of the Origin, Formation, and
Adoption of the Constitution of the United States,
with Notices of the principal Framers. New
edition. 2 vols. 8vo. . . . . . 4 00   *Harper & Bros.*

Cutting, S. S., Historical Vindications; a Discourse on
the Province and Uses of Baptist History. With
Appendices, containing Historical Notes and Confessions of Faith. 12mo. . . .. 1 00   *Gould & Lincoln.*

Cyclopædia of Literary and Scientific Anecdote : illustrative of the Characters, Habits, and Conversation of Men of Letters and Science. Edited by
William Keddie. From the London edition. . 1 25   *Follett, Foster & Co.*

—— of Wit and Humor. Edited by W. E. Bur-
ton. 2 vols. 8vo. . . . . . . 7 00   *D. Appleton & Co.*

—— of Commerce and Commercial Navigation.
Edited by J. Smith Homans. 8vo. . . . 10 00   *Harper & Bros.*

D

Dablon, R. P. C., Relation de ce qui s'est passé de plus
remarquable aux missions des Pères de la Compagnie de Jesus en la Nouvelle France dans les
Années 1673 à 1679. Par le R. P. Claude Dablon, Recteur du College de Quebec et Superieur
des Missions de la Compagnie de Jesus en la
Nouvelle France. 8vo. . . . . . 5 00   *J. G. Shea.*

Dagg, J. L. (Rev.), The Elements of Moral Science. 12mo. 1 00 *Sheldon & Co.*
Daily Thoughts for a Child   By Mrs. Thomas Geldart. 18mo. . . . . . . 0 60 "
Daisy; or, the Lost Lamb. 18mo. . . . . . 0 15 *Am. S. S. Union.*
—— Downs; or, What the Sabbath School can Do. 16mo. 0 38 *Carlton & Porter.*
Dale, S., Life and Times of Gen Sam. Dale, the Mississippi Partisan. By J. F. H. Claiborne. 12mo. 1 00 *Harper & Brothers.*
Dall, C. H. (Mrs.), Historical Pictures Retouched; a Volume of Miscellanies. 12mo. . . . . 1 25 *Walker, Wise & Co.*
Dalton, J. C. (M. D.), A Treatise on Human Physiology. Designed for the Use of Students and Practitioners of Medicine. 8vo. . . . . 4 00 *Blanchard & Lea.*
—— W., The War Tiger; or, Adventures and Wonderful Fortunes of the Young Sea Chief and his Lad Chow. 16mo. . . . . 0 75 *Townsend & Co.*
—— W., The White Elephant; or, the Hunters of Ava and the King of the Golden Foot. 16mo. . 0 75
Dana, C. A. (Editor), The Household Book of Poetry. 8vo. 3 50 *D. Appleton & Co.*
—— Jas. H., A System of Mineralogy. Illustrated by Six Hundred Wood-cuts. 4th edition, rewritten, rearranged, and enlarged. 8vo. . . . 3 50 "
—— R. H., To Cuba and Back; A Vacation Voyage. 16mo. 0 75 *Ticknor & Fields.*
Dark (The) Mountains. An Allegory. By the Rev. Edward A. Monro. 18mo. . . . . . 0 35 *H. Hooker.*
—— " River. An Allegory. By the Rev. Edward A. Monro. 18mo. . . . . . . 0 35 "
. Darlington, W. (M. D.), American Weeds and Useful Plants, being a Second and Illustrated Edition of Agricultural Botany. Revised, with Additions, by George Thurber, Prof. of Mat. Med. and Botany, &c. 12mo. . . . . . . 1 50 *Moore & Co.*
Darwin, C., The Origin of Species by Means of Natural Selection; or, the Preservation of Favored Races in the Struggle for Life. 12mo. . . . 1 25 *D. Appleton & Co.*
Dasent, G. W., Popular Tales from the Norse. 12mo. . 1 00 "
Davenport Dunn. A Man of Our Day. By Charles Lever. 8vo. pap. . . . . . . 0 50 *Peterson & Bros.*
The Same. With Illustrations. 8vo. cl. . . . 1 50 "
Davies, C., Elements of Analytical Geometry, and of the Differential and Integral Calculus. 12mo, sheep. 1 25 *Barnes & Burr.*
—— G. C., Songs of the Church; or, Psalms and Hymns of the Protestant Episcopal Church, arranged to appropriate Melodies. 12mo. . . . 1 25 *Applegate & Co.*
—— Thomas A., Answer to Hugh Miller and Theoretical Geologists. 12mo. . . . . . . 1 00 *Rudd & Carleton.*

Davis, A. J., The Great Harmonia; being a Progressive
    Revelation of the Eternal Principles which
    Inspire Mind and Govern Matter. Vol. V. 12mo. 1 00 *A. J. Davis & Co.*
——— " The History and Philosophy of Evil. 8vo. .   *Bela Marsh.*
———M. S., The Harvest of Love. A Story for the Home
    Circle. . . . . 0 75 *A. Tomkins.*
———W., The Beautiful City, and the King of Glory. 0 75 *Lindsay & Blak'n*
Day, H. A., The Art of Elocution, exemplified in a Sys-
    tematic Course of Exercises. Revised ed. 12mo. 1 00 *Moore, W., K.& Co·*
Days at Muirhead; or, the Lessons of Little Olive's Mid-
    summer Holidays. 18mo. . . . 0 50 *Carter & Bros.*
——— of Old. Three Stories from Old English History.
    For the Young. 16mo. . . . . 0 75   "
D'Azeglio, M., Ettore Fieramosca; or, the Challenge of
    Barletta. 16mo. . . . .. 1 00 *Phillips, S. & Co.*
———M., Niccolo dei Lapi; or, the Last Days of
    the Florentine Republic. 12mo. . . 1 25 *Lippincott & Co.*
Deaf (The) Shoemaker. By Philip Barrett. 18mo. cl. . 0 50 *M. W. Dodd.*
Dean, Wm. (Rev.), The China Mission, embracing a His-
    tory of the Various Missions of all Denominations
    among the Chinese, with Biographical Sketches
    of Deceased Missionaries. 12mo. cl. . 1 00 *Sheldon & Co.*
Dear Experience: a Tale. By Ruffini. 12mo. cl. . 1 00 *Rudd & Carleton.*
Death to the Traitor; or, Claude Duval and the Poachers. 0 25 *R. M. De Witt.*
Debate (The) between the Church and Science; or, the
    Ancient Hebraic Idea of the Six Days of Crea-
    tion. 12mo. . . . . 1 25 *Warren F. Draper.*
De Forest, J. W., Seacliff; or, the Mystery of the Wester-
    velts. 12mo. . . . . . 1 25 *Phillips, S. & Co.*
Degerando, Self-Education; or, the Means and Art of
    Moral Progress. Third edition, with Addi-
    tions. 12mo. . . . . 1 25 *T. O.H.P.Burnh'm*
Demi-Monde (The); a Satire on Society, from the French
    of Alexandre Dumas, jr. 12mo. pap. . 0 50 *Lippincott & Co.*
Denison, M. A., The Days and Ways of the Cocked Hats;
    or, the Dawn of the Revolution. 12mo. . 1 00 *S. A. Rolle.*
——— "Antoinette, the original of "The Child An-
    gel." 16mo. . . . . . 0 65 *H. Hoyt.*
De Plancy, J. C., Legends of the Blessed Virgin. Col-
    lected from approved sources. 12mo. . 0 50 *P. O'Shea.*
De Quincey, Thomas, Logic and Political Economy, and
    Other Papers. A new volume. 16mo. cl. . 0 75 *Tickner & Fields.*
——— " The Avenger, a Narrative; and other Papers. . 0 75   "
De Soto, F., The Life, Travels, and Adventures of. By
    Lambert A. Wilmer. 8vo. . . . 2 50 *J. T. Lloyd.*

De Stael (Madame), Corinne; or, Italy. Translated by
    Isabel Hill; with Metrical Versions of the Odes,
    by L. E. Landon. 12mo. .   .   .   . 1 25   *Derby & Jackson.*
—————— Germany; with Notes and Appendices, by O.
    W. Wight, A. M. 2 vols., 12mo. .   . . 2 50   "
Detroit, Diary of the Siege of, in the War with Pontiac.
    Also, a Narrative of the Principal Events of the
    Siege, by Major Robert Rogers; a Plan for
    conducting Indian Affairs, by Colonel Brad-
    street, and other Authentic Documents, never
    before printed. Edited with notes by Franklin
    B. Hough. 4to. .   .   .   .   . 5 00   *J. Munsell.*
Deuel, Caroline R., Scripture Lessons for Sunday-Schools
    and Families. 24mo. .   .   .   . 0 25   *Carlton & Porter.*
Devereux, J. C., The Most Material Parts of Kent's Com-
    mentaries reduced to Questions and Answers. . 3 50   *Lewis & Blood.*
Devotional Exercises for Schools and Families. 12mo. 0 50   *J. Munroe & Co.*
De Wette, W. M., A Critical and Historical Introduction
    to the Canonical Scriptures of the Old Testa-
    ment. From the German of Wilhelm Martin
    Leberecht de Wette. Translated and enlarged
    by Rev. Theodore Parker. Third edition. 2
    vols., 8vo. .   .   .   .   .   . 8 75   *Little, Brown & Co.*
Dewitt, Mrs., Original Dialogues and Conversations for
    Children. 18mo. .   .   .   .   . 0 40   *Robert Clarke & Co.*
Dexter, H. M. (Rev.), Street Thoughts. 16mo. cl. .   *Crosby, N., L. & Co.*
Diary (The) of a Samaritan. By a Member of the How-
    ard Association, of New Orleans. 12mo.   : 1 00   *Harper & Bros.*
Dickens, C., Little Folks. Illustrated by Darley. Little
    Nell; Smike; The Child-Wife; Oliver Twist
    and the Jew Fagin; Florence Dombey; Little
    Paul; The Boy Joe and Sam Weller; Sissy
    Jupe; The Two Daughters; Tiny Tim and Dot
    and the Fairy Cricket; Dame Durden; and
    "Dolly Varden, the Little Coquette." Each. 0 63   *Clark, A., M. & Co.*
—————— Tale of Two Cities. 8vo. pap. .   .   . 0 50   *Peterson & Bros.*
—————— Journey in Search of Nothing, and the Lazy
    Tour of Two Idle Apprentices. 8vo. .   . 0 50   *F. A. Brady.*
—————— Short Stories, containing thirty-one stories never
    before published. 12mo. cl. .   .   . 1 50   *Peterson & Bros.*
Dickerman, The Sisters. A Memoir of Elizabeth, Abbie
    A., and Sarah F. Dickerman. By the Rev.
    Israel P. Warren. 12mo. .   .   .   . 0 50   *Am. Tract So.*

Dickeson, M. W., The American Numismatical Manual
of the Currency and Money of the Aborigines,
and Colonial, State, and United States Coins,
with Historical and Descriptive Notices of each
Coin or Series. 4to. . . . . . 6 00 *Lippincott & Co.*

Dictionary (The) of Love. 12mo. . . . . . 1 00 *Dick & Fitzgerald.*

Disturnel, J., Influence of Climate in a Commercial,
Social, Sanitary, and Humanizing Point of
View. 4to. pp. 24. . . . . . 1 00 *C. Scribner.*

Ditson, G. L., The Crescent and French Crusaders. . *Derby & Jackson.*

———— The Para Papers on France, Egypt, and Ethiopia. 1 25 *Mason Brothers.*

Dixon, F. B., Abridgment of the Maritime Law; comprising, in a succinct and practical form, nearly
the whole Law of Shipping and Insurance.
Second Edition. 8vo. . . . . . 2 50 *D. Eggert & Son.*

Doane, George Washington, D. D., LL. D., Bishop of
New Jersey, a Memoir of the Life of. By his
son, William Croswell Doane. 4 vols. 8vo. . 10 00 *D. Appleton & Co.*

Dobell, Sidney, Poems of. 18mo. Blue and Gold. . 0 75 *Ticknor & Fields.*

Doctor Oldham at Greystones, and his Talk There. . 1 00 *D. Appleton & Co.*

———— Thorne, A Novel. By Anthony Trollope. 12mo. 1 00 *Harper & Bros.*

Dodd, J. B., Elements of Trigonometry, Plane and
Spherical. 12mo. . . . . . . 1 00 *Pratt, Oakley & Co.*

Doesticks, The Witches of New York, as encountered by
Q. K. Philander Doesticks, P. B. 12mo. . 1 00 *Rudd & Carleton.*

Doing and Not Doing; or, the Convert Guide. By W.
M. Thayer. 16mo. cl. . . . . . *Henry Hoyt.*

Dolce Far Niente, and other Poems. By John R. Tait. 0 50 *Parry & McMillan.*

Domestic Animals; a Pocket Manual of Cattle, Horse,
and Sheep Husbandry. 16mo. . . . 0 50 *Fowler & Wells.*

Donaldson, S. J., Lyrics and other Poems. 12mo. . 1 00 *Lindsay & B.*

Donkersley, R. (Rev.), Facts about Girls, for Girls. . 0 85 *Carlton & Porter.*

Donne, A., Mothers and Infants, Nurses and Nursing.
A Treatise on Nursing, Weaning, and the Gen-
eral Treatment of Young Children. 12mo. . 1 00 *Phillips, S. & Co.*

Dora Barton, the Banker's Ward. A Tale of Real Life
in New York. By Charles Burdett.

———— Deane; or, the East India Uncle; and Maggie
Miller; or, Old Hagar's Secret. By Mrs. Mary
J. Holmes. 12mo. cl. . . . . . 1 00 *Saxton & Barker.*

Dorchester, History of. By a Committee of the Dorchester Antiquarian and Historical Society. 8vo. 3 00 *E. Clapp, jr.*

Douai, A., Fata Morgana. Deutsch Amerikanische
Preis-Novelle. 8vo. . . . . . 0 60 *Westermann & Co.*

Douglas, Stephen A., Life of. With his most Important
    Speeches and Reports. By a Member of the
    Western Bar. 12mo. . . . . . 1 00 *Derby & Jackson.*

Dow, New Patent Sermons, Machine Poetry, and Lec-
    tures on Animals, etc. By Dow, Junior. 12mo. 1 00 *F. A. Brady.*

Drake, C. D., A Treatise on the Law of Suits by Attach-
    ment in the United States. Second Edition, Re-
    vised and Enlarged, with an Appendix contain-
    ing the leading Statutory Provisions of the
    several States and Territories of the United
    States in relation to Suits by Attachment, and a
    Treatise on Foreign Attachment in the Lord
    Mayor's Court of London. By John Locke. . 5 50 *Little, B. & Co.*

—— J. R., The Culprit Fay. 12mo. . . . . 0 50 *Rudd & Carleton.*

—— " and Halleck, F. G., The Croakers. By
    Joseph Rodman Drake, and Fitz-Greene Hal-
    leck. First complete edition. 4to. . . 10 00 *Bradford ClubNY*

Drama (The) of Drunkenness; or, Sixteen Scenes in the
    Drunkard's Theatre. 18mo. . . . . 0 25 *A. S. S. Union.*

Drew, W. H., The Freemason's Hand-Book; containing
    the Ritual of Freemasonry, as practised in the
    Lodges of the United States. With Symbolical
    Illustrations. 32mo. . . . . . 0 50 *Macoy & Sickels.*

Driftwood on the Sea of Life. By Willie Ware. 12mo. 1 00 *J. Challen & Son.*

Drunkard's Daughter (The). By the author of the " Old
    Red House," &c. 16mo. . . . . . 0 65 *Henry Hoyt.*

Drury, Anna H., Misrepresentation. A Novel. 8vo. 0 50 *Harper & Bros.*

Duben, G., Treatise on Microscopical Diagonosis. With
    71 engravings. Translated, with additions, by
    Professor Lewis Bauer, M. D. 8vo. . . 1 00 *John Wiley.*

Du Cauret, Life in the Desert; or, Recollections of
    Travel in Asia and Africa. Translated from
    the French. 12mo. . . . . . . 1 25 *Mason Brothers.*

Duff, Alex. (Rev.), The Indian Rebellion; its Causes and
    Results. In a series of Letters. 16mo. . . *Carter & Bros.*

Dufferin, Lord, Letters from High Latitudes. . . 1 00 *Ticknor & Fields.*

Dufresne, A., Stories of Henry and Henrietta. Trans-
    lated from the French. 12mo. . . . 0 75 *T. O. H. P. Burnh'm.*

Duganne, A. J. H., The Tenant House; or, Embers from
    Poverty's Hearth-Stone. 12mo. . . . 1 25 *R. M. De Witt.*

—— " The War in Europe, being a retrospect of Wars
    and Treaties, showing the remote and recent
    Causes and Objects of a Dynastic War in con-
    nection with the Balance of Power in Europe. 0 25 "

Dumas, A., Royalists and Republicans; or, the Companions of Jehu. Paper, 8vo. . . . . 0 50 *E. D. Long & Co.*
———— " The Guillotine; or, the Death of Morgan. A Sequel to "Royalists and Republicans " 8vo. 0 50 "
———— " The Man with Five Wives. 8vo. paper. . 0 50 *Peterson & Bros.*
———— " The Mohicans of Paris. 8vo. paper. . . 0 50 "
Duncan, M. L., Memoir of Mary Lundie Duncan; being Recollections of a Daughter, by Her Mother. . 0 75 *Am Tract So.*
———— W. C. (Rev.) The Tears of Jesus of Nazareth. 0 75 *Sheldon & Co.*
Duniway, A. J., Captain Gray's Company; or, Crossing the Plains and Living in Oregon. 12mo. cl. . 1 50 *S. J. McCormick.*
Dunlap (S. F.), Vestiges of the Spirit History of Man. . 3 50 *D. Appleton & Co.*
Durffee, C. (Rev.), A History of Williams College, Williamstown, Mass. 8vo. . . . . . 2 00 *A. Williams & Co.*
Durkee, S. (M. D.), A Treatise on Gonorrhœa and Syphilis. 3 00 *J. P. Jewitt & Co.*
Dust and Foam; or, Two Continents and Three Oceans. By T. Robinson Warren. 12mo. cl. . . . 1 25 *Chas. Scribner.*
Dwight, B. W., The Higher Christian Education. 12mo. 1 00 *Barnes & Burr.*

E

Eadie, John (Rev.), A Commentary on the Greek Text of the Epistle of Paul to the Philippians. 8vo. . *Carter & Brothers.*
———— John (Rev.), Paul, the Preacher; or, a popular and practical exposition of his Discourses and Speeches, as recorded in the Acts of the Apostles. 12mo. . . . . 1 25 "
Eames, Jane A., The Budget Closed. 12mo. . . . 1 00 *Ticknor & Fields.*
Earth, Sea, and Sky; or, the Hand of God in the Works of Nature. By the Rev. John M. Wilson. 12mo. 1 25 *T. Nelson & Sons.*
East, John (Rev.), My Saviour; or, Devotional Meditations, in Prose and Verse, on the Names and Titles of the Lord Jesus Christ. 18mo. . . 0 50 *Carter & Brothers.*
———— John (Rev.), Peace in Believing; exemplified in the Memoirs of Mrs. Ann East. Written by her husband, Rev. John East. 18mo. . . . 0 50 "
Easter Holidays at Cedar Grove. By Mrs. Wm. Wood Seymour. 24mo. . . . . . . *D. Dana, Jr.*
Eaton, J. S., A Treatise on Arithmetic. 12mo. . . *Brown & Taggard.*
Ebony Idol (The). By a Lady of New England. 12mo. cl 1 00 *D. Appleton & Co.*
Echoes of Europe; or, Word Pictures of Travel By E. K. Washington. 8vo. . . . . . . 1 50 *Jas. Challen & Son.*

Eclectic Tune Book. Edited by Wm. B. Bradbury. 8vo.	1 00	*Mason & Brothers.*
Eddy, D. C., A Visit to Ireland. 16mo.	0 63	*A. F. Graves.*
—— " Paris to Amsterdam. 16mo.	0 63	"
—— " The Alps and the Rhine.	0 50	"
—— " The Baltic to Vesuvius.	0 50	"
—— " Through Scotland and England. 16mo.	0 63	"
Eddey Ellerslie; or, Old Friends with New Faces. By A. L. O. E. 18mo.	0 30	*Carter & Brothers.*
Edgar, John G., The Crusades and the Crusaders. 16mo.	0 75	*Ticknor & Fields.*
—— " The Wars of the Roses; or, Stories of the Struggle of York and Lancaster. 16mo.	0 60	*Harper & Bros.*
Edgar Poe, and his Critics. By Sarah Helen Whitman.	0 75	*Rudd & Carleton.*
Edgarton, W. P., The Western Orator. Dialogue, Poetry, Humor, &c.	1 25	*Ingham & Bragg.*
Edith Vaughan's Victory, or How to Conquer. By Ellen Wall Pierson. 16mo.	0 63	*D. Appleton & Co.*
—— the Backwoods Girl. By Mrs. L. C. Tuthill. 16mo.	0 63	*C. Scribner.*
Edith's Ministry. By Harriet B. McKeever. 12mo.	1 00	*Lindsay & B.*
Education; Intellectual, Moral and Physical. By Herbert Spencer.	1 00	*D. Appleton & Co.*
Edwards, Arthur M., Life beneath the Waters; or, the Aquarium in America. Illustrated by plates and wood-cuts drawn from Life. 16mo.	1 50	*H. Ballière.*
—— C. M. (Mrs.), Sylvia Austin; or, the Girl who Stole a Cent. 12mo.	0 25	*Carlton & Porter.*
—— " " " The Rainbow Side; a Sequel to "The Itinerant." 16mo.	0 70	"
—— M., The Boy Inventor; a Memoir of Matthew Edwards, Mathematical Instrument Maker. 16mo.	0 50	*Walker, Wise & Co.*
Egan, Pierce, Love Me, Leave Me Not. 8vo.	0 50	*Frederick A. Brady*
—— " The Snake in the Grass. 8vo.	0 50	"
Ehninger, J. W., Illustrations of the Courtship of Miles Standish, from original Drawings.	0 00	*Rudd & Carleton.*
Eighteen (The) Christian Centuries. By the Rev. James White. 12mo.	1 25	*D. Appleton & Co.*
Eiderhorst, W., A Manual of Blowpipe Analysis and Determinate Mineralogy. 12mo.	0 88	*T. Elwood Zell.*
Eldredge, Abby, Ella Graham; or, Great Effects from Small Causes. 18mo.	0 25	*Presb. B. of Pub.*
Electron; or, The Pranks of the Modern Puck; a Telegraphic Epic for the Times. William O. Richards. 16mo.	0 50	*D. Appleton & Co.*
El Fureidis. By the author of "The Lamplighter," and "Mabel Vaughan." 12mo.	1 00	*Ticknor & Fields.*

Eliot, G., Adam Bede. 12mo. . . . . . 1 00 *Harper & Bros.*
——— " The Mill on the Floss. 12mo. . . . 1 00 "
El Khuds, the Holy; or, Glimpses in the Orient. By
    W. M. Turner, M. D. 8vo. . . . 8 50 *Challen & Son.*
Ella Graham; or, Great Effects from Small Causes. By
    Abby Eldredge. 18mo. . . . . 0 25 *Presb. B. of Pub.*
Ellen; or, The Fanatic's Daughter. By Mrs. V. G.
    Cowdin. 12mo. . . . . . . *S. H. Goetzel & Co.*
——— Akenza; or, the Female Sailor Boy. 8vo. . 0 25 *F. A. Brady.*
Ellet, E. F. (Mrs.), Women Artists in all Ages and
    Countries. 12mo. cl. . . . . . 1 00 *Harper & Bros.*
Ellicott, C. J., A Commentary, Critical and Grammatical,
    on St. Paul's Epistle to the Galatians, with a
    Revised Translation. 8vo. . . . . 1 50 *W. F. Draper.*
Ellie Randolph; or, the Good Part. By Kitty Neely. . 0 75 *Carter & Bros.*
Elliott, F. R., Fruit Book; or, the American Fruit-
    Grower's Guide in Orchard and Garden.
    Fourth edition, revised, enlarged, and improved. 1 25 *Saxton & Barker.*
——— J., The Debates in the several State Conventions
    on the Adoption of the Federal Constitution, as
    recommended by the General Convention at
    Philadelphia, in 1787.¶ Together with the
    Journal of the Federal Convention, Luther
    Martin's Letter, Yates' Minutes, Congressional
    Opinions, Virginia and Kentucky Resolutions
    of '98, '99, and other Illustrations of the Con-
    stitution; including the Madison Papers, con-
    taining the Debates on the Adoption of the
    Federal Constitution, in the Convention held at
    Philadelphia in 1787, with a Diary of the De-
    bates of the Congress of the Confederation, as
    Reported by James Madison. Published under
    the sanction of Congress, by Jonathan Elliott.
    New Edition. 5 vols. 8vo. . . . . 15 00 *Lippincott & Co.*
——— W., Carolina Sports by Land and Water. 12mo. 1 00 *Derby & Jackson.*
Ellis, J. (M. D.), The Avoidable Causes of Disease, In-
    sanity, and Deformity. . . . . . 1 00 *Mason Bros.*
——— Sarah (Mrs.), Chapters on Wives. 12mo. . 1 00 *Harper & Bros.*
——— " " Housekeeping Made Easy. A Complete
    Instructor in all Branches of Cookery and Do-
    mestic Economy. Edited by Mrs. Mowatt. . 0 25 *Townsend & Co.*
——— W. (Rev.), Three Visits to Madagascar during the
    years 1853, 1854, 1856. Including a Journey
    to the Capital; with Notices of the Natural
    History of the Country, and of the present
    Civilization of the People. 8vo. . . . 2 50 *Harper & Bros.*

Elmer, W. (M. D.), and L. Elsberg, M. D., The Physician's
    Handbook of Practice for 1860. 18mo. . . 1 25   *Townsend & Co.*

Eloquence a Virtue; or, Outlines of a Systematic Rhe- '
    toric. Translated from the German of Dr.
    Francis Theremin. By William G. T. Shedd.
    Revised edition. 12mo. Half r. . . . 0 75   *W. F. Draper.*

Elsie Lee; or, Impatience Cured. By Mary Grey. 16mo. 0 20   *Presb. B., Phila.*

Elwell, J. J. (M. D.), A Medico-Legal Treatise on Mal-
    practice and Medical Evidence; comprising the
    Elements of Medical Jurisprudence. 8vo. . 5 50   *John S. Voorhies.*

Elwes, A., Paul Blake; or, a Boy's Perils in the Islands
    of Corsica and Monte Christo. 16mo. . . 0 75   *Thomson Brothers.*

Elwyn, A. L. (M. D.), Glossary of Supposed American-
    isms. 12mo. . . . .   *Lippincott & Co.*

Emancipation of Faith. By the late Henry Edward Sche-
    del, M. D. Edited by George Schedel. 2 vols., 8vo. 4 00   *D. Appleton & C.*

Emerson, L. O., Sabbath Harmony. A new Collection of
    Original and Sacred Music. . . . . 1 00   *Chase, N. & H.*

——— R. W., Conduct of Life. 12mo. . . . 1 00   *Ticknor & Fields.*

Emilie, the Peacemaker. By Mrs. T. Geldart. 18mo. . 0 50   *Sheldon & Co.*

Emmons, E., Manual of Geology: designed for the use of
    Colleges and Academies. Second edition. 8vo. 1 50   *Barnes & Burr.*

Emphatic Diaglott (The), containing the original Greek
    Text of the New Testament, with an Interline-
    ary Translation; a new emphatic version, based
    on the literal translation of the most eminent
    Biblical Critics and Translators, to be completed
    in 27 numbers. No. 1. . . . . 0 20   *Wilson & Cockroft.*

Empress Eugenie's Boudoir; or, the Mysteries of the
    Court of France. By G. W. M. Reynolds. 8vo. 0 50   *F. A. Brady.*

Engel, Mary, A Memorial of. 18mo. limp cloth. . 0 25   *Carter & Bros.*

Engineering Precedents. By B. F. Isherwood, Chief
    Engineer, &c., U. S. Navy. Vol. II. 8vo. . 2 50   *Baillière Brothers.*

England, a Popula History of. By Mrs. Thomas Gel-
    dart. 16mo. . . . . 0 75   *Sheldon & Co.*

English Reports in Law and Equity. Vol. XL., contain-
    ing Cases in the House of Lords, the Privy
    Council, the Courts of Queen's Bench, Common
    Pleas and Exchequer, and also Crown Cases
    reserved for the year 1857. 8vo. . . . 2 50   *Little, Brown & Co.*

Episodes of French History during the Consulate and the
    First Empire. By Miss Pardoe. 12mo. . 1 00   *Harper & Bros.*

Eric; or, Little by Little: a Tale of Roslyn School. By
    Frederick W. Farrar. 12mo. . . . 1 00   *Rudd & Carleton.*

Ernest Bracebridge; or, Schoolboy Days. By W. H. G.
    Kingston. 16mo. . . . . . . 0 76   *Ticknor & Fields.*

Ernestin; or, the Heart's Longing. By Aleth. 12mo. .   1 25   *Stanford&Delisser*
Ernst, L., Intermediate French Course, in accordance
    with the Robertsonian System of Teaching Mo-
    dern Languages. 12mo.   .   .   .   .   1 00   *Lockwood & Son.*
Errym, M. J., Ben Ratcliffe, the Wrecker. 8vo. pap. .   0 25   *F. A. Brady.*
——— " The Incendiaries; or, the Haunted Manor. 8vo.   0 25   "
——— " The Young Shipwright: a Tale of the Sea. 8vo.   0 25   "
——— " True Blue; or, Sharks on Shore. 8vo.   .   0 25   "
Eschatology; or, the Scripture Doctrine of the Coming of
    the Lord, the Resurrection, and the Judgment.
    By Samuel Lee. 12mo.   .   .   .   .   1 00   *J. E. Tilton & Co.*
Esperanzo: My Journey Thither, and What I Saw There.   1 00   *V. Nicholson.*
Essay on Intuitive Morals: Being an Attempt to Pop-
    ularize Ethical Science.   Part I.   Theory of
    Morals. First American Edition, with Additions
    and Corrections by the author. 12mo.   .   1 00   *Crosby, N., L.&Co.*
Essays on Practical Piety and Divine Grace. By L.
    M. J. 18mo. cl.   .   .   .   .   .   0 25   *T. E. Zell.*
——— upon some of the Testimonials of Truth as held
    by the Society of Friends. 18mo. cl.   .   .   0 25   "
Essence (The) of Science; or, the Catechism of Positive
    Sociology and Physical Mentality. By a Student
    of Auguste Comte. 12mo. pap.   .   .   .   0 38   *O. Blanchard.*
Esterbrook, W. P., The American Stair Builder. 4to. .   6 00   *Baker & Godwin.*
Esther and her Times.   A series of Lectures on the Book
    of Esther. By John M. Lowrie. 12mo.   ..   0 60   *Presb. Bd. of Pub.*
Ethel Trevor; or, the Duke's Victim. By G. W. M.
    Reynolds. 8vo.   .   .   .   .   .   0 50   *F. A. Brady.*
Ethel's Love Life. A New England Novel. By Mrs. M.
    J. M. Sweat. 12mo.   .   .   .   .   .   1 00   *Rudd & Carleton.*
Etiquette, and the Usages of Society. By Henry P. Wil-
    lis. 12mo.   .   .   .   .   .   .   0 25   *Dick & Fitzgerald.*
Ettore Fieramosca; or, the Challenge of Barletta.   The
    Struggles of an Italian against Foreign Invaders
    and Foreign Protectors. By Massimo d'Aze-
    glio. 16mo.   .   .   .   .   .   .   1 00   *Phillips, S. & Co.*
Euripides ex Recensione.   Frederici A. Paley, accessit
    verborum et nominum index. Vol. I. 18mo. .   0 40   *Harper & Bros.*
European Civilization; Protestantism and Catholicity
    compared.   By the Rev. J. Balmes. 8vo.   .   2 00   *Murphy & Co.*
——— Life, Legend, and Landscape. By John R. Tait.   1 00   *Jas. Challen &Son.*
Evan Harrington; or, He would be a Gentleman. By
    George Meredith. 12mo. .   .   .   .   1 00   *Harper & Bros.*
Evans, Augusta J., Beulah. A Novel. 12mo.   .   .   1 25   *Derby & Jackson.*

Evans, F. W., Shakers. Compendium of the Origin,
    History, Principles, Rules and Regulations, Gov-
    ernment, and Doctrines of the United Society of
    Believers in Christ's Second Appearing. With
    Biographies of Ann Lee, William Lee, James
    Whittaker, J. Hocknell, J. Meacham, and Lucy
    White. 16mo. . . . . 0 75   *D. Appleton & Co.*

—— R. W. (Rev.), The Rectory of Valehead; or, the
    Edifice of a Holy Home. 12mo. cl. . . 0 75   *Daniel Dana, jr.*

—— W. F. (Rev.), The Happy Island; or, Paradise
    Restored. 16mo. cl. . . . . .   *H. V. Degen & Son.*

Evelyn Gray; or, Flowers thrive in Sunshine. 12mo. . 0 50   *A. S. S. Union.*

Evening (The) of Life; or, Light and Comfort Amidst
    the Shadows of Declining Years. By Rev. Je-
    remiah Chaplin, D. D. 12mo. . . . . 1 00   *Gould & Lincoln.*

Evenings at the Microscope; or, Researches among the
    Minute Organs and Forms of Animal Life. By
    Philip Henry Gosse, F. R. S. 12mo. cl. . . 1 50   *D. Appleton & Co.*

Everett, Edward, The Mount Vernon Papers. 12mo. cl. 1 25   "

——   "   The Speeches of. Vol. III. 8vo. cl. . 2 50   *Little, Brown & Co.*

Every-Day Book of History and Chronology. By Joel
    Munsell. 8vo. . . . . 2 50   *Appleton & Co.*

Evil Eye (The); or, the Black Spectre. By William
    Carleton. 12mo. . . . . . . 1 25   *Patrick Donahue.*

Evolutions of the Line, as practised by the Austrian In-
    fantry, and adopted in 1853. Translated by
    Lieut. O. M. Wilcox, 7th Regiment, U. S. Infan-
    try. 12mo. . . . . 1 00   *D. Van Nostrand.*

Ewbank, T., Thoughts on Matter and Force; or, Marvels
    that Encompass Us: comprising Suggestions Il-
    lustrative of the Theory of the Earth and of the
    Universe. 16mo. . . . . . . 0 75   *D. Appleton & Co.*

Exploits and Triumphs in Europe, of Paul Morphy, the
    Chess Champion, by his late Secretary. 12mo. cl. 0 75   "

Exposé of the Science of Gambling. Containing a Com-
    plete Disclosure of the Secret of the Art, as
    practised by Professional Gamblers. Written
    by an Adept. 18mo. . . . . . 0 50   *Frederick A. Brady.*

Extent (The) of the Atonement in its Relation to God
    and the Universe. By Rev. Thomas W. Jenkyn,
    D. D. 12mo. . . . . 1 00   *Gould & Lincoln.*

4

F

Faber, F. W. (Rev.), The Foot of the Cross : or, the Sor-
          rows of Mary. 12mo.   .   .   0.75 *Marphy & Co.*
———   "   Spiritual Conferences. 12mo.   . 0 75 "
Factory Girls (The) ; or, "Trust in God." By the author
        of "Matty Gregg," &c., &c. 18mo. cl. . 0 40 *Henry Hoyt.*
Fairbairn, R. B. (Rev.), Child of Faith. 18mo. . . 0 80 *F. D. Harriman.*
——— P. (Rev.), Hermeneutical Manual ; or, Introduc-
      tion to the Exegetical Study of the Scriptures
      of the New Testament. 12mo.   .   . 1 50 *Smith, E. & Co.*
Fairbanks, C. B., Memorials of the Blessed. A Series of
      Short Lives of the Saints. 12mo.   .   . 0 75 *Patrick Donahue.*
——— G. R., The History and Antiquities of the City of
      St. Augustine, Florida, founded A. D. 1565. 8vo. 1 50 *Chas. B. Norton.*
Fairchild, E. R. (Rev.), Memorial of the Life and Services
      of the late Rev. Henry A. Rowland, D. D. . 0 75 *M. W. Dodd.*
Fairfield, C. E., Our Bible-Class, and the Good that Came
      of It. 12mo. cl.   .   .   .   . 1 00 *Derby & Jackson.*
——— J., The Autobiography of Jane Fairfield ; em-
      bracing a few Select Poems of Sumner Lincoln
      Fairfield. 12mo.   .   .   .   . 1 00 *Bazin & Ellsworth.*
Fairy (The) Nightcaps. 16mo.   .   .   .   . 0 50 *D. Appleton & Co.*
Fairy Dreams ; or, Wanderings in Elf-Land. By Jane G.
      Austin. Sq. 16mo.   .   .   .   . 0 75 *J. E. Tilton & Co.*
Faith and Patience. A Story, and Something More, for
      Boys. 18mo.   .   .   .   .   . 0 75 *Walker, Wise & Co.*
Faithful Bridget : or, the Story of a Poor Woman who
      worked for the Lord. 18mo. .   .   . 0 20 *Carlton & Porter.*
Faithful Forever. By Coventry Patmore. 16mo. cl. . 1 00 *Ticknor & Fields.*
Faithful (The) Promiser. 18mo.   .   .   . 0 15 *E. P. Dutton & Co.*
Familiar Conversations on the Queries. By Harriet
      Stockly. 18mo. cl.   .   .   .   . 0 38 *T. E. Zell.*
Family Altar (The) ; or, Prayers for Family Worship.
      compiled by the Rev. James A. Bolles, D. D. . 0 50 *Daniel Dana, jr.*
Family Choral (The), Being a Collection of Hymns and
      Tunes. By Rev. A. C. Rose. 18mo.   .   *H. V. Degen.*
Family of Bethany (The) ; or, Meditations on the 11th
      Chapter of the Gospel of John. By L. Bonnet. 0 40 *Carter & Brothers.*
Fankwei ; or, the San Jacinto in the Seas of India, China,
      and Japan. By William Maxwell Wood, M. D.,
      U. S. N. 12mo.   .   .   .   .   . 1 25 *Harper & Brothers.*

Fanny. From the French of Ernest Feydeau. 12mo. pap. . 0 50 *E. D. Long & Co.*
——— the Flower Girl; or, Honesty Rewarded. By
    Selina Bunbury. 18mo. . . . . . 0 30 *Carter & Brothers.*
Faraday, M., Lectures on the Physical Forces. 16mo. cl. 0 75 *Harper & Bros.*
Farley, F. A. (Rev.), Unitarianism Defined. 12mo. . 0 75 *Walker, Wise & Co.*
Farnham, Eliza W., My Early Days. 12mo. . . . 1 25 *Burt, H. & A.*
Farrar, A. S. (Rev.), Science in Theology. Sermons
    preached in St. Mary's, Oxford, before the Uni-
    versity. 12mo. . . . . . . 0 85 *Smith, E. & Co.*
——— F. W., Eric; or, Little by Little: a Tale of Roz-
    lyn School. 12mo. . . . . . 1 00 *Rudd & Carleton.*
——— " Julian Home. A Tale of College Life. 12mo. 1 25 *Lippincott & Co.*
Fätä Morgana. Deutsch Amerikanische Preis-Novelle.
    By Adolph Douai. 8vo. . . . . 0 60 *Westermann & Co.*
Father Larkin's Mission in Jonesville; a Tale of the
    Times. By T. L. Nichols, M. D. 18mo. . 0 25 *Kelly, Hedian & P.*
——— Laval; or, the Jesuit Missionary; A Tale of the
    North American Indians. By James McSherry. *John Murphy & Co.*
——— and Daughter; a Portraiture from Life. By
    Fredrika Bremer. 12mo. cl. . . . 1 25 *Peterson & Bros*
Favorite Authors; a Companion Book of Prose and
    Poetry. 12mo. . . . . . 2 50 *Ticknor & Fields.*
——— English Poems of the Last Two Centuries. Illus-
    trated. Small 4to. cl. full guilt; 8$. Morocco. 9 00 *D. Appleton & Co.*
——— Fairy Tales; For Little Folks, with seventy illus-
    trations. By Twaites and others. Square cl. . 0 50 *James Miller.*
Felton, J. H., The Decimal System; an Argument for
    American Consistency in the Extension of the
    Decimal Scale to Weights and Measures, in Har-
    mony with the National Currency. 12mo. cl. 0 75 *Wiley & Halsted.*
Female Skeptic (The); or, Faith Triumphant. 12mo. . 1 25 *R. M. De Witt.*
Fenelon, Adventures of Telemachus. By Fenelon.
    Translated by Dr. Hawkesworth. With a Life
    of Fenelon, by Lamartine. Edited by O. W.
    Wight, A. M. 12mo. . . . . 1 25 *Derby & Jackson.*
Fernald, W. M., God in his Providence; a Comprehen-
    sive View of the Principles and Particulars of
    an Active Divine Providence over Man. 12mo. 1 00 *Otis Clapp.*
Feuchtwanger, L., A Popular Treatise on Gems, in refer-
    ence to their scientific value. 12mo. cl. 3 00 *D. Appleton & Co.*
——— " A Treatise on Fermented Liquors. 2 00 *L. Feuchtwanger.*
Feuillett, O., Onesta; or, a Marriage by Will. 8vo. . 0 25 *E. D. Long & Co.*
——— " The Romance of a Poor Young Man. 8vo. 0 25 *Townsend & Co.*
——— " The same. 12mo. cl. . . . . 1 00 *Rudd & Carleton.*

Fidgety Skeert. By the author of "The Babes in the
    Basket." 16mo.   .   .   .   .   .   . 0 50 *A. D. F. Randolph.*
Field, H. M., Summer Pictures; from Copenhagen to
    Venice. 12mo.   .   .   .   .   .   , 1 00 *Sheldon & Co.*
——— M., Bertha Percy; or, L'Esperance. 12mo.   .   *D. Appleton & Co.*
Fifty Years among the Baptists. By David Bene-
    dict, D. D. 12mo.   .   .   .   .   . 1 00 *Sheldon & Co.*
Fights for the Championship of England; or, Accounts
    of all the Prize Battles for the Championship,
    from the days of Figg and Broughton to the
    Present Time. 8vo. pap.   .   .   . 0 25 *R. M. Dewitt.*
Fiji and the Fijians. By Thomas Williams and James
    Calvert, late Missionaries in Fiji. 8vo.   . 2 50 *D. Appleton & Co.*
First (A) Lesson in Natural History. By Actæa. 16mo. 0 62 *Little, Brown & Co.*
——— Things; or, The Development of Church Life.
    By Baron Stow. 16mo.   .   .   .   . 0 60 *Gould & Lincoln.*
——— Quarrels, and First Discords in Married Life; to
    which is added a Matrimonial Peace Offering.
    Edited by James H. Burk. 12mo. cl.   .   .   *Applegate & Co.*
First (The) and Last Journey. 18mo.   .   .   . 0 40 *Carter & Brothers.*
    The same. .   .   .   . 0 35 *F. D. Harriman.*
Fish, H. C. (Rev.), Select Discourses : translated from the
    French and German. By the Rev.
    H. C. Fish, and D. W. Poor, D. D. 1 00 *Sheldon & Co.*
——— "   The Price of Soul Liberty, and Who Paid
    It. 18mo., cl.   .   .   .   .   .   . 0 40   "   .
Fisher, S. W., Occasional Sermons and Addresses. 8vo. 2 00 *Mason Brothers.*
——— W. L., An Inquiry into the Laws of Organized
    Societies, as applied to the alleged
    Decline of the Society of Friends. 12mo. 0 25 *T. Ellwood Zell.*
——— "   History of the Institution of the Sabbath
    Day, its Uses and Abuses. With Notices of the
    Puritans, Quakers, &c. 12mo.   .   .   .   *T. B. Pugh.*
Fiske, D. W., The Book of the First American Chess
    Congress; containing the Proceedings of that
    Celebrated Assemblage, held in New York, in
    the year 1857. 12mo.   .   .   .   . 1 50 *Rudd & Carleton.*
Five Years in China, with an Account of the Great Re-
    bellion, and a Description of St. Helena. By
    Charles Taylor, M. D. 12mo.   .   .   . 1 25 *Derby & Jackson.*
Flanders, H., An Exposition of the Constitution of the
    United States. Designed as a Manual of
    Instruction. 12mo.   .   .   .   . 1 12 *E. H. Butler & Co.*

Flanders, H., Chief Justices. The Lives and Times of the
Chief Justices of the Supreme Court of the
United States. Comprising the Lives of John
Jay, John Rutledge, William Cushing, Oliver
Ellsworth, and John Marshall, and a History of
their Times from 1754 to 1835. 2 vols. 8vo.   5 00 *Lippincott & Co.*

Flash, Henry L., Poems. 12mo. . . . . .   75 *Rudd & Carleton.*

Fleming, W. (Rev.), A Vocabulary of Philosophy, Mental, Moral, and Metaphysical; with Quotations
and References for the Use of Students, with
additions by Charles P. Krauth, D. D. 12mo.   1 75 *Smith, Eng. & Co.*

Fletcher, J. C., Rosa; or, the Parisian Girl. From the
French of Madame De Presence. 16mo.   0 60 *Harper & Brothers*

———— M., The Methodists; or, Incidents and Characters
from Life in the Baltimore Conference. With
an Introduction by W. P. Strickland, D. D. 2
vols., 12mo. . . . .   2 00 *Derby & Jackson.*

Flint, A., M. D., A Practical Treatise on the Diagnosis,
Pathology, and Treatment of the Diseases of the
Heart. 8vo. . . . .   2 75 *Blanchard & Lea.*

———— C. L., Milch Cows and Dairy Farming; comprising the Breeds, Breeding, and Management, &c., &c.; to which is added
Horsfall's System of Dairy Manage-
ment. 8vo. . . . . . .   1 25 *Crosby, N., L. & Co.*

———— " Grasses and Forage Plants. A Practical
Treatise on. Fifth edition, revised and
enlarged. 8vo. . . . . . .   1 25   "

Flora; or, Self-Deception; and other Tales. By A. L.
O. E. 18mo. . . . .   0 50 *Carter & Brothers.*

Florence Erwin's Three Homes. By a Lady. 16mo., cl. 0 75 *Crosby, N., L. & Co.*

Flounced Robe (The), and What it Cost. By Harriet B.
McKeever. 12mo. . . . . . .   0 50 *Lindsay & B.*

Flourens, P., A History of the Circulation of the Blood.
Translated from the French by J. C. Reeve,
M. D. 12mo. . . . .   0 75 *Rickey, M. & Co.*

Flower Basket (The). A Catholic Tale, from the German
of Schmid. 32mo. cl. . . . . .   0 87 *H. McGrath.*

———— Pictures. By Elise Polko. Translated from the
German by S. W. Lander. 16mo. . .   0 50 *D. Appleton & Co.*

Floyd, M. (Rev.), Travels in France and the British
Islands. 18mo. . . . .   1 25 *Lippincott & Co.*

Following the Drum; a Glimpse of Frontier Life. By
Mrs. Veile. 12mo. cl. . . . . .   1 00 *Rudd & Carleton.*

Fontana, G. B., An Elementary Grammar of the Italian Language, progressively arranged for the Use of Schools and Colleges. 12mo. . . . . 1 00 *D. Appleton & Co.*

Food for Babes; or, Artificial Human Milk, and the Manner of Preparing it and Administering it to Young Children. By Wm. Henry Cumming, M. D. 18mo. . . . . 0 85 *A. D. F. Randolph.*

Fool of Quality (The). By Henry Brooke. With a Biographical Preface. By Rev. Chas. Kingsley. 12mo. 2 00 *Derby & Jackson.*

Foot (The) of the Cross; or, the Sorrows of Mary. By F. W. Faber, D. D. 12mo. cl. . . . . 0 75 *Murphy & Co.*

Foote, Samuel E., Memoirs of the Life of. By his brother, John P. Foote. 12mo. . . . . 0 75 *Robt. Clarke & Co.*

Footfalls on the Boundary of Another World. With Narrative Illustrations. By Robert Dale Owen. 1 25 *Lippincott & Co.*

Footprints of Popery; or, Places where Martyrs have Suffered. 18mo. . . . . . . 0 30 *Presb. B. of Pub.*

Forbes, John (M. D.), Nature and Art in the Cure of Disease. 12mo. . . . . . . 0 75 *S. S. & W. Wood.*

Ford, S. R., Mary Bunyan, the Dreamer's Blind Daughter. A Tale of Religious Persecution. 12mo. . . 1 00 *Sheldon & Co.*

Forester, F., Hints to Horse Keepers. A Complete Manual for Horsemen. By the late Henry William Herbert (Frank Forester). 12mo. . . . 1 25 *Saxton & Barker.*

Forrest, Mary, Women of the South distinguished in Literature. 4to. . . . . . . 9 00 *Derby & Jackson.*

Forrester, F., Glen Morris Stories. Dick Duncan—the Story of a Boy who loved Mischief. 16mo. 0 60 *Howe & Ferry.*

———   "   Guy Carleton. 16mo. . . . . 0 60   "

———   "   Jessie Carlton. 18mo. . . . . 0 60   "

Fort, O. M. (Mrs.), Alurid Lind. 18mo. . . . *Jas. Challen & Sons.*

Forty Years' Experience in Sunday Schools. By Stephen H. Tyng, D. D., 18mo. cl. . . . 0 60 *Sheldon & Co.*

——— Years in the Wilderness of Pills and Powders; or, the Cogitations and Confessions of an Aged Physician. 12mo. . . . . . 1 00 *J. P. Jewett & Co.*

Forty-four Years of the Life of a Hunter; being Reminiscences of Meshach Browning, a Maryland Hunter, roughly written down by Himself. . 1 25 *Lippincott & Co.*

Fory, W. R. (Rev.), Premature Church Membership. With an Introduction by the Rev. Baron Stow, D. D., 16mo. . . . . . . 0 50 *A. D. F. Ran'lph.*

Foster, L., Way-Side Glimpses, North and South. 12mo. 1 00 *Rudd & Carleton.*

Foster Brothers (The); being a History of the School and College Life of two Young Men. 12mo. . 1 00 *D. Appleton & Co.*

Four Years aboard the Whale Ship. Embracing Cruises in the Pacific, Atlantic, Indian, and Antarctic Oceans, in the years 1855–'59. By William B. Whitecar, jr. 12mo. . . . . 1 00 *Lippincott & Co.*

Fowls, W. B., The Hundred Dialogues, New and Original. 12mo. hf. roan. . . . . 1 00 *Collins & Bro.*

Fowler, W. C., Elementary Grammar, Etymology and Syntax. Abridged from the Octavo Edition of the English Language in its Elements and Forms. 12mo. . . . . . 0 50 *Harper & Bros*

——— O. S. & N. L., The Illustrated Self-Instructor in Phrenology and Physiology. 16mo. pap. . 0 30 *Fowler & Wells.*

Fragments from the Study of a Pastor. By Rev. George W. Nichols, A. M. 12mo. . . . . 0 75 *Henry B. Price.*

Francatelli, C. E., The Modern Cook. 8vo. cl. . . 3 00 *Peterson & Bros.*

France, History of. From the Earliest Times to the French Revolution of 1789. Vol. I. (Ancient Gaul.) By Parke Godwin. 8vo. . . . 2 00 *Harper & Bros.*

——— History of, from the Earlier Times to 1848. By the Rev. James White, author of the "Eighteen Christian Centuries." 8vo. cl. . . . 2 00 *D. Appleton & Co.*

Francis, John W. (M. D.), Old New York; or, Reminiscences of the past Sixty Years. 12mo. . . 1 25 *Charles Roe.*

——— L., Racine's Grecques appartenant desormais a la Langue Francaise. 5 numbers. No. 1. 8vo. 0 50 *Westermann & Co.*

Frank Elliott; or, Wells in the Desert. A Religious Novel. By Rev. James Challen. 12mo. . 1 00 *J. Challen & Son.*

——— Elston; or, Patience in Well-Doing. A Story for Lads. 18mo. . . . . . . 0 35 *Carlton & Porter.*

——— Wildman's Adventures on Land and Water. By Frank Gerstaecker. 16mo. cl. . . . 1 00 *Crosby, N., L. & Co.*

Franklin, B., Letters to Benjamin Franklin, from his Family and Friends. 1751–1790. 8vo. . . 3 00 *C. B. Richardson.*

——— Josephine. Nelly's First School Days. 12mo. 0 50 *Brewn & Taggard.*

——— " Nelly and her Boat. 16mo. . . . 0 50 "

——— " Nelly and her Friends. 16mo. cl. . 0 50 "

Franklin Globe Manual (The). Small 4to. . . 0 40 *Moore & Nims.*

Fred Freeland; or, The Chain of Circumstances. . 0 75 *E. O. Libby & Co.*

——— Laurence; or, The World College. By Margaret E. Teller. 18mo. cl. . . . . 0 63 *M. W. Dodd.*

——— Markham in Russia; or, the Boy Travellers in the Land of the Czar. By Wm. H. Kingston. . 0 75 *Harper & Bros.*

Freddy, the Runaway; or, the Lost One Found. 18mo. 0 20 *Am. S. S. Union.*

Frederick the Great (Life of). By Macaulay. 18mo. . 0 50 *Sheldon & Co.*

Freemason's (The) Hand-Book; containing the Ritual of
Freemasonry, as practised in the Lodges of the
United States. By William H. Drew, Grand
Lecturer for the State of New York. 32mo. . 0 50 *Macoy & Sickels.*

French, B. F., History of the Rise and Progress of the
Iron Trade of the United States, from 1621 to
1857. With numerous Statistical Tables, relating
to the Manufacture, Importation, Exportation,
and Prices of Iron for more than a Century. 8vo. 2 00 *Wiley & Halstead.*

—— H. F., The Principles, Processes and Effects of
Draining Land with Stones, Wood, Ploughs, and
open Ditches, especially with Tiles, Including
Tables of Rain Fall; Evaporation, Filtration, Ex-
cavation, Capacity of Pipes, Cost and Number
to the Acre of Tiles, &c. 12mo. . . . 1 00 *Saxton & Barker.*

French (The) Revolution of 1789, as viewed in the Light
of Republican Institutions. By John S. C. Abbott. 8vo. . . . . . . 2 50 *Harper & Bros.*

Frore, T., Morphy's Game of Chess, and Frere's Problem
Tournament. 18mo. cl. . . . . . 0 50 *T. W. Strong.*

Fresh Hearts that Failed Three Thousand Years Ago.
With other Poems. By the author of "The
New Priest in Conception Bay." 12mo. . . 0 50 *Ticknor & Fields.*

Friarswood Post-Office. By the author of "The Heir of
Redclyffe." 18mo. . . . . . . 0 50 *D. Appleton & Co.*

Friends in Council; a Series of Readings and Discourses
Thereon. A New Series. 2 vols. 16mo. . *Jas. Munroe & Co.*

Friese, H. S., Virgil's Æneid: with Explanatory Notes. 1 25 *D. Appleton & Co.*

From Dawn to Daylight; or, the Simple Story of a Western Home. By a Minister's Wife. 12mo. cl. . 1 00 *Derby & Jackson.*

—— Hay Time to Hopping. By the author of "Our
Farm of Four Acres." 12mo. . . . . 1 00 *Rudd & Carleton.*

—— New York to Delhi, by way of Rio de Janeiro,
Australia, and China. By Robert B. Minturn,
jr. 12mo. . . . . . . 1 75 *D. Appleton & Co.*

—— Poor-House to Pulpit; or, the Triumphs of the late
Dr. John Kitto, from Boyhood to Manhood. By
Wm. M. Thayer. . . . . . . *E. O. Libby & Co.*

Frost, S. A., Parlor Charades and Proverbs, intended for
the Parlor or Saloon, and requiring no Expen-
sive Apparatus of Scenery or Properties for their
Performance. 12mo. . . . . . 0 75 *Lippincott & Co.*

Fruits and Flowers of Palestine. By Rev. Henry S. Osborn. 8vo. . . . . 3 50   *Challen & Son.*
Fry, S. M., The Young Hop-Pickers. 18mo. . . . 0 20   *Carlton & Porter.*
—— W. H., Republican Campaign Text-Book for the Year 1860. 12mo. pap. . . . . . 0 25   *A. B. Burdick.*
Fuller, M., Life Without, and Life Within; or, Reviews, Narratives, Essays, and Poems. Edited by her brother, Arthur B. Fuller. 12mo. . . . 1 25   *Brown & Taggard.*
—— Richard (Rev.), Sermons. 12mo. . . . 1 00   *Sheldon & Co.*
—— Samuel (Rev.), Loutron; or, Water Baptism. A series of Discourses on the Modes, Subjects, Advantages, and Conditions of Baptism. 12mo. . 0 50   *D. Dana, jr.*
Fulton, L. S., and Eastman's Bookkeeping, Single and Double Entry. . . . . 0 75   *Moore & Nims.*
   Blanks to the above, 6 in set, ... 0 75   "
Furman, R., The Pleasures of Piety, and other Poems.   *Courtenay & Co.*
Furness, W. H. (Rev.), Thoughts on the Life and Character of Jesus of Nazareth. 12mo. . . .   *Phillips, S. & Co.*
Future Life; or, Scenes in Another World. By Geo. Wood. 1 00   *Derby & Jackson.*
Fyfe, R. A. (Rev.), The Teaching of the New Testament in regard to the Soul, and the Nature of Christ's Kingdom. 18mo. . . . . . . 0 31   *Sheldon & Co.*

G

Gage, W. L. (Rev.), Trinitarian Sermons to a Unitarian Congregation. 16mo. . . . . . 0 50   *J. P. Jewett.*
Gallery of Distinguished English and American Female Poets, with an introduction by Henry Coppee, A. M. Illustrated with one hundred Steel Engravings, mostly from Original Designs. . 12 50   *E. H. Butler & Co.*
Garden (The): a Pocket Manual of Practical Horticulture. 12mo. . . . . . . 0 50   *Fowler & Wells.*
Gardner, D., Institutes of International Law, Public and Private, as settled by the Supreme Court of the Union and by our Republic. With References to Judicial Decisions. 8vo. . . . . 5 00   *John S. Voorhies.*
Garibaldi (Gen.), The Life of Gen. Garibaldi. Written by Himself. With Sketches of his Companions in Arms. Translated by his Friend and Admirer, Theodore Dwight. 12mo. . . . 1 00   *Barnes & Burr*
—— His Boyhood and Youth, as Written by Himself. From Theodore Dwight's Translation of Garibaldi's Autobiography. 16mo. pap. . . 0 50   "

Garratt, A. C. (M. D.), Electro-Physiology and Electro-
    Therapeutics, showing the Best Methods for the
    Medical Uses of Electricity. 8vo. .   .   4 00   *Tickner & Fields.*
Garrett, A. R., The Precious Stones of the Heavenly
    Foundation, with Illustrative Selections in Prose
    and Verse. 12mo.   .   .   .   .   .   1 00   *Sheldon & Co.*
Geskell, Mrs., My Lady Ludlow; a Novel. 8vo. .   .   0 12   *Harper & Bros.*
————   "   Right at Last, and Other Tales. 12mo. .   0 75   "
Gathered Pearls. 18mo.   .   .   .   .   .   0 25   *J. Challen & C.*
Gatty, A. (Mrs.), Alice and Adolphus; or, Worlds not
    Realized. 18mo. cl.   .   .   .   .   0 30   *Carter & Brothers.*
————   "   Aunt Judy's Tales. 18mo.   .   .   0 50   "
————   "   The Circle of Blessing, and other Para-
            bles from Nature. 18mo.   .   .   0 80   "
————   "   Motes in the Sunbeam, and other Par-
            ables from Nature. 18mo.   .   .   0 30   "
Gaussen, L., The World's Birth-day; a Book for the
    Young. 18mo. cl. .   .   .   .   .   *Am. Tract So.*
Gantrelet, F. (Rev.), Month of the Sacred Heart of Jesus. 0 37   *Dunigan & Bro.*
Geddings, E. (M. D.), Outlines of a Course of Lectures
    on the Principles and Practice of Surgery.
    Prepared by Thomas S. Waring, M. D., and
    Samuel Logan, M. D., from Notes taken during the
    course. Published with the consent, and revised
    by Professor Geddings. 8vo. .   .   .   3 50   *Courtenay & Co.*
Geldart, T. (Mrs.), Daily Thoughts for a Child. 18mo. 0 50   *Sheldon & Co.*
————   "   Emilie, the Peacemaker. 18mo. cl. 0 50   "
————   "   Memorials of Samuel Gurney. 12mo. 0 50   *Henry Longstreth.*
————   "   A Popular History of England. 16mo. 0 75   *Sheldon & Co.*
————   "   Stories of Scotland and its Adjacent
            Islands. 18mo. cl.   .   .   .   0 50   "
————   "   Sunday Evening Thoughts; or, Great
            Truths in Plain Words. 18mo. cl. 0 50   "
————   "   Sunday Morning Thoughts; or, Great
            Truths in Plain Words. 18mo. cl. 0 50   "
————   "   Truth is Everything. 18mo.   .   0 50   "
Gellert, A., Trust in God; or, Three Days in the Life of
    Adam Gellert. 16mo.   .   .   .   .   0 25   *Carter & Brothers.*
Gems of Masonry. Emblematic and Descriptive. By
    John Sherer.   .   .   .   .   .   0 50   *Moore, W., K. & Co.*
Genealogy of the Descendants of John Sill, who settled
    in Cambridge, Mass., in 1637. 16mo., cloth. . 1 00   *Munsell & R.*
General Fitzgerald, "The Chevalier." A Novel. By
    Charles Lever. Paper, 8vo.   .   .   .   0 50   *Harper & Bros.*

Gentle Grace; or, Trying to do Good. 18mo. . . 0 52　*A. D. F. Randolph*

George Lee; or, The Boy who became a Great Artist; and the Shadow in the House. By Mrs. O. A. S. Beale. 18mo. . . . . . 0 25　*Carlton & Porter.*

George Molville; an American Novel. By C. Hatch Smith. 12mo. . . . . . 1 25　*W. R. C. Clark & Co.*

Georgia, from its First Discovery by Europeans, to the Adoption of the present Constitution, in MDCCXCVIII. By Rev. Wm. Bacon Stevens, M.D., D.D. 2 vols. 12mo. cl. . . 2 00　*E. H. Butler & Co.*

Gerald Kopt, the Foundling, the Fisherman of Heligoland, and Joseph Massena; or, the Jewish Convert. 18mo. . . . . . . 0 22　*Carlton & Porter*

―― and his friend Philip; or, Patience to Work and Patience to Wait. By Marion E. Weir. Abridged from the London edition. 18mo. . . 0 37　　"

Gerard, G. Le Cabinet des Fees; or, Recreative Readings, arranged for the Express Use of Students of French. 12mo. . . . . 1 00　*D. Appleton & Co.*

Gerhard's Sacred Meditations, translated from the Latin, by Rev. W. M. Blackburn. 18mo. . . . 　*T. N. Kurtz.*

Germaine. By Edmund About. 12mo. . . 1 00　*J. E. Tilton & Co.*

Germany; by Madame the Baroness de Stael-Holstein. With Notes and Appendices, by O. W. Wight, A. M. 2 vols. 12mo. cl. . . . 2 50　*Derby & Jackson.*

Gerstaecker, F. Frank Wildman's Adventures on Land and Water. 16mo. cloth. . . 1 00　*Crosby, N., L. & Co.*

―― " Wild Sports in the Far West. 12mo. . 1 00　　"

Gosner, A. A Practical Treatise on Coal, Petroleum, and other Distilled Oils. 8vo. . . . 1 50　*Ballière Bros.*

Giant Hunting; or, Little Jacket's Adventures. . 0 75　*Mayhew & Baxter.*

Giants (The), and How to Fight them. By the Rev. Richard Newton, D. D. 18mo. . . 0 50　*Carter & Bros.*

Gibbes, R. W., (M. D.) Cuba for Invalids. 12mo. . 0 75　*Townsend & Co.*

Gibbon, Edward. Life of Mahomet. With Notes by Dean Milman, and Dr. Wm. Smith. 18mo. . 0 50　*Sheldon & Co.*

―― J. The Artillerist's Manual; compiled from Various Sources, and adapted to the Service of the United States. Illustrated by Engravings. By John Gibbon, Capt. 4th Artillery, U. S. N. 8vo. 5 00　*D. Van Nostrand.*

Gibbons, J. S. The Banks of New York, their Dealers; the Clearing House, and the Panic of 1857. With a Financial Chart. 12mo. . . . 1 50　*D. Appleton & Co.*

Gibson, W. (Rev.) The Year of Grace: a History of the Revival in Ireland in 1859. With an Introduction by Baron Stow, D. D. 12mo., cloth. . 1 25   *Gould & Lincoln.*

Giffin, J. E. Why Do You Wear it. 16mo. . .   *Murray, Y. & Co.*

Gifts of Genius, a Miscellany of Prose and Poetry, by American authors. Printed for O. A. Davenport. 1 50   *A. D. F. Randolph.*

Gilbert Harland; or, Good in Everything: being the Early History of a City Boy. By Mrs. Barwell. 0 50   *Carlton & Porter.*

Gildas Salvianus. The Reformed Pastor. By the Rev. Richard Baxter. 8vo. . . . . 2 00   *Carter & Bros.*

Gilham, W. (Maj.) A Manual of Instruction for Volunteers and Militia. Small 8vo. cl. . . . 2 50   *C. Desilver.*

Gill, J. (Rev.), The Word and Works of God. 12mo. . 0 25   *H. Dayton.*

Gillian, and other Poems. By George M. Ryder. 12mo.   *Charles Desilver.*

Gilpin, W., The Grain, Pastoral, and Gold Regions of North America. 8vo. . . . . 1 25   *Sower, Barnes & Co*

Giovagnoli, A. F., The Life of St. Margaret of Cortona. 0 50   *P. F. Cunningham.*

Girard, C., Herpetology of the United States Exploring Expedition under Commodore Wilkes. 1 vol. 4to. With a Folio Atlas of over Thirty Elegant Engravings, colored from nature. Executed under the supervision of Dr. Charles Girard, of the Smithsonian Institution. . . . . . 30 00   *Lippincott & Co.*

Girls at School; or, the Boarding-School Life of Julia and Elizabeth. By Mrs. J. P. Wallace. 18mo. 0 80   *Carlton & Porter.*

Glaciers (The) of the Alps. Being a Narrative of Excursions and Ascents, an Account of the Origin and Phenomena of Glaciers, &c. By Professor John Tyndall. 12mo. cl. . . . . . . 1 50   *Ticknor & Fields.*

Glaubrecht, O., Anna, the Leech Vender. A Narrative of Filial Love. 18mo. . . . . .   *Presb. B. of Pub.*

Gleaners (The), and the Field which they choose. 18mo. 25   *A. D. F. Randolph.*

Glenarvon; or, Holidays at the Cottage. 16mo. . 0 75   *M. W. Dodd.*

Glimpses of Europe; or, Notes drawn at Sight. By a Merchant. 12mo. . . . . . .   *Rickey, M. & Co.*

——— of Jesus. By Rev. W. P. Balfern. 18mo. .   *Sheldon, B. & Co.*

Glory (The) of the House of Israel; or, the Hebrew's Pilgrimage to the Holy City. By Fred'k Strauss. 1 25   *Lippincott & Co.*

Godwin, Parke, The History of France. From the Earliest Times to the French Revolution of 1789. Vol. I. Ancient Gaul. 8vo. . . . . 2 00   *Harper & Bros.*

Goethe, J. W., Correspondence with a Child. A new and carefully revised edition. 12mo. . . . 1 25   *Ticknor & Fields.*

——— " Poems and Ballads of. Translated by W. Edmonstoune Aytoun, D. C. L., and Theodore Martin. 0 75   *Delisser & Procter.*

Goffine, L. (Rev.), Devout Instructions on the Epistles
and Gospels, for the Sundays and Holydays.
Translated from the German by the Rev. Theo-
dore Noethen. 12mo. cl.   .   .   .   .   .   . 1 50   *Dunigan & Bro*

Gold (The) Fields of St. Domingo; with a Description of
the Agricultural, Commercial, and other Advan-
tages of Dominica. By W. S. Courtney, Esq.   0 75   *Anson P. Norton.*

—— Foil, Hammered from Popular Proverbs. By Timo-
thy Titcomb. 12mo. cl.   .   .   .   .   .   . 1 00   *Charles Scribner.*

Golden Age. By Luther W. Peck, A. M. 12mo.   . 0 60   *E. Goodenough.*

—— Rule; or, Stories Illustrative of the Ten Commandments. By the author of "A Trap to
Catch a Sunbeam." 18mo.   .   .   .   .   . 0 75   *A. D. F. Randolph.*

Goldsmith, O. B., and Renville, W. J., System of Double
Entry Book-keeping. 8vo.   .   .   .   . 0 75   *Sheldon & Co.*

Good Fight (A), and other Tales. By Chas. Reade. 12mo.   0 75   *Harper & Bros.*

Goodhue, J. A. (Rev.), The Crucible: or, Tests of a Re-
generate State. 12mo.   .   .   .   .   . 1 00   *Gould & Lincoln*

Goodrich, F. B., Man upon the Sea; or, a History of
Maritime Adventure. 8vo. cl.   .   3 00   *Lippincott & Co.*

—— " Women of Beauty and Heroism, from
Semiramis to Eugenie. 4to. Turkey
antique, or Turkey full gilt.   .   . 12 50   *Derby & Jackson.*

—— S. G., Illustrated Natural History of the Animal Kingdom. With 1500 engravings. 2 vols. 12 00   "

Goodwin, E., Lily White: a Romance. 12mo.   .   *J. B. Lippincott.*

—— W. W., Syntax of the Moods and Tenses of the
Greek Verb.   .   .   .   .   .   .   *Sever & Francis.*

Gospel (The) in Burmah. By Mrs. Macleod Wylie.   . 1 00   *Sheldon & Co.*

—— " in Leviticus; or, an Exposition of the He-
brew Ritual. By Joseph A. Seiss, D. D. 12mo.   1 00   *Lindsay & B.*

Gosse, P. H., Evenings at the Microscope; or, Researches
among the minute Organs and Forms of
Animal Life. 12mo. cl.   .   .   . 1 50   *D. Appleton & Co.*

—— " The Romance of Natural History. 12mo.   1 25   *Gould & Lincoln.*

Gotthold's Emblems; or, Invisible Things Understood
by Things that are Made. By Christian Scriver.   1 00   "

Gould, B. A., Reply to the Statements of the Trustees of
Dudley Observatory. 8vo.   .   .   .   . 1 00   *Westermann & Co.*

Grace O'Gara, the Little Mountain Guide. 18mo.   . 0 27   *Carlton & Porter.*

Grafted Trees (The); or, the Two Natures.   .   .   . 0 25   *A. D. F. Randolph.*

Graham, C. (M. D.), Man, from his Cradle to his Grave. 1 25   *C. Blanchard.*

———— J., The Opening Speech of John Graham, Esq.,
to the Jury, on the part of the Defence, on the
Trial of Hon. Daniel E. Sickles, in the Criminal
Court of the District of Columbia, April 9 and
11, 1859. 8vo. pap. . . . . . 0 25   *Townsend & Co.*

———— Thomas, Elements of Inorganic Chemistry, including the Applications of the Science to the
Arts. Edited by Henry Watts, F. C S., and
Robert Bridges, M. D. Second American, from
the second revised and enlarged London
edition. 8vo. . . . . . 4 00   *Blanchard & Lea.*

Grains of Gold suited to enrich Youthful Minds. 18mo. 0 35   *Presb. B. of Pub.*

Grand (A) Exposé of the Science of Gambling. Written
by an Adept. 18mo. . . . . . 0 50   *F. A. Brady.*

Grandmama Wise; or, Visits to Rose Cottage. 18mo. 0 25   *Presb. B. of Pub.*

Grandmother True; or, When I was a Little Girl. 18mo. 0 25   *Henry Hoyt.*

Grandmother's Scrap-Book ; or, Western Gleaner. 12mo. 1 25   *Lippincott & Co.*

Grant, J., Harry Ogilvie; or, the Black Dragoons. 8vo. 0 50   *Dick & Fitzgerald.*

Gray, Asa (M. D.), How Plants Grow : Botany for Young
People. Small 4to. . . . 0 75   *Ivison & Phinney.*

————   "   Introduction to Structural and Systematic Botany, and Vegetable
Physiology. . . . 2 00   "

————   "   Manual of the Botany of the Northern United States. A Revised edition; including
Virginia, Kentucky, and all East of the Mississippi. The Mosses and Liverworts by Wm. S.
Sullivant. 8vo. . . . . 2 50   "

———— Henry, Anatomy. Descriptive and Surgical. . 6 50   *Blanchard & Lea.*

———— M., Elsie Lee ; or, Impatience Cured. 18mo. . 0 20   *Presb. B. of Pub.*

Great Concern (The); or, Man's Relation to God and a
Future State. By Nehemiah Adams, D. D. . 0 85   *Gould & Lincoln.*

———— Exemplar (The); or, The Life of our Ever
Blessed Saviour Jesus Christ. By Jeremy
Taylor, D. D. 2 vols. 12mo. . . . 2 00   *Carter & Bros.*

———— Facts. A popular History and Description of the
Most Remarkable Inventions during the present
century. By Frederick C. Bakewell. 12mo. 1 00   *D. Appleton & Co.*

———— Harmonia (The). By Andrew Jackson Davis.
Vol. V. 12mo. . . . . 1 00   *A. J. Davis.*

———— Preparation (The); or, Redemption Draweth
Nigh. By the Rev. John Cumming, D. D.
First Series. 12mo. . . . . 1 00   *Rudd & Carleton.*

Great Tribulation (The); or, Things Coming on the
    Earth. By the Rev. John Cumming, D. D.
    First and second series. 12mo.   .   Each 1 00 *Rudd & Carleton.*

Greece, A Smaller History of, from the Earliest Times
    to the Roman Conquest. By William Smith,
    LL. D. 12mo. .   .   .   .   . 0 60 *Harper & Bros.*

Greeley, Horace, Overland Journey to California in the
    Summer of 1859. 12mo., cl. .   .   . 1 00 *Saxton & Barker.*

Green's Nursery Annual. With Original Contributions
    from the Pens of Mrs. S. O. Hall, Mrs. Abdy,
    Mary Howitt, and others. 12mo., extra cloth,
    gilt edges. .   .   .   .   .   . 1 00 *D. Appleton & Co.*

—————— B. (Rev.), Sermons and other Discourses, with
    Brief Biographical Hints. 12mo. .   . 1 25 *S. W. Green.*

—————— H. (M. D.), Selections from Favorite Prescriptions
    of Living American Practitioners. 8vo. 2 00 *John Wiley.*

——————   " On the Surgical Treatment of Polypi of
    the Larynx, and Œdema of the Glottis. 8vo. 1 25 *John Wiley.*

Greene, G. W., Biographical Studies. 12mo. .   . 0 75 *G. P. Putnam.*

Greenwood, Grace, Bonnie Scotland. Tales of her His-
    tory, Heroes, and Poets. 18mo. .   . 0 75 *Ticknor & Fields.*

——————   " Stories from Famous Ballads. For
    children. Sq. 18mo. .   .   .   . 0 50   "

Grey, Mary, Elsie Lee; or, Impatience Cured. 16mo. . 0 20 *Presb. Bd. of Pub.*

—————— Mrs., Cousin Harry. 12mo., cl. .   .   . 1 25 *Peterson & Bros.*

Griffin, Gerald, The Life of. By his Brother. 12mo. . 1 00 *D. & J. Sadlier.*

Grimm's German Popular Tales, and Household Stories.
    By the Brothers Grimm. 2 vols. 16mo., cl. . 2 50 *Crosby, N., L. & Co.*

Griscom, John, Memoir of. With an Account of the New
    York High-school Society for the Prevention of
    Pauperism, the House of Refuge, and other In-
    stitutions. Compiled from an Autobiography
    and other sources. By John H. Griscom, M. D. 2 00 *Carter & Brothers.*

Griswold, A. D. (D. D.), Prayers Adapted to Various
    Occasions of Social Worship, for which Provi-
    sion is not made in the Book of Common Prayer.
    New edition. 12mo. .   .   .   .   . 0 75 *E. P. Dutton.*

Groser, W. H., Illustrative Teaching; or, Practical Hints
    to Sunday-school Teachers. 18mo. .   . 0 25 *A. D. F. Randolph.*

Gross, S. D. (M. D.), A System of Surgery; Pathological,
    Diagnostic, Therapeutic, and Operative. 2 vols. 12 00 *Blanchard & Lea.*

Grou, J., Mary, the Morning Star; or, a Model of Interior
    Life. 24mo. .   .   .   .   .   . 0 38 *H. McGrath.*

Gruber, Jacob, The Life of. By W. P. Strickland. 1 00 *Carlton & Porter.*

Grund, F. J., Thoughts and Reflections on the Present
Position of Europe, and its Probable Conse-
quences to the United States. 12mo.   .   .   0 75   *Childs & Peterson.*

Guardian Angel (The). A Poem in three Books. By
James Scott, D.D. 12mo.   .   .   .   0 75   *D. Appleton & Co.*

Guernsey, L. E., The Christmas Earnings; or Ethel
Fletcher's Temptation.   .   .   .   0 80   *F. D. Harriman.*

————   "   Straight Forward; or, Walking in the
Light. 18mo.   .   .   .   .   0 75   *Henry Hoyt.*

————   "   Tabby's Travels; or, the Holiday Adventures of a Kitten. 18mo. cl.   .   0 50   *A. D. F. Randolph.*

Guerrazzi, F. D., Isabella Orsini; an Historical Novel.
Translated from the original Italian by Luigi
Monti. 12mo. cl.   .   .   .   .   1 25   *Rudd & Carleton.*

Guesses at Truth. By Two Brothers. 8vo.   .   .   1 50   *Ticknor & Fields.*

Guide Book to the Central Park; containing a Description of the Park, as far as completed, and
of Work yet to be done. 12mo.   .   .   0 25   *Saxton & Barker.*

———— to the Knowledge of Life, Vegetable and Animal; being a comprehensive Manual of Physio-
logy. By Robt. James Mann, M.D. 12mo.   .   0 88   *C. S. Francis & Co.*

Guild, R. A., The Librarian's Manual. Small 4to.   .   5 00   *Chas. B. Norton.*

Guillotine (The); or, the Death of Morgan. A Sequel to
"Royalists and Republicans." By Alex. Dumas.   0 50   *E. D. Long & Co.*

Guinness, H. G., The Revival in Ireland. Letters from
Ministers and Medical Men in Ulster, on the Re-
vival of Religion in the North of Ireland. 18mo.   0 25   *W. S. & A. Martien.*

Gurney, Samuel, Memorial of. By Mrs. Thomas Gel-
dart. 12mo.   .   .   .   .   .   0 50   *Henry Longstreth.*

Gurowski, A., Slavery in History. 12mo.   .   .   1 00   *A. B. Burdick.*

Guthrie, T. (Rev.), Christ the Inheritance of the Saints.   1 00   *Carter & Bros.*

————   "   "   Seed Time and Harvest of Ragged
Schools. 16mo.   .   .   .   .   0 60   "

Gutzkow, Carl, Der Zauberer von Rom. Roman in
Neuen Buechern. Vols. I., II., III., IV.,
and V. 12mo.   .   .   .   Each   0 75   *Westerman & Co.*

————   "   Uriel Acosta. A Tragedy in Five Acts.   0 50   *M. Ellenger & Co.*

Guy Carleton. 16mo.   .   .   .   .   .   *Howe & Ferry.*

Gwynne, A. E., On the Law of Sheriff and Coroner in
Ohio, Indiana, and Kentucky. 8vo.   .   .   2 00   *Robert Clarke & Co.*

H

Habershon, S. O. (M. D.), Pathological and Practical
Observations on Diseases of the Alimentary
Canal, Œsophagus, Stomach, Cæcum and Intes-
tines. 8vo. . . . . 1 75 *Blanchard & Lea.*

Habits (The) of Good Society. For Ladies and Gentle-
men. 12mo. . . . . 1 25 *Rudd & Carleton.*

Hackett, H. B. (Rev.), A Commentary on the Original
Text of the Acts of the Apostles. 8vo. 2 25 *Gould & Lincoln.*
———— " Illustrations of Scripture, suggested
by a Tour through the Holy Land. New edition,
greatly enlarged and improved. 12mo. .. . 1 00

Hadji in Syria; or, Four Years in Jerusalem. By
Mrs. S. Barclay. 12mo. cl. . . . 0 75 *J. Challen & Sons.*

Hadley, J., A Greek Grammar for Schools and Colleges. 12mo. . . . . . . , 1 25 *D. Appleton & Co.*

Haldane, R. & J. A., Memoir of Robert Haldane, and
James Alexander Haldane. 12mo. cloth. . . 0 45 *Am. Tract Soc.*

Haldeman, J. J., Trevelyan Prize Essay. Analytic Orthography; an Investigation of the Sounds of
the Voice, and their Alphabetic Notation,
including the Mechanism of Speech, and its
bearing upon Etymology. 4to. . . . 1 75 *Lippincott & Co.*

Hale, E. E., Ninety Days' Worth of Europe. 16mo. . 0 75 *Walker, Wise & Co.*

———— G. S., and Smith, H. F., United States Digest; containing a Digest of the Decisions of the Courts
of Common Law, Equity, and Admiralty of the
United States and in England. Vol. XIII. An-
nual Digest for 1859. 8vo. . . . . 5 00 *Little, Brown & Co.*

Haliburton (Judge), The Sayings and Doings of Samuel
Slick, Esq., together with his Opinion on Matrimony 12mo. . . . . 0 75 *Dick & Fitzgerald.*

Hall, B. H., History of Eastern Vermont, from its earliest Settlement to the Close of the 18th Century. With a Biographical Chapter and Ap-
pendixes. 8vo. . . . . . . 3 50 *D. Appleton & Co.*

———— John (Rev.), History of the Presbyterian Church in
Trenton, New Jersey, from the first Settlement
of the Town. 12mo. . . . . . 1 50 *A. D. F. Randolph.*

5

Hall, James, Contributions to the Palæontology of New
    York, being some of the Results of Investiga-
    tions made during the Years 1855, '56, '57 and
    '58. With Woodcuts. Paper. . . . . 0 25   *Westermann & Co.*
—— ' and Whitney, J. D., Report of the Geological Sur-
    vey of the State of Iowa, embracing the Results
    of Investigations made during portions of the
    Years 1855, '56, and '57. Vol. I., Part 1;
    Geology. Part 2; Palæontology. . . . 8 00   "
—— N., Now. By Newman Hall, Author of "Come
    to Jesus." 18mo., cloth. . . . . 0 25   *Carter & Brothers.*
—— " Quenob not the Spirit. 18mo. . . . 0 25   "
—— W. W. (M. D.), Health and Disease. A Book for
    the People. 12mo. . . . . . . 1 00   *H. B. Price.*
Hallam, H., View of the State of Europe during the
    Middle Ages. 3 Vols. 12mo. . . . 3 75   *Crosby, N., L.&Co.*
Halleck, F. G., The Poetical Works of. New Edition.
    18mo. . . . . 0 75   *D. Appleton & Co.*
Hallick, H. W., Elements of Military Art and Science.
    Second Edition. With Critical Notes on the
    Mexican and Crimean Wars. 12mo. . . . 1 50   "
Halliday, S. B., The Lost and Found: or, Life among the
    Poor. 12mo. . . . . . . 1 00   *Phinney, B. & M.*
Halsey, L. J. (Rev.), The Literary Attractions of the
    Bible; or, a Plea for the Word of God, consid-
    ered as a Classic. 12mo. . . . . 1 25   *C. Scribner.*
Hamilton, A. (Rev.), May I Believe? or, The Warrant of
    Faith. 18mo. . . . . . .   *Presb. B. of Pub.*
—— F. H., A Practical Treatise on Fractures and
    Dislocations. 8vo. . . . . . 4 50   *Blanchard & Lea.*
—— J. (Rev.), Earnest Thoughts. 18mo. . . 0 20   *Am. Tract So.*
—— " Our Christian Classics; Reading from the best
    Divines. With Notices, Biographical and
    Critical. 4 vols. 12mo. cl. . . . 4 00   *Carter & Bros.*
—— J. C., History of the Republic of the United
    States of America, as traced in the
    Writings of Alexander Hamilton, and of
    his Contemporaries. Vols. IV. and V.
    8vo. . . . . . . each 2 50   *D. Appleton &Co.*
—— William (Sir), Lectures on Metaphysics and Logic.
    Edited by the Rev. Henry L. Mansell, B. D., and
    John Veitch. 2 vols. 8vo. cl. . . . 6 00   *Gould & Lincoln.*
Hammond, Memoir of Captain M. M. Hammond, Rifle
    Brigade. 12mo. . . . . . . 1 00   *Carter & Bros.*

Hampden, A., Hartley Norman. A Tale of the Times. 1 00 *Rudd & Corleton.*
Hand (The) but not the Heart. By T. S. Arthur. 12mo. 1 00 *Derby & Jackson.*
Handbook of Artillery, for the Service of the United
   States (Army and Militia). By Captain Joseph
   Roberts, U. S. Army. 18mo. cl. .   .   . 0 75 *D. Van Nostrand.*
—— of Family Knowledge for the People. Comprising
   the Standard Handbook of Household Economy:
   Sayer's Standard Cooking, and the New Standard Letter Writer. 12mo. .   .   .   *Charles Desilver.*
—— of Horticulture, Agriculture, and Landscape Gar-
   dening. By R. Morris Copeland. 8vo. .   . 2 50 *J. P. Jewett & Co.*
—— of Literature. By Anne C. Botta. .   .   1 50 *Derby & Jackson.*
—— of Practical Receipts; or, Useful Hints in Every-
   Day Life. By an American Gentleman and
   Lady. 16mo. .   .   .   .   .   . 0 40 *Barnes & Burr.*
—— to the Gold Fields of Nebraska and Kansas. By
   William N. Byers and John H. Kellom. 16mo. 0 50 *D. B. Cooke & Co.*
Handful of Pearls. 18mo. .   .   .   .   . 0 25 *Jas. Challen&Sons.*
Hanger, C. H., Proverbial and Moral Thoughts. In a
   Series of Essays. 16mo. .   .   .   .·0 68 *Mayhew & Baker.*
Hanna, Sarah B., Bible History. 12mo. .   . 1 00 *Barnes & Burr.*
Hannah Lee; or, Rest for the Weary. 18mo. cl. . 0 45 *Henry Hoyt.*
Hannibal, Life of. By Thomas Arnold. 18mo. cl. . 0 50 *Sheldon & Co.*
Hans and his Northern Home. 12mo. .   . 0 70 *Am. S. S. Union.*
Happy Home (The). By Kirwan (Rev. N. Murray),
   author of "Letters to Bishop Hughes." 16mo. 0 50 *Harper & Bros.*
Happy Island (The); or, Paradise Restored. By Rev.
   W. F. Evans. 16mo. cl. .   .   .   . *H. V. Degen & Son*
Harbaugh, H. (Rev.), Poems. 12mo. .   .   . *Lindsay & Blak'n.*
——   "The True Glory of Woman, as portrayed
   in the Beautiful Life of the Virgin Mary. 12mo. 0 75   "
Hard Maple. By the author of "Dollars and Cents." 0 63 *Shep. Clark & Br'n.*
Harkness, A., First Greek Book. 12mo. .   . 0 75 *D. Appleton & Co.*
Harland, Marion., Nemesis; a Novel. 12mo. cl. . 1 25 *Derby & Jackson.*
Harp (The) of a Thousand Strings; or, Laughter for a Life-
   time. 12mo. .   .   .   .   . 1 25 *Dick & Fitzgerald.*
Harper, R. D. (Rev.), The Church Manual, containing
   important Historial Facts and Reminiscences
   connected with the Associate and Associated
   Reformed Churches. .   .   .   . *Fleming & H.*
Harrington: a Story of True Love. By the author of
   "What Cheer." 12mo. cl. .   .   . 1 25 *Thayer & Eldridge*
Harris, C. A., The Principles and Practice of Dental Sur-
   gery. Seventh edition. 8vo. .   .   . 4 00 *Lindsay & B.*

Harris, John (D. D.), Sermons and Addresses delivered on special occasions. Second series. 12mo.   *Gould & Lincoln.*

—— J. L. (Rev.), A New Age for the New Church. 8vo.   0 25   *New Ch. Pub. Asso.*

Harrison, D., A Voice from the Washingtonian Home.   *Redding & Co.*

—— W. C., Bees and Bee-keeping ; a plain, practical Work. 12mo. cl.   .   .   .   .   1 00   *Saxton & Barker.*

Harry Lee ; or, Hope for the Poor. 12mo. cl.   .   .   0 75   *Harper & Bros.*

—— Ogilvie ; or, the Black Dragoons. By Captain James Grant. 8vo. pap.   .   .   .   0 50   *Dick & Fitzgerald.*

Harry's Summer in Ashcroft. Square 8vo.   .   .   0 50   *Harper & Bros.*

Hart, A. M., Life in the Far West ; or, the Adventures of a Hoosier. 8vo. pap.   .   .   .   .   0 25   *W. Skelley.*

Hartley, Cecil B., Life of the Empress Josephine. 12mo.   1 00   *G. G. Evans.*

—— " Life and Adventures of Lewis Wetzel, the Virginia Ranger. 12mo.   .   .   1 00   "

—— Florence, The Ladies' Hand Book of Fancy and Ornamental Work. Small 4to. cl.   .   .   1 00   "

Hartley Norman. A Tale of the Times. By Allen Hampden. 12mo.   .   .   .   .   .   1 00   *Rudd & Carleton.*

Hartmann, T., Charity Green ; or, Varieties of Love. 12mo..   1 25   *J. W. Norton.*

Hartshorne, H. (M. D.), Memoranda Medica ; or, Note-book of Medical Principles. 12mo.   .   1 00   *Lippincott & Co.*

Harvest (The) of Love. A Story for the Home Circle. By Minnie S. Davis. 16mo.   .   .   0 75   *A. Tomkins.*

—— " and the Reapers ; Home Work for All, and How to Do it. By Rev. Harvey Newcomb.   0 63   *Gould & Lincoln.*

Hase, C., Life of Jesus. 12mo.   .   .   .   .   0 75   *Walker, W., & Co.*

Haskell, E. F. (Mrs.), The Housekeeper's Encyclopædia of Cookery. 12mo.   .   .   .   1 25   *D. Appleton & Co.*

Haskins, D. G. (Rev.), Selections from the Scriptures of the Old and New Testaments. 12mo.   .   1 25   *E. P. Dutton & Co.*

Hassan Abdallah ; or, the Enchanted Keys, and other Tales. 12mo.   .   .   .   0 75   *Kelly, H., & P.*

Haste to the Rescue ; or, Work while it is Day. By Mrs. Charles W. 16mo.   .   .   .   0 75   *Carter & Brothers.*

       The same. 16mo cl.   .   .   .   0 30   *Am. Tract Soc.*

Hastings, T., Church Music ; or, Musical Compositions for Devotional Use. Music 8vo.   .   .   0 75   *Mason Brothers.*

—— " The Mother's Hymn. Third edition. Revised and enlarged. 32mo.   .   .   0 30   *A. D. F. Randolph.*

—— " and T. S., Church Melodies ; a Collection of Psalms and Hymns, with appropriate Music for the use of Congregations. 12mo.   .   .   0 75   "

Haswell, C. H., Mensuration and Practical Geometry.   0 75   *Harper & Bros.*

Hatch, Cora L. V. (Mrs.), Discourses. First Series. 12mo. 1 00 *S. T. Munson.*

Hatty and Marcus; or, First Steps in the Better Path.
By Aunt Friendly. 18mo. . . . 0 25 *A. D. F. Randolph.*

Haunted Homestead (The); and other Novellettes. By
Mrs. Emma D. E. N. Southworth. 12mo. . 1 25 *Peterson & Bros.*

Havelock, Henry (Genl.), A Biographical Sketch of. By
the Rev. William Brock. 16mo. . . 0 75 *Carter & Brothers.*

——— " The Life of. By J. T. Headley. 12mo. cl. 1 25 *C. Scribner.*

Haven, Alice B., The Coopers; or, Getting Under Way. 0 75 *D. Appleton & Co.*

——— " Loss and Gain; or, Margaret's Home. 0 75 "

——— " Where there is a Will there is a Way. 0 75 "

——— J. (D. D.), Moral Philosophy, including Theoretical and Practical Ethics. 12mo. . . 1 25 *Gould & Lincoln.*

Hawarden, E. (Rev.), Charity and Truth; or, Catholics
not Uncharitable in Saying that none are Saved
out of the Catholic Church. 12mo. . 0 63 *P. F. Cunningham.*

Hawkins, John H. W., Life of. Compiled by his Son,
Rev. William George Hawkins, A. M. 12mo. . 1 00 *J. P. Jewett & Co.*

Hawks, F. L. (Rev.), History of North Carolina. With
Maps and Illustrations. Vol. II. Embracing
the period of the Proprietary Government, from
1663 to 1729. 8vo. . . . . . *E. J. Hale & Son.*

Hawksview; a Family History of our Own Times. By
Holme Lee. . . . . . . 1 00 *Townsend & Co.*

Hawthorne, Nathaniel, The Marble Faun; or, the Romance of Monte Beni. 2 vols. 16mo. . . 1 50 *Ticknor & Fields.*

Hayes, E., The Ballads of Ireland. 8vo. . . 1 00 *P. Donahoe.*

——— I. I., An Arctic Boat Journey in the Autumn of
1854. 12mo. . . . . . . 1 25 *Brown & Taggard.*

Hayne, P. H., Avolio: a Legend of the Island of Cos.
With Poems, Lyrical, Miscellaneous, and Dra-
matic. 16mo. . . . . . . 0 75 *Ticknor & Fields.*

Hazel, H., The Rebel and the Rover. 8vo. pap. . 0 25 *Peterson & Bros.*

Hazlett, Helen, The Cloud with a Golden Border. 12mo. 1 00 *T. Elwood Zell.*

——— " The Heights of Eidelberg. 18mo. . 0 75 *W. S. & A. Martien.*

Head, J. H., Home Pastimes. 12mo. . . . 1 00 *J. E. Tilton & Co.*

Health and Disease. A Book for the People. By Dr.
W. W. Hall. 12mo. . . . . . 1 00 *H. B. Price.*

Heart Whispers. By William Atson. 12mo. . . *Cowperthwait & Co.*

Heaven's Antidote to the Curse of Labor. A Prize
Essay. By John Allen Quinton. 18mo. . 0 80 *J. Challen & Son.*

Heavenly (The) Pathway; or, Going Home. By Rev.
R. A. Carden. . . . . . . 1 00 *Lippincott & Co.*

Heber (Bishop), The Life of. By Rev. J. N. Norton. . 0 30 *F. D. Harriman.*

Hecker, I. T., Aspirations of Nature. Third edition. 0 75 *Dunigan & Bro.*

Hedge, F. H., Recent Inquiries in Theology. By Eminent English Churchmen. 12mo. . . . 1 25 *Walker, Wise & Co.*

Heights (The) of Eidelberg. By Helen Hazlett. 18mo. 0 75 *W.S.& A. Martien.*

Helen McGregor. By Rev. Joseph H. Saunders. 2 vols. 0 50 *J. Challen & Sons.*

Helper, H. R., Compendium of the Impending Crisis of the South. 12mo. cl. . . . . . 1 00 *A. B. Burdick.*

Helps for the Pulpit; or, Sketches and Skeletons of Sermons. By a Minister. 12mo. . . . 1 25 *Smith, Eng. & Co.*

Hemlock Ridge; or, Only Dan White's Son. 16mo. . 0 40 *Henry Hoyt.*

Hempel, C. J. (M. D.), A New and Comprehensive System of Materia Medica and Therapeutics. . . 5 00 *William Radde.*

Homstead, T., Poems by Rev. T. Homstead. 12mo. cl. 0 75 *M. W. Dodd.*

Henderson, E. (D. D.), The Book of the Twelve Minor Prophets. 8vo. . . . . . . 8 00 *W. F. Draper.*

Hengstenberg, E. W. (D. D.), Commentary on Ecclesiastes, with other Treatises. Translated from the German, by D. W. Simon. 8vo. . . . 2 00 *Smith, Eng. & Co.*

Henry, C. S. (D. D.), Considerations on some of the Elements and Conditions of Social Welfare and Human Progress. 12mo. . . . . 1 00 *D. Appleton & Co.*

—— J., Sketches of Moravian Life and Character. . 1 25 *Lippincott & Co.*

Henry St. John, Gentleman. A Tale of 1774-'75. By John Esten Cooke. 12mo. . . . . 1 00 *Harper & Brothers.*

Henry's Fireside, with Peeps at his Grandpa's Farm. . 0 20 *Carlton & Porter.*

Heqnembourg, C. S. (Rev.), Plan of the Creation; or, Other Worlds, and Who Inhabit them. 12mo. 1 25 *Phillips, S. & Co.*

Herbert, H. W., Pierre, the Partisan; a Tale of the Mexican Marches. pap. . . . . 0 25 *F. A. Brady.*

—— George, The Life of. By G. L. Duyckinck. . 0 35 *F. D. Harriman.*

Here and Beyond; or, The New Man—The True Man. By Hugh Smith Carpenter. 12mo. . . 1 00 *Mason Brothers.*

—— " There; or, Earth and Heaven Contrasted. . 0 25 *D. Appleton & Co.*

Hermit (The) of the Pyrenees, and other miscellaneous Poems. By Wm. D. S. Alexander. 18mo. . *Washington, D.C.*

Herod the Great, as connected Historically and Prophetically with the Coming of Christ. By William M. Willett. 12mo. . . . . . . 1 00 *Lisnday & Blak'n.*

Herodotus, The History of Herodotus. A new English version, edited with copious Notes and Appendices, By Geo. Rawlinson, M. A. Assisted by Col. Sir Henry Rawlinson and Sir J. G. Wilkinson. 4 vols., 8vo. . . . . . . 10 00 *D. Appleton & Co.*

Heroes (The) of Europe: a Biographical Outline of Euro-
    pean History. From A. D. 700 to A. D. 1700.
    By Henry G. Hewlett. 12mo. . . . 1 00 *Ticknor & Fields.*
———— of the Indian Rebellion. By D. W. Bartlett.   *Follett, F. & Co.*
———— (The) of the Last Lustre. A Poem. 12mo. cl. . 0 63 *D. Dana, Jr.*
Herpetology of the United States Exploring Expedition
    under Commodore Wilkes. 1 vol. 4to. With a
    Folio Atlas of over Thirty Elegant Engravings,
    colored from nature. Executed under the super-
    vision of Dr. Charles Girard, of the Smithsonian
    Institution. . . . . . . 30 00 *Lippincott & Co.*
Herzen, A., Memoirs of the Empress Catherine II. Writ-
    ten by Herself. 12mo. . . . . 1 00 *D. Appleton & Co.*
Hesper, the Home Spirit. By Elizabeth Doten. 18mo. 0 75 *A. Tompkins.*
Hester, A Poem. By Sylvester B. Beckets. 12mo. . 0 75 *Bailey & Noyes.*
———— and I; or, Beware of Worldliness. By Mrs. Man-
    ners. 16mo. . . . . . . 0 60 *Sheldon & Co.*
Hewlett, H. G., The Heroes of Europe: a Biographical
    Outline of European History. From A. D. 700
    to A. D. 1700. 12mo. . . . . 1 00 *Ticknor & Fields.*
Hewson, W., Principles and Practice of Embanking Lands
    from River Floods, as applied to "Levees on
    the Mississippi." 8vo. . . . . 2 00 *D. Van Nostrand.*
Hexamer, A. C., Die Hinde-Cholera, oder Summer Com-
    plaint in den Veresiriglen Staaten, ihre Natur,
    Verhulnage und reihtgestige Erkemunig. 16mo. 0 38 *Westermann & Co.*
Hickcox, J. H., An Historical Account of American
    Coinage. 8vo. . . . . . 2 50 *Joel Munsell.*
Hickok, L. P. (D. D.), Rational Cosmology; or, the Eternal
    Principles and the Necessary Laws of the Uni-
    verse. 8vo. . . . . . . 1 75 *D. Appleton & Co.*
Hidden (The) Gem. A Drama in Two Acts. By H. E. 0 75 *Kelly, Hedian & P.*
———— " Treasure; or, the Value and Excellence of
        the Holy Mass. 32mo. . . . 0 25 *J. P. Walsh.*
———— " " or the Secret of Success in Life. By
    Miss Sarah A. Babcock. 16mo. . . . 0 60 *Carlton & Porter.*
Hide and Seek. A Novel. By Wilkie Collins. 8vo. . 0 50 *Dick & Fitzgerald.*
Hierophant (The); or, Gleanings from the Past. By G.
    C. Stewart. 12mo. . . . . . 1 00 *Ross & Tousey.*
Higgins, S., Illustrations of the Divine Government in
    Remarkable Providences. Collected and ar-
    ranged by S. Higgins and W. H. Brisbane. . .   *Higgins & Perk't.*
High Life in New York. By Jonathan Slick, Esq. 12mo. 1 25 *Peterson & Bros.*
Higher (The) Christian Education. By Benjamin W.
    Dwight. 12mo. . . . . . 1 00 *Barnes & Burr.*

Higher (The) Christian Life. By Rev. W. E. Boardman.   1 00   *Henry Hoyt.*
Highways (The) of Travel; or, a Summer in Europe. By
    Margaret J. M. Sweat. 12mo.   .   .   .   1 00   *Walker, Wise & Co.*
Hill, D. H., A Consideration of the Sermon on the Mount.   0 75   *W.S.& A. Martien.*
———— " The Crucifixion of Christ. 12mo.   .   1 00   "
———— T., Jesus, the Interpreter of Nature; and Other
    Sermons. 12mo.   .   .   .   .   .   0 75   *Walker, Wise & Co.*
———— W. W. (D. D.), Twyman Hogue; or, Early Piety
    Illustrated. A Biographical Sketch. 18mo.   .   0 80   *Presb. Bd. of Pub.*
Hilliard, F., The Law of Torts or Private Wrongs. 2 vols.   10 00   *Little, Brown & Co.*
———— " The Law of Vendors and Purchasers of Real
    Property. 8vo. pap.   .   .   .   .   6 00   "
Hilles, M. W., The Pocket Anatomist. 18mo. cl.   .   .   0 63   *Lindsay & Blak'n.*
Hillside, A. M., Familiar Compend of Geology. 12mo.   .   0 75   *J. Challen & Son.*
Hilton, H., Reports of Cases argued and determined in
    the Court of Common Pleas for the City and
    County of New York. Vol. 1. 8vo.   .   .   5 00   *Banks & Bros.*
Hines, E. L., Hyder, Dost Rajah of Soonderbaoh. 16mo.   0 50   *So. Bap. Pub. So.*
———— R. K., Legal Forms for Common Use in Geor-
    gia. 12mo. law sheep.   .   .   .   .   *J. M. Cooper & Co.*
Hints to Common School Teachers, Parents, and Pupils;
    or, Gleanings from School Life Experience. By
    Hiram Orcutt. 18mo.   .   .   .   .   .   0 50   *Brown & Taggard.*
———— " Horse Keepers. By the late Henry William
    Herbert (Frank Forester). With Additions,
    including "Rarey's Method of Horse-Taming"
    and "Baucher's System of Horsemanship."   .   1 25   *Saxton & Barker.*
Hiscox, E. T. (D. D.), The Baptist Church Directory.   .   0 60   *Sheldon & Co.*
Historical Pictures Retouched; a Volume of Miscel-
    lanies. By Mrs. Dall. 12mo.   .   .   .   1 25   *Walker, Wise & Co.*
———— Tales for Young Protestants. 16mo.   .   .   0 75   *Am. S. S. Union.*
———— Vindications; or, the Province and Uses of Bap-
    tist History. By S. S. Cutting, D. D. 12mo.   .   0 75   *Gould & Lincoln.*
———— (The) and Genealogical Researches and Recorder
    of Passing Events of Merrimack Valley. 4to.   2 00   *A. Poor.*
History of the Early Church, from the First Preaching
    of the Gospel to the Council of Nice. By the
    author of "Amy Herbert." 16mo.   .   .   0 60   *D. Appleton & Co.*
———— " the Great Italian War of 1859.   .   .   .   0 25   *E. M. De Witt.*
———— " the Patriarchs, for the Young — English and
    German. 18mo.   .   .   .   .   .   .   0 35   *Am. Tract Soc.*
———— " the Pontificate and Captivity of Pius the
    Sixth. Together with a glance at the Catholic
    Church. Translated from the French. 18mo.   0 75   *P. O'Shea.*

History of the Reformation in Germany, Switzerland,
England, Ireland, Scotland, the Netherlands,
France, and Northern Europe. By M. T. Spal-
ding. 2 vols. 8vo. . . . . . . 2 50 *Webb & Levering.*
—— and Progress of Education, from the Earliest
Times to the Present. With an Introduction
by Hon. Henry Barnard. 12mo. . . . 1 00 *Barnes & Burr.*
Hitchcock, E. (D. D.), Elementary Anatomy and Physi-
ology. 12mo. . . . . . . 1 00 *Ivison, Phin & Co.*
—— Ichnology of New England. 4to. . . . 5 00 *Phillips, S. & Co.*
Hitchman, W. (M. D.), Consumption, its Nature, Prevention
and Homœopathic Treatment. 12mo. . . 75 *William Radde.*
Hits at American Whims, and Hints for Home Use. By
Frederick W. Sawyer. 12mo. . . . 1 00 *D. Appleton & Co.*
Hobart, J. H. (D. D.), Instruction and Encouragement for
Lent. 16mo. . . . . 50 *D. Dana, Jr.*
Hodge, A. A. (Rev.), Outlines of Theology. 8vo. . . 2 00 *Carter & Brothers.*
—— C. (D. D.), An Exposition of the Second Epistle to
the Corinthians. 12mo. . . . . 1 00 "   "
—— H. L. (M. D.), On Diseases Peculiar to Women, in-
cluding Displacements of the Uterus. 8vo. . 3 25 *Blanchard & Lea.*
Hodges, R. M. (M. D.), Practical Dissections. 16mo. . 2 75 *John Bartlett.*
Hofman, E. A. (Rev.), The Weekly Eucharist; the "Old
Path" and "Good Way" of the Church. 32mo. . 20 *D. Dana, Jr.*
Hoffman, V. H., a Life of Mrs. Virginia Hale Hoffman,
By the Rev. Geo. D. Cummins, M. D. 16mo. . 75 *Lindsay & Blak'n.*
Hoge, W. J. (Rev.), Blind Bartimeus; or, the Story of a
Sightless Sinner, and his Great Physician. . 75 *Sheldon & Co.*
Holbrook, Alfred, The Normal; or, Methods of Teaching
the Common Branches, Orthoepy, Orthography,
Grammar, Geography, Arithmetic, and Elocu-
tion. 12mo. . . . . 1 00 *Barnes & Burr.*
Holcombe, Jas. R., Introduction to Equity Jurisprudence. 3 00 *R. Clarke & Co.*
—— W. H. (M. D.), Poems. 8vo. . . . . 1 50 *Mason Brothers.*
Holidays, and the Reasons why they are Observed. 18mo. 20 *Presb. Bd. of Pub.*
Holland, John, Poems. 12mo. . . . . . 50 *A. Williams & Co.*
Holmby House; a Tale of Old Northamptonshire. No. 2. 50 *Ticknor & Fields.*
Holmes, Arthur, Parties and their Principles; a Manual
of Political Intelligence. . . . . . 1 00 *D. Appleton & Co.*
Holland, J. G., Bitter-Sweet. A Poem. 12mo. . . 75 *Charles Scribner.*
—— " Miss Gilbert's Career; an American
Story. 12mo. . . . . . . 1 25 "   "
Holly and Mistletoe. Tales translated from the Ger-
man. 16mo cloth. . . . . . 75 *Crosby, N., L. & Co.*

Holmes, Mary J. (Mrs.), Dora Deane ; or, The East India
          Uncle; and Maggie Miller. .   .   1 00   *C. M. Saxton.*
———   " Cousin Maud and Rosamond. . . 1 00   *Saxton, Barker & Co.*
——— Oliver W., The Professor at the Breakfast Table ;
      with the story of Iris. 12mo.   .   . 1 00   *Ticknor & Fields.*
Homans, J. S., A Cyclopedia of Commerce and Commer-
      cial Navigation. 8vo.   .   . 10 00   *Harper & Bros.*
———   " The Merchants' and Bankers' Register for
      1860. 8vo.   .   .   .   1 25   *J. Smith Homans.*
Home Ballads and Poems. By John G. Whittier. . 75   *Ticknor & Fields.*
—— Circle (The) : a collection of Piano-Forte Music. .   *Ditson & Co.*
—— Hits and Hints. By William T. Coggeshall. 12mo. 1 00   *J. S. Redfield.*
—— Jewels ; or Maggie Ella Cotton and her Brothers. 20   *Presb. Bd. of Pub.*
—— (The) Melodist : a Collection of Songs and Ballads
      for the Voice only. 16mo.   .   .   *Ditson & Co.*
—— Memories ; or, Echoes of a Mother's Voice. By
      Mrs. Carey Brock. 12mo. cl.   .   75   *D. Appleton & Co.*
—— Pastimes. By J. H. Head. 12mo. .   . 1 00   *J. E. Tilton & Co.*
—— Songs, Songs for Little Darlings. 18mo. . 0 38   *Mayhew & Baker.*
—— Story Book. 4to. .   .   .   . 1 00   *Lindsay & Blak'n*
—— and College. By F. D. Huntington, D. D. 18mo. 0 50   *Crosby, N., L. & Co.*
Homilist (The) ; a Series of Sermons for Preachers and
      Laymen. Original and Selected. By Erwin
      House, A. M. 12mo. .   .   . 1 00   *Carlton & Porter.*
Honey Blossoms for Little Bees. Square. . . 0 50   *M. W. Dodd.*
Hood, Thomas, Memorials of. Collected, Arranged, and
      Edited by his Daughter. With a Preface
      Notes by his Son. 2 vols. 12mo. . . 1 75   *Ticknor & Fields.*
———   " Tylney Hall. 12mo. . . 1 25   *J. E. Tilton & Co.*
———   " Whims and Waifs. 12mo. . 1 25   *Derby & Jackson.*
Hooker, W. (M. D.), Natural History for the Use of
      Schools and Families. 12mo. .   . 1 00   *Harper & Bros.*
Hope, James B., A Collection of Poems. 16mo. .   *A. Morris.*
Hopes and Fears. By the author of the "Heir of Red-
      clyffe." 2 vols. 12mo. .   .   1 50   *D. Appleton & Co.*
Hopkins, S., Lessons at the Cross ; or, Spiritual Truths,
      with an introduction by Rev. George W. Blag-
      den, D. D. 12mo. .   .   . 0 75   *J. E. Tilton & Co.*
Hopkins, S., The Puritans ; or, The Court, Church, and
      Parliament of England, during the Reigns of Ed-
      ward VI. and Elizabeth. 3 vols. 8vo. Vol. I.
      and II. .   .   .   . Each 2 50   *Gould & Lincoln.*
Horace, The Odes of. Tanslated into English Verse, with
      a Life and Notes. By Theodore Martin. Blue
      and Gold. 32mo. .   .   .   0 75   *Ticknor & Fields.*

Horace, Quinti Horatii Flacci Opera Omnia ex-recensione
    A. J. Macleane. 18mo. . . . . . 0 40   *Harper & Bros.*
Hornby, E. (Mrs.), In and Around Stamboul. 12mo. cl. 1 25 *Lindsay & Blak'n.*
Horne, T. H. (D. D.), Introductions to the Books of the
    New Testament. Revised, Corrrected, and
    brought down to the Present Time, by Samuel
    Prideaux Tregelles, LL. D. 18mo. . . . 1 00 *T. H. Stockton.*
Hortense; or, Pride Corrected. 18mo. . . . . 0 25 *Kelly, Hedian & P.*
Hosmer, H. L., Adelia, the Octoroon. 12mo. . . 1 00 *Follett, Foster & Co.*
Houdin, Robert, Memoirs of, Ambassador, Author, and
    Conjuror. Written by Himself. Edited by Dr.
    R. Shelton Mackenzie. 12mo. . . . 1 00 *G. G. Evans.*
Hough, F. B., A History of Lewis County, in the State
    of New York. 8vo. . . . .   *Munsell & Row'd.*
——   "   The Comprehensive Farm Record; with
    Directions for its Use. 8vo. . . . 3 00 *Saxton & Barker.*
——   "   Diary of the Siege of Detroit in the War
    with Pontiac. Also, a Narrative of the Princi-
    pal Events of the Siege, by Major Robert Rog-
    ers. Edited with notes by Franklin B. Hough. 5 00 *J. Munsell.*
Hour, An, and a Half in a Country Sunday School. 18mo. 0 30 *Carlton & Porter.*
Hours with my Pupils; or, Educational Addresses, &c.
    By Mrs. Lincoln Phelps. 12mo. . . . 1 00 *Charles Scribner.*
—— with the Evangelists. By J. Nichols, D. D. 2
    vols. 8vo. Vol. I. . . . .   *Crosby, N., L. & Co.*
House, E., The Homilist; a Series of Sermons for Preach-
    ers and Laymen. Original and Selected. 12mo. 1 00 *Carlton & Porter.*
—— " The Missionary in Many Lands. 12mo. . 0 80   "
Household Book of Poetry. Collected and edited by
    Charles A. Dana. 8vo. . . . . 3 50 *D. Appleton & Co.*
—— (The) of Bouverie; or, the Elixir of Gold. A
    Romance. By a Southern Lady. 2 vols. 12mo. cl. 2 00 *Derby & Jackson.*
Housekeeper and Gardener. By Rebecca A. Upton. 12mo. 0 75 *Crosby, N., L. & Co.*
Housekeeper's (The) Encyclopædia of Cookery, and all
    other Branches of Domestic Economy. By Mrs.
    L. F. Haskell. 12mo. . . . . 1 25 *D. Appleton & Co.*
Houston, Samuel, The Life of. 12mo. . . . 1 00 *G. G. Evans.*
——   "   Speech of, Exposing the Malfeasance and
    Corruption of John Charles Watrous, Judge of
    the Federal Court in Texas, and of his Con-
    federates. 12mo. . . . . . 0 50 *Pudney & Russell.*
Hovey, A. (D. D.), The State of the Impenitent Dead. . 0 75 *Gould & Lincoln.*
How Could he Help it? or, the Heart Triumphant. By
    A. S. Roe. 12mo. . . . . . 1 25 *Derby & Jackson.*

How to Cook, and How to Carve. 16mo. . . . 0 25 *F. A. Brady.*
—— " Enjoy Life: or, Physical and Mental Hygiene.
By William M. Cornell, M. D. 12mo. . . 1 00 *J. Challen & Son.*
—— " Live; Illustrated in the Lives of Frederick Per-
thes, Gerhard Tersteegen, and James Montgom-
ery. 12mo. . . . . 0 50 *Am. S. S. Union.*
Howard, Nathan, Practice Reports in the Supreme Court
and Court of Appeals of the State of
New York. Vol. XV. 8vo. . . 3 50 *Banks & Brothers.*
—— " The Code of Procedure of Pleadings and
Practice of the State of New York, 1860. Sec-
ond edition, enlarged and improved, with Com-
plete Notes and References. 8vo. . . 6 00   "
Howard and his Teacher, the Sister's Influence, and Other
Stories. By Mrs. Madeline Leslie. 16mo. . 0 75 *Shepard, Clark&B.*
Howe, E., Ball-Room Hand-Book. Sq. 12mo. . . 0 38 *A. Williams & Co.*
—— H., Adventures and Achievements of Americans.
A Series of Narratives illustrating their Hero-
ism, Self-Reliance, Genius, and Enterprise. 8vo. 3 25 *George F. Tuttle.*
—— E. P., The Young Citizen's Catechism. 18mo. . 0 50 *Barnes & Burr.*
—— J., The Speeches and Public Letters of. Edited
by William Armand. 2 vols. 8vo. . .   *J. P. Jewett & Co.*
—— Julia W. (Mrs.), A Trip to Cuba. 16mo. . . 0 75 *Ticknor & Fields.*
Howeis, T. (Rev.), The Communicant's Spiritual Com-
panion. . . . . 0 38 *Prot.Epis.Book So.*
Howitt, Mary, A Popular History of the United States.
2 vols. 12mo. . . . . . . 2 00 *Harper & Bros.*
—— Mary and John, Jack and Harry; or, Pictures for
the Young. Small 4to. . . . . 1 00 *J. E. Tilton & Co.*
Hows, J. W. S., The Ladies' Reader. 12mo. . . 1 13 *E. H. Butler &Co.*
Hoyt, J. (Rev.), The Mountain Society; a History of the
First Presbyterian Church, Orange, N. J. 12mo. 1 00 *Saxton & Barker.*
Hubbard, S., The New Temperance Melodist. 12mo. .   *J. P. Jewett & Co.*
Huc, M., Recollections of a Journey through Tartary,
Thibet, and China, during the years 1844, 1845,
and 1846. 16mo. cloth. . . . . 1 00 *D. Appleton & Co.*
Hudson, C. J., Christ our Life. The Scriptural Argu-
ment for Immortality through Christ alone. . 0 75 *J. P. Jewett & Co.*
Hughes, E. B., The New York Church Year Book for
1859-60. 18mo. cl. . . . . 0 38 *D. Dana, Jr.*
—— Sallie E. (Mrs.), Lucy Hall; or, Responsibility
Realized. 18mo. . . . . . 0 30 *So. Bap. Pub. Soc.*
Humanics. By T. Wharton Collins. 8vo. . . . 1 75 *D. Appleton & Co.*

Humboldt, Alex. Von. Cosmos. A Description of the
    Universe. Vol. V. 12mo. . . . 0 35 *Harper & Bros.*
———— " The Life, Travels, and Books of. With
    an Introduction by Bayard Tayler. 12mo. 1 25 *Rudd & Carlston.*
———— " Letters of, to Varnhagen Von Ense, from
    1827 to 1858. With Extracts from Varn-
    hagen's Diaries, and Letters of Varnhagen
    and others to Humboldt. Translated from
    the Second German Edition. By Fred-
    erick Kapp. 12mo. . . . . 1 25 "
Humphrey, H. (Rev.), Revival Sketches and Manual. . 0 50 *Am. Tract Soc.*
Hundley, D. R., Social Relations in our Southern States. 1 00 *H. B. Price.*
Hungerford, J., The Old Plantation, and what I gathered
    there in an Autumn Month. 12mo. . . . 1 00 *Harper & Bros.*
Hunt, E. M. (M. D.), The Patient's and Physician's Aid;
    or, How to Preserve Health. 12mo. . . 1 00 *Saxton & Barker.*
———— F. W. (M. D.), A Practical Class Book of the His-
    tory of the World. 4to. . . . . . 1 25 *Ivison, Phin. & Co.*
———— W. (Rev.), Songs of Devotion. 8vo. paper. . 0 15 *J. L. Read.*
Huntington, F. D. (Rev.), Christian Believing and Living.
    A Series of Discourses. 12mo. cl. . 1 25 *Crosby, N., L. & Co.*
———— " Home and College. 18mo. . . 0 50 "
———— " Hymns of the Ages. 8vo. . . *Phillips, S. & Co.*
———— " Religious and Moral Sentences culled
    from the Works of Shakespeare, compared
    with Sacred Passages from Holy Writ. . 0 75 *Monroe & Co.*
———— " " Graham Lectures. Human Society;
    its Providential Structure, Relations, and Offices.
    Eight Lectures. 8vo. . . . . . 1 75 *Carter & Brothers.*
———— J. V., Rosemary; or, Life and Death. 12mo. . 1 25 *D. & J. Sadlier & Co.*
Hurd, J. C., The Law of Freedom and Bondage in the
    United States. Vol. I. 8vo., cl. 3.50; law sheep 4 00 *D. Van Nostrand.*
———— R. C., A Treatise on the Right of Personal Liber-
    ty, and on the Writ of Habeas Corpus and the
    Practice connected with it. 8vo. . . . *W. C. Little & Co.*
Hyde, Anna M., Bible Stories in Verse for the Little
    Ones at Home. 4to. . . . . 0 50 *Challen & Son.*
———— " A Ladder to Learning for Little Climbers. 0 25 "
———— " English History, condensed and simplified
    for Children. 18mo. . . . . . 0 25 "
Hyder, Dost Rajah of Soonderbach. By Eugene L. Hines. 0 50 *So. Bap. Pub. Soc.*
Hymns for Mothers and Children. Compiled by the
    author of "Violet." 12mo. . . . 1 25 *Walker, Wise & Co.*
———— " the Sick Room. 16mo. . . . 0 40 *A. D. F. Randolph.*

Hymns from the Land of Luther; translated from the
  German. New and enlarged edition. 24mo.   0 50   *A.D.F. Randolph.*
—— of Worship, designed for use especially in the
  Lecture-room, the Prayer-meeting, and the
  Family. 24mo. . . . . 0 40   *W.S.&A. Martien.*
—— " the Ages. Second Series. Being selections
  from Wither, Crashaw, Southwell, Habington,
  and other sources. 16mo. . . . . 1 25   *Ticknor & Fields.*

I

I Would Not Live Alway, and other pieces, in verse. 0 50   *A.D.F. Randolph.*
Ida Randolph, of Virginia; a Poem, in three cantos. 0 50   *Willis P. Hazard.*
Idolette Stanley; or, the Beauty of Discipline, 16mo. . 0 75   *W. S&A. Martien.*
Idols in the Heart. A Tale. By A. L. O. E. 18mo. : 0 50   *Carter & Brothers.*
Idyls of the King. By Alfred Tennyson. 16mo. cl. . 0 75   *Ticknor & Fields.*
Igdrasyl; or, the Tree of Existence. By James Challen. 1 00   *Lindsay &Blak'n*
I'll Try; or, the Young Housekeeper. By Mrs. Madeline
  Leslie. 16mo. . . . . 0 75   *Shepard, Clark&B.*
Illustrations of Scripture. By H. B. Hackett. New
  edition, greatly enlarged and improved. 12mo. 1 00   *Gould & Lincoln.*
Imogene Hartland; or, the Star of the Circus. By Geo.
  W. M. Reynolds. 8vo. pap. '. . . . 0 50   *F. A. Brady.*
In and Around Stamboul. By Mrs. Edmund Hornby. 1 25   *Lindsay&Blak'n.*
Incendiaries (The); or, the Haunted Manor. By M. J.
  Errym. 8vo. . . . . 0 25   *F. A. Brady.*
Ingalls, M. B. (Mrs.), Ocean Sketches of Burmah. 24mo. 0 55   *Am. Bap. Pub. Soc.*
Ingraham, J. H. (Rev.), The Pillar of Fire; or, Israel in
  Bondage. 12mo. . . . . 1 25   *Pudney & Russell.*
—— " The Throne of David; from the
  Consecration of the Shepherd of Bethlehem to
  the Rebellion of Prince Absalom. 12mo. . 1 25   *G. G. Evans.*
Ink, The History of Ink, including its Etymology, Chem-
  istry, and Biography. 16mo. . . . 0 60   *Thad. Davids&Co.*
Inside Views of Methodism; or, a Hand-Book for Inquir-
  ers and Beginners. By Wm. Reddy. 18mo. . 0 35   *Carlton & Porter.*
Instruction for Field Artillery. Prepared by a Board of
  Artillery Officers. 12mo. . . . . 2 50   *Lippincott & Co.*
Introductory Lectures on Mind. By the author of "Les-
  sons on Reasoning," etc. 12mo. . . . 0 75   *Jas. Munroe & Co.*
Ireland, J. B., Wall street to Cashmere; a Journal of Five
  Years in Asia, Africa, and Europe. 8vo. . 4 00   *S. A. Rollo & Co.*

rving, W., Works. National Edition (*now publishing*).
    Illustrated. Crown 8vo. cl.   .   .   per vol.   1 50   *G. P. Putnam.*
Irvingiana : a Memorial of Washington Irving. Small 4to.   0 75   *C. B. Richardson.*
Isabella Orsini : an Historical Novel. Translated from the
    Original Italian by Luigi Monti. 12mo. cl.   . 1 25   *Rudd & Carleton.*
Isherwood, B. F., Engineering Precedents for Steam Ma-
    chinery. 8vo. . .   .   .   .   .   1 25   *H. Baillière.*
Isle of the Dead ; or, the Keeper of the Lazaretto. 18mo.   0 25   *Kelly, H., & P.*
Italian Legends and Sketches. By J. W. Cummings, D.D.   0 75   *Dunigan & Bro.*
Italy, from the Earliest Period to the Present Day. By
    John S. C. Abbott. 8vo. . .   .   .   1 50   *Mason Brothers.*
—— in Transition ; Public Scenes and Private Opinions
    in the Spring of 1860. By William Arthur. .   1 00   *Harper & Bros.*
—— and the War of 1859. With Biographical Notices
    of Sovereigns, Statesmen, and Military Com-
    manders. By Julie de Marguerittes. 12mo. .   1 25   *G. G. Evans.*

J

Jack Hopeton ; or, the Adventures of a Georgian. By
    W. W. Turner. 12mo. cl.   .   .   .   1 00   *Derby & Jackson.*
—— in the Forecastle ; or, Incidents in the Early Life
    of Hawser Martingale. 12mo.   .   .   1 25   *Crosby, N., L. & Co.*
—— the Chimney Sweep, and Other Stories.   16mo.   0 75   *Shepard, C. & B.*
—— and Harry ; or, Pictures for the Young. By
    Mary and John Howitt. Small 4to.   . 1 00   *J. E. Tilton & Co.*
Jackson, Andrew, Life of. By James Parton. 3 vols. .   5 00   *Mason Brothers.*
—— J. O., Jesus Only. 16mo.   .   .   0 25   *W. S. & A. Martien.*
—— R. M. S. (M. D.), The Mountain. 12mo. .   1 50   *Lippincott & Co.*
Jacobus, M. W. (D. D.), Notes on the Acts of the Apos-
    tles. Critical and Explanatory. 12mo. .   1 00   *Carter & Bros.*
Jaques, D. H., Hints towards Physical Perfection. .   1 00   *Fowler & Wells.*
Jaeger, B., The Life of North American Insects. 12mo.   1 25   *Harper & Bros.*
James, J. A., Christian Hope. 16mo. .   .   0 75   *Carter & Bros.*
Jameson, Anna (Mrs.), Legends of the Madonna, as rep-
    resented in the Fine Arts. 32mo.   0 75   *Ticknor & Fields.*
——   "   Memoirs of the Early Italian Paint-
    ers. 32mo.   .   .   .   0 75   "
——   "   Studies, Stories, and Memoirs.
    32mo. .   .   .   .   0 75   "

Jamieson, R. (D. D.), The Historical Books of the Holy
   Scriptures. 12mo. . . . 0 75 *W.S.&A.Martien.*
——— " The Pentateuch and the Book of Joshua.
  With an Original and Copious Critical and Ex-
  planatory Commentary. 12mo. . . 0 75 *W.S.&A. Martien.*
Jamison, F. B. (Rev.), Catechism of Perseverance; an
  Historical, Doctrinal, Moral, and Liturgical Ex-
  position of the Catholic Religion. 18mo. . 0 38 *Kelly, Hedian&P.*
Jane Horton; or, The Wife's Martyrdom. By Jacob Brace. 0 25 *Frederic A.Brady.*
Janney, S. M., An American View of the Causes which
  have led to the Decline of the Society of
  Friends in Great Britain and Ireland.
  12mo. cl. . . . . 0 25 *T. E. Zell.*
——— " Conversations on Religious Subjects between
  a Father and his two Sons. 18mo. . 0 60 "
——— " History of the Religious Society of Friends,
  from its Rise to the year 1828. 12mo. . 1 25 "
Janvier, F., The Skeleton Monk and other Poems. 12mo. 1 00 *J. Challen & Son.*
Jarman, T., A Treatise on Wills. Fourth American edi-
  tion. With large additions to the Text and
  Notes, and References to American Decisions.
  By Hon. John C. Perkins. 2 vols., 8vo. . 10 00 *Little,Brown & Co.*
Jarves, J. J., Art Studies. The Old Masters of Italy.
  Painting. 8vo. . . . 6 00 *Derby & Jackson.*
Jealous Husband (The), A story of the Heart. By Mrs.
  Annette Marie Maillard. 12mo. . . 1 25 *Peterson & Bros.*
Jefferson, Thomas, Life of. By Henry S. Randall. 3 vols. 7 50 *Derby & Jackson.*
Jenks, Cornelia H., The Land of the Sun; or What Kate
  and Willie Saw There. 16mo. . . 0 63 *Crosby, N., L.&Co.*
Jenkyn, T. W. (Rev.), The Extent of the Atonement in its
  Relation to God and the Universe. 12mo. . 1 00 *Gould & Lincoln.*
Jennings, R., The Horse and his Diseases. 12mo. . 1 00 *John E. Potter.*
Jerusalem and its Environs; or, The Holy City as it Was
  and Is. By Rev. Dr. Tweedie. 18mo. cloth. . 0 75 *T. Nelson &. Sons.*
Jerram, C. (Rev.), A Tribute of Parental Affection to my
  Beloved and Only Daughter, Hannah Jerram. 0 30 *Carter & Brothers.*
Jerrold, Douglas, The Life and Remains of. By his son
  Blanchard Jerrold. 18mo. . . . 1 00 *Ticknor & Fields.*
Jervis, J. B., Railway Property. A Treatise on the Con-
  struction and Management of Railways. 12mo. 1 00 *Phinney, B. & M.*
Jessie Cameron; a Highland Story. 8vo. . . 0 25 *R. M. De Witt.*
Jessie; or, Trying to be Somebody. By Walter Aim-
  well. 16mo. . . . . . 0 63 *Gould & Lincoln.*
Jesus, the Interpreter of Nature; and other Sermons.
  By Thomas Hill. 12mo. . . . . 0 75 *Walker, Wise & Co.*

Jewish Prisoner (The); or, Sketch of the Life of Hernan
    S. Ollendorff, a Christian Israelite.   .   0 15   *Am. Tract Soc.*
Jewish (The) Twins. By Aunt Friendly. 18mo. . . 0 50   *Carter & Brothers.*
Joan of Arc; or, The Maid of Orleans. From Micholet's
    History of France. 18mo. cl. .   .   . 0 50   *Sheldon & Co.*
Joe Carton; or, The Lost Key. 18mo. . .   .   .   *Henry Hoyt.*
John Ellard, the Newsboy. 18mo. . .   .   . 0 50   *W.S.& A. Martien.*
    "   Howard and Laura Bridgeman. 18mo. . . 0 25   *Challen & Sons.*
    "   Wheeler's Two Uncles; or, Launching into Life. . 0 25   *Carlton & Porter.*
Johnes, M., Prince Charlie, the Young Chevalier. 16mo. 0 75   *D. Appleton & Co.*
———— " The Boy's Book of Modern Travel and Ad-
    venture. 12mo. . .   .   .   . 0 75   "   "
Johnnot, J., A Treatise on School-house Architecture. 2 00   *Ivison & Phinney.*
Johnson, Anna C. (Miss), The Cottages of the Alps; or,
    Life and Manners in Switzerland. 12mo. 1 25   *Charles Scribner.*
———— " Peasant Life in Germany. 12mo. . 1 25   "   "
———— J., A Daily Scriptural Watchword and Gospel
    Promise. 16mo., cl. .   .   .   . 0 37   *T. E. Zell.*
———— S. W., Essays on Peat, Muck, and Commercial .
    Manures. 8vo. .   .   .   .   . 0 75   *Brown & Gross.*
Johnston, J., Manual of Chemistry, on the basis of Turner's
    Elements of Chemistry; sixth Revised Edi-
    tion. 12mo. .   .   .   .   . 1 50   *C. Desilver.*
———— " Manual of Natural Philosophy. 12mo. . 1 00   "
Jones, J. (Rev.), Notes on Scripture. 8vo. .   . 2 50   *W.S.& A. Martien.*
———— J. B., Border War: a Tale of Disunion. 12mo. . 1 25   *Rudd & Carleton.*
———— J. H. (Rev.), Man, Moral and Physical; or, the
    Influence of Health and Disease on Religious
    Experience. 12mo. . .   .   . 1 00   *W.S.& A. Martien,*
———— T., Paradoxes of Debit and Credit Demolished. 0 50   *John Wiley.*
Joseph; or, The Model Young Man. By William B.
    Sprague, D.D. 18mo. . .   .   . 0 50   *A.D. F. Randolph.*
Josephine (Empress), Life of. By John Frost. 12mo. . 1 00   *G. G. Evans.*
Josephus, Flavius, The Works of, with a Life written by
    Himself. Translated from the Original Greek.
    Including Explanatory Notes and Observations,
    by William Whiston, A. M.. 4 vols. small 8vo. 5 00   *Lindsay & Blak'n.*
Josie Gray, and other Sketches. By Mrs. Louise B.
    Wright. 18mo. .   .   .   .   . 0 20   *F. D. Harriman.*
Journey Home (The), an Allegory. By the Rev. Edward
    A. Monro. 18mo., cl. . .   .   . 0 50   *H. Hooker.*
———— (A) in Search of Nothing. 8vo., paper. . . 0 50   *F. A. Brady.*
———— " in the Back Country. By Frederick Law
    Olmsted. 12mo. . .   .   .   . 1 25   *Mason Brothers.*

Jubilee (The) at Mount St. Mary's, October 6, 1858. 12mo.   1 00   *Dunigan&Brother*
Judson, A. (D. D.), A Memoir of the Life and Labors of.
       By Francis Wayland, D. D. 12mo. .   . 1 25   *Sheldon & Co.*
———— Emily C. (Mrs.), The Life and Letters of. By A.
       C. Kendrick. 12mo.   .   .   . 1 25   ''
Jukes, Harriet M., Memoirs, Letters, and Journals of.
       Compiled and edited by Mrs. H. A. Gilbert.   . 0 75   *Carter & Brothers.*
Julian Home. A Tale of College Life. By Frederick W.
       Farrar. 12mo. .   .   .   .   . ,   . 1 25   *Lippincott & Co.*
Julius Cæsar, Life of. By Henry G. Liddell, D. D. 18mo. 0 50   *Sheldon & Co.*
Juvenal.—The Satires of Juvenal, Persius, Sulpicia, and
       Lucilius, literally translated into English Prose,
       with Notes, Chronological Tables, Arguments,
       &c. By the Rev. Lewis Evans. To which is
       added the Metrical Version of Juvenal and Per-
       sius, by the late William Gifford, Esq. 12mo. . 0 75   *Harper &Brothers.*
Juvenile Tourist (The); or, Political Geography of Eu-
       rope. By an Irish Lady. 12mo. cl.   .   . 1 00   *C. P. Perry.*

K

Kangaroo Hunters (The); or, Adventures in the Bush.
       By Anne Bowman. 16mo.   .   .   . 0 75   *Crosby,N., L.&Co.*
Kansas in Eighteen Fifty-eight; being chiefly a History of
       the Recent Troubles in the Territory. By Wil-
       liam P. Tomlinson. 12mo.   .   .   . 1 00   *H. Dayton.*
———— Territory and Rocky Mountain Gold Region. By
       James Redpath and R. J. Hinton. 18mo.   . 0 75   *J. H. Colton.*
Karl Keigler; or, the Fortunes of a Foundling. 16mo. 0 50   *Phillips, S. & Co.*
Kate Darley; or, "It will All Come Right." By Aunt
       Friendly. 18mo.   .   .   .   . 0 25   *A. D.F. Randolph.*
———— and Effie; or, Prevarication. By Margaret Douglass
       Pinchard. 18mo.   .   .   .   . 0 50   *Carter & Bros.*
Katherine Morris: An Autobiography. 12mo.   . 1 00   *Walker, W. & Co.*
Katie Seymour; or, How to Make Others Happy. 18mo. 0 40   *Presb. Bd. of Pub.*
Kavanagh, Julia, Adele. 12mo.   .   .   . 1 25   *D. Appleton & Co.*
————   " Seven Years and Other Tales. 8vo. pap. 0 50   *Ticknor & Fields.*
————   " Seven Years and Other Tales. 12mo. 0 50   *D. Appleton & Co.*
Keddie, W., Cyclopædia of Literary and Scientific Anec-
       dote. 12mo.   .   .   .   .   . 1 25   *Follett,Foster&Co.*
Keil, G., New Fairy Stories for My Grandchildren.
       Translated from the German, by S. W. Lander. 0 50   *D. Appleton & Co.*

Kellys (The) and O'Kellys. A Novel. By Anthony
    Trollope. 12mo. . . . . . 1 25   *Rudd & Carleton.*

Kemble, Fanny (Mrs.), Poems. 16mo. cl . . . 1 00   *Ticknor & Fields.*

Kemp, E., on Landscape Gardening; or, How to Lay Out
    a Garden. 12mo. cl. . . . . . 2 00   *Wiley & Halsted*

Kendrick, F. P., The Pentatouch. Translated from the
    the Vulgate. . . . . . . 3 00   *Kelly, Hedian & P.*

——— " Job and the Prophets. Translated from
    Vulgate.. With Notes, critical and explanatory. 2 50   "

Kennedy, O., Corn in the Blade. Poems and Thoughts
    in Prose. 12mo. . . . . . 1 00   *Derby & Jackson.*

——— Grace, Dunallan; or, Know What you Judge. . 1 00   *J. P. Jewett & Co.*

——— " Father Clement: a Roman Catholic
    Story. 12mo. . . . . . 1 25   "

——— W. S., Messianic Prophecy, and the Life of
    Christ. 12mo. . . . . . 1 00   *Barnes & Burr*

Kenneth Forbes; or, Fourteen Ways of Studying the
    Bible. 12mo. . . . . . 0 40   *Am. S. S. Union.*

Kenny, O., The Manual of Chess, containing the Ele-
    mentary Principles of the Game, illustrated
    with numerous Diagrams, recent Games, and
    Original Problems. 18mo. . . . 0 50   *D. Appleton & Co.*

Kenny. By George B. Taylor, of Virginia. 16mo. . 0 50   *Sheldon & Co.*

Kerl, S., System of Arithmetic on an Original Plan. . 0 30   *C. Desilver.*

——— " A Treatise on the English Language. 8vo. .   *Moore, W., K. & Co.*

Kernan, F., Reports of Cases Argued and Determined in
    the Court of Appeals, of the State of New
    York, with Notes, References, and an Index.
    Vol. IV. 8vo. . . . . . 2 00   *Banks & Brothers.*

Ker?, Thomas, Bishop of Bath and Wells, Life of. By
    George L. Duyckinek. 12mo. . . 0 60   *F. D. Harriman.*

Killen, W. D. (Rev.), The Ancient Church; its History,
    Doctrine, Worship, and Constitution, traced for
    the first Three Hundred Years. 8vo. . . 3 00   *Charles Scribner.*

Kincaid, E. (Rev.), a History of the Labors of. By Alfred
    S. Patton. 12mo. . . . . . 1 00   *H. Dayton.*

Kind Words for Children, to Guide them to the Path of
    Peace. By Rev. Harvey Newcomb. 16mo. . 0 42   *Gould & Lincoln.*

King, D. (M. D.), Quackery Unmasked. 12mo. . .   *S. S. & W. Wood.*

——— E. F., Ten Thousand Wonderful Things, compris-
    ing the Marvelous and Rare. 12mo. . . 1 00   *Dick & Fitzgerald.*

——— J. (M. D.), New American Dispensatory. Revised
    and enlarged from the " American Eclectic Dis-
    pensatory." 8vo. . . . . .   *Moore, W., K. & Co.*

King, John (M. D.),, The Microscopist's Companion. . 1 50 *R. Clarke & Co.*
———— W. H., Lessons and Practical Notes on Steam,
    the Steam Engine, Propeller, &c. Revised by
    Chief Engineer J. W. King, U. S. N. 8vo. . 1 50 *F. A. Brady.*
———— M. M., Lucy Lambert; or, the Shrine in the
    Forest. 24mo. . . . . . . 0 25 *H. M'Grath.*
King, (The) of the Golden River; or, the Black
    Brothers. By John Ruskin, M. A. Sq. 16mo. 0 75 *Mayhew & Baker.*
———— (The) of the Mountains. From the French of
    Edmond About. 12mo. . . . . 1 00 *J. E. Tilton & Co.*
King's (The) Highway; or, Illustrations of The Com-
    mandments. By the Rev. Richard New-
    ton, D. D. 16mo. . . . . . 0 75 *Carter & Brothers.*
Kingsley, Charles, Andromeda and other Poems. 16mo. 0 50 *Ticknor & Fields.*
———— " New Miscellanies. 12mo. . 1 00 "
———— " Sir Walter Raleigh and His Times,
    with other Papers. 12mo. cl. . . 1 25 "
———— Charles, The Good News of God. Sermons. . 1 00 *Burt, Hutch'n & A.*
———— Henry, The Recollections of Geoffrey Hamlyn. 1 25 *Ticknor & Fields.*
Kingston, W. H. G., Annual for Boys, 1860. Small 4to. 1 75 "
———— " Ernest Bracebridge; or, Schoolboy
    Days. 16mo. . . . . . 0 75 "
———— W. H. G., Fred. Markham in Russia; or, the Boy
    Travelers in the Land of the Czar. Sq. 16mo. 0 75 *Harper & Bros.*
———— W. H. G., The Early Life of Old Jack; a Sea
    Tale. 16mo. . . . . . . 0 75 *T. Nelson & Sons.*
Kip, Lawrence (U. S. A.), Army Life on the Pacific, in
    the Summer of 1858. 12mo. . . . 0 50 *J. S. Redfield.*
———— W. I. (D. D.), The Catacombs of Rome; as Illus-
    trating the Church of the First Three Cen-
    turies. 12mo. . . . . . . 0 75 *Daniel Dana, Jr.*
———— The History, Object, and Proper Observance of
    the Holy Season of Lent. 12mo. . . 0 75 *Delisser & Proct'r.*
Kirby, Mary and E., Truth is always best; or, the Fatal
    Necklace. 24mo. . . . . . 0 25 *Carter & Brothers.*
Kirk, C. D., Wooing and Warring in the Wilderness. 1 00 *Derby & Jackson.*
Kirk, J., The Cloud Dispelled; or, the Doctrine of Pre-
    destination Examined. 12mo. . . 0 75 *N. Tibbals & Co.*
Kit Kelvin's Kernels. With Illustrations. 12mo. cl. . 1 00 *S. A. Rollo.*
Kitty Maynard; or, to Obey is better than Sacrifice. 0 55 *Am. S. S. Union.*
Klippart, J. H., The Wheat Plant; its Origin, Culture,
    Growth, Development, Composition, Varieties,
    Diseases, etc. Together with a few remarks on
    Indian Corn, its Culture, etc. 12mo. . . 1 50 *Moore, W., K. & Co.*

Knapp, M. L. (M. D.), Researches on Primary Pathology.
2 vols. 8vo. . . . . *Author, Philada.*

Knill, Richard (Rev.), The Life of; being Selections from
his Reminiscences, Journals, and Correspond-
ence. By Charles M. Birrell. 16mo. . . 0 75 *Carter & Brothers.*

Knitting-Work; a Web of Many Textures, wrought by
Ruth Partington (B. P. Shillaber). 12mo. . 1 25 *Brown & Taggard.*

Knowledge (A) of Living Things, with the Laws of their
Existence. By A. N. Bell. 12mo. . . . 1 50 *Baillière Brothers.*

Kormak, an Icelandic Romance of the Tenth Century.
In six cantos. 12mo. . . . . . 0 75 *Walker, W. & Co*

Krapf, J. L., Travels, Explorations, and Missionary Labors
in Eastern Africa. 12mo. cl. . . . 1 25 *Ticknor & Fields.*

Kurtz, J. H. (D.D.), History of the Old Covenant. Translated, annotated, and prefaced by a condensed
abstract of Kurtz's "Bible and Astronomy."
By Rev. Alfred Edersheim. 3 vols. 8vo. Vols.
1 & 2. . . . . . . each 2 00 *Lindsay & Blak'n.*

—— Text Book of Church History. Vol. 1. To the
Reformation. 12mo. . . . . . 1 50 "

—— Manual of Sacred History; a Guide to the under-
standing of the Divine Plan of Salvation according to its Historical Development. 12mo. . 1 25 "

L

La Borde, M. (M. D.), History of the South Carolina
College. 8vo. . . . . 2 00 *McCarter&Daw'n.*

Ladder to Learning for Little Climbers. By Anna M.
Hyde. 18mo. . . . . . . 0 25 *J. Challen & Son.*

Ladies' (The) Manual of Fancy Work. By Mrs. Pullan. 1 25 *Dick & Fitzgerald.*

—— " Reader. By John W. S. Hows. 12mo. . 1 13 *E. H. Butler & Co.*

Lady (The) of the Isle. A Romance from Real Life.
By Mrs. Emma D. E. N. Southworth. 12mo. 1 25 *Peterson & Bros.*

Lafayette (The Life of), Written for Children. By
E. Cecil. 16mo. cl. . . . . . . 0 75 *Crosby, N., L.&Co.*

La Fontaine (Fables of). Illustrated by J. J. Grand-
ville. Translated from the French, by Elizur
Wright, Jr. 2 vols. 12mo. . . . . 2 50 *Derby & Jackson.*

Laidlaw, A. H., an American Pronouncing Dictionary
of the English Language. . . . . . 1 00 *Crissy & Markley.*

Laing, C. H. B., the Old Farm House. 12mo. . . 1 00 *G. G. Evans.*

Laird (The) of Norlaw : a Scottish Story. 12mo. cl. . 1 00 *Harper & Bros.*

Lake House. By Fanny Lewald. Translated from the
German by Nathaniel Greene. 12mo. . . 0 75 *Ticknor & Fields.*

Lake Regions of Central Africa (The); a Picture of
Explorations. By Richard F. Burton. 8vo. cl. 2 50 *Harper & Bros.*

Lamar, J. S., The Organon of Scripture; or, the Inductive Method of Biblical Interpretation. 12mo. 1 00 *Lippincott & Co.*

Lamartine, A., Life of Mary Stuart, Queen of Scots. 0 50 *Sheldon & Co.*

Lamb, Charles, Essays of Elia. 12mo. . . . . 1 25 *Crosby,N.,L.&Co.*

————— " The Works of. A new Edition in four volumes, crown 8vo. cl. . . . . . 5 00 . "

Lamson, A. (D. D.), The Church of the First Three Centuries ; or, Notices of the Lives and Opinions of
some of the Early Fathers. 8vo. . . . 1 75 *Walker, W. & Co.*

Land (The) of the Sun ; or, What Kate and Willie Saw
There. By Cornelia H. Jenks. 16mo. . . 0 63 *Crosby,N., L. & Co*

Landells, E., The Boy's Own Toy-Maker. Square 16mo. 0 50 *D. Appleton & Co.*

Lander, M., Fading Flowers. Small 4to. . . . 2 00 *J. E. Tilton & Co.*

Landis, R. W., The Immortality of the Soul and the
Final Condition of the Wicked carefully considered. 12mo. . . . . . . 1 25 *Carlton & Porter.*

Lanman, C., Dictionary of the United States Congress,
containing Biographical Sketches of its Members, from the foundation of the Government:
with an Appendix, compiled as a Manual of
Reference for the Legislator and Statesman. 8vo. 2 00 *Lippincott & Co.*

La Plata, the Argentine Confederation, and Paraguay.
Being a Narrative of the Exploration of the
Tributaries of the River La Plata and Adjacent
Countries, during the years 1853, '54, '55, and
'56, under the orders of the United States
Government. By Thomas J. Page, U. S. N. 8 00 *Harper & Bros.*

Larcom, Lucy, Ships in the Mist, and other Stories. 18mo. 0 20 *Henry Hoyt.*

Lasar, S., The Cœcilia. A collection of Vocal Music. 4to. 0 62½ *Mason Brothers.*

Lasselle, N. P. (Mrs.), The Belle of Washington: a True
Story of the Affections. 12mo. . . . 1 25 *Peterson & Bros.*

Lavinia: a Novel. By Ruffini. 12mo. . . . 1 25 *Rudd & Carleton.*

Law, J., The Mississippi Bubble: a Memoir of John Law.
By Adolphe Thiers, author of "The Consulate
and Empire," &c. To which are added Authen-
tic Accounts of the Darien Expedition, and the
South Sea Scheme. Translated and edited by
Frank S. Fiske. 12mo. . . . . . 1 00 *Townsend & Co.*

Lawrence, S., The Moral Design of Freemasonry, de-
duced from the Old Charges of a Freemason. 1 00 *Macoy, S. & Co.*

Lawrence, W. B., Visitation and Search; or, an Historical Sketch of the British Claim to exercise a
Maritime Police over the Vessels of all nations,
in Peace as well as in War, with an Inquiry into
the Expediency of Terminating the Eighth Ar-
ticle of the Ashburton Treaty. . . . 3 00 *Little, Brown&Co.*

Lays of the Kirk and Covenant. By A. Stewart Men-
teath. 18mo. . . . . . . 0 50 *Carter & Brothers.*

Leaves from a Bachelor's Book of Life. By Francis
Copcutt. 12mo. cl. . . . . . . 1 00 *S. A. Rollo.*

——— from an Actor's Note Book. By George Vandenhoff. 12mo. . . . . . . 1 00 *D. Appleton & Co.*

——— of Grass. 12mo. . . . . . 1 25 *Thayer&Eldridge.*

Leaving Home; a Story for Boys. 18mo. . . 20 *Henry Hoyt.*

Lectures delivered before the Young Men's Christian Association in Exeter Hall, from November, 1858,
to February, 1859. 12mo. . . . . 1 00 *Carter & Bros.*

Lee, C., The Treason of Charles Lee, Major General,
second in command in the American Army of
the Revolution. By George H. Moore. 8vo. 1 50 *Chas. Scribner.*

——— Holme. Against Wind and Tide. 12mo. . 1 00 *Townsend & Co.*

——— " Hawksview; a Family History of Our Own
Times. . . . . 1 00 " "

——— " Sylvan Holt's Daughter. 12mo. . . 1 00 *Harper & Bros.*

——— Leila, Wee-WeeSongs, for Our Little Pets. 18mo. 0 50 *Phinney, B. & M.*

——— S., Eschatology; or, the Scripture Doctrine of the
Coming of the Lord, the Resurrection, and
the Judgment. 12mo. . . . . 1 00 *J. E. Tilton & Co.*

Leech, D. D. T., A List of Post Offices in the United
States on the 13th of June, 1858. 8vo. . 1 00 *Chas. T. Evans.*

Legal, E., School of the Guides; designed for the Use of
the Militia of the United States. 18mo. . . 0 50 *D. Van Nostrand.*

Legends of the Blessed Virgin. Collected from approved
sources. By J. Collin de Plancy. 12mo. . 0 50 *P. O'Shea.*

——— of the Madonna, as represented in the Fine Arts.
By Mrs. Jameson. Blue and Gold. . . 0 75 *Ticknor & Fields.*

——— and Lyrics. A Book of Verse. By Adelaide
Anne Proctor. 12mo. . . . . 0 75 *D. Appleton & Co.*

Legouve, E., The Moral History of Women. Translated
from the fifth Paris edition, by J. W. Palmer,
. M. D. 12mo. . . . . . 1 00 *Rudd & Carleton.*

Leidy, J. (M. D.), An Elementary Treatise on Human Anatomy. 8vo. . . . . . *Lippincott & Co.*

Leighton, Robert (D. D.), The Works of. To which is prefixed a Life of the Author, by John Norman Pearson, M. A. 8vo. . . . . . 2 00 *Carter & Bros.*

Leisure Moments. By Miss Martha Haine Butt. 12mo. 1 25 *E. D. Long & Co.*

Lesley, J. P., The Iron Manufacturer's Guide to the Furnaces, Forges, and Rolling Mills of the United States. 8vo. . . . . . . 5 00 *John Wiley.*

Leslie, C. R., Autobiographical Recollections. By Chas. Robert Leslie, R. A. Edited with Prefatory Essay on Leslie as an Artist, and Selections from his Correspondence. By Tom Taylor, Esq. 1 25 *Ticknor & Fields.*

—— Madeline (Mrs.), Howard and his Teacher, the Sister's Influence, and Other Stories. 0 75 *Shepard, C. & B.*

—— " I'll Try; or the Young Housekeeper. 0 75 "

—— " Jack the Chimney Sweep, and Other Stories for Children. 16mo. . . 0 75 "

—— " Little Agnes; or, the Rich Poor, and the Poor Rich. 18mo. . . . 0 50 *A. D. F. Randolph.*

—— " Little Frankie Stories. Six volumes. 1 80 *Crosby, N., L.& Co*

—— " Play and Study. 12mo. cl. . . 0 75 *Shepard, C. & B.*

—— " Robin Nest Stories. Six vols. 16mo. 1 80 *Crosby, N., L.& Co.*

—— " The Motherless Children. 12mo. cl. 0 75 *Shepard, C., & B.*

—— " Trying to be Useful. 16mo. . . 0 75 "

—— E., Behavior Book. 12mo. cl. . . . 1 25 *Peterson & Bros.*

Lessons at the Cross. By Samuel Hopkins and Rev. George W. Blagden, D. D. 12mo. . . . 0 75 *J. E. Tilton & Co.*

Lever, Charles, Davenport Dunn. 8vo. paper, 50c., cl. 1 50 *Peterson & Bros.*

—— " Gerald Fitzgerald, "The Chevalier." 8vo. paper. . . . . . . 0 50 *Harper & Bros.*

Lewald, Fanny, Lake House. Translated from the German by Nathaniel Greene. 12mo. . . . 0 75 *Ticknor & Fields.*

Lewellyn, E., Piety and Pride. 16mo. . . . 0 65 *Henry Hoyt.*

—— " Walter Stockton; or, My Father's at the Helm. . . . . . . 0 35 *Presb. Bd. of Pub.*

Lewes, G. H., Studies in Animal Life. 12mo. . 0 40 *Harper & Bros.*

—— " Physiology of Common Life. 2 vols. 12mo. 2 00 *D. Appleton & Co.*

Lewis, C. T., & Vincent, M. R., Bengel's Gnomon of the New Testament, newly translated from the original Latin. Vol. I. 8vo. cloth. . . . 2 50 *Perkinpine & H.*

Lewis, E., A Treatise on Plain and Spherical Trigonometry. 8vo. hf. roan. . . . . 1 25 *Hunt & Son.*

—— J. N. (Rev.), The Presbyterian Manual. 18mo. 0 38 *Presb. Pub. Com.*

—— Taylor, The Divine Human in the Scriptures. . 1 00 *Carter & Brothers.*

Lewis, Theresa, The Semi-Detached House. A Novel.
Edited by Lady Theresa Lewis. 12mo. . . 0 75 *Ticknor & Fields.*
—— W. H. (D. D.), Christian Union, and the Protestant
Episcopal Church in its relation to Church
Unity. 16mo. cl. . . . . . . 0 38 *F. D. Harriman.*
Librarian's Manual. By R. A. Guild. Small 4to. . . 5 00 *Chas. B. Norton.*
Lichen Tufts from the Alleghanies. By Elizabeth C.
Wright. 12mo. cl. . . . . . . 1 00 *M. Doolady.*
Liddell, H. G., Life of Julius Cæsar. 18mo. . . 0 50 *Sheldon & Co.*
Liebig, Baron Von, Letters on Modern Agriculture.
Edited by John Blyth, M. D. 12mo. . . 0 75 *John Wiley.*
Lieber, Francis, On Civil Liberty and Self Government.
Enlarged edition. 8vo. . . . . . 2 75 *Lippincott & Co.*
Liefde, J. De, The Signet Ring and other Gems. From
the Dutch of the Rev. J. De Liefde. 16mo. . 0 63 *Gould & Lincoln.*
Life among the Children. 12mo. . . . . . 0 68 *R. L. Delisser.*
—— Before Him, A Novel. 12mo. . . . . 1 00 *Townsend & Co.*
—— Memories, and other Poems. By Edward Sprague
Rand, Jr. 16mo. . . . . . . 0 75 *J. Munroe & Co.*
—— Sketches. 18mo. . . . . . . 0 25 *Challen & Sons.*
—— Without and Life Within; or, Reviews, Narratives,
Essays, and Poems. By Margaret Fuller Ossoli.
Edited by her Brother, Arthur B. Fuller. 12mo. 1 25 *Brown & Taggard.*
—— at Three Score. A Sermon delivered in the First
Presbyterian Church, Philadelphia, Nov. 28th,
1858. By the Rev. Albert Barnes. cl. . . 0 38 *Parry & McMillan.*
—— in Tuscany. By Mabel Sharman Crawford. 12mo. 1 00 *Sheldon & Co.*
—— in the Desert; or, Recollections of Travel in
Asia and Africa. By Colonel L. Du Couret
(Hadji-Abd'el-Hamid-Bey). 12mo. . . . 1 25 *Mason Brothers.*
—— in the Far West; or, The Adventures of a Hoosier. By Adolphus M. Hart. 8vo., paper. . 0 25 *W. Skelly.*
—— (A) for a Life. By Miss Muloch. 8vo., paper . 0 50 *Harper & Bros.*
—— and Liberty in America; or, Sketches of a Tour
in the United States and Canada in 1857-'8.
By Charles Mackay. 12mo. . . . . 1 00 "
—— (The) of St. Bridget. By an Irish Priest. 16mo. 0 38 *P. O'Shea.*
—— (The) of St. Francis Xavier. From the Italian of
D. Bartoli and J. P. Maffei. With a Preface by
the Very Rev. Dr. Faber. 16mo. . . . 1 00 *Murphy & Co.*
—— of Te-ho-ra-gwa-ne-gen, alias Thomas Williams,
a Chief of the Caughnawaga Tribe of Indians in
Canada. By the Rev. Eleazer Williams. . . *Munsell & Rowl'd.*
Life's Morning; or, Counsels and Encouragements for
Youthful Christians. 12mo. . . . . 0 65 *J. E. Tilton & Co.*

Life's Evening; or, Thoughts for the Aged. 12mo. cl.	0 65	*J. E. Tilton & Co.*
Light (A) for the Line; or, the Story of Thomas Ward.	0 25	*Carter & Brothers.*
—— in the Valley; or, the Life and Letters of Mrs. Hannah Bocking. By Miss M. Annesley. 18mo.	0 30	*Carlton & Porter.*
Light-Hearted Girl (The); a Tale for Children. By Joseph Alden, D. D. 18mo.	0 34	*J. E. Tilton & Co.*
Liguori, A., The Eternal Truths, Preparation for Death.	0 50	*Dunigan & Bro.*
Lillie, J. (D. D.), Lectures on the Epistle of Paul to the Thessalonians. 8vo.	2 00	*Carter & Brothers.*
Lily White; a Romance. . By E. Godwin. 12mo. cl. .		*Lippincott & Co.*
Lincoln, Abraham, The Life, Speeches, and Public Services of, together with a Sketch of the Life of Hannibal Hamlin. 16mo. pap.	0 25	*Rudd & Curleton.*
—— " The Life and Public Services of. By D. W. Bartlett. 12mo. cl. .	1 00	*Derby & Jackson.*
—— and Douglas, Popular Sovereignty and Democracy *vs.* Republicanism. The Debates held in Illinois between Abraham Lincoln and Stephen A. Douglas. 8vo.	0 50	*Follett, Fos. & Co.*
—— and Hamlin, Lives and Speeches of Abraham Lincoln and H. Hamlin. 12mo.	1 00	"
Lindsley, P. (D. D.), The Works of. Vol. I. Educational Discourses. 8vo.	2 00	*Lippincott & Co.*
Line upon Line. 18mo. cl.	0 25	*Moore & Nims.*
Linton Family (The); or, The Fashion of this World. By Sarah H. Bradford. 12mo.	1 00	*Pudney & Russell.*
Lionello. A Sequel to the Jew of Verona. By Rev. A. Bresciana. 12mo.	1 00	*Kelly, Hedian & P.*
Lippincott, L. K., (Grace Greenwood,) Old Wonder-Eyes, and other Stories for Children. 16mo.	0 50	*Gaut & Volkmar.*
Lisa; or, The Mesmerist's Victim. By Lady Clara Cavendish. 8vo. pap.	0 50	*E. D. Long & Co.*
Little Agnes; or, the Rich Poor, and the Poor Rich. By Mrs. Madeline Leslie. 18mo.	0 50	*A. D. F. Randolph.*
—— Annie's New or Third Book. By her Mother.	0 45	"
—— Beauty (The). By Mrs. Grey. 12mo.	1 25	*Peterson & Bros.*
—— Commodore (The). By Mary Rambler.	0 75	*Sheldon & Co.*
—— Frankie Stories. By Mrs. Madeline Leslie. Six volumes. 16mo. sq. cl.	1 80	*Crosby, N., L. & Co.*
—— Haymakers (The) and Other Tales. 12mo.	0 75	*Williams & Co.*
—— Jerry; a Story for Boys. 18mo.	0 20	*Henry Hoyt.*
—— Joe Ashton; or, Forbidden Ground. 18mo.	0 20	*Carlton & Porter.*
—— Leaven (A), and what it wrought at Mrs. Blake's School. 18mo. cl.	0 60	*A. D. F. Randolph.*

Little Lychetts, (The) and Other Stories. 16mo. . 0 75 *Carter & Brothers.*
———— Mabel and her Sunlit Home. 18mo. . . . 0 27 *Carlton & Porter.*
———— May; or, Of What Use am I? 18mo. . . 0 30 "
———— Mountain Guide (The); or, How to be Happy. . 0 35 *Henry Hoyt.*
———— Musicians (The). By Aunt Friendly. 18mo. . 0 25 *A. D. F. Randolph.*
———— Nightcap Letters (The). 16mo. . . . 0 50 *D. Appleton & Co·*
———— Orator (The); or, Primary School Speaker. By
    Charles Northend. 18mo. . . . . 30 *Barnes & Burr.*
———— Pilgrims in the Holy Land. By Rev. H. S. Os-
    born. 16mo. cl. . . . . . 0 75 *Challen & Son.*
———— Songs for Little People. 16mo. . . . 0 35 *Carlton & Porter.*
———— Tiger Lily, and her Cousin Alice; or, how a Bad
    Temper was cured. 18mo. . . . 0 28 "
———— Vesper Book. 12mo. . . . . 0 50 *Kelly, Hedian & P.*
Little by Little; or, the Cruise of the Flyaway. By
    Oliver Optic. 16mo. . . . . 0 63 *Crosby, N., L.& Co.*
Livermore, Kate, Mary Lee. By Kate Livermore. . 0 63 *D. Appleton & Co.*
Lives of Eminent Philadelphians. . . . . *W. Brotherhead.*
———— of General Henry Lee and General Thomas
    Sumpter. 12mo. . . . . . 1 00 *G. G. Evans.*
———— of Southern Heroes and Patriots, including Gen-
    eral Marion, Governor Rutledge, &c. 12mo. . 1 00 "
———— and Times of the Chief Justices of the Supreme
    Court of the United States. Comprising the
    Lives of John Jay, John Rutledge, William
    Cushing, Oliver Ellsworth, and John Marshall,
    and a History of their Times from 1754 to
    1835. 2 vols. 8vo. . . . . 5 00 *Lippincott & Co.*
Lizars, J., The Use and Abuse of Tobacco. 16mo. . 0 38 *Lindsay & Blak'n.*
Lizzy Glen; or, The Trials of a Seamstress. By T. S.
    Arthur. 12mo. cl. . . . . . 1 25 *Peterson & Bros.*
Llewellyn, E. L., Title Hunting. 12mo. . . . 1 00 *Lippincott & Co.*
Lobdell, Henry (Rev.), Memoir of. By the Rev. W. S.
    Tyler, D. D. 12mo. . . . . 0 75 *Am. Tract Soc.*
Locke, R. A., The Moon Hoax; or, a Discovery that the
    Moon has a Vast Population of Human Beings. 0 50 *William Gowans.*
Lockhart, J. G., Ancient Spanish Ballads, Historical and
    Romantic. A new revised edition. 12mo. . 0 75 *Ticknor & Fields.*
Logic in Theology, and other Essays. By Isaac Taylor. 1 25 *William Gowans.*
Longfellow, H. W., The Courtship of Miles Standish, and
    other Poems. 16mo. . . . . 0 75 *Ticknor & Fields.*
Loomis, Elias, Elements of Natural Philosophy. 12mo. 1 00 *Harper & Bros.*
———— I. C., Mispah; Prayer and Friendship. 12mo. 1 25 *Lippincott & Co.*
Lord, E., The Prophetic Office of Christ. 12mo. . . 30 *A. D. F. Randolph.*
———— " The Psalter Readjusted. 12mo. . . . 1 00 "

Lord, J., A New History of the United States of Ameri-
 ca, for the use of Schools. 12mo. .   .   .   1 00   *C. Desilver.*
——— "A Modern History, from the time of Luther to
 the Fall of Napoleon; for the use of Schools.   1 50   "
Lorimer, P. (D. D.), The Scottish Reformation; a His-
 torical Sketch. 8vo. .   .   .   .   .   8 00   *Carter & Bros.*
Loss (The) of the Kent East Indiaman. 24mo. .   .   0 25   *Henry Hoyt.*
—— and Gain; or, Margaret's Home. By Alice B.
 Haven. 12mo. .   .   .   .   .   .   0 75   *D. Appleton & Co.*
Lossing, B. J., The Life and Times of Philip Schuyler. .   1 50   *Mason Brothers.*
——— " Mount Vernon and its Associations, Historic-
 al, Biographical, and Pictorial. Small 4to. .   8 50   *Townsend & Co.*
Lost Hunter (The). A Tale of Early Times. By John
 T. Adams. 12mo. .   .   .   .   .   1 25   *M. Doolady.*
—— Key (The). By the author of the "Little Water-
 cress Sellers." 18mo. cl.   .   .   .   0 88   *Am. S. S. Union.*
—— Love (A). By Ashford Owen. 8vo. paper. .   .   0 25   *T. J. Crowen.*
—— Principle (The); or, The Sectional Equilibrium;
 how it was created, how destroyed, how it may
 be restored. By "Barbarossa." 8vo. cl.   .   2 00   *J. Woodhouse & Co.*
—— Will (The). By Ann E. Porter. 16mo. .   .   0 70   *Henry Hoyt.*
—— and Found (The); or, Life Among the Poor. By
 Samuel B. Halliday. 12mo. .   .   .   .   1 00   *Phinney, B. & M.*
Lottie's Thought Book. 12mo. .   .   .   .   0 50   *Am. S. S. Union.*
Louie's Last Term at St. Mary's. 12mo. cloth. .   .   1 00   *Derby & Jackson.*
Loutron; or, Water Baptism; a Series of Discourses.
 By Rev. Samuel Fuller, D. D. 12mo. cl.   .   0 50   *D. Dana, Jr.*
Love ("L'Amour"). From the French of M. J. Michelet.
 Translated from the fourth Paris edition by J.
 W. Palmer, M. D. .   .   .   .   .   .   1 00   *Rudd & Carleton.*
—— Me, Leave Me Not. By Pierce Egan. 8vo. .   .   0 50   *F. A. Brady.*
—— Me Little, Love Me Long. By Charles Reade. .   0 75   *Harper & Bros.*
—— and Mock Love; or, How to Marry to the End of
 Conjugal Satisfaction. By George Stevens.   0 25   *B. Marsh.*
—— and Penalty; or, Eternal Punishment consistent
 with the Fatherhood of God. By J. P. Thomp-
 son, D. D. 16mo. cl.   .   .   .   .   0 75   *Sheldon & Co.*
Lovell the Widower. A Novel. By W. M. Thackeray.
 Paper, 8vo. .   .   .   .   0 25   *Harper & Bros.*
Lover, S., The Songs of Ireland. 12mo. .   .   .   1 00   *Dick & Fitzgerald.*
Loves (The) and Heroines of the Poets; illustrated
 with real and ideal Portraits from designs by
 Barry and others. By Richard Henry Stod-
 dard. 4to. Full gilt Turkey, or Turkey antique. 12 00   *Derby & Jackson.*

Lowrie, J. M., Esther and her Times. A series of Lectures on the Book of Esther. 12mo. .   . 0 60 *Pres. Bd. of Pub.*

Loyal Verses (The) of Joseph Stansbury and Doctor Jonathan Odell; relating to the American Revolution. Now first edited by Winthrop Sargent. Small 4to. . . . . . . 3 00 *J. Munsell.*

Lucille. By Owen Meredith. 32mo. blue and gold. . 0 75 *Ticknor & Fields.*

Luck of Ladysmede (The). 8vo. paper. . . . 0 50 *Littell, Son & Co.*

Luckey, S. (D.D.), The Lord's Supper. 18mo. . . 0 40 *Carlton & Porter.*

Lucy Crofton. By the author of "Margaret Maitland." 12mo. . . . . . 0 75 *Harper & Bros.*

—— Hall, or, Responsibility Realized. By Mrs. Sallie E. Hughes. 18mo. . . . . . 0 30 *So. Bap. Pub. So*

—— Lambert; or, the Shrine in the Forest. By Mary M. King. 24mo. . . . . 0 25 *H. McGrath.*

Luther, Martin, Life of. By Chevalier Bunsen. With an Estimate of Luther's Character and Genius. By Thomas Carlyle. 18mo. . 0 50 *Sheldon & Co.*

——   " The Epistles of St. Peter and St. Jude, preached and explained by Martin Luther. Translated by E. H. Gillet. 12mo. . 1 00 *A. D. F. Randolph.*

Lyons, J. G., Rev., Christian Songs, Translations, and other Poems. 12mo. . . . . 0 80 *Smith, E. & Co.*

—— R. D., A Hand Book of Hospital Practice, or an Introduction to the Practical Study of Medicine at the Bedside. 12mo. . . . . 1 00 *S. S. & W. Wood.*

M

Mabel; or, Heart Histories. By Rosella Rice. 12mo. . 1 00 *Follett & Foster.*

Macaulay, T. B., Critical and Miscellaneous Essays and Poems. New and revised edition. . 1 00 *D. Appleton & Co.*

——   " Critical, Historical, and Miscellaneous Essays. With an Introduction and Biographical Sketch, by E. P. Whipple, Esq. 6 vols. crown 8vo. . . 7 50 *Sheldon & Co.*

——   " The Life of Frederick the Great. . 0 50   "

——   " The Life of William Pitt. 18mo. . 0 50   "

Macduff, John R. (D. D.), Grapes of Eshcol; or Gleanings from the Land of Promise.   0 60 *Carter & Brothers*

Macduff, John R. (D.D.), The Mind and Words of Jesus;
and the Faithful Promiser. . 0 30 *Carter & Brothers.*
———— " " The Morning Watches and
Night Watches. 32mo. . 0 30 "
———— " " Story of Bethlehem. A Book
for the Young. 16mo. . . 0 60 "
———— " " The Hart and the Water-brooks;
a Practical Exposition of the Forty-second
Psalm. 16mo. . . . . . 0 60 "
Mackay, Charles, Life and Liberty in America; or
Sketches of a Tour in the United States and
Canada in 1857–'8. 12mo. . . . . 1 00 *Harper & Brothers.*
Mackenzie, R. S., Tressilian and his Friends. 12mo. . 1 00 *Lippincott & Co.*
Mackey, A. G., The Book of the Chapter; or, Monitorial
Instructions, in the Degrees of Mark, Past and
Most Excellent Master, and the Holy Royal
Arch. 12mo. . . . . 1 00 *Robert Macoy.*
———— " A Text Book of Masonic Jurisprudence, Illus-
trating the Written and Unwritten Laws of
Freemasonry. 12mo. cl. . . . . 1 50 "
Maclean, G. M. (M. D.), Elements of Somatology; a
Treatise on the General Properties of Matter. . 0 75 *John Wiley.*
Madagascar during the years 1853—1854—1856. Includ-
a Journey to the Capital; with Notices of the
Natural History of the Country, and of the pre-
sent Civilization of the People. 8vo. . . 2 50 *Harper & Brothers.*
Mademoiselle Mori; a Tale of Modern Rome. 12mo. . 1 25 *Ticknor & Fields.*
Madison, James, The Life and Times of. By Hon.
William C. Rives. Vol. I., 8vo. . . . 2 25 *Little, Brown & Co.*
Magdala and Bethany. By the Rev. S. C. Malan. 18mo. 0 40 *Carter & Brothers.*
Magdalen the Enchantress. Founded on fact. 12mo. . 1 00 *Lippincott & Co.*
Magic Mirror (The), a Christmas Story. 12mo. . 0 30 *Daniel Dana, Jr.*
Magician's (The) Own Book; or the Whole Art of Con-
juring. 12mo. . . . . . . 1 00 *Dick & Fitzgerald.*
Maguire, John F., Rome; its Ruler and its Institutions. . 1 25 *D. & J. Sadlier & Co.*
Mahan, M. (D. D.), A Church History of the First Three
Centuries, from the Thirtieth to the Three Hun-
dred and Twenty-third Year of the Christian
Era. 12mo. . . . . 1 50 *Daniel Dana, Jr.*
Maid of the Ranche; or, the Regulators and Moderators.
By D. J. H. Robinson. Paper. 8vo. . . 0 25 *F. A. Brady.*
Maillard, A. M. (Mrs.), The Jealous Husband. A Story of
the Heart. 12mo. . . . . . 1 25 *T. B. Peterson.*

Maine, The Ancient Dominion of; embracing the Earliest Facts, the Recent Discoveries of the Remains of Aboriginal Towns, &c., &c. By Rufus King Sewall. . . . . . 2 00 *E. Clarke & Co.*

Mallary, C. D. (D. D.), Soul-Prosperity, its Nature, its Fruits, and its Culture. 12mo. . . . 0 75 *So. Bap. Pub. Soc.*

Malon, S. C., Magdala and Bethany. 18mo. . . 0 40 *Carter & Brothers.*

Mamma's Lessons about Jesus. By a Mother. 12mo. . 0 75 *W. S.&A.Martien.*

Mammalogy and Ornithology of the United States Exploring Expedition under Commodore Wilkes. 1 vol. 4to. With a Folio Atlas of over Fifty Colored Steel Engravings. Prepared under the Superintendence of John Cassin, Member of the Academy of Natural Sciences. . . . 50 00 *Lippincott & Co.*

Man, Moral and Physical; or, The Influence of Health and Disease on Religious Experience. By Rev. Joseph H. Jones, D. D. 12mo. . . . 1 00 *W. S.&A.Martien.*

——— upon the Sea; or, a History of Maritime Adventure, Exploration, and Discovery, from the Earliest Ages. By Frank B. Goodrich. 8vo. cl. . 3 00 *Lippincott & Co.*

——— from his Cradle to his Grave. By C. Graham, M. D. 12mo. . . . . . . 1 25 *C. Blanchard.*

——— and his Dwelling-place: an Essay towards the Interpretation of Nature. 12mo. . . . 1 00 *J. S. Redfield.*

Manesca, L., Serial and Oral Method of Teaching Languages, adapted to the French. 12mo. . . 1 25 *C. Desilver.*

Mangan, J. C., Poems. With a Biographical Introduction by John Mitchell. 12mo. . . . 1 00 *P. M. Haverty.*

Maniac's Secret; or, the Privateer of Massachusetts Bay. 8vo., paper. . . . . . 0 25 *F. A. Brady.*

Mann, R. J. (M. D.), A Guide to the Knowledge of Life, Vegetable and Animal. 12mo. . . . 0 88 *C. S. Francis & Co.*

Manners, Mrs., Hester and I; or, Beware of Wordliness. 0 60 *Sheldon & Co.*

Mansel, H. L. (Rev.), Prolegomena Logica: An Inquiry into the Psychological Character of Logical Processes. 12mo. . . 1 00 *Gould & Lincoln.*

——— " " The Limits of Religious Thought Examined in Eight Lectures. 12mo. 1 00 "

Mansfield, E. D., Political Manual. 12mo. . . 1 00 *Barnes & Burr.*

Manual (A) of Bookbinding, Designed for the Practical Workman, the Amateur, and the Book-Collector. . . . . . . *Pawson&Nichols'n*

Manual (A) of Naval Tactics; together with a Brief Critical Analysis of the Principal Modern Naval Battles. By James H. Ward, Commander U. S. N. 8vo. . . . .   2 50   *D. Appleton & Co.*

—— " of Roman Chant; Compiled from Authentic Roman Sources. 4to. . . . .   1 50   *Kelly, Hedian & P.*

—— " of Scientific and Practical Agriculture. By J. L. Campbell. 12mo. . . . .   1 00   *Lindsay & Blackn.*

Many a Little makes a Mickle. From the German. 16mo.   0 75   *Crosby, N., L. & Co.*

Marcy, R. B. (Capt. U. S. A.), The Prairie Traveler. A Handbook for Overland Emigrants. With Maps, Illustrations, &c., of the Principal Routes between the Mississippi and the Pacific. 12mo. .   1 00   *Harper & Brothers.*

Margaret Maxham. A Book for Young Ladies. By Marianna H. Bliss. 18mo. . . . .   0 25   *Carlton & Porter.*

—— Moncrieffe: the First Love of Aaron Burr. A Romance of the Revolution. By Charles Burdett. 12mo. . . . . .   1 25   *Derby & Jackson.*

Marguerittes, Julia De, Italy and the War of 1859. With Biographical Notices of Sovereigns, Statesmen, and Military Commanders.   1 25   *Geo. G. Evans.*

—— " Parisian Pickings; or, Paris in all States and Stations. 12mo. cl. . . .   1 25   *J. S. Cotton & Co.*

Marian Elwood; or, How Girls Live. By One of Themselves. 12mo. cl. . . . . .   0 75   *E. Dunigan & Bro.*

Marie Lessair; or, the Bullet Girl's Love. 8vo. pap.   0 25   *W. Skelley.*

Marion Leslie; or, the Light at Home. 18mo. cl.   0 45   *Presb. Bd. of Pub.*

Marion's Sundays; or, Stories on the Ten Commandments. By Miss Kitty Neily. 18mo. . . .   0 40   *Carter & Brothers.*

Mark Noble; or, the Button Necklace. 18mo. .   0 30   *W. S. & A. Martien.*

Marryat (Miss), Temper. A Novel. 12mo. . .   1 00   *Dick & Fitzgerald.*

Marsh, G. P., Lectures on the English Language. 8vo.   2 50   *Charles Scribner.*

—— " (Mrs.), Wolfe of the Knoll, and other Poems.   1 00   "

Marshal, T. F., Speeches and Writings of. Edited by W. L. Barre. 8vo.   *Applegate & Co.*

Marshman, J. C., The Life and times of Carey, Marshman, and Ward; embracing the History of the Serampore Mission. 2 vols. 8vo. . . .   5 00   *Sheldon & Co.*

Martha's Hooks and Eyes. 18mo. . .   0 37   *D. Appleton & Co.*

Martin's Natural History. Translated from the Thirty-fifth German Edition. By Sarah A. Myers. 2 vols, 12mo. . . . .   3 00   *Phinney, B. & M.*

Martin, T., Odes (The) of Horace; an English Metrical Translation. Blue and gold. 32mo. . .   0 75   *Ticknor & Fields.*

Martin Rattler; or, a Boy's Adventures in the Forests
of Brazil. By Robert Michael Ballantyne. . 0 75 *T. Nelson & Sons.*
Martineau, James (Rev.), Studies of Christianity; or,
Timely Thoughts for Religious Thinkers. . 1 00 *Am. Unitarian As.*
Martyrs (The). By M. De Chateaubriand. Edited by
O. W. Wight, A. M. 12mo. . . . . 1 25 *Derby & Jackson.*
—— of the Mutiny; or, Trials and Triumphs of
Christians in Hindostan. 16mo. . . . *Presb. Pub. Com.*
Marvelous Adventures and Rare Conceits of Master Tyll
Owlglass. By Kenneth R. M. Mackenzie. . 2 50 *Ticknor & Fields.*
Marvels; or, Facts in a Fairy Form. 18mo. . . 0 25 *J. Challen & Sons.*
Marvin, W., A Treatise on the Law of Wreck and
Salvage. 8vo. . . . . . . 3 00 *Little, Brown & Co.*
Mary Coverley, the Young Dressmaker. 12mo. cl. . 0 75 *J. E. Tilton & Co.*
—— Derwent. By Mrs. Ann S. Stephens. 12mo. cl. 1 25 *Peterson & Bros.*
—— Bunyan, the Dreamer's Blind Daughter. By
Sallie Rochester Ford. 12mo. . . . 1 00 *Sheldon & Co.*
—— Humphreys; or, Light Shining in a Dark Place. 0 20 *Presb. B. of Pub.*
—— Lee. By Kate Livermore. 18mo. . . . 0 63 *D. Appleton & Co.*
—— Staunton; or, the Pupils of Marvel Hall. 12mo. 1 00 "
—— Stuart, Queen of Scots. By Alphonse de
Lamartine. 18mo. . . . . . 0 50 *Sheldon & Co.*
Mason, John, An Inquiry into the Laws which regulate
the Circulation and Distribution of Wealth. . 1 00 *Wiley & Halsted.*
—— W., The Parlor Preacher. 18mo. . . . 0 20 *Presb. B. of Pub.*
Masson, D., British Novelists and their Styles. 12mo. 1 00 *Gould & Lincoln.*
—— " The Life of John Milton. Vol. 1. 8vo. . 2 75 "
Matrimonial Brokerage in the Metropolis. By a Reporter
of the New York Press. 12mo. cl. . . 1 00 *Thatcher & H.*
Matt Peel's Banjo; being a Collection of the most Popular
and Laughable Negro Melodies. . . . 0 12 *R. De Witt.*
Matthew Caraby, A Narrative of his Adventures in Coun-
try and in Town. By Benaulay. 12mo. . . 1 25 *Mason Brothers.*
Matthews, H. E., Plymouth Sabbath School Collection of
Hymns and Tunes. . . . . . 0 25 *Barnes & Burr.*
Maud: a Story for Girls. Written and Illustrated by
Cousin Fannie. 12mo. . . . . . 0 75 *A. K. Loring.*
Maurice, J., K. N. Pepper and other Condiments, put up
for general use. 12mo. cl. . . . . 1 00 *Rudd & Carleton.*
Maury, M. F., Explanations and Sailing Directions to
accompany the Wind and Current Charts.
Vol. XI. 4to. . . . . . . *Washington, D. C.*
Maxwell, W. H., Stories of Waterloo. 8vo. paper. . 0 50 *Peterson & Broth's.*
May, E. J., Bertrand Noel; a Story for Youth. 12mo. . 0 75 *D. Appleton & Co.*

7

May, S., Christmas Fairies. 16mo. . . . . *Geo. Pattison & Co.*

May Coverley, the Young Dressmaker. 16mo. . . 0 75 *J. E. Tilton & Co.*

May I Believe; or the Warrant of Faith. By the Rev.
Alfred Hamilton, D.D. 18mo. . . . *Pres. Board of Pub.*

Mayfield, M., Progression; or, the South Defended. . *Applegate & Co.*

Mayhew, E., The Illustrated Horse Doctor. 8vo. . . 2 50 *D. Appleton & Co.*

Mayo, A. D., Symbols of the Capital; or, Civilization in
New York. 12mo. . . . . . . 1 00 *Thatcher & H.*

McCall, H. S., Precedents or Practical Forms in Actions
at Law in the Supreme Court of the State of
New York, the Superior Court and Court of
Common Pleas for the City of New York.
Adapted to the Code and Rules of 1828. And
the Practice of States having a Similar Code.
Second Edition, Enlarged and Improved. 8vo. 3 00 *Banks & Brothers.*

McCalla, M., Why was I left; or, He hath done All
Things Well. 18mo. . . . . . 0 25 *Pres. Board of Pub.*

McClelland, A., A Brief Treatise on the Canon and Interpretation of the Holy Scriptures. 12mo. . 0 75 *Carter & Brothers.*

McClintock, Captain, The Voyage of the "Fox" in the
Arctic Seas. 12mo. . . . . . 1 50 *Tickner & Fields.*

McCord, W. J., Lot's Wife; a Warning against Bad Ex-
amples. 18mo. . . . . . . 0 20 *Pres. Board of Pub.*

McCormick, R. C., St. Paul's to St. Sophia; or Sketchings
in Europe. 12mo. . . . . . . 1 00 *Sheldon & Co.*

McCosh, J., The Institutions of the Mind inductively
investigated. 8vo. . . . . . . 2 00 *Carter & Brothers.*

McDonald, D., Treatise for Justices and Constables in
Indiana. 8vo. Law sheep. . . . . 4 50 *Robt. Clarke & Co.*

McIntosh, Maria J., Meta Gray; or, What Makes Home
Happy. 12mo. . . . . . 0 75 *D. Appleton & Co.*

——— " A Year with Maggie and Emma; a
True Story. Edited by Maria J. McIntosh. . 0 63 "

McKeever, Harriet B., Edith's Ministry. 12mo. . . 1 00 *Lindsay & B.*

——— " Sunshine; or, Kate Vinton. 16mo. 0 75 "

——— " The Way to the Pit. 16mo. ol. . 0 45 *Henry Hoyt.*

McSherry, J., Father Laval; or, The Jesuit Missionary;
a Tale of the North American Indians. 18mo. *John Murphy & Co.*

Meat Eaters; With Some Account of their Haunts and
Habits. 12mo. cl. . . . . . 1 00 *Am. S. S. Union.*

Mechanics' (The) and Builders' Price Book. To which is
added a Dictionary of Mechanical Terms; also,
a Treatise on Architecture. By J. Wilson. . 1 00 *D. Appleton & Co.*

Meggie of "The Pines." By Aunt Friendly. 18mo. cl. 0 50 *A. D. F. Randolph.*

Meigs, Mary N., Cousin Bertha's Stories. 16mo. cl.   . 0 50   *A.D.F. Randolph.*
—— " Our Summer at Sunny Brook, and the Boys
  and Girls There. 16mo.   .   .   .   .   . 0 60   "
Melodies of Childhood. 12mo. cl.   .   .   .   . 0 75   *Stanford & Delisser.*
Melville, G. J. W., Holmby House; A Tale of Old North-
  amptonshire. No. 2, 8vo. paper   .   .   . 0 50   *Tickner & Fields.*
—— The Interpreter; a Tale of the War. 8vo. paper. 0 50   *Stanford & Delisser.*
Memoir of the Pilgrimage to Virginia of the Knights
  Templars of Massachusetts and Rhode Island,
  May, 1859. Published by authority of the "De
  Molay Encampment." 12mo.   .   .   .   *A. Williams & Co.*
Memoirs of my Life Work. The Autobiography of Mrs.
  Harriet B. Cooke. 12mo. cl.   .   .   . 1 00   *Carter & Brothers.*
Memoranda Medica; or, Note-book of Medical Princi-
  ples. By Henry Hartshorne, M. D.   .   . 1 00   *Lippincott & Co.*
Memorial (A) of the Dedication of Monuments erected by
  the Moravian Historical Society, to mark the
  sites of ancient missionary stations in New
  York and Connecticut. 8vo.   .   .   .   . 1 25   *C. B. Richardson.*
Men of the Olden Time. By Rev. Charles A. Smith. . 0 75   *Lindsay & B.*
—— Who Have Risen, a book for Boys. 18mo. cl. . . 0 75   *Townsend & Co.*
Mento-Theology, The New Science; or, Mento-Theology.
  The Parables for Clergy, but Intelligence for the
  People. By Sciencia. 12mo.   .   .   .   . 1 00   *James Miller.*
Mercein, T. F. R., Childhood and the Church. 16mo. 0 80   *A D. F. Randolph.*
Meredith, G., Evan Harrington; or, He Would be a Gen-
  tleman. 12mo.   .   .   .   .   .   . 1 00   *Harper & Brothers*
—— O., Lucille. 32mo. Blue and gold.   .   . 0 75   *Tickner & Fields.*
Meroke; or, Missionary Life in Africa. 18mo.   .   . 0 45   *Am. S. S. Union.*
Messianic Prophecy, and the Life of Christ. By William
  S. Kennedy. 12mo.   .   .   .   .   . 1 00   *Barnes & Burr.*
Meta Gray; or, What makes Home Happy. By M. J.
  McIntosh. 12mo.   .   .   .   .   .   . 0 75   *D. Appleton & Co.*
Metcalf, D. (Rev.), An Inquiry into the Nature, Founda-
  tion, and Extent of Moral Obligation. 12mo.   *Crosby, N., L. & Co.*
Methodism Successful; and the Internal Causes of its
  Success. By the Rev. B. F. Tefft. 12mo.   cl. 1 25   *Derby & Jackson.*
Mexican's Bride (The); or, the Ranger's Revenge. By
  William Linn Tidball. Paper, 8vo.   .   .   25   *W. Skelley.*
Michelet, M. J., Love ("L'Amour"). From the French.
  By J. W. Palmer, M. D. 12mo. .   . 1 00   *Rudd & Carleton.*
—— " Woman (La Femme). From the French.
  By J. W. Palmer, M.D.   .   .   . 1 00   "
Michener, E. (M. D.), A Retrospect of Early Quakerism.
  12mo. cloth.   .   .   .   . 1 50   *T. E. Zell.*

Microscopist's Companion (The). By John King. 8vo. 1 50 *Robt. Clarke & Co.*

Mid-Day Thoughts for the Weary. 32mo. . . . *Jas. Munroe & Co.*

Middleton, E., Sappho: a Tragedy in Five Acts. After
    the German of Franz Grillparzer. 8vo. . . 2 00 *D. Appleton & Co.*

—— H. W., The Truth Unmasked, and Error Exposed,
    in Theology and Metaphysics, Moral Govern-
    ment, and Moral Agency. 12mo. . . . *Lippincott & Co.*

Midgley, R. L., Boston Sights; or Hand-Book for Visit-
    ors. 18mo. . . . . 0 50 *Jas. Munroe & Co.*

Midnight, and other Poems. 16mo. . . . . 0 50 *T. J. Crowen.*

Miggie of the Pines. By Aunt Friendly. 18mo. . 0 85 *A. D. F. Randolph.*

Milburn, W. H. (Rev.), Ten Years of Preacher-Life; or,
    Chapters from an Autobiography. 12mo. 1 00 *Derby & Jackson.*

—— " The Pioneers, Preachers, and People of
    the Mississippi Valley. 12mo. . . . 1 25 "

Miles Lawson; or the Yews. 18mo. cloth. . . 0 80 *Henry Hoyt.*

Mill (The) on the Floss. By George Eliot. 12mo. . 1 00 *Harper & Bros.*

Millard, H. B., A Monograph upon Aconite. Translated
    from the German of Dr. Reil, by Henry B. Mil-
    lard, M. D., A. M. 8vo. . . . . 0 75 *William Radde.*

Millen, J. M., Digest of the Decisions of the Supreme
    Court of Georgia, from vol. 10 to 20 inclusive. 6 00 *J. M. Cooper & Co.*

Millennial Experience; or, God's Will Known and Done.
    By Rev. Almon Underwood. 12mo. . . 1 00 *Henry Hoyt.*

Miller, G. B. (Rev.), Sermons on Some of the Fundamen-
    tal Principles of the Gospel. 12mo. . . 1 25 *N. Tibbals & Co.*

—— Hugh, the Cruise of the Betsey; or a Summer
    Ramble among the Fossiliferous Deposits
    of the Hebrides, with Rambles of a
    Geologist. 18mo. . . . . . 1 25 *Gould & Lincoln.*

—— " The Life and Times of. By Thomas N.
    Brown. 12mo. . . . . . . 1 00 *Rudd & Carleton.*

—— " The Old Red Sandstone; or, New Walks
    in an Old Field. A new, improved, and
    enlarged edition. 12mo. . . . . 1 00 *Gould & Lincoln.*

—— " Sketch Book of Popular Geology. 12mo. 1 25 "

—— J., Alcohol; its Place and Power. 16mo. . 0 50 *Lindsay & B.*

—— S. F., Wilkins Wylder; or, the Successful Man. *Lippincott & Co.*

—— New York as It Is; or, Stranger's Guide-Book
    to the Cities of New York, Brooklyn, and ad-
    jacent Places. 18mo. . . . . . 0 50 *James Miller.*

Milman, H. H. (D. D.), History of Latin Christianity, in-
    cluding that of the Popes to the Pontificate of
    Nicholas V. 8 vols. 12mo. . . . . 12 00 *Sheldon & Co.*

Milton, John, The Life of. By Professor Masson. With
    an Estimate of his Genius and Character. By
    Lord Macaulay. 18mo. . . .. . . 0 50   *Sheldon & Co.*
Mine (The); or Darkness and Light. By A. L. O. E. 0 40   *Carter & Brothers.*
Minister's (The) Wooing. By Harriet Beecher Stowe. 1 25   *Derby & Jackson.*
Ministerial (The) Legacy. By a Lady. 12mo. . . 0 75   *Darrow & Brother.*
Ministering Children: a Tale dedicated to Childhood. 1 00   *Carter & Brother.*
Ministry of Life. By Maria Louisa Charlesworth. 12mo. · 1 00   *D. Appleton & Co.*
Minnesota, from the Earliest French Explorations to the
    Present Time. By Rev. Edward Duffield Neill. 2 00   *Lippincott & Co.*
Minnie Wingfield and Polly Bright; or Wings and
    Stings. By A. L. O. E. 18mo. . . 0 25   *Carlton & Porter.*
Minster, A. M., Glenalvan; or, Morning Draweth Nigh. 1 00   *A. B. Burdick.*
Minturn, R. B., From New York to Delhi, by way of Rio
    de Janeiro, Australia and China. 12mo. . . 1 25   *D. Appleton & Co.*
Mispah; Prayer and Friendship. By Lafayette C.
    Loomis. 12mo. . . . . . . 1 25   *Lippincott & Co.*
Miss Gilbert's Career; An American Story. By Dr. J.
    G. Holland. 12mo. . . . . 1 25   *C. Scribner.*
—— Slimmens' Widow, and other Papers. By Mrs.
    Mark Peabody. 12mo. cl. . . . . 1 00   *Derby & Jackson.*
Missing Link (The); or, Bible-Women in the Homes of
    the London Poor. By L. N. R. 12mo. . . 0 75   *Carter & Brothers*
Missionary (A) among Cannibals; or the Life of John
    Hunt, who was eminently Successful in Con-
    verting the People of Fiji from Cannibalism
    to Christianity. By George Stringer Rowe. 0 65   *Carlton & Porter.*
—— (The) Prince. The Brothers. A Wayside
    Lesson. 18mo. . . . . 0 80   *F. D. Harriman.*
—— " Sisters; a Memorial of Mrs. Seraphina
    Haynes Everett, and Mrs. Harriet Martha
    Hamlin. By Mrs. M. G. Benjamin. . 0 75   *Am. Tract. So.*
—— " in many Lands; A Series of Interest-
    ing Sketches of Missionary Life. By Erwin
    House. 12mo. . . . . . . 0 80   *Carlton & Porter.*
Mississippi Bubble (The); A Memoir of John Law. By
    Adolphe Thiers. 12mo. . . . . 1 00   *Townsend & Co.*
Mitchel, O. M., Popular Astronomy. 12mo. . . 1 25   *Phinney, B. & M.*
Mitchell, J. K. (M. D.), Five Essays. Edited by S. Weir
    Mitchell (M. D.) 12mos . . . . 1 25   *Lippincott & Co.*
—— J. W. S., The History of Freemasonry and Mason-
    ic Digests: embracing an Account of the Order
    from the building of Solomon's Temple; its
    Progress thence throughout the Civilized World   *[Ga.*
    to 1858. 2 vols. 8vo. . . . . 6 00   *Author, Marietta,*

Mitchell, S. (Rev.), The Church, its Constitution and
　　　Government. 18mo. . . . . . 0 25　*Presb. Bd. of Pub.*

—— S. A., An Ancient Geography, Classical and
　　　Sacred. 12mo. . . . . . 1 00　*E. H. Butler & Co.*

—— " First Lessons in Geography for Young
　　　Children. Square 16mo. . . 0 25　　"

—— " New Intermediate Geography. . . . 1 12　　"

—— " New Primary Geography. . . . C 50　　"

Mock Auction (The), Ossawattomie Sold. A Mock
　　　Heroic Poem. 12mo., cloth. . . . 0 75　*J. W. Randolph.*

Modern Fancies and Follies. By Le Roy Pope. . 1 00　*Applegate & Co.*

—— Philology; its Discoveries, History, and Influence.
　　　By Benjamin W. Dwight. 8vo. . . . 1 75　*Barnes & Burr.*

Modesty and Merit; or, The Graybird's Story of Little
　　　May, Rose, and John. . . . . 0 75　*Walker, Wise & Co.*

Mohicans (The) of Paris. By Alexander Dumas. . . 0 50　*Peterson & Bros.*

Money King (The), and other Poems. By John G. Saxe. 0 75　*Ticknor & Fields.*

—— or, the Ainsworths. A Prize Book. By the
　　　author of "Day Dreams," &c. 16mo. . . 0 60　*Presb. Pub. Com.*

Monod, A. (D. D.), Saint Paul; Discourses. Translated
　　　from the French, by Rev. J. H. Myers, D. D. . 1 25　*W. F. Draper.*

—— A., Woman: Her Mission and Life. 16mo. . . 0 50　*Sheldon & Co.*

Monro, E. A. (Rev.), The Dark Mountains. An Allegory. 0 35　*H. Hooker.*

—— " The Dark River; an Allegory. 18mo. . 0 35　　"

—— " The Journey Home, an Allegory. 18mo., cl. 0 50　　"

Monroe, J., Science and Art of Chess. 12mo. . . 1 00　*Charles Scribner.*

Montaigne, M., Works of, comprising his Essays, Journey
　　　into Italy, and Letters. With notes from all the
　　　Commentators, Biographical and Bibliographical
　　　Notices. By W. Hazlitt. Edited by O. W.
　　　Wight. 4 vols. 12mo. . . . . 5 00　*Derby & Jackson.*

Monteith, A. H., French, German, Spanish, Latin and
　　　Italian Languages, without a Master. 12mo., cl. 1 25　*Peterson & Bros.*

—— J., Youth's History of the United States. . . 0 50　*Barnes & Burr.*

Montez, Lola, Anecdotes of Love. 12mo. . . . 1 00　*Dick & Fitzgerald.*

—— " The Arts of Beauty; or, Secrets of a
　　　Lady's Toilet. 16mo., cl. . . . 0 50　　"

—— " The Lectures of. With a full and com-
　　　plete Autobiography. 12mo. . . . 1 25　*Peterson & Bros.*

Moon Hoax (The): or, a Discovery that the Moon has a
　　　Vast Population of Human Beings. By Richard
　　　Adams Locke. 8vo. paper. . . . . 0 50　*William Gowans.*

Moorcroft Hatch; or, Darkness and Light. By A. L. O. E. 0 40　*Henry Hoyt.*

Moore, Augusta, Notes from Plymouth Pulpit. With a
　　　Sketch of Henry Ward Beecher. 12mo. . 1 00　*Derby & Jackson.*

Moore, Frank, Diary of the American Revolution. 2 vols.   5 00   *Charles Scribner.*
——— Franklin (Rev.), Descriptive and Didactic Sermons
    of the Seasons. 16mo. . . . . .   0 60   *Perkinpine & H.*
——— H. J. (Mrs.), Wild Nell: the White Mountain Girl.   1 00   *Sheldon & Co.*
——— N. F., Ancient Mineralogy; or, an Inquiry respect-
    ing Mineral Substances, mentioned by the An-
    cients. A New and Revised Edition. 16mo. .   0 75   *Harper & Bros.*
——— T. V. (D. D.), The Last Days of Jesus; or, the
    Appearance of our Lord during the Forty Days
    between the Resurrection and Ascension. 12mo.   *Presb. Bd. of Pub.*
Moorman, J. J. (M. D.), The Virginia Springs, and Springs
    of the South and West. 12mo. . . .   1 25   *Lippincott & Co.*
Moral History of Women. From the French of Ernest
    Legouvé. Translated by J. W. Palmer, M. D. .   1 00   *Rudd & Carleton.*
——— Emblems and Aphorisms, Adages and Proverbs, of
    all Ages and Nations, from Jacob Catz and Rob-
    ert Farlie. With Illustrations freely rendered,
    from designs found in their works, by John
    Leighton, F. S. A. Translated and edited, with
    additions, by Richard Pigot. 4to. . . .   7 50   *D. Appleton & Co.*
——— and Religious Quotations from the Poets. Com-
    piled by Rev. William Rice, A. M. 8vo. . .   1 50   *Carlton & Porter.*
Moravian Life; or, an English Girl's account of a Mora-
    vian Settlement in the Black Forest. 12mo. cl.   0 75   *D. Dana, Jr.*
More about Jesus. By the author of "Peep of Day,"
    etc. 18mo. . . . .   0 63   *Harper & Bros.*
Morel: a Compendium of Human Histiology. Trans-
    lated and edited with copious Notes. By Dr.
    W. H. Van Buren. Illustrated. 8vo. . .   3 00   *Baillière Bros.*
Morford, H., Rhymes of Twenty Years. 12mo. . .   1 00   *H. Dexter & Co.*
Mordecai, S., Virginia, especially Richmond, in By-Gone
    Days; with a Glance at the Present; being
    Reminiscences and Last Words of an Old Citi-
    zen. By Samuel Mordecai. Second edition,
    with many corrections and additions. 12mo. .   *West & Johnston.*
More, M., Mendip Annals; or, a Narrative of Charitable
    Labors of Hannah and Martha Moore in their
    Neighborhood. 16mo. . . . . .   0 60   *Carter & Brothers.*
Morgan, R. W. (Rev.), Christianity and Modern Infidel-
    ity, their relative intellectual claims compared.   1 25   *Daniel Dana, Jr.*
——— S., Passages from My Autobiography. By Syd-
    ney, Lady Morgan. 12mo. . . . .   1 00   *D. Appleton & Co.*

Morin, A., Fundamental Ideas of Mechanics, and Experimental Data. Revised, translated, and reduced to English Units of Measure. By Joseph Bennett, Civil Engineer. 8vo. . . . . . 8 00   *D. Appleton & Co.*

Morison, J. H. (Rev.), Disquisitions and Notes on the Gospels—Matthew. 12mo. . . . 1 25   *Walker, W. & Co.*

Morland, W. W. (M. D.), Diseases of the Urinary Organs. A Compendium of their Diagnosis, Pathology, and Treatment. 8vo. . . . . 3 50   *Blanchard & Lea.*

Mormoniad. A National Epic. 12mo. cl. . . . 0 63   *A. Williams & Co.*

Morning Hours in Patmos. By A. C. Thompson. 12mo. 1 00   *Gould & Lincoln.*

—— Star (The); History of the Children's Missionary Vessel, and of the Marquesan and Micronesian Missions. By Mrs. Jane S. Warren. 18mo. 0 60   *Am. Tract Society.*

—— Watches (The). By the author of "The Night Watches," &c. 32mo. cl. . . . 0 20   *F. D. Harrriman.*

—— and Evening Hymns for a Week. By a Lady. 0 25   "   "

Morphy's Games; a Selection of the Best Games played by, in Europe and America, with Analytical and Critical Notes, by J. Lowenthal. 12mo. . 1 25   *D. Appleton & Co.*

Morphy Game of Chess, and Frere's Problem Tournament. By Thomas Frere. 18mo. cl. . 0 50   *T. W. Strong.*

—— Match Games. Being a Full and Accurate Account of his Successes Abroad. 18mo. . . 0 38   *Robert M. De Witt.*

Morris, C. (M. D.), An Essay on the Pathology and Therapeutics of Scarlet Fever. 8vo. cl.   1 25   *Lindsay & B.*

—— George P., Poems of; with a Memoir of the Author. 18mo. Blue and Gold. . . 0 80   *Charles Scribner.*

—— J. G. (D. D.), Quaint Sayings and Doings concerning Luther. 12mo. . . . 0 75   *Lindsay & B.*

—— R., Courtship and Matrimony; with other Sketches. 12mo. . . . . 1 25   *Peterson & Bros.*

Mortimer, C. B., Bethlehem and Bethlehem School. 0 63   *Stanford & D.*

Mosaics. By the author of "Salad for the Solitary," &c. 1 25   *Charles Scribner.*

Mother Goose for Grown Folks. A Christmas Reading. Illustrated by Billings. 12mo. cl. . . 0 75   *Rudd & Carleton.*

Mother's (A) Gift to her Little Ones at Home. . 0 40   *Carlton & Porter.*

—— " Prayers Answered. 18mo. cl. . . 0 30   *Presb. Bd. of Pub.*

—— " Trials. By the author of "My Lady." . 1 00   *Harper & Bros.*

—— (The) Dream, and other Poems. By Enrica.   *Lippincott & Co.*

—— Mission (The). Sketches from Real Life. By the author of "The Object of Life." 16mo. . 0 75   *Henry Hoyt.*

Motherless Children. By Mrs. Madeline Leslie. 12mo. cl. 0 75   *Shepard, Clark & B.*

Mothers (The) of the Bible. B~ Mrs. S. G. Ashton ; with
    an Introductory Essay, by Rev. A. L. Stone. . .   *J. E. Tilton & Co.*
Motherwell, William, The Poetical Works of. With a
    Memoir of his Life. Fourth edition, greatly
    enlarged. 32mo. Blue and Gold. .   .   . . 0 75   *Ticknor & Fields.*
Moulton, Louise C., My Third Book. A Collection of
    Tales. . 12mo. . . .   . 1 00   *Harper & Brothers.*
Mount Vernon. A Letter to the Children of America.
    By the author of " Rural Hours." 16mo.   : 0 50   *D. Appleton & Co.*
—————— Vernon Papers. By Edward Everett. 12mo. cl. 1 25   "
——————   "   and its Associations, Historical, Biograph-
    ical, and Pictorial. By Benson J. Lossing. 3 50   *Townsend & Co.*
——————   "   and Other Poems. By B. H. Rice.   . 0 75   *J. P. Jewett & Co.*
Mountain (The). By R. M. S. Jackson, M. D., corre-
    sponding member of the Academy of Natural
    Sciences, of Philadelphia, &c. 12mo. .   . 1 50   *Lippincott & Co.*
Mr. Sponge's Sporting Tour. By the author of " Ask
    Mamma," &c. Edited by the late Frank For-
    ester. 8vo. Paper.   . . .   . 0 75   *Townsend & Co.*
Mrs. Cooper's Story ; or, the Golden Mushroom. 18mo. 0 40   *Am. S. S. Union.*
Muirhead, J. P., The Life of James Watt, with Selec-
    tions from his Correspondence. 12mo. .   . 1 25   *D. Appleton & Co.*
Mullaly, J., The Laying of the Cable ; or, the Ocean
    Telegraph ; a Narrative of the Attempt to lay
    the Cable across the entrance to the Gulf of St.
    Lawrence in 1855. 8vo. Paper.   .   .   . 0 50   "
Muloch (Miss), Studies from Life. 12mo., cl.   .   . 0 75   *Harper & Bros.*
——————   "   A Woman's Thoughts about Women.   . 1 00   *Rudd & Carleton.*
Municipalists (The). In two parts ; the National Govern-
    ment and the State Government of New York. 1 00   *Geo. Savage.*
Munsell, Joel, The Every-Day Book of History and Chro-
    nology. 8vo.   .   .   . . 3 50   *D. Appleton & Co.*
——————   "   Guide to the Hudson River by Railroad and
    Steamboat. 18mo. .   .   .   .   .   . 0 25   *Munsell & R.*
Murdoch, David (Rev.), The Dutch Dominie of the Cats-
    kills of the Times of the " Bloody Brandt."   . 1 25   *Derby & Jackson.*
Murdock, J. (D. D.), The New Testament ; or, the Book
    of the Holy Gospel. 8vo.   .   .   .   : 2 00   *Carter & Brothers.*
Murray, G., Aunt Gracie's Library for Little Folks who
    want to be Good. 10 vols., 32mo. In case. . 1 00   *Carlton & Porter.*
—————— N. (D. D.), Preachers and Preaching. 12mo. . . 0 75   *Harper & Bros.*
Musteo (The) ; or, Love and Liberty. By B. F. Pres-
    bury. 12mo. cl.   .   . .   .   .   . 1 25   *Shepard, C. & B.*
My Bootmaker and I on Modes of Baptism. By an Old
    Student. 12mo., cl.   .   . .   .   . . 0 40   *D. Dana, Jr.*

My Early Days. By Eliza W. Farnham. 12mo. . 1 25 *Burt, H. & A.*
—— Holiday Gift: a Book of Poems, Stories, and
    Sketches, for Boys and Girls. 16mo. . . 0 75 *Carlton & Porter.*
—— Journey Thither, and What I Saw There. 12mo. 1 00 *V. Nicholson.*
—— Lady Ludlow: a Novel. By Mrs. Gaskell. 8vo. 0 12 *Harper & Bros.*
—— Little Neigbbors. 18mo. . . . . 0 50 *Walker, Wise & Co.*
—— Lost Home, and other Tales. 8vo., pap. . . 0 50 *F. A. Brady.*
—— Novel. By Sir Edward Lytton Bulwer. 4 vols. . 4 00 *Lippincott & Co.*
—— Ride to the Barbecue; or, Revolutionary Remin-
    iscences of the Old Dominion. 12mo., pap. . 0 25 *S. A. Rollo.*
—— Saviour; or, Devotional Meditations in Prose
    and Verse. By the Rev. John East, A. M. .   *Brooks & Brother.*
—— Third Book. A Collection of Tales by Louise
    Chandler Moulton. 12mo. . . . . 1 00 *Harper & Bros.*
—— Thirty Years out of the Senate. By Major Jack
    Downing. (Seba Smith, Esq.) 12mo., cl. . 1 25 *Oaksmith & Co.*
Myers, Sarah A., Aunt Carrie's Budget; or, Fireside
    Stories. 18mo., cl. . . . . . . 0 35 *Pres. Bd. of Pub.*
Mylne, G. W., Intercessory Prayer, its Duties and Effects. 0 30 *E. P. Dutton & Co.*
Mysteries (The) of Human Nature, Explained. By J.
    Stanley Grimes. New edition. 12mo. . .   *Jas. Monroe & Co.*
Mystic Hours; or, Spiritual Experiences. By G. A.
    Redman, M. D. 12mo. . . . . . 1 25 *Chas. Partridge.*

N

Nack J., The Romance of the Ring, and Other Poems. 1 00 *Delisser & Procter.*
Nall, J., The Widow's Sixpence; or, Go Thou and Do
    likewise. 18mo. . . . . . .   *Pres. B. of Pub.*
Napoleon III. in Italy. And other Poems. By Eliza-
    beth Barrett Browning. 16mo. . . . 0 50 *C. S. Francis & Co.*
Napoleon III., The Man of Prophecy; or, the Revival of
    the French Emperorship anticipated from the
    Necessity of Prophecy. By G. S. Faber, B. D. 0 87 *D. Appleton & Co.*
Napoleonic Ideas, Des Idées Napoleoniennes, par le
    Prince Napoleon Louis Bonaparte. Brussels,
    1839. Translated by James A. Dorr. 12mo. . 0 50   "
Narrative (A) of the Causes which led to Philip's Indian
    War, of 1675 and 1676, by John Easton. . . 5 00 *J. Munsell.*

Nash, S., Digest of the first twenty volumes of the Ohio
    Reports. 8vo., law shp.   .   .   .   .   4 50   *R. Clarke & Co.*
———— " Morality and the State. 12mo.   .   .   1 25   *F., Foster & Co.*
———— " Pleading and Practice under the Civil Code of
    Ohio. 8vo., law shp.   .   .   .   .   5 00   *R. Clarke & Co.*
National Book-keeper. By H. B. Bryant, H. D. Stratton,
    and S. S. Packard. 8vo.   .   .   .   1 75   *Ivison, P. & Co.*
———— Orator. By Charles Northend, A. M. 12mo. .   0 75   *Barnes & Burr.*
Natural History of the Human Temperament. By W. B.
    Powell. 8vo.   .   .   .   .   .   1 50   *R. Clarke & Co.*
Nature's School; or, Lessons from the Garden and the
    Field. 12mo.   .   .   .   .   0 75   *Am. S. S. Union.*
Neal, E. (M. D.), Diet for the Sick and Convales-
    cent. 12mo.   .   .   .   .   0 50   *J. Challen & Son.*
——— J., True Womanhood. A Tale. 12mo.   .   .   1 25   *Ticknor & Fields.*
Neale, E. (Rev.), Shadows and Sunshine, as Illustrated
    in the History of Notable Characters. 18mo.   0 50   *M. W. Dodd.*
Neill, E. D. (Rev.), History of Minnesota. 8vo. .   2 00   *Lippincott & Co.*
Neily, K. Marion's Sundays; or, Stories on the Ten
    Commandments. 18mo.   .   .   0 40   *Carter & Brothers.*
Nelly and her Boat. By Josephine Franklin. 16mo., cl.   0 30   "
——— and her Friends. By the same author. 18mo., cl.   0 50   *Brown & Taggard.*
Nelly's First School Days. By the same author.   . 0 50   "
Neligan, Wm. H. (Rev.), Rome: Its Churches, its Chari-
    ties, and its Schools. 12mo.   .   .   1 00   *Dunigan & Bro.*
———— " Saintly Characters recently Presented for
    Canonization. 12mo.   .   .   .   "
Nellie Russell; or, the Little Girl who was easily Fright-
    ened. 18mo.   .   .   .   .   0 21   *Carlton & Porter.*
Nemesis; a Novel. By Marion Harland. 12mo., cl. .   1 25   *Derby & Jackson.*
New American Cylopædia; a Popular Dictionary of
    General Knowledge. Edited by George Rip-
    ley and Charles A. Dana. Now publishing.
    8vo., per volume, cloth,   .   .   .   8 00   *D. Appleton & Co.*
——— Dictionary of Quotations from the Greek, Latin
    and Modern Languages. 12mo.   .   .   1 50   *Lippincott & Co.*
——— Discussion of the Trinity. 16mo.   .   .   0 62   *Walker, Wise & Co.*
——— Fairy Stories for My Grandchildren. By George
    Keil. 18mo.   .   .   .   .   0 50   *D. Appleton & Co.*
——— Glories (The) of the Catholic Church. Translated
    from the Italian. 12mo.   .   .   0 75   *J. Murphy & Co.*
——— Pantheon (The); or, The Age of the Black Paper.   0 25   *S. A. Rollo.*
——— Priest (The) in Conception Bay. A Novel. By the
    Rev. Robert T. S. Lowell. 2vols. 12mo. .   1 75   *Phillips, S. & Co.*

New (The) and the Old; or, California and India in Ro-
mantio Aspects. By J. W. Palmer, M. D. . . 1 25 *Rudd & Carelton.*

New England's Chattels; or, Life in the Northern Poor
House. 12mo. . . . . . . 1 25 *H. Dayton.*

New England during the Stuart Dynasty. By John
Gorham Palfrey. 2 vols. 8vo. . . 4 50 *Little, Brown & Co.*

——— " Theocracy: a History of the Congregation-
alists of New England to the Revivals of 1740.
By H. F. Uhden. 12mo. . . . 1 00 *Gould & Lincoln.*

New York Civil and Criminal Justice: a Treatise
on the Civil, Criminal, and Special Powers
and Duties of Justices of the Peace in the
State of New York, with a numerous and
copious Index. Second edition, revised and
enlarged. 8vo. . . . . . . 5 00 *C. M. Saxton.*

——— Pulpit (The) in the Revival of 1858: A Memorial Volume of Sermons. 12mo. . . . 1 00 *Shelden, B. & Co.*

——— State Business Directory. 8vo. . . . 3 00 *John F. Trow.*

——— (A History of the City of), from its earliest
Settlement to the Present Time. By Mary L.
Booth. 8vo. . . . . . . 3 50 *Clark & Meeker.*

Newcomb, H. (Rev.), Kind Words for Children. 16mo. . 0 42 *Gould & Lincoln.*

——— " " The Harvest and the Reapers; Home
Work for All, and How to Do It. 16mo. . 0 63 " "

Newton, R. (D. D.), Rills from the Fountain of Life; or,
Sermons to Children. 12mo. . 0 75 *Carter & Brothers.*

——— " " The Best Things. 16mo. . . 0 75 " "

——— " " The Giants, and How to Fight Them. 0 50 " "

——— " " The King's Highway; or, Illustrations of the Commandments. . 0 75 " "

——— W. (Rev.), Lectures on the First Two Versions
of the Book of Daniel. 12mo. . . . 0 75 *W. S. & A. Martien.*

Nicaragua: Past, Present, and Future. By Peter F.
Stout. 12mo. . . . . . . 1 25 *J. E. Potter.*

——— (The War in), Written by General Wm. Walker. 1 50 *Goetzel & Co.*

Nichols, G. W. (Rev.), Fragments from the Study of a
Pastor. 12mo. . . . . . . 0 75 *Henry B. Price.*

——— J. (Rev.), Remembered Words from the Sermons
of. 12mo. . . . . . . 0 50 *Crosby, N., L. & Co.*

——— " Hours with the Evangelists. 2 vols. Vol I. "

——— T. L., Father Larkin's Mission in Jonesville. . 0 25 *Kelly, Hedian & P.*

Nicholson, J. B., a Manual of Bookbinding. . . . *Pawson & N.*

Night Caps (The New) told to Charlie. By the author
of " Aunt Fanny's Stories." 18mo. . . . 0 50 *D. Appleton & Co.*

Night Lessons from Scripture. 18mo. . . . . 0 60 *D. Appleton & Co.*
—— Watches (The). By the author of "The Morning
    Watches." 32mo., cloth. . . . . 0 20 *Prot. Ep. Book So.*
Nightingale, Florence, Notes on Nursing. 12mo. . . 0 60 *D. Appleton & Co.*
No Lie Thrives. A Tale. By the author of "Charlie
    Burton," etc. 18mo. . . . . . 0 50 *W.S.& A.Martien.*
Nœggerath, E., Contributions to Midwifery, and Diseases
    of Women and Children, with a Report on the
    Progress of Obstetrics, and Uterine and Infan-
    tile Pathology in 1858. By E. Nœggerath, and
    A. Jacobi. 8vo. . . . . . . 2 50 *Ballière Brothers.*
Noisy Herbert, and other Stories, for small children. . 0 50 *Walker, Wise & Co.*
Northend, C., Entertaining Dialogues. 12mo. h. r. . 0 75 *Barnes & Burr.*
——   " Little Orator. 18mo. Half roan. . . 0 30   "
——   " The National Orator. 12mo. . . . 0 75   "
Northrop, E. L. (Mrs.), Aunt Charity. 16mo. . . 0 75 *F. D. Harriman.*
Norton, C. B., Hand-book to Europe; or, How to Travel
    in the Old World. By J. H. Siddons. 16mo. . 1 00 *Chas. B. Norton.*
—— C. E., Notes of Travel and Study in Italy. . 0 75 *Ticknor & Fields.*
—— J. H., Lectures on the Life of David. 18mo. .   *H. Hooker.*
—— J. N., Life of Bishop Claggett, of Maryland. . 0 30 *F. D. Harriman.*
——   " The Life of Bishop Henshaw, of Rhode
    Island. 18mo. . . . . . . 0 30   "
Notes from Plymouth Pulpit. By Augusta Moore. . 1 00 *Derby & Jackson.*
—— of Travel and Study in Italy. By Charles Eliott
    Norton. 12mo. . . . . . . 0 75 *Ticknor & Fields.*
—— on Nursing. By Florence Nightingale. 12mo. . 0 60 *D. Appleton & Co.*
—— on Prophecy and Difficult Passages of Scripture. .   "
    By Joel Jones, LL. D. 8vo. cl. . . . 2 50 *W.S.& A.Martien.*
Noyce, E., The Boy's Book of Industrial Information. . 1 25 *D. Appleton & Co.*
Nugamenta: a Book of Verse. By George Edward Rice. 0 75 *J. E. Tilton & Co.*

O

O'Callaghan, J., The Holy Bible Authenticated. 12mo. 0 50 *Sadliers & Co.*
—— E. B., Orderly Book of Lieut. Gen. John Bur-
    goyne. Small 4to. . . . . . 3 50 *J. Munsell.*
Ocean Sketches of Burmah. By Mrs. M. B. Ingalls. . 0 55 *Am. Bap. Pub. So.*
Odd People. Being a Popular Description of Singular
    Races of Men. By Captain Mayne Reid. 12mo. 0 50 *Harper & Brothers*
    The same, 16mo. cl. . . . . . 0 75 *Ticknor & Fields.*

Odes and Sonnets, Selected from the Most Eminent
    Authors. Sq. 8vo. extra cloth, gilt $3 50, mor.   5 00   *D. Appleton & Co.*
Odic-Magnetic Letters. By Baron Reichenbach. 12mo.   0 80   *Calvin Blanchard.*
Officer, M. (Rev.), African Bible Pictures. 18mo. .   *Lutheran B. Pub.*
Ogden, E. D., Tariff or Rates of Duties Payable on Goods,
    Wares and Merchandise Imported into the
    United States of America. 8vo. . . . 1 50   *W. H. Arthur & Co.*
—— J., The Science of Education and Art of Teach-
    ing. 12mo. . . . . 1 25   *Moore, W., K. & Co.*
Olcott, H. S., Outlines of the First Course of Yale Agri-
    cultural Lectures. 12mo. . . . . 5 00   *Saxton & Baker.*
Old Battle Ground (The). By J. T. Trowbridge. 18mo.   0 50   *Sheldon & Co.*
—— Cabinet (The). By Helen W. Pierson. 18mo. cl. . 0 50   *Challen & Son.*
—— Farm House (The) By Caroline H. Butler Laing. . 1 00   *G. G. Evans.*
—— Friends with New Faces. By A. L. O. E. 18mo. cl. 0 40   *T. Nelson & Sons.*
—— Leaves; Gathered from Household Words. By W.
    Henry Wills. 12mo. . . . . . 1 00   *Harper & Brothers.*
—— Log Schoolhouse (The). By Alexander Clark. .   *Leary, Getz & Co.*
—— Mackinaw; or, the Fortress of the Lakes and its
    Surroundings. By W. F. Strickland. 12mo. . 1 00   *J. Challen & Son.*
—— New York; or, Reminiscences of the Past Sixty
    Years. By John W. Francis, M. D. 12mo. cl. 1 25   *Charles Roe.*
—— Nurse's Book of Rhymes, Jingles, and Ditties. Edited
    and Illustrated by Charles H. Bennett. 4to. .   *Jas. Monroe & Co.*
—— Plantation (The), and What I Gathered There in an
    Autumn Month. By James Hungerford. 12mo. 1 00   *Harper & Bros.*
—— Red House (The). By the author of "Ellen
    Dacre," &c. 16mo. . . . . . 0 80   *Henry Hoyt.*
—— Robin and His Proverb. By Mrs. Henry F. Brock. 0 40   *Am. Tract So.*
—— South Chapel Prayer Meeting. Its Origin and
    History 12mo. . . . . . . 0 50   *J. E. Tilton & Co.*
—— Red Sand Stone (The); or, New Walks in an Old
    Field. By Hugh Miller. 12mo., cl. . . 1 00   *Gould & Lincoln.*
—— Stone Mansion (The). By Charles J. Peterson. . 1 25   *Peterson & Bros.*
—— Wonder-Eyes, and other Stories for Children. By
    Mr. and Mrs. L. K. Lippincott (Grace Green-
    wood). 16mo. . . . . . . 0 50   *Gaut & Volkmar.*
—— and New. By the Rev. James Craik, D. D. . 0 80   *Daniel Dana, Jr.*
Older than Adam. By the author of "Violet." 16mo. 0 63   *Brown & Taggard.*
Oliphant, L., Narrative of the Earl of Elgin's Mission to
    China and Japan, in the years 1857, '59. 8vo. 2 75   *Harper & Bros.*
—— (Mrs.), Adam Graeme of Mossgray. 12mo. . 1 00   *D. & Fitzgerald.*
—— " Agnes Hopetoun's Schools and Holidays. . 0 63   *Gould & Lincoln.*
Olive Branch (The). A Collection of Sacred Music. By
    T. J. Cook, and T. E. Perkins. 8vo. . . 0 75   *F. J. Huntington.*

Olmsted, D., Rudiments of Natural Philosophy and As-
    tronomy. Revised edition. 18mo. . . 0 56 *Collins & Brother.*
—— F. L., A Journey in the Back Country. 12mo. . 1 25 *Mason Bros.*
—— " Walks and Talks of an American Farmer in
    England. 12mo. . . . . . . 1 25 *J. H. Riley & Co.*
Olshausen, H. (D. D.), Biblical Commentary on the New
    Testament. Continued after his death by Dr.
    John Henry Augustus Ehrard and Lic. Augustus
    Wiesinger. Revised by A. C. Kendrick, D. D.
    6 vols., 8vo., cl. . . . . . . 12 00 *Sheldon & Co.*
One Hundred Songs of Ireland. Music and Words. 8vo. 0 50 *O. Ditson & Co.*
—— and Twenty. By the author of "Wildflower," &c. 0 50 *R. M. De Witt.*
O'Neall, J. B., The Annals of Newberry District. . . 1 25 *Courtenay & Co.*
—— " Biographical Sketches of the Bench and
    Bar of South Carolina. 2 vols., 8vo. . . 5 00   "
O'Neill, J. W., New Standard Letter Writer for the Peo-
    ple. 12mo. . . . . . *Charles Desilver.*
—— " Carpenter's Guide in Stair Building and Hand
    Railing. Folio. . . . . . 2 00 *J. W. Randolph.*
Onesta; or, a Marriage by Will. Translated from the
    French. 8vo. . . . . . . 0 25 *E. D. Long & Co.*
Only a Pauper. By A. S. M. 12mo. . . . 1 00 *Henry Hoyt.*
—— One Way of Salvation. By the Rev. J. C. Ryle. . *Am. Tract Soc.*
Onward; or, the Mountain Clamberers. By Jane Anne
    Winscom. 12mo. . . . . . 0 75 *D. Appleton & Co.*
Opera Dancer; or, the Mysteries of London Life. By
    George W. M. Reynolds. Paper. 8vo. . . 0 50 *Peterson & Bros.*
Opportunity for Industry and the Safe Investment of
    Capital; or, a Thousand Chances to Make Money.
    By a Retired Merchant. 12mo. . . . 1 25 *Lippincott & Co.*
Opposite the Jail. By the author of "Carrie Hamilton,"
    etc. 16mo. cl. . . . . . . 0 75 *Henry Hoyt.*
Optimism: The Lesson of Ages. By B. Blood. 16mo. cl. 0 60 *B. Marsh.*
Orange Plume (The); or, The Bride of the Bastile. 8vo. 0 50 *E. D. Long & Co.*
—— Seed (The). By Aunt Friendly. 18mo. . . 0 25 *A. D. F. Randolph.*
Orchard House (The); or, Culture of Fruit-Trees in Pots
    under Glass. By Thomas Rivers. 8vo. . . 0 40 *Saxton & Barber.*
Orcutt, H., Hints to Common School Teachers, Parents,
    and Pupils. 18mo. . . . . . 0 50 *Brown & Taggard.*
Orderly Book of the Northern Army, at Ticonderoga
    and Mt. Independence, from October 17, 1776,
    to January 8, 1777, with Biographical and Ex-
    planatory Notes and an Appendix. Small 4to. . 5 00 *J. Munsell.*
O'Reilly, John (M. D.), The Anatomy and Physiology of
    the Placenta. . . . . . . *Hall, Clayton & Co.*

Organon (The) of Scripture; or, the Inductive Method of
     Biblical Interpretation. By J. S. Lamar. 12mo.   1 00   *Lippincott & Co.*
Oriental Tales of Fairy Land. 16mo. cl.   .   .   .   0 63   *Stanford&Delisser*
Origin of Species by Means of Natural Selection; or, the
     Preservation of Favored Races in the Struggle
     for Life. By Charles Darwin, M. A. 12mo. .   1 25   *D. Appleton & Co.*
Original Dialogues and Conversations for Children. By
     Mrs. Dewitt. 18mo.   .   .   .   .   0 40   *Robt. Clarke & Co.*
Oriola; a New and Complete Hymn and Tune Book.
     By William B. Bradbury. 16mo.   .   .   .   0 87   *Moore, W., K.& Co.*
Orkney Islands, Excursions to. By Jacob Abbott. 16mo.   0 50   *Sheldon & Co.*
Orleans (Duchess), Memoirs of. By the Marquis de H——.
     Together with Biographical Souvenirs and Ori-
     ginal Letters. Collected by Prof. G. H. DeSchu-
     bert. 12mo.   .   .   .   .   .   .   1 00   *Charles Scribner.*
Ormsby, R. M., A History of the Whig Party. 12mo. .   1 00   *Crosby, N., L,& Co.*
Osborn, H. S. (Rev.), Fruits and Flowers of Palestine. .   8 50   *J. Challen & Son.*
——— "   " Little Pilgrims in the Holy Land. .   0 75   "
Osceola, the Seminole; or, the Red Fawn of the Flower
     Land. By Capt. Mayne Reid. 12mo.   .   .   1 25   *R. M. De Witt.*
Osgood, Frances S. (Mrs.), The Poems of. 32mo. .   .   0 75   *Clark, A., M.& Co.*
——— Samuel, Student Life; Letters and Recollec-
     tions for a Young Friend. 12mo.   .   .   0 75   *James Miller.*
Our Bible Chronology, Historic and Prophetic. By the
     Rev. R. C. Schimeall.   .   .   .   .   2 00   *Barnes & Burr.*
——— Class, and the Good that Came of It. By Miss
     Caroline E. Fairfield. 12mo. cloth.   .   .   1 00   *Derby & Jackson.*
—— Charley, and What to Do with Him. By Mrs. H.
     B. Stowe. 18mo.   .   .   .   .   0 50   *Phillips, S. & Co.*
—— Farm of Four Acres, and the Money We Made
     by It. 16mo. paper, 25c.; cloth,   .   .   0 50   *Saxton & Barker.*
—— Father's House; and Days of my Youth. 18mo .   0 25   *Henry Hoyt.*
—— Little Girls. By the author of "A Little Leaven,
     and What it Wrought." 18mo. cloth.   .   .   0 40   *A. D.F. Randolph.*
—— Little Ones in Heaven. Edited by the author of
     the "Aimwell Stories," etc. 18mo.   .   .   0 50   *Gould & Lincoln.*
—— Living Representative Men. From Official and Ori-
     ginal Sources. By John Savage. 12mo. .   1 25   *Childs & Peterson.*
—— Modern Athens; or, Who is First? A Poem. By
     Anicetus. 12mo.   .   .   .   .   .   0 50   *Redding & Co.*
—— Old Favorites; Songs for the Nursery. 12mo. cl. .   0 50   *D. Appleton & Co.*
——Press Gang; or, An Exposition of the Corruptions and
     Crimes of the American Newspapers. By Lam-
     bert A. Wilmer. 12mo.   .   .   .   .   1 00   *J. T. Lloyd.*

Our Summer House, and What was Said and Done in It. 0 62 *Brown & Taggard.*
——Summer at Sunnybrook, and the Boys and Girls
  There. By Mary Noel Meigs. 16mo. . . 0 60 *A.D.F. Randolph.*
—— Year; a Child's Book, in Prose and Verse. By Miss
  Muloch. 16mo. . . . . . . 0 75 *Harper & Bros.*
Out of the Depths: the Story of a Woman's Life. 12mo. 1 00 *Townsend & Co.*
Outlines of Theology. By the Rev. A. Alex. Hodge. 2 00 *Carter & Brothers.*
Over the Cliffs. By Charlotte Chanter. 12mo. . . 1 00 *Ticknor & Fields.*
Owen, Ashford, A Lost Love. 8vo. paper. . . 0 25 *T. J. Crowen.*
Owen, D. D., First Report of a Geological Reconnoisance
  of the Northern Counties of Arkansas, made
  during the years 1857 and 1858, assisted by Wil-
  liam Elderhorst and Edward T. Cox. 8vo. . 2 00 *John E. Reardon.*
—— G. (Rev.), Materials for Thought. Designed for
  Young Men. 16mo. . . . . . *W.S.&A.Martien.*
—— J. J. (D. D.), A Commentary, Critical, Expository,
  and Practical, on the Gospel of John. 12mo. . 1 00 *Leavitt & Allen.*
—— Robert Dale, Footfalls on the Boundary of Anoth-
  er World. With Narrative Illustrations. 12mo. 1 25 *Lippincott & Co.*

P

Page, T. J., La Plata, the Argentine Confederation, and
  Paraguay. Being a Narrative of the Explora-
  tion.of the Tributaries of the River La Plata
  and Adjacent Countries, during the years 1853,
  '54, '55, and '56. 8vo. . . . . . 3 00 *Harper & Bros.*
Paget, J., Lectures on Surgical Pathology. Second
  American edition. 8vo., sheep. . . . 3 50 *Lindsay & B.*
Paine, Caroline, Tent and Harem: Notes of an Oriental
 . Trip. 12mo. . . . . . . 1 00 *D. Appleton & Co.*
——— Thos., The Philosophy of Creation. 18mo. . 0 25 *B. Marsh.*
Painstaking. By the author of "Edward Clifford." 18mo. 0 25 *A.D.F.Randolph*
Palace (The) of Ice. By Alexander Dumas. 8vo. . 0 50 *E. D. Long & Co.*
——— " of the Great King. By Rev. Hollis Read. 1 25 *Charles Scribner.*
Paleario, A., The Benefit of Christ's Death; or, The
  Glorious Riches of God's Free Grace. 16mo. 0 38 *Gould & Lincoln.*

8

Palestine, Past and Present. By Rev. Henry S. Osborn.	8 50	*J. Challen & Son.*
Paley, W., View of the Evidences of Christianity. 8vo.	1 75	*James Miller.*
Palfrey, J. G., A History of New England during the Stuart Dynasty. 2 vols. 8vo., cloth.	4 50	*Little, Brown & Co.*
Palissy, the Huguenot Potter. A True Tale. By C. L. Brightwell. 16mo.	0 55	*Pres. Bd. of Pub.*
The same. 16mo., cloth.	0 75	*H. Hoyt.*
Palmer, J. W., The New and the Old; or, California and India in Romantic Aspects. 12mo.	1 25	*Budd & Carleton.*
—— " Folk Songs: a Book of Golden Poems made for the Popular Heart. Royal 8vo., mor.	10 00	*Chas. Scribner.*
—— R. (D. D.), Hints on the Formation of Religious Opinions. 12mo.	1 00	*Sheldon & Co.*
Para Papers (The), on France, Egypt, and Ethiopia. By George L. Ditson. 8vo., cloth.	1 25	*Mason Brothers.*
Parables of Our Lord. Folio.	10 00	*Lippincott & Co.*
Pardoe, Julia, A Life Struggle. 12mo.	1 25	*W. I. Pooley & Co.*
—— " The Adopted Heir. 12mo.	1 25	*Peterson Brothers.*
—— " Episodes of French History during the Consulate and the First Empire. 12mo.	1 00	*Harper & Bros.*
Paris with Pen and Pencil; its People and Literature, its Life and Business. By David W. Bartlett.	1 00	*C. M. Saxton.*
Parisian Pickings; or, Paris in all States and Stations. By Julie de Marguerittes. 12mo., cl.	1 25	*J. S. Cotton & Co.*
Park, E. A. (D. D.), The Sabbath Hymn-Book. 16mo.	1 00	*Mason Brothers.*
Parker, J. M., Boy Missionary. 18mo.	0 30	*F. D. Harriman.*
—— R. G., The National Fifth Reader. 12mo.	1 00	*Barnes & Burr.*
Parlor Charades and Proverbs. By S. Annie Frost. 12mo.	0 75	*Lippincott & Co.*
—— Preacher (The); or, Short Addresses to Those who are determined to Win Christ. By W. Mason. 18mo.	0 20	*Pres. Bd. of Pub.*
—— Theatricals; or, Winter Evenings' Entertainment.	0 75	*Dick & Fitzgerald.*
Parrish, E., An Introduction to Practical Pharmacy. Second Edition. 8vo.	3 50	*Blanchard & Lea.*
Parsons, T., The Law of Contracts. Fourth Ed. 2 vols.	11 00	*Little, Brown & Co.*
—— " Laws of Business for Business Men in all the States of the Union. 8vo.	2 50	"
—— " A Treatise on Maritime Law, including the Law of Shipping, the Law of Marine Insurance, and the Law and Practice of Admiralty. By Hon. Theophilus Parsons, LL.D., Dane Professor of Law in Harvard University. 2 vols., 8vo.	11 00	*Little, Brown & Co.*

Parsons, T., Memoir of; with Notices of some of his
    Contemporaries. By his Son, Theophilus
    Parsons. 12mo. .   .   .   .   .   1 50   *Ticknor & Fields.*
Parton, J., Life of Andrew Jackson. 3 vols., 8vo. . 5 00   *Mason Brothers.*
Pascal, Blaire, The Thoughts, Letters, and Opuscules of.
    Translated from the French by O. W. Wight,
    A. M.; with Introductory Notices, and Notes
    from all the Commentators. 12mo. .   .   . 1 25   *Derby & Jackson.*
Pasha Papers (The). Epistles of Mohammed Pasha, Rear
    Admiral of the Turkish Navy. Written from
    New York to his friend Abel Ben Hassan. 12mo. 1 25   *C. Scribner.*
Passing Thoughts on Religion. By the author of "Amy
    Herbert," etc. 16mo. .   .   .   . 0 75   *D. Appleton & Co.*
Path (The) which led a Protestant Lawyer to the Catho-
    lic Church. By Peter H. Burnet. 8vo. .   . 2 50   "
Patient's (The) and Physician's Aid; or, How to Pre-
    serve Health. By E. M. Hunt, M. D. 12mo. . 1 00   *Saxton & Barker.*
Patmore, C., Faithful Forever. 16mo., cl. .   . . 1 00   *Ticknor & Fields.*
Patriot Cruiser (The). By Sylvanus Cobb, jr. Pap. , 0 25   *F. A. Brady.*
———— Preachers of the American Revolution. .   . 1 00   *Osborne & D.*
Pattison, R. E. (D. D.), A Commentary, Explanatory,
    Doctrinal, and Practical, on the Epistle to the
    Ephesians. 12mo. .   : .   .   . 0 85   *Gould & Lincoln.*
Patton, A. S., The Losing and Taking of Mansoul; or,
    Lectures on the Holy War. 12mo. .   .   . 1 00   *Sheldon & Co.*
Paul Blake; or, a Boy's Perils in the Islands of Corsica
    and Monte Christo. By Alfred Elwes. 16mo. 0 75   *Thomson Brothers.*
———— Winslow; or, Blessings in Disguise. By Helen
    Chapman. 18mo. .   .   .   .   . 0 25   *Presb. Board Pub.*
———— the Preacher. By John Eadie, D.D., LL.D. . . 1 25   *Carter & Brothers.*
———— and Harry Fane; or, the Two Sons. 18mo. . 0 20   *Carlton & Porter.*
Payson's (E.) Works; Being the Memoir, Select Thoughts
    and Sermons of the late Rev. Edward Payson,
    D. D. Compiled by Asa Cummings, D. D. . 3 75   *W. S & A. Martien.*
Peabody, M., Miss Slimmens' Widow and other Papers. . 1 00   *Derby & Jackson.*
———— E. P., Universal History. Arranged to Illustrate
    Bem's Chart of Chronology. .   .   .   . 1 25   *Sheldon & Co.*
Peace in Believing. By Rev. John East. 18mo. .   . 0 50   *Carter & Brothers.*
Pearce, S., Annals of Luzerne County: From the First
    Settlement of Wyoming to 1860. 8vo. .   . 2 50   *Lippincott & Co.*
Pearls for the Little Ones. By Mrs. Mary Jane Phillips. 0 25   *Carlton & Porter.*
———— of Thought, Religious and Philosophical, gathered
    from Old Authors. 32mo. .   .   .   . 0 38   *Stanford & D.*
Peasant Life in Germany. By Mrs. Anna C. Johnson. . 1 25   *Charles Scribner.*

Peck, George (D. D.), Early Methodism within the Bounds
     of the Old Genesee Conference, from 1788
     to 1828. 12mo. . . . . . 1 00   *Carlton & Porter.*
—— " Wyoming; its History, Stirring Incidents,
     and Romantic Adventures. 12mo. . . . 1 25   *Harper & Brothers.*
—— J. T. (D. D.), What Must I Do to Be Saved? . 0 35   *Carlton & Porter.*
—— L. W., The Golden Age. 12mo. . . . 0 60   *E. Goodenough.*
—— W. G., Elements of Mechanics. 12mo. . . 1 25   *Barnes & Burr.*
—— " Introductory Course of Natural Philo-
     sophy. Edited from Ganot's Popular Physics. 1 00   "
Peep of Day. 18mo. cl. . . . . 0 25   *Moore & Nims.*
Pen and Pencil. By Mrs. Balmanno. Illustrated with
     120 engravings, consisting of Portraits, Views,
     and Poetical Subjects. Small 4to., ex. cl. gilt. 5 00   *D. Appleton & Co.*
Pendleton, W. N. (D. D.), Science a Witness for the Bible. 1 00   *Lippincott & Co.*
Percival, James G., The Poetical Works of. With a
     Biographical Sketch. 2 vols. Blue and gold. . 1 75   *Ticknor & Fields.*
Perils of the Deep. 18mo. . . . . . . 0 25   *J. Challen & Sons.*
Perry, J. (Rev.), A Full Course of Instruction for the Use
     of Catechists. 18mo. . . . . . 0 63   *Sadlier & Co.*
Personal Recollections of the American Revolution. A
     Domestic Diary. By Sidney Barclay. 12mo. 1 00   *Rudd & Carleton.*
Perthes, F. C., Caroline Perthes, the Christian Wife.
     Condensed from the Life of Frederick Chris-
     topher Perthes. By Mrs. L. C. Tuthill. 12mo. 1 25   *Carter & Brothers.*
Peter the Great, History of. By Jacob Abbott. 16mo. 0 60   *Harper & Bros.*
—— " Life of. Compiled from Schlosson,
     Vulehofs; Bruce, Segur, Voltaire, Staehlin,
     Peiz, Von Halem, Sevesque, &c. 2 vols. 18mo. 1 00   *Sheldon & Co.*
Peterchen and Gretchen; or Tales of Early Childhood. . 0 75   *A. D. F. Randolph*
Peterson, C. J., The Old Stone Mansion. 12mo. cl. . 1 25   *Peterson & Bros.*
Petty Annoyances (The) of Married Life. From the
     French of Honoré de Balzac. Translated by O.
     W. Wight and F. B. Goodrich. 12mo. . 1 00   *Rudd & Carleton.*
Phelps, A., The Still Hour; or, Communion with God. . 0 88   *Gould & Lincoln.*
—— Anson G., A Memorial of. By Professor H. B.
     Smith, D. D. 12mo. . . . . . 0 75   *Charles Scribner.*
—— L. (Mrs.), Hours with my Pupils; or, Educational
     Addresses, &c. 12mo. . . . . . 1 00   "
—— R. H., A History of Newgate of Connecticut, at
     Simsbury. Small 4to. . . . . . 1 25   *J. Munsell.*
Philip Blandford; or How to Win a Sweetheart. By J.
     F. Smith. 8vo. Paper. . . . . 0 50   *Dick & Fitzgerald.*
Phillipo, J. M., The United States and Cuba. 12mo. . 1 50   *Sheldon & Co.*

Phillips, M. J. (Mrs.), Pearls for the Little Ones. 18mo. 0 25 *Carlton & Porter.*
——— " " Sweet Corabelle, and other Authentic Sketches. 18mo. . . 0 25 "
——— " " Home Pictures for the Little Ones. 0 22 "
——— " " Little Things for Little Folks. . 0 22 "
——— " " The Young Gold Seeker, and other
Authentic Sketches. A book for Youth. 18mo. 0 22 "
Philosophy of Creation. By Thomas Paine. 18mo. . 0 25 *B. Marsh.*
——— (The) of Natural History. By John Ware, M. D. 1 25 *Brown & Taggard.*
Physical and Moral Aspects of Geology. By William J.
Barbee, M. D. 12mo. cl. . . . . . 1 00 *Challen & Son.*
Physician's (A) Counsels to his Professional Brethren.
18mo. . . . . 0 20 *Presb. Bd. of Pub.*
Physiology (The) of Common Life. By George Henry
Lewes. 2 vols. 12mo. . . . . . 2 00 *D. Appleton & Co.*
Piaget, H. F., The Watch; How to Choose and How to
Use. . . . . 0 25 *Author, N. Y.*
Pic-Nic Papers (The). By Charles Dickens, Thomas
Moore, Leitch Ritchie, Horace Smith, W. H. Maxwell, Agnes Strickland, W. H. Ainsworth,
James Erskine Murray, Allen Cunningham, and
other Writers. Paper. 8vo. . . . , 0 50 *Peterson & Bros.*
Pictures from the History of Spain. 16mo. . . . 0 67 *Brown & Taggard.*
——— from the History of the Swiss. 16mo. . . 0 75 "
——— of Country Life. By Alice Carey. 12mo. . 1 00 *Derby & Jackson.*
——— and Flowers for Child Lovers. 16mo. . . 0 50 *Walker, W. & Co.*
Pierre, the Partisan; a Tale of the Mexican Marches.
By Henry William Herbert. Paper. . . 0 25 *F. A. Brady.*
Pierson, Helen W., Edith Vaughan's Victory, or How to
Conquer. 16mo. . . . . . . 0 63 *D. Appleton & Co.*
——— " The Old Cabinet. 18mo. . . . 0 50 *J. Challen & Son.*
Piety and Pride. By E. L. Lewellyn. 16mo. . . 0 65 *Henry Hoyt.*
Pigot, R., Moral Emblems and Aphorisms, Adages, and
Proverbs, of all Ages and Nations, from Jacob
Catz and Robert Farlie. 4to. . . . . 7 50 *D. Appleton & Co.*
Pike, S. (Rev.), Religious Cases of Conscience Answered
in an Evangelical Manner. 12mo. . . . 1 00 *Smith, E. & Co.*
Pilgrim Memorials, and Guide to Plymouth. By Wm.
S. Russell. 12mo. . . . . . . 0 75 *Crosby, N., L. & Co.*
Pillar (The) of Fire; or, Israel in Bondage. By Rev. J.
H. Ingraham. 12mo. . . . . . 1 25 *Pudney & Russell.*
Pinchard, Margaret D., Kate and Effie; or, Prevarication. 18mo. . . . . 0 50 *Carter & Brothers.*
Piney Woods Tavern; or, Sam Slick in Texas. By the
author of "A Stray Yankee in Texas." 12mo. 1 25 *Peterson & Bro.*

Pioneer Preachers (The) and People of the Mississippi
    Valley. By William Henry Milburn. 12mo. . 1 25   *Derby & Jackson.*
Plain Words to Young Men. By A. Woodbury. 12mo. 1 00   *E. C. Eastman.*
Plan of the Creation; or, Other Worlds, and Who Inhabit
    them. By Rev. O. I. Hequembourg. 12mo. . 1 25   *Phillips, S. & Co.*
Plato, The Divine and Moral Works of. Translated
    from the original Greek; with Introductory
    Dissertations and Notes. 12mo. . . . 1 25   *C. Blanchard.*
—— The Gorgias of, chiefly according to Stallbaum's
    Text. With Notes, by Theodore D. Wolsey. . 1 00   *J. Munroe & Co.*
Plato's Apology and Crito. With Notes. By W. S.
    Tyler. 12mo. . . . . 0 75   *D. Appleton & Co.*
Play and Study. By Mrs. Madeline Leslie. 12mo. cl. . 0 75   *Shepard, C. & B.*
Pleasant Paths for Little Feet, a Juvenile. . . .   *E. O. Libby & Co.*
—— Pathways; or Persuasives to Early Piety. By
    Daniel Wise. 16mo. . . . . . 0 60   *Carlton & Porter.*
Pleasures (The) of Piety, and other Poems. By Richard
    Furman. 12mo. . . . . . .   *Courtenay & Co.*
Plymouth Sabbath School Collection of Hymns and
    Tunes. By H. E. Matthews. . . . 0 25   *Barnes & Co.*
Pocket Anatomist; for the Use of Students. By M. W.
    Hilles. 18mo., cl. . . . . . . 0 63   *Lindsay & B.*
—— Critical Greek and English Testament, in Paral-
    lel Columns. 18mo., cl. . . . . 1 75   *John Wiley.*
—— Guide for Americans Going to Europe. 18mo. . . 0 50   *Townsend & Co.*
Poe, Edgar A., The Poetical Works of. With an Origi-
    nal Memoir. Illustrated with more than one
    hundred original designs. 8vo., morocco. . 0 60   *J. S. Redfield.*
    The same. 82mo., blue and gold. . . 0 75   *W. J. Widdleton.*
Poems. By Matilda. 12mo., cl. . . . . 1 00   *A. Morris.*
Poets (The) of the West: a Selection of Favorite Ameri-
    can Poems, with Memoirs of their Authors. . 3 00   *A.D.F. Randolph.*
—— and Poetry of Vermont. Edited by Abby Maria
    Hemenway. . . . . . .   *G. A. Tuttle & Co.*
Political Manual. By E. D. Mansfield. 12mo. . . 1 00   *Barnes & Burr.*
Polko, E., Flower Pictures. Translated from the Ger-
    man. By S. W. Lander. 16mo. . . . 0 50   *D. Appleton & Co.*
Poll-Pegg, and other Sketches. 18mo. . . . . 0 25   *J. Challen & Sons.*
Pollard, E. A., Black Diamonds! Gathered in the Dar-
    key Homes of the South. 12mo. . . . 0 50   *Pudney & Russell.*
Pond, E. (D. D.), The Church. Second edition revised. 0 33   *E. F. Duren.*
Poor (The) Girl and True Woman; or, Elements of
    Woman's Success. Drawn from the Life of
    Mary Lyon and Others. By William M. Thayer. 0 75   *Gould & Lincoln.*

Poor Little Joe. By Aunt Friendly. 18mo.	0 25	*A.D.F. Randolph.*
—— and Proud; or, the Fortunes of Katy Redburn.	0 63	*Phillips, S. & Co.*
Pope, Le Roy, Modern Fancies and Follies: Considered upon the Basis of Human Nature. 12mo.	1 00	*Applegate & Co.*
Pope or President? Startling Disclosures of Romanism as Revealed by its Own Writers. 12mo.	1 00	*R. L. Delisser.*
Popular Tales from the Norse. By George Webbe Dasent. 12mo.	1 00	*D. Appleton & Co.*
Porter, Ann E., The Lost Will. 18mo.	0 70	*Henry Hoyt.*
—— E. (D. D.), Letters on the Religious Revivals.	0 40	*B. Cong. B. of P.*
—— J. (D. D.), A Commonplace Book; designed to assist Students, Professional Men, and General Readers in treasuring up Knowledge for future Use. 4to.	1 75	*Carlton & Porter.*
—— " " The True Evangelist; or, an Itinerant Ministry. 16mo.	0 35	"
—— S. (Rev.), A Daily Walk with God. 32mo.	0 25	*E. Darrow & Bro.*
—— William T., Life of. By Francis Brinley. 12mo.	1 00	*D. Appleton & Co.*
Potter, Alonzo (Bishop), Discourses, Charges, Addresses, Pastoral Letters, &c., &c. 12mo.	1 25	*E. H. Butler & Co.*
—— R. S., The Life and Adventures of Major Roger Sherman Potter. 12mo.	1 25	*Stanford & D.*
Powell, A. W. (Mrs.), Familiar Letters; or, Ministerial Legacy. 12mo.	1 00	*E. Darrow & Bro.*
—— W. B., Natural History of the Human Temperament. 8vo.	1 50	*R. Clarke & Co.*
Power of Faith (The). A Narrative of Sarah Johnson. By Mrs. P. L. Upham. 18mo.	0 33	*Henry Hoyt.*
—— (The) of Grace; or, Incidents and Narratives of Wonderful Conversions. 12mo.	1 00	*Saxton & Barker.*
Practical Calculator. By Martin Rohrer. 18mo., cloth.	0 50	*Lippincott & Co.*
—— Cook-book. By Mrs. Sylvia Cambell. 12mo.	0 38	*Munsell&Rowland*
—— Miner's Guide. 8vo. cloth.	2 00	*Geo. M. Newton.*
—— " Own Book and Guide. By J. Bridge, with Additions, by J. Atkins. 12mo.	2 00	*J. W. Randolph.*
—— Treatise on Dyeing and Calico Printing. 8vo.	5 00	*John Wiley.*
Praed, W. M., The Poetical Works of. New and enlarged edition. 2 vols. 12mo.	2 00	*J. S. Redfield.*
Prairie Farming in America, with Notes by the Way on Canada and the United States. By James Caird. 12mo.	0 50	*D. Appleton & Co.*
—— Traveler (The). A Hand-Book for Overland Emigrants. By Randolph B. Marcy, Captain U. S. Army. 12mo.	1 00	*Harper & Bros.*

Pratt, J. J., Poems of Two Friends. By J. J. Pratt and
W. D. Howells. 16mo. . . . . . 0 75   *Follett, Foster & Co.*

Prayer at Home; or, Short Family Prayers for Every
Morning and Evening in the Week. 18mo. . 1 00   *F. D. Harriman.*

Preachers and Preaching. By the Rev. Nicholas Murray, D. D. 12mo. . . . . . . 0 75   *Harper & Bros.*

Precept upon Precept. 18mo. cl. . . . . 0 25   *Moore & N.*

Precepts in Practice; or, Stories Illustrating the Proverbs. By A. L. O. E. 18mo. . . . 0 50   *Carter & Brothers.*

Prenticeana; or, Wit and Humor in Paragraphs. By the
Editor of the *Louisville Journal.* 12mo., cloth. 1 00   *Derby & Jackson.*

Prerequisites to Communion. The Scriptural Terms of
Admission to the Lord's Supper. By Rev. A.
N. Arnold. 16mo. pap. . . . . . 0 38   *Gould & Lincoln.*

Presbury, B. F., The Mustee; or, Love and Liberty. . 1 25   *Shepard, Clark & B.*

Prescott, G. B., History, Theory, and Practice of the
Electric Telegraph. 12mo. . . . . 1 75   *Ticknor & Fields.*

—— W. H., History of the Reign of Philip II. of
Spain. 3 vols. 8vo. cl. . . . . 6 75   *Lippincott & Co.*

Preston, L., Treatise on Bookkeeping. New Edition Revised, Improved, and Enlarged. 8vo. . 1 12   *Collins & Brother.*

Pretty Stories for Little Boys. 16mo. . . . 0 30   *Carlton & Porter.*

Priestley, J., The Christian Maiden. Memorials of Eliza
Hessel. 16mo. . . . . . . 0 75   "

Prime, S. I. (Rev.), The Bible in the Levant; or, The
Life and Letters of the Rev. Chester
N. Righter. 18mo. . . . . 0 75   *Sheldon & Co.*

——   "   Letters from Switzerland. 12mo. . 1 00   "

——   "   The Power of Prayer, as Illustrated
in the Wonderful Displays of Divine Grace in
the Fulton Street and other Meetings in New
York, and Elsewhere, in 1857–'58. 12mo. . 1 00   *Charles Scribner.*

Prince Charles; or, The Young Pretender. By J. F.
Smith. Pap. . . . . . . 0 50   *Dick & F.*

—— Charlie, the Young Chevalier. By Meredith
Johnes. 16mo. . . . . . . 0 75   *D. Appleton & Co.*

—— (The) of Peace; or, Songs of Bethlehem, with 32
Illustrations. Sq. 12mo. ex. cl. gilt, $2 50; mor. 4 00   "

Prince's Ball (The). A Brochure from "Vanity Fair."
By Edmund C. Stedman. 12mo. . . . 0 50   *Rudd & Carleton.*

Prison Life; or, Interesting Biographies of Picciola,
Heroine of Siberia, Silvio Pellico, and Baron
Trenck. 16mo. . . . . . . 0 50   *Barnes & Burr.*

Prisoner's Child (The) and other Stories. 18mo. . . 0 20   *Sheldon & Co.*

Prissner, E., The American Question in its National
    Aspects. 12mo. cl. . . . . 0 60   *H. H. Lloyd & Co.*
Private Diaries (The) of George Washington, from Octo-
    ber, 1789, to June, 1792. Edited by Benson J.
    Lossing. 12mo. . . . . 1 00   *Richardson & Co.*
Proclamations for Thanksgiving, issued by the Con-
    tinental Congress, President Washington, by the
    National and State Governments on the Peace
    of 1815, and by the Governors of New York
    since the Introduction of the Custom. 4to. . 2 00   *Munsell&Rowland*
Proctor, Adelaide A., Legends and Lyrics. 12mo. . 0 75   *D. Appleton & Co.*
Profits (The) of Godliness. By the author of "Scenes in
    Chusan," etc. 18mo. . . . . . . 0 25   *Presb. Bd. of Pub.*
Progress of Philosophy in the Past and in the Future.
    By Samuel Tyler. 12mo. cl. . . . . 1 00   *Lippincott & Co.*
Progression; or, the South Defended. By Millie May-
    field. 12mo. cl. . . . . . .   *Applegate & Co.*
Prolegomena Logica: an Inquiry into the Psychological
    Character of Logical Processes. By H. Longue-
    ville Mansel. 12mo. . . . . . ., 1 00   *Gould & Lincoln.*
Proverbial and Moral Thoughts. By Charles Henry
    Hanger. 16mo. . . . . . . 0 63   *Mayhew & Baker.*
Pujol, L., and Van Norman, D. C., The Complete French
    Class Book. 8vo. . . . . . . 1 00   *Barnes & Burr.*
Pullan, The Ladies' Manual of Fancy Work. 8vo. cl. . 1 25   *Dick & Fitzgerald.*
Pulpit (The) of the American Revolution; or, the Poli-
    tical Sermons of the Period of 1776. With a
    Historical Introduction, Notes, and Illustrations.
    By John Wingate Thornton. 12mo. . . 1 25   *Gould & Lincoln.*
—— Themes and Preacher's Assistant. By the author
    of "Helps for the Pulpit." 12mo. cl. . . 1 00   *Smith & English.*
—— (The) and the Pew. From the Leaves of a Pas-
    tor's Journal. 12mo. . . . . . 1 00   *A. B. Burdick.*
Punshon, W. M. (Rev.), Select Letters and Sermons of.
    With an Introduction by Rev. George
    O. Robinson. 12mo. . . . 1 00   *C. Moore.*
—— " Sermons by. To which is prefixed a Plea
    for Class Meetings, and an Introduction by Rev.
    William H. Milburn. 12mo. cl. . . . 1 00   *Derby & Jackson.*
Purefoy, G. W., A History of the Sandy Creek Baptist
    Association from its Organization in A. D. 1758,
    to A. D. 1858. 12mo. . . . . . 1 00   *Sheldon & Co.*
Puritan (The) Hymn and Tune Book. 8vo. . . .   *Cong. Bd. of Pub.*

Puritans (The); or, the Church, Court, and Parliament
    of England during the Reigns of Edward VI.
    and Elizabeth. By Samuel Hopkins. 2 vols. 8vo.   5 00   *Gould & Lincoln.*
Putnam, A. W., History of Middle Tennessee; or, Life
    and Times of General James Robertson. 8vo.   3 50   *C. B. Richardson.*
—— Mrs., Receipt Book, and Young Housekeeper's
    Assistant. New and Enlarged edition. 12mo.   0 75   *Phinney, B. & M.*

Q

Quackenbos, G. P., A Natural Philosophy. 12mo.   .   1 00   *D. Appleton & Co.*
——   "   Primary History of the United States.   0 50   "
Quackery Unmasked; or, a Consideration of the most
    Prominent Empirical Schemes of the Present
    Time. By Dan King, M. D. 12mo. .   .   .   *S. S. & W. Wood.*
Quaint Sayings and Doings concerning Luther. Collected
    and arranged by John G. Morris, D. D. 12mo.   0 75   *Lindsay & B.*
Quaker (The) Soldier; or, the British in Philadelphia.
    A Historical Novel. 12mo.   .   .   .   1 25   *Peterson & Bros.*
Queen of Hearts. A Novel, by Wilkie Collins. 12mo.   1 00   *Harper & Brothers.*
Queen's Domain and other Poems. By William Winter.   *E. O. Libby & Co.*
Queens and Princesses of France. By George White.   .   0 50   *Murphy & Co.*
—— of Society. By Grace and Philip Wharton.   .   1 50   *Harper & Bros.*
Quench not the Spirit. By Newman Hall. 18mo.   .   0 25   *Carter & Brothers.*
Questions on the Bible Hand-Book; an Introduction to
    the Study of Sacred Scripture. 24mo.   .   .   0 20   *W. S. & A. Martien.*
—— and Answers on the Books of the Bible. 12mo.   0 18   *A. D. F. Randolph.*
Quiet Thoughts for Quiet Hours. By the author of
    "Life's Morning," &c. 16mo., cl.   .   .   .   0 75   *Tilton & Co.*
Quinby, G. W., Marriage, and the Duties of the Marriage
    Relations. 18mo., cl.   .   .   .   .   0 40   *U. P. James.*
Quincy, Essays on the Soiling of Cattle. 8vo.   .   .   0 40   *Jno. Wilson & Son.*
Quinton, J. A., Heaven's Antidote to the Curse of Labor.   0 30   *J. Challen & Son.*
Quitman, John A., Life and Correspondence of. By J.
    F. Claiborne. 2 vols. 12mo. .   .   .   .   3 00   *Harper & Bros.*
Quodlibet. 12mo. .   .   .   .   1 00   *Lippincott & Co*

R

Rabb and his Friends. By John Brown, M. D. 16mo. 0 15 *Ticknor & Fields.*

Raccolta (The); or, Collection of Indulgenced Prayers.
By Ambrose St. John. 18mo. . . . 0 50 *Sadlier & Co.*

Rachel Johnson: a Tale. By the author of "The Widow's Son," etc. 18mo. . . . . . 0 25 *Daniel Dana, Jr.*

Raff, George W., Guide for Executors and Administrators in Ohio. 8vo. law sheep. . . . 1 50 *Robt. Clarke & Co.*

Ragged Homes and How to Mend Them. 12mo. . 0 60 *Am. S. S. Union.*

Raikes, Robert (the Founder of Sabbath-Schools), Life of .
By William M. Cornell. 18mo. . . . 0 20 *Henry Hoyt.*

Rainbow Side (The), a Sequel to "The Itinerant." By
Mrs. C. M. Edwards. 16mo. . . . 0 70 *Carlton & Porter.*

Ralston, S. S., the Revelation of John, the Divine; A
New Theory of Apocalypse. 8vo. . : *Smith, E. & Co.*

Rambles about Portsmouth. Sketches of Persons, Localities, and Incidents of Two Centuries. Principally from Tradition and Unpublished Documents. . . . . . . 1 75 *Brewster & Co.*

—— among Words. Their Poetry, History, and Wisdom. By William Swinton. 12mo. . . 1 00 *Charles Scribner.*

—— (The) of a Rat. By A. L. O. E. . . 0 30 *F. D. Harriman.*

Ramsay, E. B., Reminiscences of Scottish Life and Character. 12mo. . . . . . . 1 00 *Ticknor & Fields.*

Ran Away to Sea: an Autobiography for Boys. By
Capt. Mayne Reid. 16mo. cl. . . 0 75 "

Rand, E. S., Life Memories, and other Poems. 16mo. . 0 75 *Jas. Munroe & Co.*

Randall, G. M. (D. D.), The Pitt Street Chapel Lecture,
in answer to the Question: "Why I am a
Churchman?" 18mo. . . . . 0 25 *F. D. Harriman.*

—— H. S., The Life of Thomas Jefferson. 3 vols. 8vo. 7 50 *Derby & Jackson.*

—— J. M. (Rev.), The Titles of Our Lord; Adopted
by Himself in the New Testament. 12mo. . 0 50 *Presb. B'd of Pub.*

Raphael, Analysis of the Cartoons of Raphael. 16mo. . 1 00 *Charles B. Norton.*

Rational Cosmology; or, The Eternal Principles and the
Necessary Laws of the Universe. By Laurens
P. Hickok, D. D. 8vo. . . . . 1 75 *D. Appleton & Co.*

Rawle, W. H., A Practical Treatise on the Law of Covenants for Title. Third Edition. Revised and
Enlarged. 8vo. . . . . . . 5 50 *Little, Brown & Co*

Rawlinson, G., The Historical Evidences of the Truth of
    the Scripture Records stated anew. 12mo. . 1 25 *Gould & Lincoln.*
—— G., The History of Herodotus. A New English
    version, edited with copious notes, &c., &c. By
    George Rawlinson, M. A. 4 vols. 8vo. cloth. 10 00 *D. Appleton & Co.*
Rawson, the Renegade. By the author of "The Regula-
    tors of Arkansas." 8vo. . . . . 0 25 *Dick & Fitzgerald.*
Read, H. (Rev.), The Palace of the Great King; or, the
    Power, Wisdom, and Goodness of God. 12mo. 1 25 *Charles Scribner.*
—— T. B., Poems. A new and enlarged edition.
    2 vols. 12mo. . . . . . 2 00 *Ticknor & Fields.*
Reade, C., A Good Fight and other Tales. 12mo. . 0 75 *Harper & Bros.*
—— " Love Me Little, Love Me Long. 12mo. . 0 75 "
—— " The Eighth Commandment. 12mo. . . 0 75 *Ticknor & Fields.*
Readings for Every Day in Lent. Compiled from the
    Writings of Bishop Jeremy Taylor. By the
    author of "Amy Herbert." 12mo. . . 0 75 *Daniel Dana, Jr.*
Reason and Revelation. By Rev. Dr. Candlish. Post 8vo. 0 75 *T. Nelson & Sons.*
—— and the Bible; or, The Truth of Religion. By
    Miles P. Squier, D. D. 12mo. . . . 1 00 *Charles Scribner.*
—— Why (The); Natural History. 12mo. . . 1 00 *Dick & Fitzgerald.*
Rebel (The) and the Rover. By Harry Hazel. 8vo. pap. 0 25 *Peterson & Bros.*
Record (The) of the Court at Upland, in Pennsylvania,
    1676 to 1681. And a Military Journal, kept by
    Major E. Denny, 1781 to 1795. 8vo. . . 2 50 *Lippincott & Co.*
Recreations (The) of a Country Parson. 12mo. . . 1 25 *Ticknor & Fields.*
—— of a Southern Barrister. 12mo. . . . 0 75 *Lippincott & Co.*
Rector's Offering. Selections from the Sermons of the
    Rev. D. R. Brewer. 18mo. . . . . 0 50 *A. D. F. Randolph.*
Rectory (The) of Moreland; or, My Duty. 12mo. . 1 00 *J. E. Tilton & Co.*
—— (The) of Valehead; or, the Edifice of a Holy
    Home. By the Rev. Robert Wilson
    Evans, D. D. 12mo. cl. . . . . 0 75 *Daniel Dona, Jr.*
Red Scout (The); or, the Outlaw's Revenge. 8vo. . 0 25 *Dick & Fitzgerald.*
Reddy, W., Inside Views of Methodism; or, a Hand-
    Book for Inquirers and Beginners. 18mo . 0 35 *Carlton & Porter.*
Redemption; a Poem. By John D. Bryant, M. D. .. 1 00 *Pennington & Son.*
Redman, G. A., Mystic Hours; or, Spiritual Experi-
    ences. 12mo. . . . . . . 1 25 *Charles Partridge.*
Redpath, J., Handbook to Kansas Territory and Rocky
    Mountain Gold Region. 18mo. . . . 0 75 *J. H. Colton.*
—— " Echoes of Harper's Ferry. 12mo. . . 1 25 *Thayer & Eldridge.*
Reformed Woman; or, Passages from the Life of Mrs.
    Anna Cooley. By Edith Rivers. 12mo. . 1 00 *Henry Hoyt.*

Reichenbach, Baron, Odic-Magnetic Letters. Translated
    from the German by John S. Hit-
    tell. 12mo. pap. . . . . 0 30 *Calvin Blanchard.*
————   "   Somnambulism and Cramp. Trans-
    lated from the German. By
    John S. Hittell. 12mo. . . 1 00   "
Reid, Mayne, The Boy Tar; or, a Voyage in the Dark. 0 75 *Tickner & Fields.*
————   " Odd People. Being a Popular Description
    of Singular Races of Men. 16mo. . 0 75   "
    The same. 12mo. cl. . . . . 0 50 *Harper & Bros.*
————   " Osceola, the Seminole; or, the Red Fawn
    of the Flower Land. 12mo. . . 1 25 *R. M. De Witt.*
————   " Ran Away to Sea; an Autobiography for
    Boys. 16mo. . . . . . 0 75 *Tickner & Fields.*
————   " The Wood Rangers; or, the Trappers of
    Sonora. 12mo. . . . . . 1 25 *R. M. De Witt.*
————   " Wild Life; or, Adventures on the Fron-
    tier. A Tale of the Early Days of the
    Texan Republic. 12mo. . . . 1 25   "
———— S. O., Scouting Expeditions of McCullough's
    Texan Rangers. 12mo. . . . . 1 00 *G. G. Evans.*
Religion (The) of Science. 12mo. . . . 0 25 *Calvin Blanchard.*
Religious Aspects of the Age (The). 12mo. pap. . 0 25 *Thatcher & H.*
Remembered Words from the Sermons of Rev. I. Nichols. 0 50 *Crosby, N., L.& Co.*
———— (The) Prayer. 18mo. . . . . 0 20 *Henry Hoyt.*
Reminiscences of a General Officer of Zouaves. By
    General Cler. 12mo. . . . . 1 00 *D. Appleton & Co.*
Representative Men of the New Testament. By George
    C. Baldwin, D. D. 12mo. . . . 1 00 *Phinney, B. & M.*
Requier, A. J., Poems. 12mo. . . . . 0 75 *Lippincott & Co.*
Rest and Unrest; or, the Story of a Year. By Cousin
    Kate (Catherine D. Bell). 16mo. . . 0 75 *A. D. F. Randolph.*
Retrospect of Early Quakerism. By Ezra Michener,
    M. D. 12mo. cl. . . . . . 1 50 *T. E. Zell.*
Revised Statutes (The) of the State of New York. Pre-
    pared by Amasa J. Parker, Geo. Wolford, and
    Edward Wade, Counselor-at-Law. 3 vols. 8vo. 15 00 *Banks & Brother.*
Revival (The) in Ireland. Letters addressed to the Rev.
    H. Grattan Guinness. 18mo. . . . 0 25 *W.S. &A. Martien.*
Revolutions in English History. By Robert Vaughan,
    D. D. Vol. I. Revolutions of Race. 8vo. . 2 00 *D. Appleton & Co.*
Reynard the Fox, after the German Version of Goethe.
    Translated by Thomas J. Arnold. With Illus-
    trations from designs of Wilhelm Von Kaul-
    bach. 8vo. . . . . . . 3 50   "

Reynolds, G. W. M., Empress Eugenie's Boudoir; or, the
       Mysteries of the Court of France. . 0 50   F. A. Brady.
———   " Ethel Trevor; or, the Duke's Victim. 0 50   "
———   " Imogene Hartland; or, the Star of
       the Circus. 8vo. Paper. . . 0 50   "
———   " The Maid of Honor. 8vo. Paper. . 0 50   "
———   " The Opera Dancer; or, the Mysteries
       of London Life. 8vo. Paper. . 0 50   Peterson & Bros.
———   " The Ruined Gamster. 8vo. Paper. 0 50   "
——— J., The Life and Discourses of Sir Joshua Rey-
       nolds. 12mo. . . . . . . 1 00   Barnes & Burr.
Rhees, W. J., An Account of the Smithsonian Institu-
       tion, its Founder, Building, Operations, &c. 0 50   Westermann & Co.
———   " Manual of Libraries, Societies, and Institu-
       tions, in the United States and British
       Provinces of North America. 8vo. . 3 00   Lippincott & Co.
Rhode Island and Providence Plantations, History of.
       By Samuel Greene Arnold. 2 vols. 8vo. cl. . 5 00   D. Appleton & Co.
Rhymes of Twenty Years. By Henry Morford. 12mo, 1 00   H. Dexter & Co.
Rhymings. By Howard Wainwright. 12mo. . 0 75   D. Appleton & Co.
Rice, G. E., Nugamenta: a Book of Verse. By George
       Edward Rice. 18mo. . . . . . 0 75   J. E. Tilton & Co.
——— H., Mount Vernon, and other Poems. 18mo. . 0 75   J. P. Jewett & Co.
——— Rosella, Mabel; or, Heart Histories. 12mo. . 1 00   Follett & Foster.
——— W. (Rev.), Moral and Religious Quotations from
       the Poets. 8vo. . . . . . 1 50   Carlton & Porter.
Richards, C. S., Latin Lessons and Tables. 12mo. . 0 62   Phillips, S. & Co.
——— W. C., Electron; or, The Pranks of the Mod-
       ern Puck: a Telegraphic Epic for the Times. . 0 50   L. Appleton & Co.
Richardson, J. F., Roman Orthoepy. A Plea for the
       Restoration of the True System of Latin Pro-
       nunciation. 12mo. . . . . . 0 50   Sheldon & Co.
——— W. H., The Boot and Shoe Manufacturer's Assist-
       ant and Guide. 12mo. . . . . 1 25   Higgins, B. & D.
Richmond, A., The First Twenty Years of my Life. , 0 65   Am. S. S. Union.
Rifles and Rifle Practice; an Elementary Treatise upon
       the Theory of Rifle Firing, with Description
       of the Infantry Rifles of Europe and the United
       States, their Balls and Cartridges. 12mo. . 1 75   D. Van Nostrand.
Right at Last; and other Tales. By Mrs. Gaskell. 12mo. 0 75   Harper & Bros.
Rills from the Fountain of Life; or, Sermons to Child-
       ren. By Rev. Richard Newton, D. D. 12mo. 0 75   Carter & Brothers.
Rion, Mary C., Ladies' Southern Florist. 12mo. . . 1 00   Peter B. Glass.
Ripley, J. B. (Rev.), Six Soundings. 18mo. . . . 0 25   J. Challen & Son.

Rita: an Autobiography. 12mo. .   .   .   .   1 00   *Mayhew & Baker.*

Ritchie, Leigh, Robert Oaklands; or, The Outcast Or-
    phan. 8vo., paper.   .   .   .   .   .   0 25   *Peterson & Bros.*

Rivers, E., The Reformed Woman; or, Passages from
    the Life of Mrs. Anna Cooley. 12mo. .   .   1 00   *Henry Hoyt.*

—— T., The Orchard House; or, Culture of Fruit
    Trees in Pots under Glass. 8vo. .   .   .   0 40   *C. M. Saxton & B.*

Robbins, C. (D. D.), Portrait of a Christian. Drawn from
    life. 18mo. .   .   .   .   0 75   *Crosby, N., L. & Co.*

Robert Oakland; or, the Outcast Orphan. By Leigh
    Ritchie. 8vo. paper.   .   .   .   .   .   0 25   *Peterson & Bro.*

—— Walton; or, a Great Idea. 18mo. .   .   .   0 50   *Henry Hoyt.*

Roberts, J. (Capt. U. S. A.) Hand-Book of Artillery.   0 75   *D. Van Nostrand.*

Robertson, F. W. (Rev.) Lectures and Addresses on
    Literary and Social Topics. 12mo. cl.   1 00   *Ticknor & Fields.*

——   "   Sermons · 1st, 2d, and 3d series. 12mo.
    cloth.   .   .   .   .   Each   1 00   "

Robin Nest Stories. By Mrs. Madeline Leslie. Six vols.
    16mo. square. cl. .   .   .   .   .   .   1 80   *Crosby, N., L. & Co.*

Robinson, (J. H.), The Maid of the Ranche; or, the
    Regulators and Moderators. Paper. 8vo.   .   0 25   *F. A. Brady.*

—— H. N., A New Elementary Algebra. 12mo. .   0 75   *Ivison & Phinney.*

——   "   The Progressive Higher Arithmetic.   .   0 75   "

—— S., How to Live; Saving and Wasting; or, Do-
    mestic Economy Illustrated. 12mo.   .   .   1 00   *Fowler & Wells.*

—— S. (Rev.), The Church of God as an Essential
    Element of the Gospel. 12mo.   .   .   .   0 60   *J. M. Wilson.*

Roby Family (The); or, Battling with the World. By
    A. L. O. E. 18mo. .   .   .   .   .   0 80   *Carlton & Porter.*

Rocket (The). 18mo. .   .   .   .   .   .   0 25   *Am. Tract Society.*

Rockwell, J. E. (Rev.), Scenes and Impressions Abroad.   1 00   *W. S. & A. Martien.*

——   "   The Young Christian Warned.   0 25   *Presb. Bd. of Pub.*

Roe, A. S., How Could He Help It? or, The Heart Tri-
    umphant. 12mo.   .   .   .   .   .   1 25   *Derby & Jackson.*

——   "   True to the Last; or, Alone on a Wide,
    Wide Sea. 12mo.   .   .   .   .   .   .   1 25   "

Roessle, T., How to Cultivate and Preserve Celery.
    Edited by Henry S. Olcott. 8vo. .   .   .   1 00   *Saxton & Barker.*

Rogers, H. D., A Government Survey, with a General
    View of the Geology of the United States;
    Essays on the Coal Formation and its Fossils;
    and a Description of the Coal-Fields of North
    America and Great Britain. 2 vols. 4to. (Vol.
    II. bound in two parts). Accompanied by a

Geological Map of Pennsylvania, and a Geological and Topographical Map of the Anthracite Fields of Pennsylvania. . . . . . 80 00 *Lippincott & Co.*

Rogers, H. D., A New Map of the State of Pennsylvania. Constructed from Original Surveys, and the most Recent Authorities, under the superintendence of Professor H. D. Rogers. Mounted on rollers. 6 00 "

—— S., Recollections. By Samuel Rogers. 16mo. . 0 75 *Bartlett & Miles.*

Rohrer, M. M., Practical Calculator. Carefully revised by Rev. Theodore A. Hopkins, A. M. New Edition, with Additions and Improvements. . 0 50 *Lippincott & Co.*

Rollo in Rome. By Jacob Abbott. 16mo. . . . 0 50 *Brown & Taggard.*

Roman Orthoepy. A Plea for the Restoration of the True System of Latin Pronunciation. By Prof. John F. Richardson. 12mo. . . . . 0 50 *Sheldon & Co.*

—— Question (The). By E. About. Translated from the French by H. C. Coupe. 12mo. 0 60 *D. Appleton & Co.*

—— " " Translated from the French of Edmond About, by Mrs. Annie T. Wood. 12mo., pap. . . . 0 45 *J. E. Tilton & Co.*

Romance (The) of History, as exhibited in the Lives of Celebrated Women of all Ages and Countries. By Henry C. Watson. . 1 25 *J. S. Cotton & Co.*

—— " of Natural History. By Philip Henry Gosse. 12mo. . . . . . 1 25 *Gould & Lincoln.*

—— " of a Poor Young Man. By Octave Feuillet. 12mo. . . . . . 1 00 *Rudd & Carleton.*

The same. 8vo., pap. . . . . 0 25 *Townsend & Co.*

—— " of the Ring, and other Poems. By James Nack. 12mo., cl. . . . . 1 00 *Delisser & Procter.*

—— " and its Hero. 12mo. . . . . 1 00 *Harper & Bros.*

Romanism in America. By the Rev. Rufus W. Clark. . *J. E. Tilton & Co.*

Rome; its Churches, its Charities, and its Schools. By Rev. Wm. Neligan. 12mo., cl. . . . 1 00 *Dunigan & Bro.*

—— its Ruler and its Institutions. By J. F. Maguire. 1 25 *Sadlier & Co.*

Roorbach, O. A., Addenda to the Bibliotheca Americana, a Catalogue of American Publications (Reprints and Original Works), from May, 1855, to March, 1858. Compiled and arranged by Orville A. Roorbach. 8vo., cloth. . . . . 3 00 *Wiley & Halsted.*

Root, G. E., Belshazzar's Feast. (Music) 8vo. . . 0 25 *Mason Brothers.*

Ropes, Hannah A., Cranston House: A Novel. 12mo. . 1 00 *Otis Clapp.*

Rosa; or, the Parisian Girl. From the French, by Mrs. J. C. Fletcher. 16mo. . . . . . 0 60 *Harper & Bros.*

Rosalie's Lessons. By Mrs. Sarah S. T. Wallace. 18mo.　0 25　*Presb. Bd. of Pub.*
Rose, A. O. (Rev.), The Family Choral. 18mo.　.　.　　　　*H. V. Degen.*
—— Cottage; or, Grandmamma Wise. 18mo.　.　.　0 75　*Henry Hoyt.*
Rosemary; or, Life and Death. By J. Vincent Hunt-
　　ington. 12mo.　.　.　.　.　.　.　.1 25　*Sadlier & Co.*
Round the Fire: Six Stories. 16mo.　.　.　.　.　0 75　*Carter & Brothers.*
Rowe, G. S., A Missionary among Cannibals; or, the
　　Life of John Hunt. 16mo.　.　.　.　.　0 65　*Carlton & Porter.*
Royalists and Republicans. Translated from the French
　　of Alexandre Dumas. Paper, 8vo.　.　.　0 50　*E. D. Long & Co.*
Royalty in the New World; or, the Prince of Wales in
　　America. By Kinahan Cornwallis. 12mo.　.　1 00　*M. Doolady.*
Ruffini. Dear Experience. A Tale. 12mo.　.　.　1 00　*Rudd & Carleton.*
—— Lavinia; a Novel. 12mo.　.　.　.　.　1 25　　　"
Ruined Cities of the East. By the Rev. Dr. Tweedie.　0 75　*Am. Tract. So.*
—— Gamester. By George W. Reynolds. 8vo., pap.　0 50　*Peterson & Bros.*
Run (A) through Europe. By Erastus O. Benedict.　.　1 25　*D. Appleton & Co.*
Rush, Richard, Occasional Productions, Political, Diplo-
　　matic, and Miscellaneous. Edited by his Exe-
　　cutors. 8vo.　.　.　.　.　.　.　.　2 25　*Lippincott & Co.*
Ruskin, J., Beauties of Ruskin; or, the True and the
　　Beautiful in Nature, Art, Morals, and Religion.
　　Selected from the works of John Ruskin.　.　1 25　*Wiley & Halsted.*
—— "Modern Painters, Parts VI., of Leaf Beauty,
　　VII., of Cloud Beauty, VIII., of Ideas of Rela-
　　tion, 1.—Of Invention Formal; IX.. of Ideas of
　　Relation, 2—Of Invention Spiritual. 12mo.　.　1 25　*John Wiley.*
—— "The Elements of Perspective, arranged for the
　　Use of Schools. 12mo.　.　.　.　.　0 63　　　"
—— "The King of the Golden River; or, the Black
　　Brothers. 16mo..　.　.　.　.　.　0 75　*Mahew & Baker.*
—— "The Two Paths, being Lectures on Art, and its
　　Application to Decoration and Manufacture.　.　1 00　*John Wiley.*
Russell, W. S., Pilgrim Memorials, and Guide to Ply-
　　mouth. 12mo.　.　.　.　.　.　.　0 75　*Crosby, N.,L.&Co.*
Rustic Rhymes. By the Author of "Winter Studies in
　　the Country." 16mo..　.　.　.　.　　　　*Parry & McM.*
Ruth and her Friends. A Story for Girls. 16mo.　.　0 50　*Carter & Brothers.*
Rutledge. A Novel. 12mo.　.　.　.　.　.　1 25　*Derby & Jackson.*
Ruttenber, E. M. Obstructions to the Navigation of
　　Hudson's River. 4to.　.　.　.　.　.　5 00　*J. Munsell.*
Ryder, G. M. Gillian, and other Poems. 12mo.　.　.　　　　*Chas. Desilver.*
Ryle, J. C. (Rev.), Expository Thoughts on the Gospels.　4 00　*Carter & Brothers.*
—— 　　"　　Only One Way of Salvation. 18mo., cl.　.　　　*Am. Tract So.*
—— 　　"　　Spiritual Songs. 32mo.　.　.　0 50　*A. D. F. Randolph*

S

Sabbath Harmony. A New Collection of Original and
    Sacred Music. By L. O. Emerson. . . 1 00 *Chase, N. & H.*
—— Hymn-Book. By Edwards A. Park, D. D., and
    Austin Phelps, D. D. 16mo. . . . 1 00 *Mason Brothers.*
—— School Bell (The). A new Collection of Choice
    Hymns and Tunes. Compiled by Horace Waters. 0 25 *Horace Waters.*
—— Talks with Little Children on the Psalms of Da-
    vid. 18mo. . . . . . . *J. E. Tilton & Co.*
Sabine, L., An Address before the New England Historic-
    Genealogical Society, September 13th, 1859; the
    Hundredth Anniversary of the Death of Major
    General James Wolfe. 8vo., paper. . . 0 50 *A. Williams & Co.*
Sackville St. Lawrence, an Autobiography. By Kinahan
    Cornwallis. 12mo. . . . . 1 50 *M. Doolady.*
Sacramental Discourses. By James W. Alexander, D. D. 1 00 *A.D.F. Randolph.*
Sacred Lyrics from the German. 8vo. . . 1 00 *Pres. Board Pub.*
—— Meditations. Translated from the Latin, by Rev.
    W. M. Blackburn. 18mo. . . . *T. Newton Kurtz.*
Sadlier, J. (Mrs.), The Confederate Chieftains: a Tale of
    the Irish Rebellion of 1641. 12mo. . . 1 25 *Sadlier & Co.*
Safe Home; or, The Last Days and Happy Death of Fan-
    nie Kenyon. 18mo. . . . . 0 25 *Gould & Lincoln.*
Saint Germain, J. T., The Art of Suffering. . . 0 25 *Sadlier & Co.*
Sala, G. A., A Journey Due North; being Notes of a
    Residence in Russia. 16mo., cl. . . . 1 00 *Ticknor & Fields.*
—— " The Adventuress; or, The Babington Peerage. 0 50 *F. A. Brady.*
Salem Witchcraft; a new edition. . . . 1 00 *Ives & Smith.*
Salisbury, Vermont (History of). By John M. Weeks. *A. H. Copeland.*
Salmagundi; or, the Whim-Whams and Opinions of
    Launcelot Langstaff, Esq., and others. By Wil-
    liam Irving, James Kirke Paulding, and Wash-
    ington Irving. 12mo. . . . . 1 50 *G. P. Putnam.*
Salzmann, C. S., Charles and Mary; or, Stories to help in
    the Training of Children. 12mo. . . 0 63 *James Miller.*
Sampson, George W. (D. D.), Spiritualism Tested. 16mo. 0 42 *Gould & Lincoln.*
Sand-Hills (The) of Jutland. By Hans Christian Ander-
    sen. 12mo. cl. . . . . . 0 75 *Ticknor & Fields.*

Sanders, C. W., Analysis of English Words. 12mo. . 0 56   *Ivison & Phinney.*

—— J. O., Analytical Definer and Higher Speller. . 0 63   *Clark A., M. & Co.*

Sanger, W. (M. D.), The History of Prostitution : its Extent, Causes, and Effects, throughout the World. 3 00   *Harper & Bros.*

Sappho : a Tragedy in Five Acts. By Edda Middleton. 2 00   *D. Appleton & Co.*

Sargent, E., Arctic Adventure by Sea and Land. 12mo. 1 25   *Brown & Taggard.*

—— " Original Dialogues. For School and Family Reading, and Representation. 12mo. 1 00   *W. I. Pooley & Co.*

—— " The Standard Speaker ; containing Exercises in Prose and Poetry. 12mo. . . . 1 50   *C. Desilver.*

Saunders, O., New Latin Paradigms, adapted to any Latin Grammar. . . . . . 0 75   *E. H. Butler & Co.*

—— J. H., Helen McGregor. 2 vols. 18mo. . . 0 50   *Challen & Sons.*

Savage, James, Genealogical Dictionary of the First Settlers of New England. 8vo. Vols. I. and II. 6 00   *Little, B. & Co.*

—— John, Our Living Representative Men : from official and original sources. 12mo. cl. . . 1 25   *Childs & Peterson.*

Sawyer, F. W., Hits at American Whims, and Hints for Home Use. 12mo. . . . . . 1 00   *D. Appleton & Co.*

—— G. S., Southern Institutes ; or, An Inquiry into the Origin and Early Prevalence of Slavery and the Slave Trade. With notes and comments in defense of the Southern Institutions. 8vo., cl.   *Lippincott & Co.*

Say, Thomas, The Complete Writings of, on the Conchology of the United States. Edited by .W. G. Binney. 8vo. . . .

hf. cf., plain, 6 00 ; colored . . 12 00   *H. Ballière.*

—— " The Complete Works of, on the Entomology of the United States. Edited by J. L. Le Conte. 2 vols., with 54 colored and 2 plain plates, 8vo. . . . . . . 20 00   *Ballière Bros.*

Say and Seal. By the author of "Wide, Wide World." 2 00   *Lippincott & Co.*

Sayings and Doings of Samuel Slick, Esq. By Judge Haliburton. 12mo. . . . . . 0 75   *Dick & Fitzg'ld.*

Saxe, J. G., The Money King, and other Poems. 16mo. 0 75   *Ticknor & Fields.*

Scattergood, D., The Game of Draughts, or Checkers, simplified and explained. 12mo. . . 0 38   *Dick & Fitzg'ld.*

Scenes in our Parish. By a Country Parson's Daughter. 1 00   *F. D. Harriman.*

—— and Incidents of Every-Day Life in Africa. By Miss Harriet G. Brittain. 12mo. . . 1 00   *Pudney & Russell.*

Schaff, P. (D. D.), History of the Christian Church. 8vo. 2 50   *Charles Scribner.*

Schedel, G. (M. D.), The Emancipation of Faith. 2 vols. 4 00   *D. Appleton & Co.*

Schem, A. J., The American Ecclesiastical Year Book. 1 00   *H. Dayton.*

Schiller, E., Cherry Blossom ; or, Love Thy Neighbor as Thyself. 12mo. . . . . . 1 00   *R. M. De Witt.*

Schiller, Frederich, The Life of, comprehending an Exam-
    ination of his Works. By Thomas Carlyle. · .   1 00 *Sheldon & Co.*
Schimeall, R. C. (Rev.), Our Bible Chronology, Historic
    and Prophetic, Critically Examined and Demon-
    strated. .   .   .   .   .   .   2 00 *Barnes & Burr.*
Schimmelpenninck, Mary A., Life of. Edited by her
    Relation, Christiana C. Hankin. 2 vols. 12mo. 2 00 *Hen'y Longstreth.*
Schmid, C., The Flower Basket; a Catholic Tale. 32mo. 0 37 *H. M'Grath.*
——— " The Wonderful Doctor; an Eastern Tale. . 0 25   "   "
Schmidt, H. L. (D. D.), Course of Ancient Geography. . 1 00 *D. Appleton & Co.*
Schmucker, S. S. (D. D.), A Commentary on Paul's Epis-
    tle to the Galatians. By Martin Luther. 8vo. 1 25 *Smith, E. & Co.*
Schoolcraft, H. R. (Mrs.), The Black Gauntlet: a Tale of
    Plantation Life in South Carolina. 12mo. . 1 25 *Lippincott & Co.*
School Days at Rugby. By an Old Boy. New edition. 1 50 *Ticknor & Fields.*
——— Days of Eminent Men. By John Timbs. 12mo. 1 00 *Follett, F. & Co.*
——— Harmonist (The). By Andrew J. Cleaveland,
    Professor of Music in the Baltimore Female
    College. 16mo. .   .   .   .   . 0 50 *Barnes & Burr.*
——— of the Guides; designed for the Use of the Militia
    of the United States. By Colonel Eugene Le
    Gal. 18mo. .   .   .   .   .   . 0 50 *D. Van Nostrand.*
Schubert, G. H., Memoir of the Duchess of Orleans. . 1 00 *Charles Scribner.*
Schultz, O., Tirocinium; or, First Lessons in Latin. . 0 40 *Ivison & Phinney.*
Schuyler, Philip (Genl.) Life and Times of. By B. J. Los-
    sing. 8vo. .   .   .   .   .   1 50 *Mason Brothers.*
Science a Witness for the Bible. By Rev. W. N. Pendle-
    ton, D. D. 12mo. cloth. .   .   .   1 00 *Lippincott & Co.*
——— in Theology. Sermons preached. By Adam S.
    Farrar. 12mo. .   .   .   .   0 85 *Smith, E. & Co.*
——— of Education and Art of Teaching. By John Og-
    den. 12mo. .   .   .   .   1 25 *Moore, W., K.& Co.*
——— and Art of Chess. By J. Monroe. 12mo. . 1 00 *Charles Scribner.*
Scott, James (D. D.), The Guardian Angel. A Poem in
    three Books. 12mo. .   .   .   0 75 *D. Appleton & Co.*
——— W. A. (Rev.), The Giant Judge; or, the Story of
    Samson. .   .   .   .   .   *Pres. B. of Pub.*
Scottish Reformation (The); a Historical Sketch. By
    Peter Lorimer, D. D. 8vo. .   .   3 00 *Carter & Brothers.*
Scouring (The) of the White Horse; or, the Long Vaca-
    tion Ramble of a London Clerk. 12mo. . . 1 00 *Ticknor & Fields.*
Sea of Ice (The); or, The Arctic Adventurers. By Percy
    B. St. John. 12mo. .   .   .   0 75 *Mayhew & Baker.*
Seacliff; or, The Mystery of the Westervelts. By J. W.
    De Forest. 12mo. .   .   .   .   1 25 *Phillips, S. & Co.*

Seaman Narratives. 16mo.	0 25	*Am. Tract Society.*
Secker, W., The Nonsuch Professor. With an Introduction by C. P. Krauth, Jr., D. D. 12mo. .	1 00	*Sheldon & Co.*
Secret History of the French Court under Richelieu and Mazarin. By Victor Cousin. 12mo., cl. .	0 63	*Delisser & Proctor.*
Secret Out (The); or, One Thousand Tricks with Cards, and other Recreations. 12mo., cl. . . .	1 00	*Dick & Fitzgerald.*
Seed-Time and Harvest. Tales translated from the German of Rosalie Koch and Maria Burg. 16mo.	0 75	*Crosby, N., L.&Co.*
—— and Harvest of Ragged Schools. By Thomas Guthrie, D. D. 16mo.	0 60	*Carter & Bros.*
Seiss, J. A. (D. D.), The Gospel in Leviticus; or, an Exposition of the Hebrew Ritual. 12mo. . .	1 00	*Lindsay & B.*
Self-Made Men. By Chas. C. B. Seymour. 12mo. .	1 25	*Harper &Brothers.*
Semi-Detached House (The). A Novel. Edited by Lady Theresa Lewis. 12mo.	0 75	*Ticknor & Fields.*
Seney, Geo. E., The Code of Civil Procedure, and the Code of Procedure before Justices of the Peace in Ohio. 8vo. Law sheep.	4 00	*Robt. Clarke & Co.*
Seraphic Manual (The). A Collection of Devotions, &c.	0 50	*Dunigan &Brother*
Seven Little Sisters (The) who Live on the Round Ball that Floats in the Air. Square 16mo. . .	0 63	*Ticknor & Fields.*
—— Years, and Other Tales. By Julia Kavanagh. .	0 50	*D. Appleton & Co.*
Sewall, R. K., The Ancient Dominions of Maine. . .	2 00	*E. Clarke & Co.*
Sewell, E. M. (Miss), Ursula. A Tale of Country Life. .	1 50	*D. Appleton & Co.*
Seymour, C. C. B., Self-Made Men. 12mo. . .	1 25	*Harper &Brothers.*
—— W. W. (Mrs.), Christmas Holidays at Cedar Grove. 18mo.	0 63	*D. Dana, Jr.*
—— " " Whitsuntide at Cedar Grove. .	0 75	"
—— " " Easter Holidays at Cedar Grove.		"
Shadow (The) on the Hearth; or, Our Father's Voice in taking away our Little Ones. By a Bereaved Parent. 16mo.	0 75	*Carter & Bros.*
Shadows and Sunshine, as Illustrated in the History of Notable Characters. By the Rev. Erskine Neale. 18mo.	0 50	*M. W. Dodd.*
Shaffner, T. P., The Telegraph Manual: a Complete History and Description of the Semaphoric, Electric, and Magnetic Telegraphs of Europe, Asia, Africa, and America, Ancient and Modern. With 625 Illustrations. 8vo.	5 00	*Pudney & Russell.*
Shahmah in Pursuit of Freedom; or, the Branded Hand.	1 25	*Thatcher & H.*
Shakespeare, H., The Wild Sports of India. 12mo. cl. .	0 75	*Ticknor & Fields.*
Shakspeare's (Wm.), Legal Acquirements, Considered by John Lord Campbell. 12mo. cl. .	0 75	*D. Appleton & Co.*

Shakspeare (Wm.), The Most Excellent Historie of the
    Merchant of Venice. Written by William Shak-
    speare. 8vo. . . . . 2 00　*D. Appleton & Co.*

Shedd, W. G. T., The Confessions of Augustine. Edited,
    with an Introduction by Rev. William G. T.
    Shedd, D. D. 12mo. . . . . . 1 00　*Warren F. Draper.*

Sheepfold (The) and the Common; or, the Evangelical
    Rambler. 12mo. . . . . . . 1 25　*Carter & Brothers.*

Sheldon, E. M. (Mrs.), The Clevelands. . . . . 0 20　*Am. Tract Soc.*

Shelley Memorials, from Authentic Sources. Edited by
    Lady Shelley. 16mo. cl. . . . . . 0 75　*Ticknor & Fields.*

Shells from the Sea Shore of Life. 12mo. . . . 0 75　*Clark & Mecker.*

Shepard, A. K., The Land of the Aztecs; or, Two Years
    in Mexico. 12mo. . . . . . . 　*Weed, P. & Co.*

Sherer, J., Gems of Masonry. Emblematic and Descrip-
    tive . . . . 0 50　*Moore, W., K.& Co.*

Sherman, D. (Rev.), Sketches of New England Divines. 1 00　*Carlton & Porter.*

Shillaber, B. P., Knitting-Work: a Web of Many Tex-
    tures, Wrought by Ruth Partington. 12mo. . 1 25　*Brown & Taggard.*

Ships in the Mist, and other Stories. By Lucy Larcom. 0 20　*Henry Hoyt.*

Short Stories, containing Thirty-one Stories. By Charles
    Dickens. 12mo., cl. . . . . . 1 50　*Peterson & Bros.*

——— Yarns. 18mo. . . . . 0 25　*Challen & Sons.*

Siberia: A Narrative of Seven Years' Exploration and
    Adventures in Siberia, Mongolia, the Kirghis
    Steppes, Chinese Tartary, and Part of Central
    Asia. By Thomas Witlam Atkinson. 12mo. . 1 25　*J. W. Bradley.*

Sidney, P., The Miscellaneous Works of Sir Philip Sid-
    ney, Knt. With a Life of the Author and Il-
    lustrative Notes. By William Gray, Esq. 8vo. 2 25　*T. O.H.P. Burn'm.*

Sidney Grey: a Tale of School Life. 16mo. . . 0 75　*F. D. Harriman.*

    The Same. 12mo., cl. . . . . . 0 75　*Carter & Bros.*

Silsbee, Mrs., Willie Winkle's Nursery Songs of Scotland. 0 75　*Ticknor & Fields.*

Sigourney, L. H. (Mrs.), Illustrated Poems. 8vo. . . 3 00　*Lindsay & B.*

——— " The Daily Counsellor. 12mo. . 1 50　*Brown & Gross.*

Silloway, T. W.. Text-Book of Modern Carpentry. 16mo. 1 25　*Crosby, N.,L.& Co.*

Silver Penny Series. 6 Vols. 16mo. . . . 1 50　*Walker, Wise & Co.*

Simms, W. G., The Cassique of Kiawah: a Romance of
    Carolina. 12mo. . . . . . . 1 25　*J. S. Redfield.*

Sims, J. M. (M. D.), Silver Sutures in Surgery. Discourse
    before the New York Academy of Medicine,
    delivered November, 1857. 8vo., pap. . . 0 50　*S. S. & W. Wood.*

Singer's Manual. By W. Williams. . . . . 0 50　*Shepard C. & B.*

Siogvolk, P., Walter Ashwood. A Love Story. 12mo. 1 00　*Rudd & Carleton.*

Sir Rohan's Ghost. A Romance. 12mo. . . . 1 00　*J. E. Tilton & Co.*

Sixty Years' Gleanings from Life's Harvest. By John
    Brown, of Cambridge. 12mo. . . . . . 1 00 *D. Appleton & Co.*
Skater's (The) Pocket Companion. 18mo. . . . 0 25 *Mayhew & Baker.*
Skeleton Monk (The), and other Poems. By F. D. H.
    Janvier. 12mo. cl. . . . . 1 00 *Challen & Son.*
Sketch Book of Popular Geology. With Descriptive
    Sketches from a Geologist's Portfolio. By Hugh
    Miller. 12mo. . . . . 1 25 *Gould & Lincoln.*
Sketches from Life; or, Illustrations of the Influence of
    Christianity. Second Series. 12mo. . . 0 60 *Am. Tract Soc.*
—— of Moravian Life and Character. By James
    Henry. 12mo. . . . . *Lippincott & Co.*
—— of New England Divines. By Rev. D. Sherman. 1 00 *Carleton & Porter.*
Slaughter, P. (Rev.), Man and Woman; or, the Law of
    Honor applied to the Solution of the Problem,
    Why are so many more Women than Men Chris-
    tians? 18mo. . . . . 0 50 *Lippincott & Co.*
Slaveholder (The) Abroad; or, Billy Buck's Visit, with
    his Master, to England. A series of Letters
    from Dr. Pleasant Jones to Major Joseph Jones,
    of Georgia. 12mo. cloth. . . . . . 1 25   "
Slavery in History. By Adam Gurowski. 12mo. . 1 00 *A. B. Burdick.*
Slick, Jonathan, High Life in New York. 12mo. . 1 25 *Peterson & Bros.*
—— Sam, The Courtship and Adventures of Jonathan
    Homebred. 12mo. . . . . . . 1 00 *Dick & Fitzgerald.*
Sloan's, S., City and Suburban Architecture. In which
    are exhibited numerous Designs and Details for
    Public Edifices, Private Residences, and Mercan-
    tile Buildings. Illustrated with 136 Folio
    Engravings, accompanied by Specifications and
    Historical and Explanatory Text. Folio. . 12 00 *Lippincott & Co.*
—— " Constructive Architecture. A Guide for the
    Builder and Carpenter; exhibiting the Construc-
    tion of a Series of Designs for Roofs, Domes,
    Spires, and the Five Orders of Architecture, se-
    lected from the best specimens of Grecian and
    Roman Art, with the figured dimensions of their
    Height, Projection, and Profile. To which is
    added a Treatise on Practical Geometry. The
    whole illustrated by 62 plates, and accompanied
    by Explanatory Text. 4to. . . . . 5 00   "
Smiles, S., Brief Biographies. 12mo. . . . . 1 25 *Ticknor & Fields.*
—— " Self-Help; with Illustrations of Character and
    Conduct. 12mo. 1 00

Smith, B. M. (Rev.), Family Religion; or the Domestic
　　　Relations, as regulated by Christian Principles.　0 60　*Presb. Bd. of Pub.*
———— C. A. (Rev.), Men of the Olden Time. 12mo. .　0 75　*Lindsay & B.*
———— E. D., New York Common Pleas Reports. Vol. 4.　5 50　*John S. Voorhies.*
———— Elizabeth E., Three Eras of Woman's Life. 12mo.　1 00　*T.O.H.P. Burn'm.*
———— E. P., Reports of Cases Argued and Determined
　　　in the Court of Appeals of the State of New
　　　York. Vol. II. 8vo. . . . . .　2 00　*Banks & Brothers.*
———— Emeline S., Poems and Ballads. . .　1 00　*Rudd & Carleton.*
———— H. B. (D. D.), History of the Church of Christ, in
　　　Chronological Tables. Folio. . . .　6 00　*Charles Scribner.*
———— J. (Rev.), The Better Land. A Book for the Aged.　0 20　*Pres. Bd. of Pub.*
———— J. F., Dick Markham; or, Smiles and Tears.　0 50　*Dick & Fitzgerald.*
———— " Philip Blandford; or, How to Win a Sweet-
　　　heart. 8vo. . . . . . .　0 50　　　"
———— " Prince Charles; or, the Young Pretender.　0 50　　　"
———— T., An Examination of the Question of Ana-
　　　thœsia. 8vo., cloth. . . . . .　　　　*John A. Gray.*
———— Wm., A Dictionary of the Bible. 2 vols. Vol.
　　　I., A to Juttah. 8vo. . . . .　5 00　*Little, Brown & Co.*
———— " A Smaller History of Greece, from the
　　　Earliest Times to the Roman Conquest. 12mo.　0 60　*Harper & Bros.*
———— W. C. (Rev.), Sketch-Book; or, Miscellaneous
　　　Anecdotes, proper to the Pulpit and the Plat-
　　　form. 12mo. . . . . . .　0 75　*Carlton & Porter.*
———— W. R., The Uses of Solitude. Small 4to. paper.　0 25　*Munsell & Rowland*
———— W. T. (M. D.), Lectures on Obstetrics. With
　　　Notes and Additions, by A. K. Gardner, M. D.　4 00　*R. M. De Witt.*
———— W. W., Juvenile Speller. . . . .　0 38　*Barnes & Burr.*
———— " and Martin, E., Book-keeping by Single
　　　and Double Entry. 4to. . . . .　0 75　　　"
Smucker, S., History of the Four Georges, Kings of
　　　England. 12mo. cl. . . . . .　1 25　*D. Appleton & Co.*
———— S. M. (LL. D.), A History of all Religions, con-
　　　　　taining a Statement of their Ori-
　　　　　gin, Development, Doctrines,
　　　　　and Discipline. 12mo. . .　1 00　*Duane Rulison.*
———— " " A History of the Modern Jews,
　　　　　from the Destruction of Jerusa-
　　　　　salem to the Present Time. .　1 00　　　"
———— " " The Life of Elisha Kent Kane
　　　and other American Explorers. 12mo. . .　1 25　*J. W. Bradley.*
Smyth, T. (D. D.), Obedience the Life of Missions. 18mo.　0 30　*Presb. Bd. of Pub.*
Snow-flakes and Sunbeams of Young Fur Traders. By
　　　R. M. Ballantyne. 16mo. cl. . . .　0 75　*Phinney, B. & M.*

Snow Storm (The). 18mo. cl. . . . . . 0 25 *Am. S. S. Union.*

Sociable (The); or, One Thousand and One Home Amusements. 12mo. . . . . . . 1 00 *Dick & Fitzgerald.*

Social Relations in our Southern States. By D. R. Hundley. 12mo. . . . . . 1 00 *Henry B. Price.*

Socialist Friend (The); containing a Collection of Meditations and Prayers. 12mo. . . . . 0 50 *P. F. Cunningham.*

Socrates, Life, Teachings, and Death of. From Grote's History of Greece. 18mo., cl. . . . 0 50 *Sheldon & Co.*

Somnambulism and Cramp. By Baron Reichenbach. Translated from the German, by John S. Hittell. 1 00 *Calvin Blanchard.*

Songs for the Sabbath School and Vestry. Edited by . B. W. Williams. . . . . . . *Henry Hoyt.*

—— " the Sorrowing. By H. N. 12mo. . . 0 75 *Phinney, B. & M*

—— in the Night; or, Hymns for the Sick and Suffering. 0 75 *J. E. Tilton & Co.*

—— of Ireland. Edited by Samuel Lover. 12mo. . 1 00 *Dick & Fitzgerald.*

—— " the Church; or, Psalms and Hymns of the Protestant Episcopal Church. By George C. Davies. 12mo. . . . . . 1 25 *Applegate & Co.*

—— " " Woodland, the Garden and the Sea. Small 4to. With six beautiful illustrations, colored. Beveled boards, gilt. . . . 2 00 *A.D.F. Randolph.*

—— and Prayers for the family Altar. By the Rev. William Staunton, D. D. 12mo., cl. . 0 63 *Daniel Dana. jr.*

Sophia De Brentz; or, the Sword of Truth. 18mo. . *Henry Hoyt.*

Sophie Krantz; or, the Cot and the Castle. By Surrey Keene. 18mo. . . . . . 0 50 *F. D. Harriman.*

Sorsby, N. T., Horizontal Plowing, and Hill-side Ditching. Paper. . . . . . 0 50 *S. H. Goetzel & Co.*

Soul Prosperity. Its Nature, its Fruits, and its Culture. By Charles D. Mallary, D. D. 12mo. . 0 75 *Sou. Bap. Pub. So.*

South Carolina College, History of, from its Incorporation, 1801 to 1857—including Sketches of its Presidents and Professors. By M. La Borde, M. D. 8vo. . . . . . 2 00 *Peter B. Glass.*

—— and North; or, Impressions Received during a Trip to Cuba and the South. By John S. C. Abbott. 12mo. . . . . . 0 75 *Abbey & Abbott.*

Southern Institutes; or, An Inquiry into the Origin and Early Prevalence of Slavery and the Slave Trade; with an Analysis of the Laws, History, and Government of the Institution in the Principal Nations, Ancient and Modern, from the Earliest Ages down to the Present Time. With Notes and Comments in Defense of Southern Institutions. By George S. Sawyer. 8vo. *Lippincott & Co.*

Southern Notes for Northern Circulation. . . .	0 25	*Thayer& Eldridge*
——— and South-western Sketches. Fun, Sentiment, and Adventure. 12mo.	0 60	*J. W. Randolph.*
Southey, Robert, The Poetical Works of. With a Memoir of the Author. 10 vols. . . .	7 50	*Little, B. & Co.*
Southgate, H. (D. D.), Parochial Sermons. 12mo. .	1 00	*Daniel Dana, jr.*
Southwold : a Novel. By Mrs. Lillie Devereux Umsted.	1 00	*Rudd & Carleton.*
Southworth, E. D. E. N., The Haunted Homestead ; with an Autobiography of the Author.	1 25	*Peterson & Bros.*
——— " The Lady of the Isle : a Romance from Real Life. 12mo. . .	1 25	"
——— " The Mother-in-Law : a Tale of Domestic Life. 12mo. . . .	1 25	"
——— " The Two Sisters. 12mo. . .	1 25	"
Souvestre, E., Isle of the Dead ; or, the Keeper of the Lazaretto. 18mo.	0 25	*Kelly, H. & P.*
Spalding, M. T. (D. D.), The History of the Reformation in Germany, Switzerland, England, Ireland, Scotland, the Netherlands, France and Northern Europe. 2 vols. 8vo.	2 50	*Webb & Levering.*
Sparks from a Locomotive ; or, Life and Liberty in Europe. 12mo. cloth.	1 00	*Derby & Jackson.*
Spaulding, J. (Rev.), Stories of the Ocean ; or, Gems from Seafaring Life. 18mo. . . .	0 30	*R. Carter & Bros.*
Specimens of Douglas Jerrold's Wit ; together with Selections, chiefly from his Contributions to Journals. 16mo.	0 75	*Ticknor & Fields.*
Spencer, H., Education : Intellectual, Moral, and Physical.	1 00	*D. Appleton & Co.*
——— Thomas (Rev.), Memoir of. By Thomas Raffles, D.D., LL.D. 12mo.	0 63	*Sheldon & Co.*
Spiritual Conferences. By Frederick William Faber, D. D. 12mo.	0 75	*J. Murphy & Co.*
——— Songs : being One Hundred Hymns not to be found in the Hymn-books commonly used. Selected by the Rev. J. O. Ryle, B. A. 24mo. Cloth, gilt edge.	0 50	*A.D.F.Randolph.*
Spiritualism : an Oral Discussion on Spiritualism, between S. B. Brittan and Dr. D. D. Hanson, at Hartford, Conn. 8vo.	0 63	*S. T. Munson.*
——— Tested. By George W. Samson, D. D. 16mo.	0 42	*Gould & Lincoln.*
Sprague, W. B. (D. D.), Annals of the American Pulpit. Vol. V. and VI. 8vo. Each.	2 50	*R. Carter & Bros.*
——— " Joseph ; or, The Model Young Man. 18mo.	0 50	*A.D.F.Randolph.*

Spurgeon, C. II. (Rev.), Sermons of. Series IV., V., and
      VI. 12mo. . . Each 1 00 *Sheldon & Co.*

————— " Smooth Stones taken from
Ancient Brooks. Being a Collection of Sentences, Illustrations, and Quaint Sayings, from
the Works of that Renowned Puritan, Thomas
Brooks. 16mo. . . . . . . 0 60   "

Spurgeon's Gems: being Brilliant Passages from the Discourses of the Rev. C. H. Spurgeon. 12mo. . 1 00   "

Squier, E. G., Collection of Rare and Original Documents
and Relations concerning the Discovery and
Conquest of America, chiefly from the Spanish
Archives. Small 4to. . . . . . 3 00 *C. B. Norton.*

—————" (Mrs.), The Demi-Monde; a Satire on Society,
from the French of Alexandre Dumas, jr. 0 50 *Lippincott & Co.*

————— M. P. (D. D.), Reason and the Bible; or, The Truth
of Religion. 12mo. . . . . . 1 00 *Charles Scribner.*

St. Augustine (Florida), History and Antiquities of. By
G. R. Fairbanks. 8vo. . . . . . 1 50 *C. B. Norton.*

St. John, P. B., The Sea of Ice; or, The Arctic Adventurers. 12mo. . . . . . . 0 75 *Mayhew & Baker.*

————— C. H., Poems. 12mo. . . . . . . 0 75 *A. Williams & Co.*

St. Paul, A Commentary on St. Paul's Epistle to the
Galatians. By Martin Luther. 8vo. . 1 25 *Smith, E. & Co.*

St. Paul's to St. Sophia; or Sketchings in Europe. By
Richard C. McCormick. 12mo. . . . 1 00 *Sheldon & Co.*

Stanley, C. H., The Chess Player's Instructor. 18mo. 0 38 *R. M. De Witt.*

Staunton, R. H., Kentucky Code of Practice in Civil and
      Criminal Cases. 8vo., law sheep . 5 00 *Rob't Clarke & Co.*

————— " Practical Manual for the Use of Executors, Administrators, Guardians, and
Trustees in Kentucky. 8vo. . . 4 50   "

————— " Practical Treatise for the Use of Justices of the Peace, Constables, Sheriffs,
Jailors, and Coroners of Kentucky. 4 00   "

————— " Revised Statutes of Kentucky to 1860. 10 00   "

————— W. (D. D.), Songs and Prayers for the Family
Altar. 12mo., cloth. . . . . . 0 63 *Daniel Dana, Jr.*

Stars (The) and the Angels. 12mo. . . . 1 25 *W. S. & A. Martien.*

Steam for the Million. A Popular Treatise on Steam
and its Application to the Useful Arts, especially
to Navigation. A New and Revised Edition.
By J. H. Ward, Commander U. S. Navy. 8vo. 1 00 *D. Van Nostrand.*

Stedman, E. C., Poems, Lyrical and Idyllic. 16mo. . 0 75 *Charles Scribner.*

Stedman, E. C., The Prince's Ball. A Brochure from
"Vanity Fair." 12mo. . . . . . 0 50 *Rudd & Carleton.*
Steele Family. A Genealogical History of John and
George Steele (settlers of Hartford, Conn.),
1635-'36, and their Descendants. By Daniel
Steele Durrie. 4to. . . . . . . 2 00 *Munsell&Rowland*
Stephens, Anna S., Mary Derwent. 12mo. . . 1 25 *Peterson & Bros.*
Stephenson, George, The Life of. By Samuel Smiles. . 1 25 *Ticknor & Fields.*
Steps Towards Heaven. A Series of Lay Sermons. By
T. S. Arthur. 12mo., cl. . . . . . 1 00 *Derby & Jackson.*
Steuben, F. W., The Life of Frederich William Von
Steuben, Major-General in the Revolutionary
Army. By Frederich Kapp. 12mo. . . 1 75 *Mason & Brothers.*
Stevens, A., The History of the Religious Movement of
the Eighteenth Century, called Methodism, Con-
sidered. Vol. I. From the Origin of Method-
ism to the death of Whitefield. 12mo. . . 1 00 *Carlton & Porter.*
—— G., Love and Mock Love; or, How to Marry to
the end of Conjugal Satisfaction. 18mo. . . 0 25 *B. Marsh.*
—— W. B. (Rev.), A History of Georgia, from its
First Discovery by Europeans to the
Adoption of the present Constitution in
MDCCXCVIII. 2 vols. . . . . 2 00 *E. H. Butler &Co.*
—— " The Book of Prayer for the House of
Prayer. 18mo. . . . . . . *G. H. & L. N. Ide.*
Stewart, Alvan, Writings and Speeches of, on Slavery.
Edited by Luther Rawdon Marsh. 12mo . 1 00 *A. B. Burdick.*
—— G. C., The Hierophant: or, Gleanings from the
Past. Being an Exposition of Biblical As-
tronomy, and the Symbolism and Mysteries on
which were founded all Religious and Secret
Societies. 12mo. . . . . . . 1 00 *Ross & Tousey.*
Stier, R., The Words of the Lord Jesus. Translated from
the Second Revised and Enlarged German Edi-
tion, by the Rev. William B. Pope. Vol. V. 8vo. 2 00 *Smith, E. & Co.*
Stiles, H. R., The History of Ancient Windsor, Connecti-
cut, including East Windsor, South Windsor,
and Ellington, prior to 1768, to the Present
Time. 8vo. . . . . 3 00 *Charles B. Norton.*
Still Hour (The); or, Communion with God. By Austin
Phelps. 16mo. . . . . . . 0 38 *Gould & Lincoln.*
Stille, A. (M. D.), Therapeutics and Materia Medica. A
Treatise on the Action and Uses of Medicinal
Agents, including their Description and His-
tory. 2 vols. 8vo. . . . . . . 8 00 *Blanchard & Lea.*

Stockly, Harriet, Familiar Conversations on the Queries.   0 38   *T. E. Zell.*
Stoddard, David T. (Rev.), Memoir of. By Joseph P.
    Thompson, D. D. 12mo. . . . . . . 1 00   *Sheldon, & Co.*
——— R. H., The Loves and Heroines of the Poets. . 12 00   *Derby & Jackson.*
Stone, B. W., The Works of. Vol. I. 12mo., cl. . . 1 25   *Moore, W. K. & Co.*
Stone Him to Death; or, the Jewish and Christian
    Dispensations compared and contrasted with
    the Fourth Commandment. 12mo., paper. . 0 25   *Townsend & Co.*
Stork, T., A Christmas Book for Children. Square cl. . 0 63   *Lindsay & B.*
Stories from famous Ballads. For children. By Grace
    Greenwood. Sq. 18mo. . . . . . 0 50   *Ticknor & Fields.*
——— of Henry and Henrietta. Translated from the
    French of Abel Dufresne. By H. B. A. . 0 75   *T. O. H. P. Burnham.*
——— " Inventors and Discoverers in Science and the
    Useful Arts. By John Timbs. 12mo. . 0 75   *Harper & Brothers.*
——— " Scotland and its Adjacent Islands. By Mrs.
    Thomas Geldart. 18mo. cl. . . . 0 50   *Sheldon & Co.*
——— " Waterloo. By William H. Maxwell. 8vo. . 0 50   *Peterson & Bros.*
——— " the Ocean; or, Gems from Seafaring Life. By
    Rev. John Spalding. 18mo. . . . 0 30   *Carter & Brothers.*
Story, Thomas S., Conversation and Discussions of. Com-
    piled by Nathaniel Richardson. 12mo. cl. . 1 00   *T. E. Zell.*
Story of Bethlehem. A Book for the Young. By John
    R. Macduff, D. D. 16mo. . . . . 0 60   *Carter & Brothers.*
——— (The) of a Needle. By A. L. O. E. 24mo. . 0 25   "
——— " of a Pocket Bible. 12mo. cl. . . 0 85   *Henry Hoyt.*
——— " of Our Darling Nellie. 18mo. . . 0 38   *J. E. Tilton & Co.*
Stout, P. F., Nicaragua: Past, Present, and Future: a
    Description of its Inhabitants, Customs, Early
    History, &c. 12mo. . . . . . 1 25   *J. E. Potter.*
Stow, Baron, First Things; or the Development of
    Church Life. 16mo. . . . . . 0 60   *Gould & Lincoln*
Stowe, Harriet B., Our Charley and What to Do with
    Him. 18mo. . . . . . 0 50   *Phillips, S. & Co.*
——— "   The Minister's Wooing. 12mo. cl. . 1 25   *Derby & Jackson.*
Strahl, M., On the True Causes of Habitual Constipation,
    and the Most Reliable Remedies for the same. 0 50   *Westermann & Co.*
Straight Forward; or, Walking in the Light. By Lucy
    Ellen Guernsey. 18mo. . . . . 0 75   *Henry Hoyt.*
Stranger's (The) Stratagem; or, the Double Deceit, and
    other Stories. By Sarah J. C. Whittlesey. . 1 00   *M. W. Dodd.*
Strains from Helen's Music Box. 18mo. . . 0 15   *F. D. Harriman.*
Strauss, F., The Glory of the House of Israel; or, the
    Hebrew's Pilgrimage to the Holy City. 12mo. 1 25   *Lippincott & Co.*

Street, A. B., Woods and Waters; or, the Saranacs and
      Racket. 12mo. .   .   .   .   .   1 25   *M. Doolady.*

Street Thoughts. By the Rev. Henry M. Dexter. 16mo.   *Crosby, N., L. & Co.*

Strickland, Agnes, Lives of the Queens of Scotland.
      Vols. VII. and VIII. 12mo. Each .   . 1 00   *Harper & Brothers.*

—— W. P., Autobiography of Dan Young, a New
      England Preacher of the Olden Time.   1 00   *Carlton & Porter.*

—— "   Old Mackinaw; or, the Fortress of
      the Lakes and its surroundings. 12mo. .   1 00   *J. Challen & Son.*

Strong, T., A Treatise on Elementary and Higher Al-
      gebra. 8vo. .   .   .   .   .   2 00   *Pratt, O. & Co.*

Struggles (The) of the Early Christians, from the Days
      of our Saviour to the Reign of Constantine. .   0 50   *J. P. Jewett & Co.*

Struggles for Life. By the Author of "Seven Stormy
      Sundays." 12mo. .   .   .   .   1 00   *Walker, Wise & Co.*

Student Life; Letters and Recollections for a Young
      Friend. By Samuel Osgood. 12mo. .   .   0 75   *James Miller.*

Student's Hume (The). A History of England, from the
      Earliest Times to the Revolution in 1688. By
      David Hume, Abridged, Incorporating the Re-
      searches of Recent Historians, and continued
      down to the year 1858. 12mo. .   .   .   1 00   *Harper & Bros.*

—— (The) Memorandum of the New Testament. .   1 00   *T. H. Stockton.*

Studies from Life. By Miss Muloch. 12mo., cloth. .   *Harper & Bros.*

—— in Animal Life. By George Henry Lewes. 12mo.   0 40   "

—— of Christianity. By Rev. James Martineau. .   1 00   *Am. Univ'n Ass'n.*

—— Stories, and Memoirs. By Mrs. Anna Jame-
      son. Blue and Gold. .   .   .   .   0 75   *Tioknor & Fields.*

Sullivan, James, The Life and Writings of. By T. C.
      Amory. 8vo. 2 vols. .   .   .   .   *Phillips, S. & Co.*

Summer (A) with the Little Grays. By H. W. P.   0 50   *Walker, Wise & Co.*

Sunday Afternoons in the Nursery; or, Familiar Narra-
      tives from the Book of Genesis. Square 16mo.   0 50   *Carter & Bros.*

—— Enjoyments; or, Religion made Pleasant to
      Children. 18mo. .   .   .   .   0 25   *Daniel Dana, Jr.*

—— Evening Thoughts; or, Great Truths in Plain
      Words. 18mo. By Mrs. Thomas Geldart. .   0 50   *Sheldon & Co.*

—— Morning Thoughts; or, Great Truths in Plain
      Words. By Mrs. Thomas Geldart. 18mo. .   0 50   "

—— Sketches for Children. By a Father. 18mo.   0 50   *M. W. Dodd.*

—— Excursion (The) and What Came of it. .   0 20   *Henry Hoyt.*

Sunny South (The); or, The Southerner at Home. Em-
      bracing Five Years' Experience of a Northern
      Governess in the Land of Sugar, Rice and
      Cotton. 12mo. .   .   .   .   .   1 25   *Geo. G. Evans.*

Sunshine; or Kate Vinton. By Harriet B. M'Keever.   0 75   *Lindsay & Blak'n.*
Swan, J. R., Pleadings and Precedents under the Ohio
    Code. 8vo., law shp. . . . .   5 00   *Robt. Clarke & Co.*
——— " Treatise for Justices and Constables in Ohio.   4 50   "
——— " and Critchfield, L. J., Revised Statutes of
    Ohio, to August, 1860. 2 vols. 8vo., law s. 10 00   "
Sweat, M. J. M. (Mrs.), Ethel's Love Life. A New Eng-
    land Novel. 12mo. . . . .   1 00   *Rudd & Carleton.*
——— " Highways of Travel; or, a Summer in
    Europe. 12mo. . . . .   1 00   *Walker, Wise & Co.*
Swedenborg, E., A Hermetic Philosopher. A Sequel to
    Remarks on Alchemy and the Alchemists. 12mo.   1 00   *D. Appleton & Co.*
Sweet, S. N., Practical Elocution. 12mo. . .   0 75   *Moore & Nims.*
Swimmers' Guide (The). By an Experienced Swimmer.   0 12   *H. Dexter & Co.*
Swinton, W., Rambles among Words. Their Poetry,
    History, and Wisdom. 12mo. . . .   1 00   *Charles Scribner.*
Switzerland, Letters from. By Samuel Irenæus Prime.   1 00   *Sheldon & Co.*
Sword and Gown. By the author of "Guy Livingstone."   0 75   *Ticknor & Fields.*
   The same. 8vo., paper. . . . .   0 25   *Harper & Bros.*
Sybil Gray; or, the Triumphs of Virtue. 8vo., paper.   .   0 25   *Peterson & Bros.*
Sydney, Philip (Sir), The Life and Times of. 16mo. . .   1 00   *Ticknor & Fields.*
Sylvan Holt's Daughter. By Holme Lee. 12mo. .   .   1 00   *Harper & Bros.*
Sylvia's World. Crimes which the Law does not Reach.
    By the author of "Busy Moments of an Idle
    Woman." 12mo. . . . . .   1 00   *Derby & Jackson.*
Symbols of the Capital; or, Civilization in New York.
    By A. D. Mayo. 12mo. . . . .   1 00   *Thatcher & H.*

T

Tabby's Travels; or, the Holiday Adventures of a Kitte·
    By Lucy Ellen Guernsey. 18mo. cl. .   0 50   *A. D. F. Randolph.*
Taft, J., A Practical Treatise on Operative Dentistry.   .   2 75   *Lindsay & Blak'n.*
Tait, J. R., Dolce Far Niente, and other Poems. 12mo.   0 50   *Parry & McMillan.*
——— " European Life, Legend, and Landscape. 8vo.   1 00   *J. Challen & Son.*
Taking a Stand. By the author of "Hugh Fisher,"   .   0 25   *Henry Hoyt.*
Tale (A) of Two Cities. By Charles Dickens. 8vo. pap.   0 50   *Peterson & Bros.*
Tales About Animals. 12mo. gilt edges. . .   1 50   *D. Appleton & Co.*

Talk (A) with the Ganges; or, an Epithalamium on the
    First Hindoo Widow Marriage. 8vo. . . 0 25 *A. D.F. Randolph.*
Talley, Susan A., Poems. 12mo. . . . . 0 75 *Rudd & Carleton.*
Tanner, T. H. (M. D.), Treatise on the Diseases of Infancy
          and Childhood. 12mo. cl. . . 1 00 *Lindsay & Blak'n.*
—— " " A Manual of the Practice of Medi-
    cine. 12mo. limp. cl. . . . . 1 25 "
Tasso, Torquato, The Life of. By J. H. Wiffen. 18mo. 0 50 *Sheldon & Co.*
Taylor, Bayard, At Home and Abroad; A Sketch Book
          of Life, Scenery, and Men. 12mo. . 1 25 *G. P. Putnam.*
—— " Travels in Greece and Russia, with an
    Excursion to Crete. 12mo. . . . 1 25 "
—— C. (M. D.), Five Years in China, with an Account
    of the Great Rebellion, and a Description of St.
    Helena. 12mo. . . . . . 1 25 *Derby & Jackson.*
—— C. B. (Rev.), The Bar of Iron; and the Conclu-
    sion of the Matter. A True Story. 18mo. . 0 25 *Pres. Board of Pub.*
—— G. B., Cousin Guy. 16mo. . . . 0 50* *Sheldon & Co.*
—— " Claiborne. 16mo. . . . . 0 50 "
—— " Kenny. 18mo. . . . . 0 50 "
—— G. H. (M. D.), An Exposition of the Swedish
    Method of Treating Disease by Movement-
    Cure. 12mo. . . . . . 1 25 *Fowler & Wells.*
—— Isaac, Logic in Theology, and Other Essays.
    With a Sketch of the Life of the Author. 12mo. 1 25 *William Gowans.*
—— Jeremy (D. D.), The Great Exemplar; or, The
        Life of Our Ever Blessed Saviour
        Jesus Christ. 2 vols. 12mo. . 2 00 *Carter & Brothers.*
—— " · The Life of. By George L. Duyck-
    inck. 18mo. . . . . . 0 40 *F. D. Harriman.*
—— J. N., A Treatise on the American Law of Land-
    lord and Tenant. 8vo. . . . 5 00 *Little, Brown & Co.*
—— Jas. W., Manual of the Ohio School System. 8vo. 1 50 *Robt. Clarke & Co.*
—— N. W. (D. D.), Essays, Lectures, &c., upon Select
        Topics in Revealed Theology. . 1 13 *Clark, A., M. & Co.*
—— " Lectures on the Moral Government
        of God. 2 vols. 8vo. . 3 00 "
—— " Practical Sermons. 8vo. . . 1 25 "
Teachers' (The) Indicator and Parent's Manual, for School
    and Home Education. 12mo. . . 1 25 *Moore, W., K. & Co.*
—— Pocket Record of Attendance, Deportment, and
    Scholarship. By J. L. Tracy. 16mo. . 0 40 *Barnes & Burr.*
Teachings of Patriots and Statesmen; or, The Founders
    of the Republic on Slavery. By Ezra B. Chase.   *J. W. Bradley.*

Teddy White; or, The Little Orange Sellers. 18mo. . 0 25 *Henry Hoyt.*

Te Deum Laudamus: set to Music in two Compositions.
A, by William Henry Monk; D, by William
Staunton, D.D. . . . . . . 0 40 *Daniel Dana, Jr.*

Tefft, B. F. (Rev.), Methodism Successful; and the Internal Causes of its Success. 12mo., cl. . . 1 25 *Derby & Jackson.*

—— J. D., The True Philosophy of Teaching the
Young to Read. 12mo. . . . . *Tibballs & Co.*

Telescope (The), An Allegory. 18mo. . . . 0 25 *Henry Hoyt.*

Teller, Margaret E., Fred Laurence; or, The World College. 18mo., cl. . . . . . . 0 63 *M. W. Dodd.*

Temper. A Novel. By Miss Marryatt. 12mo. . . 1 00 *Dick & Fitzgerald.*

Ten years of Preacher-Life; or, Chapters from an Autobiography. By William Henry Milburn. 12mo. 1 00 *Derby & Jackson.*

Tenant-House (The); or, Embers from Poverty's Hearth-
Stone. By A. J. H. Duganne. 12mo. . . 1 25 *R. M. De Witt.*

Tenney, S., Geology for Teachers, Classes, and Private
Students. 12mo. . . . . . . 1 18 *Butler & Co.*

Tennyson, Alfred, Idyls of the King. 16mo., cl. . . 0 75 *Ticknor & Fields.*

Tent and Harem: Notes of an Oriental Trip. By Caroline Paine. 12mo. . . . . . 1 00 *D. Appleton & Co.*

Terence (The Comedies of). Literally Translated into
English Prose, with Notes. By Henry Thomas
Riley, B.A. To which is added the blank verse
translation of George Colman. 12mo. . . 0 75 *Harper & Bros.*

Terry, Rose. Poems. 12mo. . . . . . 0 75 *Ticknor & Fields.*

Texas; her Resources and her Public Men. A Compan-
ion to J. De Cordova's new Map of Texas. 12mo. 1 25 *Lippincott & Co.*

Text-Book in Intellectual Philosophy. By J. T. Champlin, D.D. 12mo. . . . . . 0 75 *Crosby, N., L.& Co.*

—— Of Modern Carpentry. By Thomas W. Silloway. 1 25 "

Thackeray, W. M., Lovell the Widower. A Novel. . 0 25 *Harper & Bros.*

—— " The Four Georges. Sketches of Manners, Morals, Court, and Town Life. 12mo. . 0 75 "

Thayer, W. M., Doing and Not Doing; or, The Convert
Guide. 16mo. . . . . *Henry Hoyt.*

—— " From Poor-House to Pulpit; or, The Triumphs of the late Dr. John Kitto, from
Boyhood to Manhood. . . . *E. O. Libby & Co.*

—— " Tales from the Bible for the Young. . *J. E. Tilton & Co.*

—— " The Bobbin Boy; or, How Nat got his
Learning. 12mo. . . . . 0 75 "

—— " The Poor Girl and True Woman; or, Elements of Woman's Success. 16mo. . 0 75 *Gould & Lincoln.*

10

The R. R. R's.: My Little Neighbors. A Story for the
"Younger Members." . . . . . *Walker, W. & Co.*

Theology of Christian Experience. By George D. Armstrong, D. D. 12mo. . . . . 1 00 *C. Scribner.*

Thirty Years in the Arctic Regions; or, The Adventures
of Sir John Franklin. 12mo. . . . 1 25 *H. Dayton.*

Three Pines (The). By Jacob Abbott. 16mo. . . 0 50 *Harper & Bros.*

Theologia Dogmatica, Quam Concinnavit Franciscus Pa-
tricius Kenrick, Archiepiscopus Baltimorensis.
3 vols. 8vo. . . . . . . 6 00 *J. Murphy & Co.*

Three Wakings (The). With Hymns and Songs. 16mo. 0 60 *Carter & Bros.*

Theremin, F., Eloquence a Virtue; or, Outlines of a
Systematic Rhetoric. Revised edition. 12mo. 0 75 *W. F. Draper.*

This One Thing I Do. A Call to Christian Earnestness. 0 31 *Presb. Pub. Com.*

Tholuck, Augustus, Commentary on the Gospel of John.
Translated from the German by
Charles P. Krauth, D. D. 8vo. . 2 25 *Smith, Eng. & Co.*

——— " Commentary on the Sermon on the
Mount. Translated by the Rev. R. Lundin
Brown. 8vo. . . . . . 2 25 "

Thomas, C. W. (Rev.), Adventures and Observations on
the West Coast of Africa, and its Islands. 12mo. 1 25 *Derby & Jackson.*

Thompson, A. C., Morning Hours in Patmos; the Opening Vision of the Apocalypse, and Christ's
Epistles to the Seven Churches of Asia. 12mo. 1 00 *Gould & Lincoln.*

——— J. P. (D. D.), Love and Penalty; or, Eternal
Punishment consistent with the Fatherhood of God. 16mo. cl. . . . 0 75 *Sheldon & Co.*

——— " The Christian Graces. A Series of Lectures on 2d Peter, 1, 5, 12. 18mo. . 0 75 "

——— W. (D. D.), An Outline of the Necessary Laws of
Thought. 12mo. . . . . . 1 00 *John Bartlett.*

——— W. M. (D. D.), The Land and the Book; or,
Biblical Illustrations, Drawn from the Manners
and Customs, the Scenes and Scenery of the
Holy Land. 2 vols., 12mo. . . . 3 50 *Harper & Bros.*

Thornbury, W., Life in Spain: Past and Present. 12mo. 1 00 "

Thorndale; or, the Conflict of Opinions. 12mo., cl. : 1 25 *Ticknor & Fields.*

Thornton, J. W., The Pulpit of the American Revolution; or, the Political Sermons of the Period of
1776. 12mo. . . . . . . 1 25 *Gould & Lincoln.*

Thoughtless Rosa, and Other Stories. 18mo. . 0 25 *Carlton & Porter.*

Thoughts of Favored Hours, upon Bible Incidents and
Characters. By Josiah Copley. 18mo. . 0 50 *Lippincott & Co.*

Three Clerks (The). By Anthony Trollope. 12mo.	1 00	*Harper & Bros.*
——— Eras of Woman's Life. By Elizabeth Elton Smith.	1 00	*T.O.H.P. Burn'm.*
Throne of David (The); from the Consecration of the Shepherd of Bethlehem to the Rebellion of Prince Absalom. By the Rev. J. H. Ingraham, LL. D. 12mo, ...	1 25	*G. G. Evans.*
Tidball, W. L., The Mexican's Bride; or, the Ranger's Revenge. 8vo. paper.	0 25	*W. Skelley.*
Tiffany, O., Brandon; or, A Hundred Years Ago. A Tale of the American Colonies. 12mo. . .	1 00	*Stanford&Delisser*
Tighe Lyfford: a Novel. 12mo. . . .	1 00	*James Miller.*
Tillotson, J., Tales about Animals. 12mo. cl., gilt edges.	1 50	*D. Appleton & Co.*
Timbs, J., School Days of Eminent Men. 12mo. .	1 00	*Follett, Foster & Co.*
——— " Stories of Inventors and Discoverers in Science and the Useful Arts. 12mo.	0 75	*Harper & Bros.*
Timrod, Henry, Poems. 12mo.	0 75	*Ticknor & Fields.*
Tin Trumpet (The); or, Heads and Tails for the Wise and Waggish. 12mo. cl.	1 25	*D. Appleton & Co.*
Titcomb's Letters to Young People, Single and Married, by Timothy Titcomb, Esq. `(Dr. J. G. Holland).	1 00	*Charles Scribner.*
Title Hunting. By E. L. Llewellyn. 12mo. . · .	1 00	*Lippincott & Co.*
Tobacco: Its Use and Abuse. By John Lizars. 16mo.	0 38	*Lindsay & Blak'n.*
Todd, John (Rev.), The Angel of the Iceberg; and other Stories. 16mo.	0 75	*Bridgman&Childs*
——— " Lectures to Children; familiarly illustrating Important Truth. 2d series.	0 50	"
——— R. B. (M. D.), Clinical Lectures on certain Acute Diseases. 8vo.	1 75	*Blanchard & Lea.*
——— S. E., The Young Farmer's Manual, describing the Manipulations of the Farm in a Plain and Intelligible Manner. 12mo. . . .	1 25	*Saxton & Barker.*
Toll Gate (The). 18mo. . . . ·. .	0 25	*Carter & Brothers.*
Tom Brown at Oxford; a Sequel to "School Days at Rugby." By the author of "School Days at Rugby." Part first. 12mo. cl.	1 00	*Ticknor & Fields.*
The Same. 12mo. cl.	0 38	*Harper & Bros.*
Tomes, J., A System of Dental Surgery. 8vo. . .	3 50	*Lindsay & Blak'n.*
Tomlinson, W. P., Kansas in Eighteen Fifty-eight; being chiefly a History of the Recent Troubles in the Territory. 12mo.	1 00	*H. Dayton.*
Touchstone (The) of Character: translated from the French of the Abbé Frederick Edward Chassay.	0 63	*P. O'Shea.*
Tounghoo Women; Ladies, will you Approve or Condemn? 8vo.	0 25	*A.D.F. Randolph.*

Towle, N. C., A History and Analysis of the Constitution
    of the United States. 12mo.   .   .   1 25   *Little, Brown & Co.*
Townsend J., The Code of Procedure of the State of New
    York, as amended to 1860. 7th edition, 8vo. . 6 00   *J. S. Voorhies.*
—— Virginia F., By-and-By. 12mo.   .   .   0 63   *R. L. Delisser.*
——   "   Buds from Christmas Boughs. 12mo. 0 63   "
——   "   While it Was Morning. 12mo.   . 1 00   *Derby & Jackson.*
Toynbee, J., The Diseases of the Ear. Their Nature, Pa-
    thology, and Treatment. 8vo.   .   .   .   *Blanchard & Lea.*
Tracts for Missionary Use. Edited by the author of
    "Letters to a Man bewildered among many
    Counselors." 2 vols. 12mo.   .   .   1 25   *D. Dana, Jr.*
Tracy, J. L., Teacher's Pocket Record of Attendance,
    Deportment, and Scholarship. 16mo.   .   0 40   *Barnes & Burr.*
Train, George F., Spread Eagleism. 12mo. .   .   0 75   *Derby & Jackson.*
Trauermantel, Seed-Time and Harvest. Tales translated
    from the German. 16mo.   .   .   0 75   *Crosby, N., L. & Co.*
——— A Will and a Way. Tales translated from the
    German. 16mo.   .   .   .   .   0 75   "
Treasury (A) of Scripture Stories. Illustrated with co-
    lored plates. 12mo.   .   .   .   0 75   *Sheldon & Co.*
Treatise (A) on The Love of God. By Saint Francis of
    Sales. 12mo.   .   .   .   .   1 25   *P. O'Shea.*
Trelawney, E. J., Recollections of the Last Days of Shel-
    ley and Byron. 16mo.   .   .   .   0 75   *Ticknor & Fields.*
Trench, R. C. (D. D.), On the Authorized Version of the
    New Testament, in connection
    with some Recent Proposals for
    its Revision. 12mo.   .   0 75   *J. S. Redfield.*
——   "   On the Study of Words. Lectures
    addressed (originally) to the
    Pupils of the Diocesan Training
    School, Winchester. 12mo. . 0 75   *W. J. Widdleton.*
——   "   "Sermons Preached in Westminster
    Abbey." 12mo.   .   .   1 00   , "
Tressilian and his Friends. By Dr. R. Shelton Mac-
    kenzie. 12mo.   .   .   .   .   1 00   *Lippincott & Co.*
Trials of a Public Benefactor, as illustrated in the Dis-
    covery of Etherization. 12mo.   .   .   1 00   *Pudney & Russell.*
Trinitarian Sermons to a Unitarian Congregation. By
    Rev. William L. Gage. 16mo.   .   .   0 50   *J. P Jewett & Co.*
Trip (A) to Cuba. By Mrs. Julia Ward Howe. 16mo. 0 75   *Ticknor & Fields.*
Trollope, Anthony, Castle Richmond. 12mo.   . 1 00   *Harper & Bros.*
——   "   Doctor Thorne. 12mo. .   .   1 00   "

Trollope, Anthony, The Kellys and O'Kellys. 12mo. . 1 25 *Budd & Carleton.*
———   "   The Three Clerks. 12mo.   .   . 1 00 *Harper & Bros.*
———   "   The West Indies and the Spanish
                Main. 12mo.   .   .   .   . 1 00   "
——— T. A., Life of Vittoria Colonna. 18mo.   .   . 0 50 *Sheldon & Co.*
Trowbridge, Catharine M., Charles Norwood; or, Erring
                and Repenting. 16mo.   . 0 75 *W.S.& A.Martien.*
———   "   Dick and his Friend Fidus. . 0 45   "
——— J. T., The Old Battle Ground. 18mo.   .   . 0 50 *Sheldon & Co.*
Troup, George M., The Life of (Ex-Governor of Georgia).
        By Edward J. Harden. 12mo.   .   .   . *E. J. Purse.*
Troy, Reminiscences of, from its Settlement in 1790 to
        1807. By John Woodworth. Small 4to.   . 1 25 *J. Munsell.*
True Blue; or, Sharks on Shore. By J. M. Errym. 8vo. 0 25 *F. A. Brady.*
—— Path (The); or, The Young Man Invited to the
        Saviour, in a Series of Lectures. By the Rev.
        Joseph H. Atkinson. 12mo.   .   .   . 0 60 *Pres. Bd. of Pub.*
—— Prince (The) of the Tribe of Judah; or, Life Scenes
        in the Messiah. By the Rev. Rufus W. Clark. 1 25 *A. Colby & Co.*
—— Stories of the Days of Washington. 18mo. .   . 0 75 *Phinney, B. & M.*
—— Womanhood: a Tale. By John Neal. 12mo.   . 1 25 *Tickner & Fields.*
—— to the Last; or, Alone on a Wide, Wide Sea. By
        A. S. Roe. 12mo. .   .   .   .   . 1 25 *Derby & Jackson.*
Trumbull, Jonathan, Sen., (the Revolutionary Governor
        of Connecticut). The Life of 8vo.   .   . 3 00 *Crocker &Brewster.*
——— J. H., The Public Records of the Colony of Con-
        necticut. With Notes and Appendix. 8vo. . *Case, L. & Co.*
Trust in God; or, Three Days in the Life of Gellert.   . 0 25 *Carter & Brothers.*
Truth (The) Unmasked, and Error Exposed, in Theology
        and Metaphysics, Moral Government and Moral
        Agency. By Elder H. W. Middleton. 12mo. . *Lippincott & Co.*
——— is Everything. By Mrs. Thomas Geldart. 18mo. 0 50 *Sheldon & Co.*
Trying to be Useful. By Mrs. Madeline Leslie. 16mo. 0 75 *Shepard, C. & B.*
Tulloch, J. (D. D.), The Leaders of the Reformation,
        Luther, Calvin, Latimer, and Knox. 12mo.   . 1 00 *Gould & Lincoln.*
Tully, J. B., The Fourth Book of Reading Lessons. 12mo. 0 63 *P. O'Shea.*
Tuppy; or, the Autobiography of a Donkey. 16mo.   . 0 50 *Carter & Brothers.*
Tuel, J. E., The Illustrated History of the War in Italy. 1 25 *John G. Wells.*
Turnbull, R. (D. D.), Christ in History. New and Re-
        vised Edition. 12mo.   .   .   .   . 1 25 *Gould & Lincoln.*
Turner, J. J., The Discovery of Franklin. 12mo. cl.   . 0 60 *Goetzel & Co.*
——— W. M. (M. D.), El-Knuds, the Holy; or, Glimpses
        in the Orient. 8vo.   .   .   .   . 3 50 *J. Challen & Son.*
——— W. W., Jack Hopeton; or, the Adventures of a
        Georgian. 12mo. .   .   .   .   . 1 00 *Derby & Jackson.*

Tuthill, L. C. (Mrs.), Edith, the Backwoods Girl. 16mo.   0 63   *C. Scribner.*

Tweedie, W. E. (Rev.), Ruined Cities of the East. 16mo.   0 75   *Am. Tract Society.*

————   "   Jerusalem and its Environs; or,
  The Holy City as it Was and Is. 18mo.   .   0 75   "

Twelfth Night at the Century Club, January 6, 1858.   1 00   *D. Appleton & Co.*

Twelve Messages from the Spirit of John Quincy Adams,
  through Joseph C. Stiles, medium, to Josiah
  Brigham. . . . .   1 50   *Bela Marsh.*

———— Years of a Soldier's Life in India; being Extracts
  from the Letters of the late Major W. S. R. Hod-
  son. Including a Personal Narrative of the
  Siege of Delhi and Capture of the King and
  Princes. Edited by his Brother, the Rev. George
  H. Hodson. 12mo. . . . . .   1 00   *Ticknor & Fields.*

Twenty Years Ago, and Now. By T. S. Arthur. 12mo.   1 00   *G. G. Evans.*

Two Millions. By William Allen Butler. 16mo.   ,   0 50   *D. Appleton & Co.*

—— Sisters (The). By Mrs. Emma D. E. N. Southworth.   1 25   *Peterson & Bros.*

—— Ways to Wedlock. A Novelette. 12mo. . .   1 00   *Rudd & Carleton.*

Twyman Hogue; or, Early Piety Illustrated. A Biographical Sketch. By W. W. Hill, D. D.   .   0 30   *Pres. Bd. of Pub.*

Tyler, B. (Rev.), Lectures on Theology. With a Memoir
  by the Rev. Nahum Gale, D. D. 8vo. . .   1 50   *J. E. Tilton & Co.,*

—— R. H., The Bible and Social Reform; or, the Scriptures as a Means of Civilization. 12mo. .   1 00   *J. Challen & Son.*

—— S., The Progress of Philosophy in the Past and in
  the Future   12mo. . . . . .   1 00   *Lippincott & Co.*

—— W. S., Plato's Apology and Crito. With Notes. .   0 75   *D. Appleton & Co.*

Tylney Hall. By Thomas Hood. 12mo. . . .   1 25   *J. E. Tilton & Co.*

Tyndall, J., The Glaciers of the Alps. Being a Narrative
  of Excursions and Ascents. 12mo. . .   1 50   *Ticknor & Fields.*

Tyng, S. H. (Rev.), The Captive Orphan; Esther, the
    Queen of Persia. 12mo. . .   1 00   *Carter & Brothers.*

——   "   The Child of Prayer; a Father's
    Memorial to the Rev. Dudley A.
    Tyng. ·32mo. . . . .   0 40   "

——   "   Forty Years' Experience in Sunday
    Schools. 18mo. . . .   0 60   *Sheldon & Co.*

Tyree, C. (Rev.), The Living Epistle; or, the Moral Power
  of a Religious Life. 18mo. . . . .   0 60   "

U

Uhden, H. F., The New England Theocracy; a History
    of the Congregationalists of New England to
    the Revivals of 1740. 12mo.   .   .   .   .   1 00   *Gould & Lincoln.*
Umsted, L. D. (Mrs.), Southwold: a Novel. 12mo.   .   1 00   *Rudd & Carleton.*
Underwood, A. (Rev.), Millennial Experience; or, God's
    Will Known and Done.   12mo.   .   .   .   1 00   *Henry Hoyt.*
Ungava; a Tale of Esquimaux-land, by R. M. Ballan-
    tine. 16mo., cl.   .   .   .   .   .   0 75   *Phinney, B. & Y.*
Unica; a Story for Girls. 18mo.   .   .   .   .   0 25   *Carter & Bros.*
Union Pulpit (The), A Collection of Sermons by Ministers
    of various denominations, with thirty-four finely
    engraved portraits. 8vo., cl.   .   .   .   .   2 50   *Wm. T. Smithson*
—— Text Book (The), containing Selections from the
    Writings of Daniel Webster; the Declaration
    of Independence; the Constitution of the United
    States; and Washington's Farewell Address.   .   1 25   *G. G. Evans.*
—— of Christians and Death of Christ. 18mo.   .   .   0 40   *Challen & Sons.*
Unitarianism Defined. A Course of Lectures, by Fred-
    erick A. Farley, D. D. 12mo.   .   .   .   .   0 75   *Walker, W. & Co.*
United States, History of. Vol. VIII. By George Ban-
    croft. 8vo.   .   .   .   .   .   .   2 25   *Little, B. & Co.*
—— A Popular History of, from the Discovery of the
    American Continent to the Present Time. By
    Mary Howitt. 2 vols., 12mo.   .   .   .   .   2 00   *Harper & Bros.*
—— Primary History of, made Easy and Interesting
    for Beginners. By G. P. Quackenbos. 12mo.   .   0 50   *D. Appleton & Co.*
—— (The), and Cuba. By James M. Philippo. 12mo.   1 50   *Sheldon, B. & Co.*
Universal-Speaker (The).   Edited by N. A. Calkins and
    W. T. Adams. 12mo., cl.   .   .   .   .   1 00   *Brown & Taggard.*
Upham, P. L. (Mrs.), The Power of Faith. A Narrative
    of Sarah Johnson. 18mo.   .   .   .   .   0 33   *Henry Hoyt.*
Upton, Rebecca A., The Housekeeper and Gardener.   .   0 75   *Crosby, N., L. & Co.*
Uriel Acosta. A Tragedy in Five Acts. By Carl Gutz-
    kow. 12mo.   .   .   .   .   .   .   0 50   *M. Ellenger & Co.*
Ursula. A Tale of Country Life. By Miss Sewell. 2 vols.   1 50   *D. Appleton & Co.*
Use (The) and Abuse of Tobacco. By John Lizars.   .   0 38   *Lindsay & Blak'n.*
Uses (The) of Solitude. By William R. Smith. 4to.   .   0 25   *Munsell & Row'd.*

V

Vagabond (The), A Volume of Piquant Sketches, Treat-
ing upon Literature, Art and Society. By Adam
Badeau. 12mo. . . . . . . 1 00   *Rudd & Carleton.*
Vandenhoff, G., Leaves from an Actor's Note Book. . 1 00   *D. Appleton & Co.*
Van Schaack, E. T. (Mrs.), A Woman's Hand; or, Plain
Instructions for Embellishing a Cottage. 16mo. 0 50   *Munsell & R.*
Varra, O., Eddies Round the Rectory. 8vo. paper. . 0 38   *Stanford&Delisser.*
Vaughan, R. (D. D.), Revolutions in English History.
Vol. I. Revolutions of Race. 8vo. . . 2 00   *D. Appleton & Co.*
Veile (Mrs.), Following the Drum; A Glimpse at Fron-
tier Life. 12mo. . . . . . . 1 00   *Rudd & Carleton.*
Vernon Grove; or, Hearts as they Are. A Novel. 12mo. 1 00   "
Vestiges of the Spirit History of Man. By S. F. Dunlap. 3 50   *D. Appleton & Co.*
Vidocq, Memoirs of. Written by Himself. 12mo. . 1 25   *Peterson & Bros.*
Vincent, J., The Pretty Plate. 12mo. . . . 0 37   *D. & J. Sadlier.*
Viola; or, A Trial of Love and Faith. 12mo. . . 1 00   *Evans & Co.*
Violet; or, The Times We Live In. 12mo., cloth. . . 1 00   *Lippincott & Co.*
Virgil's Æneid: With Explanatory Notes. By Henry S.
Frieze. 12mo. . . . . 1 25   *D. Appleton & Co.*
Virginia, History of the Colony and Ancient Dominion
of. By Charles Campbell. 8vo. . . . 2 50   *Lippincott & Co.*
Virginians (The). A Tale of the Last Century. By W.
M. Thackeray. 8vo. . . . . . 2 00   *Harper &Brothers.*
Vision (The) of Old Andrew the Weaver. 18mo. . . 0 37½ *Kelly, Hedian & P.*
Voice (The) of Christian Life in Song; or, Hymns and
Hymn-Writers of Many Lands and Ages. 16mo. 0 75   *Carter & Brothers.*
Vogdes and Alsop's Elements of Practical Arithmetic. .   *Biddle & Co.*
Voltaire, M. De, The Henriade, with the Battle of Fonte-
noy, Dissertations on Man, Law of Nature, De-
struction of Lisbon, Temple of Taste, and Tem-
ple of Friendship. Edited by O. W. Wight. . 1 25   *Derby & Jackson.*
Volunteer's (The) Hand-Book. 18mo. . . . .   *West & Johnston.*
Voyage (The) of the "Fox" in the Arctic Seas. A Nar-
rative of the Discovery of the Fate of Sir John
Franklin and his Companions. By Captain
McClintock, R. N. 12mo. . . . . 1 50   *Ticknor & Fields.*

W

Wainwright, H., Rhymings. 12mo.	0 75	*D. Appleton & Co.*
——— J. M. (Bishop), Life of. By John N. Norton.	0 30	*F. D. Harriman.*
Wall Street to Cashmere: a Journal of Five Years in Asia, Africa, and Europe, during 1851, '2, '3, '4, '5 and '6. By John B. Ireland. 8vo.	4 00	*S. A. Rollo.*
Walker, J., Rhyming Dictionary. 12mo.	0 50	*Barnes & Burr.*
——— P., History and Habits of Animals. Square.	1 00	*Presb. Bd. of Pub.*
——— T., Introduction to American Law. Fourth Edition. Enlarged and thoroughly revised. By Edward L. Pierce. 8vo.	5 00	*Little, Brown & Co.*
——— W. (Gen.), The War in Nicaragua. Written by Gen. Wm. Walker. With a Colored Map of Nicaragua. 12mo.	1 50	*Goetzel & Co.*
Wallace, J. P. (Mrs.), Girls at School; or, the Boarding School Life of Julia and Elizabeth. 18mo.	0 30	*Carlton & Porter.*
——— S. S. T. (Mrs.), Rosalie's Lessons. 18mo.	0 25	*Presb. Bd. of Pub.*
Walshe, W. H. (M. D.), A Practical Treatise on the Diseases of the Lungs. 8vo.	2 25	*Blanchard & Lea.*
Walt Whitman's Leaves of Grass. 12mo.	1 25	*Thayer & Eldridge.*
Walter, W. H., Manual of Church Music. 4to.	1 00	*D. Appleton & Co.*
Walter, Ashwood: a Love Story. By Paul Siogvolk.	1 00	*Rudd & Carleton.*
——— Leyton: a Story of Rural Life in Virginia.	0 50	*Phillips, S. & Co.*
——— Stockton; or, My Father's at the Helm. By E. Llewellyn. 18mo.	0 35	*Presb. Bd. of Pub.*
——— Thornley; or, A Peep at the Past. 12mo.	1 00	*Harper & Bros.*
Walton, Izaak, The Lives of Dr. John Donne, Sir Henry Wotton, Richard Hooker, George Herbert, and Dr. Robert Sanderson. With some account of the Author and his Writings. By Thomas Zouch. New edition, with illustrated notes.	1 25	*Crosby, N., L. & Co.*
War Tiger (The): a Tale of the Conquest of China. By William Dalton. Illustrations by H. S. Melville.	0 75	*Townsend & Co.*
Wars (The) of the Roses; or, Stories of the Struggle of York and Lancaster. By J. G. Edgar. 16mo.	0 60	*Harper & Bros.*
Ward, J. H. (U. S. N.), A Manual of Naval Tactics. 8vo.	2 50	*D. Appleton & Co.*

Ward, J. H. (U. S. N.), Steam for the Million: a Popular
  Treatise on Steam and its Application to the
  Useful Arts, especially to Navigation. A new
  and Revised edition. 8vo. . . . . 1 00 *D. Van Nostrand.*
Warden, R. B., A Familiar Forensic View of Man and
  Law. 8vo. . . . . . . 2 25 *Follett, F. & Co.*
Ware, J. (M. D.), The Philosophy of Natural History. . 1 25 *Brown & Taggard.*
—— W., Driftwood on the Sea of Life. 12mo. . 1 00 *J. Challen & Son.*
Warfare and Work; or, Life's Progress. 18mo. . . 0 50 *F. D. Harriman.*
  The same. 18mo. . . . . . 0 50 *Carter & Brothers.*
Warren, John Collins (M. D.), The Life of. Compiled
  chiefly from his Autobiography and Journals.
  By Edward Warren, M. D. 2 vols. 8vo. . 3 50 *Ticknor & Fields.*
—— Jane S. (Mrs.), The Morning Star; History of
  the Children's Missionary Vessel, and of the
  Marquesan and Micronesian Missions. 18mo. . 0 60 *Am. Tract Society.*
Warren, S. E., General Problems from the Orthographic
  Projections of Descriptive Geometry. 8vo. . 3 00 *John Wiley.*
Washburn, E., Treatise on the American Law of Real
  Property. Vol. 1. 8vo. . . . . 5 50 *Little, B. & Co.*
Washington, George, Life of. By Washington Irving.
  National Ed'n, 5 vols. cl. 7 50 *G. P. Putnam.*
——   "   " Written for Children. By E.
  Cecil. 16mo., cl. . . 0 75 *Crosby, N., L. & Co.*
——   "   " By Edward Everett. 12mo. 1 00 *Sheldon & Co.*
——   "   " By John N. Norton. 16mo. *F. D. Harriman.*
——   " The Character and Portraits of.
  By H. T. Tuckerman. Illustrated
  with all the prominent Portraits,
  Proofs on India Paper. Quarto. 6 00 *G. P. Putnam.*
——   " The Recollections and Private Me-
  moirs of. By his Adopted Son,
  George Washington Park Custis. 2 50 *Derby & Jackson.*
—— E. K., Echoes of Europe; or, Word Pictures of
  Travel. 8vo. . . . . . 1 50 *J. Challen & Son.*
Watchword (The). 16mo.. . . . . . 0 75 *Carter & Brothers.*
Watson, A., The American Home Garden. Being Prin-
  ciples and Rules for the Culture of Vegetables,
  Fruits, Flowers and Shrubbery. 12mo. . . 1 50 *Harper & Bros.*
—— H. C., The Romance of History, as exhibited in
  the Lives of Celebrated Women of all Ages and
  Countries. 12mo. . . . . . 1 25 *J. S. Cotton & Co.*
Waverley Gallery (The) of the Principal Female Charac-
  ters in Sir Walter Scott's Romances. 8vo. . 10 00 *D. Appleton & Co.*

Wa-wa-wanda. A Legend of Old Orange. 12mo. . 1 00 *Rudd & Carleton.*

Way-Side Glimpses, North and South. By Lilian Foster. 12mo. . . . . . . 1 00 "

Way (The) of the Pit. By Harriet B. McKeever. 16mo. 0 65 *Henry Hoyt.*

—— " to the Pit. By Harriet B. McKeever. 16mo. 0 45 "

Wayland, F. (Rev.), Salvation by Christ. A Series of Discourses. 12mo. . . . 1 00 *Gould & Lincoln.*

——— " Sermons to the Churches. 12mo. . 1 00 *Sheldon & Co.*

Webb, T. S., The Freemason's Monitor. To which is added a Monitor of the Ancient and Accepted Rite, Thirty-three Degrees, including those generally known as the Ineffable Degrees. By E. T. Carson. 12mo. . . . . . 1 00 *Applegate & Co.*

Webster, D., and Hayne's Celebrated Speeches in the United States Senate, January, 1830. 8vo. pap. 0 25 *Peterson & Bros.*

Wee-Wee Songs, for Our Little Pets. By Leila Lee. 0 50 *Phinney, B & M.*

Weeks, J. M., History of Salisbury, Vermont. 12mo. . *A. H. Copeland.*

Weir, M. E., Gerald and his Friend Philip; or, Patience to Work and Patience to Wait. 18mo. . . 0 37 *Carlton & Porter.*

Wells, D. A., Annual of Scientific Discovery; or, Year-Book of Facts in Science and Art for 1859, '60, '61. Edited by David A. Wells. 12mo. Each. 1 25 *Gould & Lincoln.*

——— " Principles and Applications of Chemistry, for the use of Academies, High Schools, and Colleges. 12mo. . . . . . . 1 00 *Ivison & Phinney.*

——— J. D., The Last Week in the Life of Davis Johnson, Jr. 16mo. . . . . . 0 60 *Carter & Brothers.*

——— W. H., A Grammar of the English Language. New and Revised edition. 12mo. . . 0 88 *Ivison & Phinney.*

——— W. S., An Epitome of Braithwaite's Retrospect of Practical Medicine and Surgery. 2 vols., 8vo. 7 00 *Charles T. Evans.*

Western Orator (The). By Warren P. Edgarton. . 1 25 *Ingham & Bragg.*

Wharton, F., A Treatise on Theism, and on Modern Skeptical Theories. 12mo. . . . 1 25 *Lippincott & Co.*

——— " & Stille, M. (M. D.), Treatise on Medical Jurisprudence. By Alfred Stille, M. D. Second and revised edition. . . . . . 7 50 *Kay & Brother.*

——— Grace & Philip, The Queens of Society. 12mo. 1 50 *Harper & Bros.*

——— J. J. S., Law Lexicon; or, Dictionary of Jurisprudence; Second Edition, with Additions. By Edward Hopper. 8vo. . . . . 5 50 *Kay & Brother.*

What may be Learned from a Tree. By Harland Coultas. 1 00 *D. Appleton & Co.*

What must i do to be Saved. By Rev. J. T. Peck. 24mo. 0 35 *Carlton & Porter.*

What Norman Saw in the West. By the author of "Four Days in July." 18mo. 0 37

Whateley, Richard (Bp.), A General View of the Rise,
    Progress, and Corruptions of Christianity.
    With a sketch of the Life of the Author. 12mo.   *William Gowans.*

Whatever is, is Right. By A. B. Child. 12mo. cl.   1 00   *R. Marsh.*

Wheat and Tares. 12mo., cloth. . . . . .   0 50   *Harper & Bros.*

Whedon, D. D. (Rev.), A Commentary on the Gospels of
    Matthew and Mark. 12mo. . . . .   1 00   *Carlton & Porter.*

Where there is a Will there is a Way. By Alice B.
    Haven. 18mo., cloth. . . . . .   0 75   *D. Appleton & Co.*

Whewell, Wm. (D. D.), History of the Inductive Sciences.
    Third edition, with additions. 2 vols. 8vo. .   4 00   "

Whildin, J. R., Memoranda on the Strength of Materials
    used in Engineering Construction. 12mo. .   0 75   *D. Van Nostrand.*

While it Was Morning. By Virginia F. Townsend. .   1 00   *Derby & Jackson.*

Whims and Oddities, with one hundred and twelve
    Illustrations, and National Tales. By Thomas
    Hood. 12mo. . . . . . .   1 25   "

Whims and Waifs. By Thomas Hood. 12mo. .   1 25   "

Whitaker, Mary A., Alice's Dream. 18mo. . .   0 50   *Walker, W. & Co.*

White, G., Queens and Princesses of France. 18mo. .   0 50   *J. Murphy & Co.*

——— Jas. (Rev.), History of France from the earlier
    times to 1848. 8vo., cloth. .   2 00   *D. Appleton & Co.*

——— " The Eighteen Christian Centuries.   1 25   "

White Elephant (The); or, the Hunters of Ava and the
    King of the Golden Foot. By William Dalton.   0 75   *Townsend & Co.*

——— Wizard (The); or, the Great Prophet of the Semi-
    noles. By Ned Buntline. 8vo. . . .   0 25   *Fred. A. Brady.*

Whitecar, W. B., Four Years aboard the Whale Ship. .   1 00   *Lippincott & Co.*

Whitehall; or, The Days and Times of Oliver Crom-
    well. 8vo., paper. . . . . .   0 50   *Peterson & Bros.*

Whitehead, C. E., Wild Sports in the South; or, the
    Camp-fires of the Everglades. 12mo. .   1 25   *Derby & Jackson.*

Whitman, W., Leaves of Grass. 12mo. . .   1 25   *Thayer & Eld'ge.*

——— S. H., Edgar Poe and his Critics. 12mo. .   0 75   *Rudd & Carleton.*

Whitney, Anne, Poems. 16mo. . . . .   0 75   *D. Appleton & Co.*

Whiton, J. M., Hand-book of Latin. 12mo. . .   1 00   *Jas. Munroe & Co.*

Whitsuntide at Cedar Grove. By Mrs. William Wood
    Seymour. 16mo. . . . . .   0 75   *Daniel Dana, Jr.*

Whittier, John G., Home Ballads and Poems. 16mo. .   0 75   *Ticknor & Fields.*

Whittlesey, Sarah J. C., The Stranger's Stratagem; or,
    the Double Deceit, and other Stories. 12mo.   1 00   *M. W. Dodd.*

Why Do you Wear It. By James E. Griffin. 16mo. .   *Murray, Y. & Co.*

Why was I Left? or, He hath done All Things Well.
    By Mary McCalla. 18mo. . . . .   0 25   *Presb. Bd. of Pub.*

Widow (The) Davis and the Young Milliners. 18mo. . 0 25 *Henry Hoyt.*
Wife's Trials and Triumphs. 12mo. . . . 1 00 *Sheldon & Co*
Wilcox, C. M. (U. S. A.), Rifles and Rifle Practice; an
     Elementary Treatise upon the
     Theory of Rifle Firing. 12mo. 1 75 *D. Van Nostrand.*
—— " " Evolutions of the Line, as Prac-
     ticed by the Austrian Infantry,
     and adopted in 1853. 12mo. 1 00   "
—— " Tabular Statement of the Com-
     position of the Austrian Army
     on a War Footing. . 0 25   "
—— " " Tabular Statement of the Com-
     position of the French Army
     on a War Footing. . . 0 25   "
Wild Flowers. Drawn and Colored from Nature by
  Mrs. C. M. Badger. With an Introduction by
  Mrs. L. H. Sigourney. Folio, 22 plates. . 12 50 *Charles Scribner.*
—— Life; or, Adventures on the Frontier. By Captain
  Mayne Reid. 12mo. . . . . . 1 25 *R. M. De Witt.*
—— Nell: The White Mountain Girl. By Mrs. H. J.
  Moore. 12mo., cloth. . . . . . 1 00 *Sheldon & Co.*
—— Scenes on the Frontiers; or, Heroes of the West.
  By Emerson Bennett. 12mo., cloth. . . 1 25 *H. Dexter & Co.*
—— Sports in the Far West. By Frederich Gerstaecker. 1 00 *Crosby, N., L. & Co.*
—— " in the South; or, the Camp-fires of the
    Everglades. By Charles E. Whitehead. 1 25 *Derby & Jackson*
—— " of India: with remarks on the Rearing and
    Breeding of Horses, and the Formation
    of Light Irregular Cavalry. By Captain
    Henry Shakespeare. 12mo., cloth. . 0 75 *Ticknor & Fields*
Wilkins Wylder; or, the Successful Man. By Stephen
  F. Miller. 12mo. . . . . . *Lippincott & Co*
Will he Find Her? A Romance of New York and New
  Orleans. By Winter Summerton. 12mo. . 1 25 *Derby & Jackson.*
Will (A) and a Way. Tales translated from the German.
  By Trauermantel. 16mo. . . . . 0 75 *Crosby, N., L. & Co.*
Willard, Emma, Astronomy, and Astronomical Geogra-
  phy, with the Use of the Globes. 12mo. . 0 75 *Barnes & Burr.*
—— Memorial; or, Life and Times of Major Simon
  Willard; with Notices of three Generations of
  his Descendants. By Joseph Willard. 8vo. . *Phillips, S. & Co.*
Willet, W. M., The Life and Times of Herod the Great. 1 00 *Lindsay & Blak'n.*
Williams, B. W., Songs for the Sabbath School and
  Vestry. . . . . *Henry Hoyt.*

Williams, O., Narratives and Adventures of Travelers in
Africa. 12mo. . . . . . . 1 00 *Dick & Fitzgerald.*
―――― F. S., English into French. A Book of Practice
in French Conversation. 12mo. . . . 1 00 *Mason Brothers.*
―――― T., Life of Te-ho-ra-gwa-ne-qua, alias Thomas
Williams, a Chief of the Caughnawaga Tribe of
Indians in Canada. By the Rev. Eleazer Williams, reputed Son of Thomas Williams, and by
many believed to be Louis XVII., son of the
last reigning monarch of France, previous to the
Revolution of 1789. 8vo. paper. . (Printed for
private circulation.) . . . . *Joel Munsell.*
―――― W., The Singer's Manual. . . . . 0 50 *Shepard, C. & B.*
Willie trying to be Manly. 18mo. . . . 0 30 *Carlton & Porter.*
―――― trying to be Thorough. 18mo. . . . . 0 30 "
―――― wishing to be Useful. 18mo. . . . 0 30 "
―――― and Harrie; a True Story for Children. By a
Mother. 18mo. . . . . . . 0 20 *F. D. Harriman.*
―――― and Nellie; or Stories about my Canaries. By
Cousin Sarah. Square 18mo. . . . *W.S.& A.Martien.*
―――― Winkie's Nursery Songs of Scotland. Edited by .
Mrs. Silsbee. 12mo. . . . . . 0 75 *Ticknor & Fields.*
Willis, H. P., Etiquette, and the Usages of Society. . 0 25 *Dick & Fitzgerald.*
―――― N. P., Poems. 32mo. Blue and Gold. . . 0 80 *Clark, A., M.& Co.*
―――― " Sacred Poems. 12mo. . . . 1 50 "
―――― W. H., Old Leaves; Gathered from Household
Words. 12mo. . . . . . . 1 00 *Harper & Bros.*
Wilson, M., History of the United States. 12mo. . . 0 88 *Ivison & Phinney*
―――― " The Fourth Reader. 12mo. . . 0 66 *Harper & Bros.*
―――― " The Third Reader. 12mo. . . 0 50 "
―――― " The Second Reader. 12mo. . . 0 30 "
―――― " The First Reader. 12mo. . . 0 20 "
―――― " The School and Family Primer. . 0 13 "
Willard, Emma, Astronomical Geography, with the use
of the Globes. 12mo. . . . . . 0 75 *Moore & Nims.*
Wilmer, L. A., Our Press Gang; or, a Complete Exposi-
tion of the Corruptions and Crimes of the
American Newspapers. 12mo. . . . 1 00 *J. T. Lloyd.*
Wilson, Daniel (Rev.), Life and Correspondence of. By
Rev. Josiah Bateman. 8vo. . . . . 3 00 *Gould & Lincoln.*
―――― J., The Mechanic's and Builder's Price Book. To
which is added a Dictionary of Mechanical
terms; also a treatise on Architecture. 12mo. 1 00 *D. Appleton & Co.*
―――― " (Rev.), Memoirs of the Life of. By James
Hamilton, D. D. 12mo. . . . . 1 00 *Carter & Brothers.*

Wilson, J. M. (Rev.), Earth, Sea, and Sky; or, the Hand
of God in the Works of Nature. 12mo. . 1 25 *T. Nelson & Sons.*

—— J. S. (M. D.), Woman's Home Book of Health . 1 25 *Lippincott & Co.*

—— R. A., A New History of the Conquest of
Mexico. 8vo. . . . . . . 2 50 *J. Challen & Son.*

—— W. D. (D. D.), The Church Identified, by a Reference to the History of its Origin, Perpetuation,
and Extension into the United States. 12mo. 1 00 *Daniel Dana, Jr.*

Win and Wear. 16mo. . . . . . . 0 75 *Carter & Bros.*

Winer, G. B., A Grammar of the New Testament Dic-
tion; intended as an Introduction to the Critical
Study of the Greek New Testament. Translated .
from the sixth enlarged and improved edition of
the original. By Edward Masson. Vol. 1, 8vo. 1 75 *Smith, E. & Co.*

Wines, E. O. (D. D.), Commentaries on the Laws of the
Ancient Hebrews. 8vo. . . . *W.S. & A.Martien.*

Winkelmann, F. T., A Course of Exercises in all Parts of
French Syntax. 12mo. . . . . . 1 00 *D. Appleton & Co.*

Winkworth, C., Lyra Germanica; Hymns for the Sun-
days and Chief Festivals of the Christian Year. *Stanford & Delis'r.*

Winnie and Walter; or, Story Telling at Thanksgiving. 0 38 *J. E. Tilton & Co.*

—— " Walter's Christmas Stories. 18mo. . . 0 38 "

—— " " Evening Talks with their Father
about Old Times. 18mo. . 0 38 "

Wiscom, J. A., Onward; or, the Mountain Clamberers. 0 75 *D. Appleton & Co.*

Winslow, F. (M. D.), On Obscure Diseases of the Brain
and Disorders of the Mind. 8vo. . . . 3 00 *Blanchard & Lea.*

—— M., Life in Jesus: a Memoir of Mrs. Mary Wins-
low. By her Son, Octavius Winslow, D. D. 1 00 *Carter & Brothers.*

—— O. (D. D.), The Precious Things of God. 16mo. 0 75 "

Winter, W., The Queen's Domain, and other Poems. *E. O. Libby & Co.*

Wise, D., Pleasant Pathways; or, Persuasives to Early
Piety. 16mo. . . . . . . 0 60 *Carlton & Porter.*

—— H. A., The Story of the Gray African Parrot. . 0 45 *Charles Scribner.*

Wiseman, H. E. (Cardinal), Recollections of the last four
Popes, and of Rome in their
Times. 8vo. . . . 1 00 *Patrick Donahoe.*

—— " " The Hidden Gem. A Drama
in Two Acts. . . 0 75 *Kelly, Hedian & P.*

his Tour in Ireland, and in
London. 12mo. . . 0 75 *Patrick Donahoe.*

Witches (The) of New York, as encountered by Q. K.
Philander Doesticks. 12mo. . . . 1 00 *Rudd & Carleton.*

Wolf-Boy (The) of China; or, Incidents and Adventures
in the Life of Lyu Payo. By William Dalton. 0 75 *Jas. Monroe & Co.*

Wolfe of the Knoll, and other Poems. By Mrs. G. P.
    Marsh. 12mo. . . . . . . 1 00 *Charles Scribner.*
Woman; Her Mission and Life. By Adolphe Monad. 0 50 *Sheldon & Co.*
—— (The) in White; a Novel. By Wilkie Collins.
    8vo. . . . Cloth, $1 00; paper, 0 75 *Harper & Bros.*
—— " of the World. By Lady Cavendish. 8vo. pap. 0 50 *E. D. Long & Co.*
Woman's (A) Hand; or Plain Instructions for embellish-
    ing a Cottage. By Mrs. Eliza T. Van Schaack. 0 50 *Munsell & R.*
—— Home Book of Health. A Work for Mothers
    and for Families on a plan, safe and efficient,
    showing in Plain Language how Disease may
    be prevented and cured, without the use of
    dangerous medicines. By Jno. Stainback
    Wilson, M. D. 12mo. . . . . . 1 25 *Lippincott & Co.*
—— (A) Thoughts about Woman. By Miss Muloch. 1 00 *Rudd & Carleton.*
Women Artists in all Ages and Countries. By Mrs. E. F.
    Ellet. 12mo., cl. . . . . . . 1 00 *Harper & Brothers.*
—— of Beauty and Heroism, from Semiramis to
    Eugenie. By Frank B. Goodrich. 4to. . . 12 50 *Derby & Jackson.*
—— " Worth. A Book for Girls. 18mo. . 0 75 *Townsend & Co.*
—— " the South distinguished in Literature. By
    Mary Forrest. 4to. . . . . . 9 00 *Derby & Jackson.*
Wonderful (The) Doctor; an Eastern Tale. By Canon
    Schmid. 24mo. . . . . . . 0 25 *H. M'Grath.*
Wood, A., Class Book of Botany. 12mo. . . 1 50 *Moore & Nims.*
—— *The same.* 8vo. . . . . . 2 00 "
—— " First Lessons in Botany. 16mo. . . 0 50 *Barnes & Burr.*
—— G., Future Life; or, Scenes in Another World. . 1 00 *Derby & Jackson.*
—— Geo. B. (M. D.), and Bache, F. (M. D.), The Dis-
    pensatory of the United States of America.
    Eleventh Edition. 8vo. . . . . 6 00 *Lippincott & Co.*
—— J. (Rev.), Grace and Glory; or, the Young Con-
    vert instructed in the Doctrines of Grace. . 0 45 *Presb. Bd. of Pub.*
—— W. M. (M. D.), Fankwei; or, the San Jacinto in
    the Seas of India, China, and Japan. 12mo. . 1 25 *Harper & Brothers.*
Wood-Cutter of Lebanon; a Story Illustrative of a Jew-
    ish Institution. 12mo. . . . . 0 35 *Am. S. S. Union.*
—— Rangers (The); or, the Trappers of Sonora. By
    Captain Mayne Reid. 12mo. . . . . 1 25 *R. M. De Witt.*
Woods and Waters; or, the Saranacs and Racket. By
    Alfred B. Street. 12mo. . . . . 1 25 *M. Doolady.*
Woodbury, A., Plain Words to Young Men. 12mo. . 1 00 *Edson C. Eastman.*
—— D. P., Theory of the Arch. A Treatise on the
    Various Elements of Stability in the Well-Pro-
    portioned Arch. With numerous Tables of the
    Ultimate and Actual Thrust. 8vo. . . 2 50 *D. Van Nostrand.*

Woodworth, J., Reminiscences of Troy, from its Settlement in 1790 to 1807. Second edition, with Notes, Explanatory, Biographical, Historical, and Antiquarian. Small quarto. . . . 1 25   *J. Munsell.*

Wooing and Warring in the Wilderness. By Charles D. Kirk. 12mo. . . . . . . 1 00   *Derby & Jackson.*

Wooley, C., A Two Years' Journal in New York and Part of the Territories in America. 8vo. . 2 00   *William Gowans.*

Woolsey, T. D., Introduction to the Study of International Law. 12mo. . . . . . . 1 25   *Jas. Munroe & Co.*

Worcester, J. E., A Dictionary of the English Language. 7 50   *Swan, Brewer & T.*

Word (The) of the Spirit to the Church. 16mo. . . 0 50   *Walker & Co.*

——— and Works of God. By John Gill, D. D. 12mo. 0 25   *H. Dayton.*

Words (The) of Jesus. By the Author of "The Morning and Night Watches," etc. 18mo. . . . 0 88   *Phinney, B. & M.*

——— that Shook the World; or Martin Luther his own Biographer. By Charles Adams. 16mo. . 0 75   *Carlton & Porter.*

Wordsworth's Pastoral Poems. Illustrated. Extra cloth, gilt, $1.50. Morocco. . . . . 3 00   *D. Appleton & Co.*

Working Boy's Sunday Improved. 12mo. . . . 0 55   *Am. S. S. Union.*

——— and Trusting; or, Sketches drawn from the Records of "The Children's Mission to the Children of the Institute." 18mo. . . . 0 40   *Crosby, N., L. & Co.*

——— and Waiting; or, Patience in Well-doing. By Mrs. O. Brock. 16mo. cl. . . . . 0 50   *W.S.&A. Martien.*

World's Birth-day (The); a Book for the Young. By Professor L. Gaussen. Cloth. . . . .   *Am. Tract Society.*

Worthen, J. W., A New Method of Computing Interest and of Averaging Accounts. 16mo. . . 0 50   *Brown & Taggard.*

Wright, E. O. Lichen Tufts, from the Alleghanies. 12mo. 1 00   *M. Doolady.*

——— L. B. Josie Gray, and other Sketches. For the Children at Home. 18mo. . . . . 0 20   *F. D. Harriman.*

Wylie, M. (Mrs.), The Gospel in Burmah. 12mo., cloth. 1 00   *Sheldon & Co.*

Wyoming; its History, Stirring Incidents, and Romantic Adventures. By George Peck, D. D., 12mo., cl. 1 25   *Harper & Bros.*

11

Y

Year (A) in Europe. By Rev. Joseph Cross, M. D. Edited by Thomas O. Summers, M. D. 12mo.   .   *So. M. Pub. House.*

—— " with Maggie and Emma; a True Story. Edited by Maria J. McIntosh. 18mo.   .   .   .   0 63   *D. Appleton & Co.*

—— of Grace (The); a History of the Revival in Ireland in 1859. By Rev. William Gibson. 12mo.   .   1 25   *Gould & Lincoln.*

Young, A. W., The American Statesman. 8vo.   .   .   8 50   *Derby & Jackson.*

——   "   The Citizen's Manual of Government and Law. 12mo.   .   .   .   .   .   1 25   *H. Dayton.*

—— J., The Province of Reason : a Criticism of the Bampton Lecture on "The Limits of Religious Thought." 12mo.   .   .   .   .   0 25   *R. Carter & Bros.*

—— American's Picture Gallery (The). 4to.   .   .   1 25   *Lindsay & Blak'n.*

—— Christian Warned. By Rev. J. E. Rockwell. 18mo.   .   .   .   .   .   .   0 25   *Presb. Bd. of Pub.*

—— Citizen's Catechism. By Elisha P. Howe.   .   0 50   *Barnes & Burr.*

—— Farmer's Manual (The), Describing the Manipulations of the Farm in a Plain and Intelligible Manner. By S. Edwards Todd. 12mo.   .   1 25   *Saxton & Barker.*

—— Housekeeper's Friend (The). By Mrs. M. H. Cornelius. New and revised edition. 12mo., ol. .   0 75   *Brown & Taggard.*

—— Lady's Oracle. 16mo.   .   .   .   .   0 88   *Jas. Munroe & Co.*

—— Men (The) of the Bible, Considered in a Series of Lectures before the Young Men's Christian Association, by Distinguished Clergymen. 12mo. 1 00   *Higgins, B. & D.*

—— Shipwright (The); a Tale of the Sea. By Malcolm J. Errym. 8vo.   .   .   .   .   0 25   *F. A. Brady.*

Youth's History of the United States. By James Monteith. Small 4to.   .   .   .   .   0 50   *Barnes & Burr.*

Z

Zacharie, L, Surgical and Practical Observations on the Diseases of the Human Foot; with Instructions for their Treatment. 12mo.   .   .   .   1 00   *Charles B. Norton.*

Zenaida. By Florence Anderson, of Paris, Ky. 12mo. 1 25   *Lippincott & Co.*